★★★★★

'...other thoroughly enjoyable read from Iris Costello'

★★★★★

'A big warm hug for a cold winter night'

★★★★★

'This story is still on my mind days after finishing'

★★★★★

'A beautiful book'

★★★★★

'Better than any history lesson, that's for sure'

★★★★★

'An enjoyable and thought-provoking novel'

★★★★★

'A well-written and beautifully crafted story'

★★★★★

'The perfect book for book clubs'

★★★★★

'Great for fans of *The Guernsey Literary and Potato Peel Pie Society*'

★★★★★

'I can imagine many people curled up, reading this in the winter months'

★★★★★

'It will make you shiver, smile, cheer and cry'

★★★★★

'Once you start you will find it very hard to put down'

★★★★★

Praise for Iris Costello's
The Secrets of Rochester Place

'A rich and tender story of fortitude, family and friendship'
Ruth Hogan, *The Keeper of Lost Things*

'The perfect winter read'
Amanda Prowse, *To Love and Be Loved*

'Simply spellbinding, very addictive and so beautifully written'
Sophie Irwin, *A Lady's Guide to Fortune-Hunting*

'Richly atmospheric, evocative and moving – a triumph
of storytelling'
Abbie Greaves, *The Ends of the Earth*

'Full of intrigue and loss, this beautifully written gothic tale makes
for a spellbinding read'
Rhiannon Ward, *The Shadowing*

'An intriguing story which skilfully entwines the past and present'
Heidi Swain, *A Christmas Celebration*

'Absorbing, moving and multi-layered . . . A book to curl up with'
Emma Curtis, *Invite Me In*

'Beautifully written with a story that draws you in'
Jane Corry, *We All Have Our Secrets*

About the Author

Iris Costello is the pseudonym of bestselling author Nuala Ellwood. She has a BA Hons degree in Sociology from Durham University and a Master's in Creative Writing from York St John University where she is a visiting lecturer. She is the author of seven highly acclaimed novels, the most recent of which was *The Secrets of Rochester Place*. *The Story Collector* is her eighth book.

THE
STORY
COLLECTOR

IRIS COSTELLO

PENGUIN BOOKS

PENGUIN BOOKS

UK | USA | Canada | Ireland | Australia
India | New Zealand | South Africa

Penguin Books is part of the Penguin Random House group of companies
whose addresses can be found at global.penguinrandomhouse.com.

First published 2023
001

Copyright © Iris Costello, 2023

The moral right of the author has been asserted

Set in 12.5/14.75pt Garamond MT
Typeset by Falcon Oast Graphic Art Ltd
Printed and bound in Great Britain by Clays Ltd, Elcograf S.p.A.

The authorized representative in the EEA is Penguin Random House Ireland,
Morrison Chambers, 32 Nassau Street, Dublin D02 YH68

A CIP catalogue record for this book is available from the British Library

ISBN: 978-0-241-99911-0

www.greenpenguin.co.uk

Penguin Random House is committed to a
sustainable future for our business, our readers
and our planet. This book is made from Forest
Stewardship Council® certified paper.

In memory of Luke and Mavis Casey

O sweet everlasting Voices, be still.
W. B. Yeats

Prologue

London

1 January 1914

All is darkness. As I am led into the room, the blindfold tied firmly around my eyes, I hold out my hands to get my bearings and lower myself onto the silk-covered dais. From this perch I can hear the chit-chat of the men and women seated below me who are sipping their cocktails and waiting.

'I hear she's very good.'

'Didn't she foretell the sinking of Titanic *a couple of years ago?'*

'A talented artist too, by all accounts.'

'How enchanting.'

'Well, let's hope she has good things to say. I fancy asking her about the stock market. See if she's really worth her salt.'

'I just want to know if I'll live a long life.'

'Don't we all, dear?'

The great and the good of London society who have made the journey to this elegant Mayfair apartment are here on the promise that my words will bring them comfort and hope. As part of my initiation process into the second tier of the Divine Order of Universal Truth, I must share my gifts with the uninitiated, the shadow souls who have yet to be brought into the light.

Yet tonight I feel more darkness than light. As I remove my blindfold and begin to shuffle the cards, placing them on the table in front of me in the shape of a Celtic cross, the words from last night echo round my mind: '*I can't do this any more. It is over.*'

As I reflect on those words, regret and sadness waltz around me like a doomed couple dancing to their death. I'd had to do it. There was no other choice. No matter how strong our union was, there are some things that cannot be saved by the power of love alone. I couldn't risk being cast out again. It had to end. For both our sakes.

The cards feel alive tonight. They are burning with intent, mirroring my brooding thoughts. I look down at the Celtic cross in front of me, not quite believing the message it is imparting. But cards do not lie, and what they are showing this evening speaks of something terrifying and bleak. What to do? Tell the truth? Or offer these people the promise of a hope that will not come?

I close my eyes. Outside on the street, a drunken voice cries out, 'Forget it!' A sign. There will be time to share this reading when the oil lamps begin to expire, when the cocktails have been drunk and the shadow souls become weary and long for their beds. For now, I will give them what they want.

Surveying the audience, my eyes rest on a young couple: the man, lithe and pale with cropped hair the colour of wheat; the woman, small-boned and delicate with large hazel eyes and a pixie-like face. Their silhouettes ripple against the wall as the candles flicker in the draught. Rising from my dais, I take the remaining cards and make my way over to them, shuffling the deck as I go. The young pair get to their feet as they see me approach. The woman smirks while the young man stares at me intently and waits for me to deliver my lines.

'Take this card and read its name aloud,' I say, drawing a card for the young woman and placing it in her hands.

'It is,' she says, firmly, her eyes twinkling in the light of the oil lamps, 'the Eight of Swords.'

As she speaks, I feel my throat tighten. I close my eyes and see a magnificent ballroom with an ornate ceiling rose and long windows decked with drapes of the finest silk. It is a scene of opulence beyond words, the stuff of dreams, and yet the young woman is curled up in the corner, her hands bound loosely with silk scarves. She appears to be trapped but the ballroom door is wide open.

'And for me?'

I open my eyes and regard the young man. He stands erect, broad shoulders filling every inch of his dark suit jacket, eyes the milky green of a winter sea, regarding me with anticipation. He is holding out his right hand, the thumb tucked against the palm, a gesture I remember from childhood. I take a deep breath, clear my mind of the ballroom prison cell and reshuffle the cards. To the delight of the gathered audience, a card flips out of the deck like a slippery fish, and lands at the feet of the young man. The audience have never seen anything like it. They probably think it is a trick.

'So, what have we here?' says the young man, smiling to the crowd as he stoops to retrieve the card.

I watch as he turns it over in his hands, his expression darkening.

'It appears we have a sequence,' he says, holding up the card for the others to see. 'I have the Nine of Swords.'

He looks at me and I stagger backwards as jolts of pain course through my body. I see a man, all alone, legs drawn up and pressed to his chest, blood pooling on the floor beside him. His despair is palpable.

'Now your turn.'

His steady voice brings me back to the room.

'What does the future hold for our gracious hostess, eh?' he says, turning to the crowd who cheer their approval.

With trembling hands, I shuffle the deck. Almost instantaneously a card jumps out. The Five of Pentacles. I scrutinize the imagery on it as I return to my dais: the ragged, shadowy figures, the golden glow of the church window. A chill breeze flutters through the air as I sit down on my cushion, the Celtic cross spread out in front of me like a dark stain. Then I turn my attention to the gathered audience, their faces half-shadowed in the fading candle-light, and a voice issues from me that is not my own.

'A gilded cage; a nightmare without end; and a young woman cast out into the cold.'

I hear the crowd mutter despondently.

I turn another card. It is the Seven of Swords. I look up. The eyes of the young couple are on me, but my words are directed at the woman. She looks up expectantly. There are a hundred different ways of interpreting this card but in that moment I choose the most damning outcome I can think of.

'This love affair is not meant to be,' I tell her, the words rushing from my mouth. 'You will not grow old together. You will make your choice and the life you lead will be prosperous but stifling. As for him? He will find his soul-mate on a distant shore.'

'Come on,' shouts a monocled young man at the back of the room. 'Enough about those two. What does the future have in store for the rest of us?'

'Yes,' adds his companion, a red-haired young lady with striking green eyes. 'That's why we came here tonight. Though please don't tell us we're going to end up on a sinking ship.'

The crowd erupt in a chorus of laughter.

'I don't know about you, old chap,' chimes a stout, ginger-whiskered man in an ill-fitting suit. 'But I intend to stay on terra firma for the foreseeable future.'

With their voices echoing around me, I look down at the Celtic cross. The meaning of the spread has lost none of its power in the moments since I drew it. I look at the central card, the burning Tower expelling its terrified inhabitants, and I am filled with a sadness so crushing I almost lose my breath.

'Tell us,' cries the monocled man. 'Surely it can't be that bad.'

My heart stuttering in my chest, I take the card and hold it aloft.

'The Tower?' says the woman with the green eyes. 'But whatever does that mean?'

I look at their faces, so full of hope and expectation, and for a moment I almost lose my nerve. But then I remind myself that forewarned is forearmed, that I am not here to scare these people but to empower them. Still the words that spill from my lips seem to come unbidden.

'That which is built on rocky foundations is destined to fall. A great battle will rage. The world as you know it will fall apart.'

'No!' cries the woman. 'That cannot be true.'

I am terrifying them. I know that. I want to stop myself, but the words continue to pour forth.

'The Tower will fall,' I cry. 'And not one person gathered here tonight will escape unscathed.'

As the room falls silent, I slump forward, every ounce of energy drained from my body. This was not meant to happen. A murmur of dissent strikes up among the crowd. They are angry and scared. I feel a pair of arms pull me up from behind.

I turn round and see, to my relief, that it is my brother.

'Time to leave,' he hisses. 'Now.'

I

EDIE

Present Day

Tarot cards. Surely only cranks use them. Or, as was the case when I was young, lovestruck teens hoping to find out if the hot guy in the upper sixth reciprocates their feelings. Sensible, rational-minded adults don't bother with that sort of thing, do they?

Yet according to Rebecca Young, thirty-something CEO of Rise, the dynamic mind, body and spirit publishing house where I was summoned this morning, times have changed.

'Tarot has had a facelift,' she told me, over breakfast in the achingly minimalist Notting Hill town house from which Rise operates. 'It's no longer seen as a fringe subject, beloved of hippies and occultists, it's now very much made its way into the mainstream. It's all about being in control of your life, creating the best version of yourself. I tell my investors that using the Tarot to forecast your life is just as important as making a five-year business plan, taking out life insurance or joining a gym. It's a lifestyle tool, one that I believe can help anyone, in any walk of life. I've had CEOs of Fortune 500 companies buy Tarot decks in bulk. That kind of thing was unthinkable ten years ago.'

She leaned forward, her glossy black hair falling around her shoulders like silk, and tapped a perfectly manicured nail, the colour of peach melba, on the glass table. I looked down at my loose linen shirt, ripped jeans and scuffed, paint-splattered Converse, wishing that I had made more of an effort. But when I'd received the email about designing Tarot cards, I'd imagined a much more informal setting, had thought Rebecca would be clad in flowing skirts and love beads and reeking of patchouli oil like the Tarot enthusiasts of my youth. Yet instead of Linda McCartney *circa* 1971, I was greeted by a vision in a crisp white shirt, tailored cigarette pants and four-inch, shiny Louboutins.

'We're moving with the times and taking Tarot into new territory,' she said emphatically, pouring us both a cup of peppermint tea. 'Updating it for a new generation. And this is where you come in, Edie.'

She told me how much she loved my art, how she had seen my paintings on display at the Brick Lane Gallery and felt an instant connection.

'I particularly loved *Golden Hour*,' she said, beaming at me with perfectly white teeth. 'The one of the man lying in bed, the sun reflecting off his sleeping form. That was exquisite, yet achingly real. Just the kind of image we want to create in this new Tarot deck. Instead of medieval knights and veiled priestesses, we want twenty-first-century life in all its glory, the good and the bad. We want people to see themselves in the cards, to resonate with the story that unfolds. Like your guy asleep in bed. Mr Everyman getting ready to greet the day.'

Mr Everyman. He was anything but that. As Rebecca scrolled her iPad for the next point, I returned to the morning I had sketched him. A lazy Sunday in our little flat in Bethnal Green, pale spring sunlight trickling through the cracks in the white plantation blinds. I had woken first and gone to the kitchen to make coffee for us both. When I returned to the bedroom, the morning sun had intensified and was pouring onto his sleeping form, bathing it in gold and making him look, for just a moment, like an angel. I'd put the coffee down and run to grab my sketchbook. His reading glasses lay on the bedside table on top of the manuscript of *On Flanders' Poppied Fields*, the biography of a forgotten African American war poet he had spent the last three years working on. He had been awake until the early hours making last-minute amends in red pen before sending it off to his editor. As I opened my sketchpad and began to draw, he was no longer a man in his fifties with salt-and-pepper hair and beard, he was the young man I fell in love with all those years ago. The proud Nigerian Londoner who had marched over to me in the college bar and asked me to vote for him in the upcoming student elections. Lying in the light of the morning sun, his body relaxed, his face serene, he was my David again, unencumbered by age. In those moments as I sat sketching him, neither of us could have imagined the horrors to come, though they crouched in the shadows outside on the street, biding their time, waiting to pounce. When he woke a couple of hours later the drawing was finished, my sketchbook put away. We sat and drank our coffee, and he chatted about the day ahead, oblivious to the fact that with a flourish of a sharpened pencil, I had just captured him in that moment for ever.

*

As the signs for Holton come into view, my shoulders loosen. This Cornish village, a few miles north of St Ives, was the place I ran to when my world fell apart eighteen months ago. Moonstone Cottage had been left to my father in his grandmother's will when I was a child and as I grew up it became a little holiday home for us. To a child born and raised in the East End, the idea of a cottage by the sea on the very edge of England had been ridiculously exciting. Fancy overseas holidays were out of the question. The earnings from my father's cake shop combined with my mum's part-time hairdressing didn't leave much spare for luxuries so Moonstone Cottage was as fantastical as its name. And yet my father, after a run of calamitous visits during which the kitchen flooded, a dead rat was found in the water pipe and he almost crashed our old Ford Cortina on the coastal path, decided the old place was becoming a liability. 'I think we should put it up for let,' he had told my mother as the train pulled out of Penzance station bound for London, on what would be our last trip to Holton as a family. 'It'll give us a nice financial cushion, help us pay for art school for Edie when the time comes.' I had protested. I loved Cornwall, loved its light, loved the sense of peace I felt there. 'Please, Dad,' I'd begged. 'We can't lose Moonstone Cottage. It's my home.' But it was no use, he had made his mind up, and after just two brief summer trips, our Cornish dream was over.

As the years went by, I put Cornwall to the back of my mind though it would always have a special place in my heart. But, like Dad, the East End of London was in my blood. I was born and grew up there, married, raised a child, lived, worked and loved in that familiar and comforting square mile, and never imagined living anywhere else.

Then, one autumn night, everything changed. In an instant my life was blown apart. And though I sat it out for another six months, I knew that I needed to escape London and its painful memories, needed to be in a place of safety, a place where I could heal. So I swam back through the silt of memory and asked myself where in the world I would find the peace I was searching for. When Dad told me that my beloved Moonstone Cottage was free of tenants for the first time in years, I knew I had found the answer. Knowing that they relied on the rental income, I made my father an offer for the cottage, but he wouldn't hear of it, telling me that it was my inheritance as much as his, and that it was now time for me to make Moonstone Cottage my own.

Though it is tiny, with just a sliver of a galley kitchen, a compact living room, a bedroom and a box room, there's an abundance of nature on the doorstep and a coastal pathway that leads all the way to Lytton Cove, an idyllic sandy beach. During the two summers I had spent there as a child, I would take my sketchbook and oil paints down to the shoreline and spend hours trying to capture the strange marine colours, the ever-changing light. It had all lodged in my head, become a well from which I could drink when I needed inspiration. For years, I nurtured dreams of retiring here one day with David.

Never did I imagine that I would make the move so soon. Or that I would do it without him.

Now as I pull up at Moonstone, I notice that the front door of Wicket End, the cottage that adjoins mine, has been left wide open. In London, this would be cause for alarm, yet here in Cornwall life works differently. It seems everyone and everything runs to a different clock. It has taken me a while to get used to but, after the bustle of London, it is strangely reassuring to step out of time. Alexander, the owner of Wicket End, assured me over a welcome coffee when I first arrived last spring that this change of pace, though shocking at first, would turn out to be liberating. However, as a busy forty-something hedge fund manager who still has a flat in West London, he is years away from a quiet retirement and I get the sense that by dipping his toes in the tranquillity of Cornwall before escaping to the bustle of the City through the week, he has made sure he can enjoy the best of both worlds. I, on the other hand, have well and truly taken the plunge and left London behind for good, a decision I still can't quite believe I was bold enough to make.

Alexander's elegant designer reading chair is perched on the grass out front, a thick hardback book laid beside it alongside a pair of reading glasses and a half-eaten sandwich. Jupiter, his plump silver cat, lounges by the apple tree, soaking up the early evening sun.

My phone beeps as I turn off the engine. It is an email from Rebecca Young, hoping that I will accept the commission. Seventy-eight Tarot cards to be designed and illustrated by the end of the summer. It is a big ask and I am still not sure if I am ready to take on work of this magnitude just yet. Since I lost David, I haven't been able to bring myself to do anything, grief stifling my ability to create. But David wouldn't want me to give up drawing. Yes, the commission will be a huge undertaking, but it will get me back in the game, give me something to focus on, something to fill the long, empty days ahead.

My head is full of thoughts as I lock the car and make

my way up the path. I'll reply to Rebecca later, I tell myself. Then, first thing tomorrow morning I shall get started on some initial sketches. As I reach the door, my phone trills. I smile when I see the initials on the screen: DD2. Darling Daughter. My nickname for our only child. David was DD1. Gathering myself, I press Accept.

'Dora, or should I say Dr Hart, how are you?' Saying the title that once belonged to her dad makes me start, though I know it is something I shall have to get used to. 'How did the first day go?'

'Really well,' she replies, her calm voice soothing my sadness. 'There was a lot of admin to get through today but I had a tour of the faculty which was amazing and tomorrow my furniture is arriving from St Andrews, so I can start making the flat feel homely. All in all, things are looking good.'

Dora has been in Scotland for two years, studying for her Master's at St Andrews before embarking on her PhD. Today is her first day joining the faculty of English Literature at Glasgow University as Senior Lecturer, a role she will take up on a full-time basis when the autumn term begins in September. For now, she is spending these last weeks of summer term familiarizing herself with the staff and the campus and settling into her new flat in the West End of the city.

'Your dad would be so proud, my darling,' I say, tears springing to my eyes unbidden. 'As am I.'

'I was thinking about him today,' she says, her voice faltering. 'When I saw the library here. There's a whole section dedicated to the First World War poets. I took my phone out to take a photo to show Dad, then I remembered.'

'Oh, Dora,' I say, slumping down onto the doorstep. 'I do that all the time. You know, I almost bought a big bag of cinder toffee from Portobello Market when I was up in London today. God, he loved that dreadful stuff.'

'And you hated it,' laughs Dora. 'I remember you saying he'd lose all his teeth if he wasn't careful.'

'Which only made him want more of it,' I say, happy to hear her laugh. 'Ah, darling, we'll always have our memories, eh?'

'Always,' she says, her steady voice faltering. 'Listen, Mum, I've got to run. I'm meeting the head of faculty for drinks in five minutes. I'll give you a call tomorrow.'

'OK, darling,' I say, wiping my eyes with the back of my hand. 'Have a good evening. Love you.'

'Love you, Mum.'

As she clicks off, I put the phone in my palm and stare at the screensaver: a photo of me and David sitting on the beach, a few New Year's Eves ago. He is wearing that old grey linen shirt he'd had since his student days and I'm in my navy painting smock. The sun is setting behind us as we hold our wine glasses aloft, toasting the year to come. We didn't know what lay ahead, how our humdrum ease would be shattered by the terror of that evening, the grim silence of its aftermath. Yet here on my phone we are happy. Like my numerous attempts to capture the changing moods and colours of the sea, I had managed to encapsulate, in a bloody selfie, a moment of pure contentedness. As I place the phone in my pocket, my stomach knots with longing. For my husband, for my daughter, for the life I once had. Yet, getting up from the step, I hear the words Ronke, my best friend and sister-in-law, wrote to me the day after the funeral: 'Though it may seem impossible now, the only way through this is forward . . .'

Walking into Moonstone Cottage, I see a strip of brown woodchip plasterboard half-hanging from the living-room wall. Though my back is aching after the drive from London, and I am longing for a warm bath, if I get another few panels of that ghastly 1970s decor removed then I am another few steps forward.

I have, perhaps over-ambitiously, set myself the task of renovating the cottage, one room at a time. I have never undertaken such a job, but I reckoned it would keep me busy, help distract me from what my GP described as Complex Post-Traumatic Stress Disorder, but what I refer to as '12 October Paralysis'. The events of that evening, its build-up and aftermath, play on a loop in my mind throughout the day. Most of the time, it is background noise, a low, anxiety-inducing hum, though at certain moments, often innocuous ones where I'm making a cup of tea or cleaning my paintbrushes, I am thrust back into the evening in all its horror, standing in the living room, my feet treading through broken glass, the cold air blowing through the open window. These flashbacks are so real it feels like I am back there in East London though I am sitting in tranquil Cornwall. I hear the whine of the police sirens as they slice through the night air, smell the dope being smoked by the art students on the roof terrace next door, hear the thud of footsteps making their way up my polished wooden stairs and David's voice, so real, so clear, shouting, 'Edie, get back!'

In the midst of such terror, the idea of stripping down a cottage and losing myself in such practicality was a life raft. A way of distracting myself that didn't involve either medication – blocking everything out – or therapy – blocking nothing out. Though now the reality of doing it all by myself is starting to sink in. As I stand here looking at the half-finished wall and the thick cloud of dust that hangs over every bit of furniture, I ask myself, for the hundredth time, whether I have bitten off more than I can chew.

'Oh, come on, Edie,' I cry, taking off my trainers and placing them on the rack by the back door. 'Enough of this pity party. There's work to be done.'

Retrieving my newly acquired metal toolbox from the cupboard under the stairs, I take out the crowbar, brace myself on the dust sheet and begin to remove the next piece of plasterboard.

It yields easily, and I can see the edges of russet-coloured brickwork peeking out from behind. Though I am sweating and covered in dust, there is something so addictive and satisfying about this work. Perhaps I should retrain as a builder, I tell myself, as the whole panel peels off in one neat piece, sending a sandstorm of white dust cascading onto the carpet – pursue a life of practical, no-nonsense graft.

But as I place the panel on the floor beside me, I am greeted by a sight that makes my heart sink. Instead of a smooth wall, there is a great big gaping hole.

'Shit,' I mutter, sitting back on my haunches, and remembering the words of my sister-in-law Ronke, a lifelong Londoner, who had been baffled when I told her I was not only moving to Cornwall but renovating an old cottage alone. 'It's bad enough living without a Tube station or a decent hairdresser or curry house,' she had exclaimed as we sat drinking champagne on the beach my first week here. 'But house renovations? You need to call in the experts for that, Edie.'

Leaning forward, I place my hand inside the hole. If it's not too deep, then I can just fill it in, surely? Yet, as my arms disappear further inside the gap, I realize that this is going to take more than Polyfilla. It must be at least a metre deep.

I am just pulling my arm out when my hand catches against something solid. Taking my torch from the tool-box, I shine it into the hole. There, wedged against the left side of the wall, is a large wooden box.

Shining the torch along the surface of the box, I see it has been carved with roses, cherubs, scrolls and what looks like a crucifix wrapped in thorns and crowned with a set of devil-like horns. As I investigate the hollow recess, a deep sense of unease creeps over me. Have I come across an urn? Placing the torch on the floor beside me, I summon up the courage to pull out the box. It can't be bodily remains, surely, I tell myself, brushing the thick dust from the box with a cloth. As far as I know, this building has never been a chapel or a church or any place that would contain a catacomb.

There is a metal latch, rusted with age, on the front of the box. I lift the latch, but the lock is jammed and will not budge. I am on my way to fetch a screwdriver to prise it open, but as I pass through the kitchen, hunger gets the better of me.

I place the box on the sideboard and reluctantly force down a slice of buttered bread while standing against the kitchen counter, remembering how David and I would always make dinner together, one of us stirring the pot, the other topping up the wine. The kitchen had been our haven right up until that night. I see the upturned white table, the broken bottles strewn across the wooden floor, and my stomach knots.

Throwing the bread crust into the bin, I take my laptop and go into the living room where, with the reassuring sound of the waves crashing onto the shore, I sit on the sofa and begin to compose my email to Rebecca. I hesitate at first, a sick feeling rising from the pit of my stomach at the thought of committing to such a huge job. Am I ready to return to work? Am I mentally strong enough to even carry this out? Then I hear David's voice in my head: 'Come on, Edie. You've got this.' A solitary tear rolls down my cheek as I type out my reply to Rebecca, thanking her for the opportunity and telling her that, yes, I would love to accept.

At this point, back in my old life, I would close the laptop and go and drag David out of his study so we could toast my new deal with a bottle of red. 'Tarot cards, Edie,' he'd exclaim. 'Hilarious!'

But there is no warm laughter or words of congratulation here, just the ticking of the clock on the mantelpiece and the susurration of the waves as they wash the sand clean. Somewhere in the distance a dog barks and the noise startles me.

'Time for bed, Edie,' I say as I haul myself from the sofa. It is almost midnight and I have to be up early to get started on the drawings.

But as I go to turn out the light, something catches my eye. The box, sitting where I left it on the sideboard. I run my fingers along the intricate carvings before trying once more to lift the latch, to no avail. But then I notice something. On the front of the box, just above the latch, are carved three words that send a shiver right through me.

Mystic. Medium. Messenger.

2

KATERINA

'Little Germany', East London

May 1915

The morning air is uncharacteristically sweet as I make my way up the Mile End Road. As is usual at this hour, the streets are packed with delivery carts, disgorging sacks of flour, crates of fruit and vegetables, ice boxes of freshly caught fish, and hulking sides of beef hanging from blood-stained hooks, bound for Atkinson's and Bardello's the grocers', Goldsmith's the butcher's and Simon's the fishmonger's, businesses that have thrived in this area since the days of Victoria. As I weave my way through the carts, which are parked nose to tail along the road, the voices of the delivery men punctuate the quiet of the morning.

Cockney, Kentish, Polish, Italian, Irish, Scottish, Punjabi, these are the voices I have grown up with, the myriad sounds of London. Yet one accent is noticeable by its absence today: the German that once dominated this square mile of the East End.

The men fall silent as I pass, and I can feel their eyes upon me as I make my way south towards Stepney Green.

I am used to this attention, and it is not down to my

dazzling good looks or strutting gait but to the fact that in their eyes I do not conform to the idea of how a woman should present herself. And though it may offend them, I have never once been tempted to modify myself in order to fit in. As far as I am concerned, the clothes I wear reflect the person I am on the inside, durable, strong, built to last, but it is also a matter of practicality. Ever since I was a child, I have found the idea of squeezing myself into stiff skirts, tight corsets and frilly blouses utterly preposterous. For one thing, I love to walk. Not pleasant perambulations along Oxford Street or the South Bank but rigorous hikes across town and heath. I could not do that if I was sewn into a voluminous skirt with petticoats and all that nonsense. It would be far too restrictive. I first started wearing trousers when I was six years old. Though my parents protested, I told them, defiantly, that if my older brother could wear them then so could I. Over the years, I have developed a uniform of sorts, a practical set of outfits that allow me to move freely without impediment. Today's ensemble of wool pants, white Henley shirt, braces and tweed overcoat is very much standard. Oh, and my hobnail boots, which are now getting perilously close to wearing out, fit my feet like a second skin. The same goes for my choice of hairstyle. Who needs waist-length hair? And as for all those fussy chignons and braids, twists and plaits, well, they are more suited to pastries and confections than the head of a grown woman. Better to feel the cool air on the nape of your neck as I do now as I thread through a maze of run-down back-to-back terraces, my cloth cap snugly fitted over my cropped blonde hair.

'Oy, missus,' cries a barefoot boy in ragged short trousers

chasing a runaway ball down the cobbled pavement. 'Catch it, will you?'

I stop the ball in its tracks and throw it back to the boy.

'Why you dressed like that?' he says, catching the ball in one. 'Can you not afford a dress?'

'I could ask you the same question,' I say, doffing my cap and leaving him with a bemused look on his face.

As I follow the cobbled pathway that runs parallel to Stepney Green Park, its shiny blue Scoria stones, imported here from the blast furnaces of Middlesbrough, glistening in the sun, I think of my father and the bakery he built up from scratch when he arrived in this country seventeen years ago. Back then, Mile End Old Town was so dominated by German immigrants it became known as 'Little Germany'. It certainly felt like that for my newly widowed father who, on arriving here with his bookish young son and rebellious daughter, was welcomed with open arms by the German expats. Despite the loss of my mother and the guilt I felt at her death, soon we had a community of surrogate mothers, uncles, aunts, cousins and grandparents. People with familiar names like Schmidt and Cohen, Brummer and Graf, who celebrated the same festivals as us, knew the old songs and ate the same food.

When I reach St Dunstan's church, I stand for a while at the entrance to take in the carvings above the door. On the right is a grotesque devil grimacing in pain as a set of tongs twist round his nose, an allusion to the church's namesake, Dunstan, who had assailed the beast with a similar instrument. As my eyes turn left to the carving of a ship riding the crest of the wave, my attention is drawn to a figure sitting on the bench by the graveyard.

I am at least two hundred yards away, yet there is no mistaking him. The pale blonde hair that almost dissolves into his milk-white skin, the long, aquiline nose, the furrowed brow, the broad shoulders that hunch as he leans over the book he is reading.

'Otto,' I cry, joy filling my tired body as I bound across the grass towards him. 'What are you—?'

Yet before I can finish my sentence, the young man turns and looks up at me. I see the dog collar, the crucifix round his neck, the Bible clutched in his hands, and my heart sinks. This is not my brother, it is the new vicar, the attractive young curate Violet has been mooning over.

'Can I help you?' he says, closing his Bible and smiling at me beatifically. 'Are you lost?'

I shake my head, embarrassed at my outburst, but as I turn and walk away across the churchyard, my shame gives way to despair. I had been sure it was my brother. I feel the curate's eyes on me as I unlatch the gate, his words reverberating in my head. 'Are you lost?'

'*Yes*,' I feel like shouting back to him. '*Yes, I am lost but there is no one here to guide me home.*'

The air seems to thicken as I head on to Mile End Road, a heaviness that settles in my lungs, weighing down on them like a stone. I feel strangely discombobulated, like someone walking out of time, and I am grateful when I reach the bakery and see the reassuring *Open* sign on the mullioned window. Thank goodness for Violet, I think to myself as I open the door. I really do not know what I would do without my diligent young assistant with her endless chatter and sunny demeanour.

'Morning, Miss Drechsler,' Violet says, looking up from

a steaming tray of breakfast rolls, her breezy voice snapping me out of my reverie. 'You were out and about early.'

'I needed some fresh air,' I reply, hanging up my overcoat. I take my apron from its hook behind the teak counter and tie it round my waist. 'The rooms upstairs can get awfully stuffy at this time of year. It seems you had an early start too, dear. It's not yet six thirty.'

'Oh, that Mrs Higgins from next door had her baby crying all night long,' says Violet, brushing a strand of auburn hair from her face. 'Pa says if it carries on much longer, he'll go round and give the bairn a pacifier himself. Tot of gin, in his case, the old ratbag. Anyway, it got to dawn, and I thought to myself it's no use lying here wide awake, I'd be better use at the bakery.'

I smile at the girl as she busies herself arranging a tray of crisp, perfectly triangular strudels in the glass cabinet. She seems older than her fifteen years, worldly wise as my father would say. Girls grow up fast round here. They have to.

'Quiet this morning,' she says, glancing at the clock. 'Usually have a dozen or more customers before seven.'

'Give it time, Violet,' I say, as I go to the kitchen to retrieve a tray of warm pumpernickel rolls. 'Once their stomachs start rumbling, they'll be knocking the door down.'

My optimism is as much for myself as for Violet. We both know that business has been dwindling since last August. As a German-owned shop selling strudels and pumpernickel bread we have fallen considerably out of favour in a district where one in every three young men have been sent off to fight the 'dreaded Kraut'. Still, I had hoped that our seventeen-year tenure, and the legacy of my father, would have afforded us some loyalty. But in these unstable times, nothing is a given.

'Miss Drechsler,' Violet cries, her face stricken, her body hunched over the morning edition of the *Daily Mail* that is spread on the counter in front of her. 'Oh, my days.'

'What is it, Violet?'

She hands me the newspaper. The headline rips through my body like an aftershock as I read.

LUSITANIA TORPEDOED BY GERMANS

'Dear God, no,' I whisper. 'Not this.'

'They say there were hundreds of little kiddies killed,' says Violet, pressing her cotton handkerchief to her eyes. 'Women too. If you'll excuse my language, Miss Drechsler, but those bloody Germans are going to get what's coming to them.'

She scurries behind the counter and begins laying out the freshly baked rolls in the display case. I stand rooted to the spot, images burning into my brain.

A great ship, packed with men, women and children, smiling and waving as they left the port. Then a darkness, black as hell, descended. Screams of terror, propellors whirring, water filling lungs.

'Our lot won't let them get away with this,' says Violet.

She gestures wildly to the street outside which, for this hour of the morning, has remained conspicuously quiet.

'Customers have been thin on the ground since war broke out,' she says, shaking her head. 'But this, this will tip them over the edge. You mark my words. My old ma said it herself; she said the likes of you are living on borrowed time.'

'Violet. Calm yourself.'

'Calm myself?' she cries, grabbing the newspaper from my hands and jabbing her finger at the headline. 'In the face of this? My ma and pa warned me about staying on working here when war broke out, but I told them that you were different, you weren't like those evil Germans who want to bayonet babies, you're just a nice lady who likes baking cakes.'

'I'm still a nice person,' I say, a feeling of dread lodging in my chest. 'This is terrible, Violet, but it has nothing to do with me.'

'I know that, miss,' she says, her voice softening. 'But that lot outside'll be baying for blood. And while I'm still working here, I'm guilty by association.'

She marches to the wooden coat stand by the door and collects her hat and jacket.

'Violet, what are you doing?' I exclaim. 'You can't leave. We'll have the breakfast rush in a moment.'

'I'm sorry, miss,' she says, her eyes filling with tears. 'I can't work here any more. Things are going to get worse after this, much worse.'

'Violet, stop,' I cry, following her out onto the street. 'This has nothing to do with me. Violet, please, I . . .'

My voice is swallowed by a set of horses' hooves as a bottle cart clatters by. The man driving it stares at me with cold grey eyes. As he pulls the reins and draws the cart to a halt, I recognize him. It is Alfred Jennings, Violet's father, known locally as a gambler and a feckless drunk.

'Violet, get yourself home,' he cries, jumping down from the cart. 'We'll deal with this ourselves.'

'Pa, don't do anything silly,' pleads Violet, glancing at me with stricken eyes. 'Miss Drechsler's done nothing wrong. It's those other Germans that are the problem. They're the murderers, not her.'

'Violet, I won't say it twice,' he says, spittle forming at the edge of his mouth. 'Get yourself home or I will take my belt to you.'

'Get away, Miss Drechsler,' cries Violet, looking back at me as she runs down the street. 'For heaven's sake, get away.'

'You don't scare me, Jennings,' I say to her father, folding my arms across my chest defiantly. 'An old drunk with a flea-bitten horse. Get away from my premises this instant or I shall summon a policeman.'

'The only thing you're going to summon is the Devil,' says Jennings, jumping down from the cart. ''Ere, lads. We'll start with this one. The mad German bint dresses like a man. Let's see if she can fight like one.'

He puts his two fingers to his mouth and gives a whistle.

I look up the street and see a herd of men and boys holding wooden spikes aloft, more like a scene from a medieval battlefield than a capital city in a civilized nation.

'Do it for our country, lads,' cries Jennings. 'No mercy.'

With that, the crowd of men seems to multiply. Scores of figures, coming from all directions, swarm towards me. I want to stay and face them, scare them off, but I know that I am pitifully outnumbered. However, I will defend my property if it is the last thing I do. Turning on my heels, I run back into the bakery, securing the latch with trembling hands.

Then I dash upstairs, smashing my arm against the wooden banister in my haste. When I reach what was my father's bedroom, I heave the iron-framed bed aside, and dart underneath, taking the metal bar Father always kept there and clutching it to my chest. If they want a fight, they can have one. As I lie beneath the bed, I hear men's voices coming from the street outside.

'Kill the Kraut.'

'Smash it all to pieces.'

There is a pause, then an almighty crash as the shop window smashes. In my haste to escape, I had forgotten to pull the shutters down. I hear metal-capped boots on the stone floor, angry voices screaming curses, and suddenly my courage deserts me.

3

MIRIAM

Dänholm Prisoner-of-War Camp, Germany

September 1918

The men lining up obediently in the exercise yard look like ghosts, half-people haunting the prison-issue uniforms that hang from their thin frames like rags. One of the men catches my eye as he is standing slightly out of line, his arms folded across his chest, a small act of defiance in this institutionalized world. His hair has been roughly shaven by the guards and his hollow eyes are outlined with vivid yellow and purple bruises. Beyond him and the exercise yard enclosed by barbed wire I can see the iron joists of the bridge that links this part of the island, known as Lesser Dänholm, to its other half, Greater Dänholm, and beyond that the sea. A ferry runs through here every few days, bringing with it more British prisoners who are held in cages in the harbour like shoals of fish before being processed and brought to the camp. The sheer volume of men that arrives here every few days is staggering and yet, according to them, the British are winning the war. Who knows what to believe? For if my time in here has taught me anything, it is to trust nothing and no one.

Not least the prisoners with their filthy language and lecherous ways. The endless crude jokes, the leering stares, the wandering hands. I must say it all took some getting used to for a young academic newly released from a women's college at the University of Freiburg. Over time, I have learned how to deal with the prisoners and their unwanted attention, finding that a quick slap stops a wandering hand in its tracks – as does the application of my cold stare, something I honed while working for a brief stint as a governess for two over-indulged eight-year-old boys back in Cologne. Whether eight years old or eighty, I have found that there is nothing a man fears more than the icy stare of a woman.

'Fräulein Ziegler,' says Herr Garn, coming over to the window where I am standing looking out at the barbed wire-framed yard. He places his pipe in his top pocket, the smell of tobacco lingering on his breath as he speaks. 'The men are about to be brought in. Best have everything ready.'

I jump to attention and go to the large cupboard at the back of the room to retrieve the equipment while Herr Garn peruses his large, leather-bound Bible, looking for a suitable verse.

'You know, today feels like a Gospel of St Luke day,' he says, his grey eyes twinkling. 'Let's see what the men can do with the Parable of the Prodigal Son.'

As Herr Garn holds the page with the ribbon bookmark, I bring the bulky recording apparatus over to the table and prepare the wax cylinder. The room is stiflingly warm and poky, a dank forgotten corner that the camp administrator deemed useless enough to give to us for what he referred to as 'your little experiment'.

'Now,' says Herr Garn, handing me the Bible. 'May I ask you to recite a few lines to test the sound levels before the men arrive?'

'Certainly,' I say, taking the Bible and stepping onto the platform.

Herr Garn nods his head and, leaning into the recording horn, I begin to speak.

'There was a man who had two sons. The younger one said to his father, "Father, give me my share of the estate." So he divided his property between them.

'How was that?' I say, looking up as Herr Garn pauses the recording.

'My word, Fräulein Ziegler,' he exclaims, a rare smile breaking across his thin, grey face. 'If I didn't know better, I would have taken you for a member of the English aristocracy. I haven't heard such perfect RP since my Oxford days. Can you do any others? What about the West Country?'

'Somerset?' I say, rolling the 'r', which causes Herr Garn to snort with laughter. 'Why, of course I can.'

I recite the second stanza of the parable in a voice I last heard a couple of days ago, a young man called Billy Taylor who had regaled us with stories of his childhood on a dairy farm in a place called Frome that, according to him, was pronounced 'Froome'.

'My dear girl,' Garn exclaims, when I have finished. 'It's a wonder you didn't choose a career on the stage. You're quite the mimic. Where did you learn how to do it?'

'I'm not sure,' I say, closing the Bible. 'Though I've always been curious about accents and voices. When I was a child, my aunt would scold me for mimicking her guests, but I didn't do it to be impertinent, I was genuinely fascinated by their voices, the pitch, the cadence, the way a voice could alter a face. Have you noticed how a lot of the officers speak out of the side of their mouth, as though the very act of talking is somehow beneath them, or a tiresome chore? Whereas the Irish friends of my aunt used to talk so fast and with such animation, even the most mundane topic was turned into a grand performance. It was mesmerizing to observe. And it's led me here, so I suppose there was more to it than childish impertinence.'

Herr Garn looks at me with a wistful expression.

'It's how it all began for me too,' he says softly. 'This life-long obsession. I have always found the voice to be a kind of sorcery. We cannot see it or touch it and yet humans have spent epochs placing their trust in this strange invisible force that has the power to break hearts, to wage wars, to stir and to soothe.'

He looks down at the phonograph, lost in his thoughts. I want to ask him about his time in Oxford, why he looked so sad when he spoke of it, but before I can there is a clatter of footsteps in the corridor outside.

'Ah, here come the men now,' says Herr Garn, snapping out of his reverie. He takes the Bible from me, placing it on the table, then stands with his hands behind his back as the prisoners file in. In an instant, he has resumed the impassive, impenetrable mantle of professor. There will be no more reflection today. There is work to be done.

It is a new group this morning, freshly processed. Some of them look exhausted and not a little shell-shocked. A desperately thin young man who doesn't look a day over fifteen trembles violently as they shuffle into the room.

Others seem ebullient, fizzing with energy, likely glad to be reprieved of an afternoon's hard labour.

'All right, darlin',' says one of them, in an accent that I recall Herr Garn referring to as Estuary English. 'Name's Harry. What's yours then?'

The young man has hair the colour of marmalade, pink pimpled skin, and a lairy smile that exposes a mouthful of grey crooked teeth.

'This is Fräulein Ziegler,' interjects Herr Garn. 'She will be recording you today, alongside myself, Professor Josef Garn of the University of Berlin. Before we begin, I would like to thank you all for agreeing to take part in this project.'

'So we just have to read something?' asks Harry, his eyes narrowing. 'And you record it?'

'That is correct,' says Herr Garn coolly. 'A short extract from the Bible. Now who would like to go first?'

As one, the men look down at their feet. All except Harry, who strides forward.

'May as well start with the best,' he says, giving me a wink as he approaches the desk. 'Now what do you want me to read?'

Herr Garn hands Harry the Bible and points to the page.

'I would like you to recite this parable in its entirety,' he says, speaking slowly and steadily. 'But first, I would like you to stand in front of the platform here while we take your photograph.'

'A photograph? Blimey. I should have worn a tie, eh, lads?' says Harry, addressing his fellow prisoners with a hollow laugh as he steps up to the platform. 'Do you want me to smile?'

'That will not be necessary,' says Herr Garn, placing his

head inside the curtained camera. 'The image is solely for our records. Now, on a count of three. One, two, three.'

With that a flash illuminates Harry's face and his image is captured.

'Right,' says Herr Garn, moving the camera to one side. 'Before you begin the recital, I would like you to introduce yourself. Tell us your name, your date of birth, where you were born and, finally, your battalion and unit number. Is that clear?'

'As mud,' says the prisoner. Then turning to me with a crooked grin, he adds, 'Make sure you're recording now, darlin'.'

I check that the wax cylinder is still in place, then flick the recording switch, nodding at the young man to begin.

'My name is Harold William Boscombe,' he says, speaking loudly into the horn. 'I was born on the sixth of June eighteen ninety-nine in Southend, county of Essex . . .'

As he talks, my mind drifts unbidden. I'm sitting, in stunned silence, in the assembly hall at the University of Freiburg, as the principal, Herr Baumer, announces that, further to the declaration of war, we female students are to cease our studies forthwith and sign up for the war effort. 'There will be time for books once the war is won,' he thunders, slamming his fist onto the lectern in a rare display of patriotic fervour. 'For now, all German women are expected to play their part and serve the brave men who are risking their lives in the muddy fields of Flanders.'

As we filed out of the hall towards an unknown future, I felt numb. This education had not come easily to me or my female contemporaries. Though it had been fourteen years since women were granted full access to university in the state of Baden, we were still considered second-class scholars by the male professors and students. We should be grateful, that is what they told us. Grateful to be thrown scraps from the banqueting table that represented centuries of male-dominated education. Our choices, when it came to the subjects we wished to study, were limited to a handful, so, though my passion was linguistics, I was only permitted to study philosophy, as that was the humanities subject deemed most suited to the 'emotional' female brain. I made the most of my studies regardless. I threw myself into the philosophy degree, while secretly immersing myself in the linguistics books housed in the magnificent university library. I would find a way to study my beloved words, even if it meant working long into the night. Now, it was being taken away from me, and the devastation was almost too much to bear.

Yet when I arrived in Flanders and began to nurse the wounded and dying men, the devastation gave way to guilt. What right had I to be complaining about my studies being cut short when these young men, teenagers most of them, were risking their lives in a war that was nothing short of organized slaughter? Still, my linguistic brain was never switched off, and I found myself listening to the men as they spoke, sorting and sifting their voices into locality and state. The melodious alto of Prussia, the monosyllabic staccato of the lower lands. I threw myself into nursing with the same intensity as I had pursued my studies and, over time, found that my calm head and gentle manner gave comfort to the scared and the dying. If only there was a way of continuing my studies while still doing my bit for the war effort, I would ponder to myself in rare quiet moments, When I was transferred to this camp, and met Herr Garn, it appeared my wish had been granted.

By the time he reached Dänholm last month, he had been to eleven camps across Germany, and gathered almost one thousand recordings. Now here we are, four years into the war, and four weeks into the recordings, and Herr Garn seems no closer to completing the project. Sometimes, I think it will never end; that his hunger for collecting dialects will see him trapped in these camps for ever.

'That will be all, Mr Boscombe.' The professor's voice brings me hurtling back to the present. 'Thank you very much.'

'Was that all right?' says Harry, his bravado faltering for a moment. 'I stumbled a bit over those long words. I could do it again if you like?'

'That won't be necessary, Mr Boscombe,' says Herr Garn briskly. 'Now, who is next?'

A thick silence settles over the room. I look up from my recording, and my heart begins to pulsate. It is the man I saw earlier in the exercise yard.

He stands motionless in front of the desk, his pale eyes fixed on me. As I return his stare, I am overcome with the feeling I had when I was watching him earlier, that he is a strange paradox of light and dark, dangerous and vulnerable all at once.

'You must be next,' says Herr Garn, coming to stand beside him. 'Now, if you'd like to step onto the platform, tell me your name and—'

'Hands on your head!'

The door bursts open and Herr Garn's voice is swallowed up by three armed guards yelling orders.

'I said hands on your head. Now!'

I am about to do as the guard says when I realize that the order is being directed at the prisoner and not to the room at large.

And yet, it seems he is the only one of us not to flinch. As the guards bear down on him, he continues to stare at me, his eyes seemingly penetrating my soul. As though he exudes some kind of powerful energy, a radio frequency of sorts. It fills the space around us. Finally, without averting his gaze, he raises his hands to his head and allows the guards to guide him to the door.

'Are you all right, Fräulein?'

I look up and see one of the guards has returned. I recognize him. His name is Dieter but the nurses have another name for him. He has a reputation that means nurses always make sure they are in pairs when he comes to inspect the sanatorium.

'Are you all right?' he repeats, flecks of spittle escaping from his mouth as he speaks. 'He didn't touch you?'

'I am fine,' I say, though the altercation and the intensity of the prisoner's gaze have left me feeling rather shaken. 'And, no, he didn't touch me. He didn't do anything at all.'

'That is good,' he says, with a nod. 'Apologies for the disruption, Herr Professor.'

'That is quite all right,' replies Herr Garn, though it is clear, as he wipes the beads of sweat from his forehead with a handkerchief, that the incident has left him just as shaken as me. 'But what is the meaning of this? What has the man done to warrant this sort of mob-handedness?'

'He's a troublemaker,' says Dieter, lowering his voice.

'Keeps getting into scraps with the guards. Won't follow orders. You see, he refuses to speak.'

'He is mute?' says Garn, his linguistic curiosity piqued.

'Apparently so,' says Dieter, with a shrug. 'He's one of the new arrivals. Found him wandering, with no clue where he was, outside the train station at Amiens, just after the Third Battle of Picardy. Hasn't uttered a word since.'

My eyes are fixed on the soldier, who is standing, stock-still, staring at the floor while the guards flank him. There is something different about this man, something solitary and insular. He reminds me of the lone leopards that used to slip from the mangrove forests into the gardens of my aunt's house in Kerala at night, wide-eyed and stealthy, a killer yet somehow vulnerable and exposed, a wild animal so out of place amongst the starched tablecloths and polished silverware.

'How odd,' says Herr Garn. 'What is his name?'

'Only God can answer that. We can't get a word out of him,' says Dieter, glancing at the door where his comrades are waiting for him patiently, the man frozen like a statue between them. 'All we know about him is his battalion, from the badges on his uniform. And the only item he had on him was a photograph of a woman in the breast pocket of his greatcoat, the words "From your darling wife" written on the back. That he's married is all we know for sure. The medic seems to think he's suffering from shell shock. I've seen a lot of it in the camps. In the absence of a name, he was registered as Prisoner X.'

How terrifying, I think to myself, glancing across at the man. To be trapped in one's own silence, to be stripped of your voice.

'I will let you get on, Professor,' says Dieter. 'We have taken up enough of your time already.'

He doffs his cap, first at Herr Garn, then at me, before joining his fellow guards at the door.

'Hands down!' he screams, his voice contorted with hatred.

Then, taking an arm each, they escort the silent prisoner from the room. But as they open the door, Prisoner X turns and flashes me one last glance. And as I watch him depart, flanked by the guards, into the darkened corridor, I feel as though in that one, short moment, no longer than the blink of an eye, I could somehow peer straight into his soul. A soul caught between two worlds, that of the living and the dead.

4

EDIE

Cornwall

Present Day

I wake to a fierce thunderstorm, the worst I have known since moving to Cornwall. The wind rattles the delicate windows and with every blow it feels like the glass is going to come crashing in on me as I lie here in my single bed. My beautiful French bed with the clawed feet and ornate carved headboard was another casualty of 12 October. I found I couldn't sleep in it any more. All that empty space where David's warm body had once been – it was no longer a place of refuge but an icy wasteland. I included the bed and every other bit of furniture in the sale of the flat. French armoire, oak bookshelves, hand-painted kitchen tables and Edwardian armchairs, all thrown in. I set out for Cornwall with a vanload of newly acquired IKEA furniture; cheap, minimalist and with no painful memories attached, this bed included.

Another gust of wind smashes against the cottage. The room shakes violently, and I hear something clatter to the ground outside. Reaching for my phone, I check the time: 2.43 a.m. I really should go and see what has been broken, inspect the damage, but my mind pulls me in several directions at once. Remember that night. Stay put. Wait till morning. Call the police. Round and round go the thoughts like bicycle wheels moving yet not getting anywhere fast. Eventually, I haul myself from the bed, put on my thick fleece-lined dressing gown and, with my phone gripped in my hands, tentatively make my way downstairs.

When I reach the narrow hallway with its dark wood panelling, I switch on the light and stand for a moment by the front door. The wind is pounding against the thin wooden frame, and I can feel the cold air as it whistles under the door. Perhaps I should call Alexander. He told me when I first moved in that he's a night owl. Maybe he can come and help me investigate, safety in numbers and all that. But then a voice inside my head, David's perhaps, tells me to stop being so silly, that this is Cornwall not London. The only threat out there is a wild summer storm and possibly a fox or two.

Unlatching the door, I slip my feet into the gardening Crocs by the door and make my way out into the night. Rain lashes at my face and I am almost blown off my feet as I stumble down the path, shining the torch from my phone all around me in search of whatever made that noise. The air smells of salt and its grittiness sticks to my face as I make my way to the front gate, which is swinging on its hinges. I place my hand on the latch in a feeble attempt to secure the gate but as I do, I catch sight of something out of the corner of my eye. I look up and see a figure cresting the road in the direction of Lytton Cove. The person is tall and slim and is wearing what looks like a padded raincoat, the hood pulled up over their head. They are carrying something in their right hand. It looks like a shopping bag of some sort, one of those hessian jute bags my mother likes to haul to Columbia Road market each Saturday.

'Hello,' I call out, but my voice is swallowed by the fierce wind and rain. 'Who is there? Can I help you?'

Wiping the rain from my eyes with the sleeve of my dressing gown, I point the phone torch out across the deserted road. The figure is nowhere to be seen and yet, as I walk back up the path towards the cottage, I can't shake the feeling that I am being watched. Quickening my step, I glance up beyond the white wicker fence that divides my garden from next door's, to Alexander's bedroom. There is a faint light coming from inside but the curtains are drawn. He may be up late, reading. I should be reassured by that but as I head back to my cottage, I feel an odd sensation throughout my body, a darkness closing in on me. It is the same feeling I had when I tiptoed into the living room that night with David striding ahead of me, telling me that the noise that had woken us was probably just foxes in the yard. A gust of wind rattles the door open in front of me. The noise and the blast of light pouring out onto the pathway like blood from an open wound sends shock waves hurtling through my body. Composing myself, I am about to step inside when I see a dark shape to the left of the doorstep, illuminated by the light.

Bending down to take a closer look, I see that it is a large roof slate, cut cleanly in two. So that was what the noise had been, I mutter to myself, somewhat relieved, as I pick it up and head inside. See, Edie, nothing to worry about. Just a broken slate. But as I enter the hallway, I hear something that makes my stomach twist.

A trickling sound that gets louder as I slowly make my way along the corridor. As I switch on the living-room light, my heart sinks. Water is gushing from the ceiling. Desperate, I take my phone and call Alexander. His light was on. Surely he is awake? But the call goes straight to voicemail. I run into the kitchen and fetch a bucket. I am just placing it under the stream of water when I hear the front door burst open. My heart leaps inside my chest as I run into the hallway.

'Who's there?' I call, tiptoeing out onto the front step. 'What do you want?'

But the freezing night air returns only silence.

'Just the wind,' I say, trying to reassure myself. 'These old doors are fragile at the best of times. Nothing to worry about.'

But as I head back inside, I remember the hooded figure hurrying away down the deserted road. With trembling hands, I pull the chain across and wedge the heavy iron doorstop against the frame.

Please, David, I whisper, as I make my way upstairs. Please keep me safe.

5

KATERINA

'Little Germany', East London

May 1915

I crouch beneath the bed, my face pressed into the dusty wooden floorboards. 'Give me courage,' I plead. 'Let Archangel Michael wrap his shield around me, now and always, and protect me from harm.'

The words I had first learned when I was initiated into the Divine Order of Universal Truth seem redundant in the face of the violence that is taking place in the bakery downstairs and out on the street. Back then, I had been a rather innocent young girl, keen to develop my gifts in a place where, my brother had assured me, I would find like-minded people. It was a world of esoteric discussions and literary salons, highballs of gin and velvet smoking jackets. A world where you might find yourself giving a reading for a poet laureate or a famous stage actress before dining by candlelight on filet mignon while sipping the finest of wines. I did not realize it then, though Otto tried to convince me, that there was no real need for protection in the Divine Order as there was no one there who wished me harm. 'The real danger, Katerina,' he would say, his intelligent eyes as blue as the pocket square he wore at all times, 'is out there on the street. I fear you are sheltered from it, hiding away with this lot and behind the counter in Father's bakery. You haven't seen the things that I have seen, and I hope you never do.'

I had thought he was patronizing me, treating me as the child I knew I was, but he was right. I was vulnerable.

I flinch as I recall the first time it happened, the first hint we had that I possessed the gift of second sight. Father, Mother, Otto and I had been gathered on the common land on the outskirts of the small German town where I was brought up, to watch a great spectacle: the inaugural flight of a hot air balloon. I stood holding my mother's hand, watching as the brightly coloured canvas began to take shape. Yet as the two men who were to fly it climbed into the basket, I was assailed with such a violent vision it almost took my breath away. I saw flames leaping at the basket, the men shrieking in terror as the balloon hurtled to the ground. I began to cry and demanded we go home. I made such a scene, it drew gasps of shock from the onlookers, most of whom were our neighbours and friends. One of them, Fräulein Holst, was heard to mutter, 'There is something odd about that child. You mark my words. She's going to be trouble,' as my poor parents hurried me away. They were embarrassed at being shown up in front of their friends, but I shall never forget their faces when the evening papers delivered to our home later had the news splashed across them:

HORROR BALLOON CRASH. INFERNO! NO SURVIVORS

Little did we know how much all of our lives would

be affected by that incident, how the world as we knew it would change beyond recognition. In the weeks following the accident, my visions had intensified and were now accompanied by voices, loud and insistent, that came to me as I drifted off to sleep. I was so young I had no idea where these voices were coming from and I would scream for my parents, begging them, as they ran into my bedroom, their faces etched with fear, to please make the voices stop. One day, exhausted from my nocturnal terrors, my mother had confided in a customer; a woman she had long considered a friend. The woman had offered sympathy, had told my mother not to worry, that it was likely just a phase, and that it would pass. But when that 'loyal' customer left that day, clutching her bag of strudels, she would tell the tale to her husband who would tell his friends at the bierkeller who would go home and tell their wives. Before long the whole town was fizzing with the news that Drechsler's daughter was being driven mad by voices in her head. Soon the gossip turned hostile, and the bakery was targeted by groups of young thugs, smashing windows and calling me a devil child. A town meeting was held to debate whether a child such as me should be allowed to attend school or whether I posed a danger to their sons and daughters. 'She belongs in an asylum!' one of our neighbours yelled at us as my mother walked me home from school one day. My poor mama, unused to such hostility, saw her health begin to fail. The thought of her daughter being taken from her was just too much to bear. She lost weight, suffered from crippling anxiety, and refused to leave the house. And though the doctors refused to acknowledge a correlation, we knew that the stroke that claimed my mother's life at the tender age of thirty-three was a direct result of the stresses my 'gift' had brought to her door. In the wake of this devastation, Father decided a fresh start was needed, and the capital city of England seemed liberal and progressive enough to offer safety and security to a girl like me. Once we arrived, he and Otto did everything they could to shield me from potential danger, from the cruelty of other people that had led to my mother's death.

Now, Father is dead too, a heart attack claiming him the day after war was declared, and Otto is fighting for Germany in the sodden fields of France. I am the only Drechsler left here, the last German standing, or so it seems.

But the danger they tried to shield me from has crept into my world. For the last few hours, I have lain here and listened as it tears down my shop, smashes the windows, prowls like a beast. And any moment now, it will burst into this room and take its vengeance on me.

'Give me courage,' I repeat, gripping the metal bar in my hands. 'Let me—'

Before I can finish, there is a heavy thud on the landing, then the door bursts open.

'This way, lads. Let's see if there's anything worth nicking.'

'Careful, Hobbsy. There might be some toothless old Hun waiting to jump you.'

'I'd like to see 'er try. I'd beat 'er with this stick till she begged me to stop.'

The voices are childish, high-spirited. These are nothing more than boys. Still, children or not, the menace of their intent is real, and it permeates the room. If they find me, they will do me harm, there is no doubt of that. I hold my breath, watching their small booted feet as they stomp around the room, upending drawers and dragging Father's old suits from the wardrobe.

'Nowt here worth stealing,' says the one called Hobbsy. 'Just a bunch of old rags. Let's go help Pa finish off downstairs. He's emptied the till, but those plates should fetch a canny bob.'

My father's silverware. Simple but precious items, passed down from his grandfather, steeped in family history.

'No, you don't,' I cry, leaping from under the bed and aiming a blow at the back of the boy's legs with the metal bar.

He crashes to the ground, yelling in pain. His accomplice stands by the open wardrobe, his face aghast.

'Run, Sid,' he cries. 'It's a fella. Run for your life.'

The boy staggers to his feet but instead of running away he charges at me and locks his hands around my throat.

'German scum,' he spits, his face so close to mine I can smell his sour breath. 'What you doing hiding under a bed like some rat? Come on, Ernie, give us a hand getting him downstairs. Let's throw him to Jennings's lot. See what they do to him.'

I glance in the other boy's direction, but he is rooted to the spot, his hands gripping the wardrobe door.

'Ernie, I said . . .'

He stops as heavy footsteps clatter up the stairs.

'Kat?'

A female voice rings out across the landing.

'Kat, are you up here?'

There is only one person who calls me that.

'Gillian,' I croak, as she hurtles into the room, her long black coat trailing behind her.

The boy whose hands are round my throat turns and I take the opportunity to smash him across the shoulders with the metal bar.

'Get out of here, you brutes,' cries Gillian, pulling the stunned boy up by his braces and throwing him onto the landing.

'You too,' she says, gesturing to the other boy who is trembling from head to foot, his hands still gripping the wardrobe door. 'Out now. Before the police arrive.'

Gillian's formidable height, almost six foot in her heeled lace-up boots, combined with her cut-glass accent, are enough to send both boys scurrying off down the stairs.

'Darling,' says Gillian, rushing to me, in a haze of orange blossom scent. 'Are you all right? Did he hurt you? Let me look at your neck.'

'I'm fine,' I say, batting her hand away and straightening my clothes. 'I was dealing with it perfectly well until you turned up.'

'What are you talking about? He had his hands around your throat,' she cries. 'He could have killed you.'

'I was in control,' I say, pulling out the bed and seeing the outline of the loose floorboard beneath it. Down there are the month's takings, some of my mother's jewellery, my father's gold watch, his stocks and bonds and, most precious of all, my Tarot cards. If those boys had found the safe, then I would have been left with nothing.

'I don't need rescuing,' I say, turning to Gillian who is standing by the window looking out onto the street. 'What are you doing here anyway?'

'I heard about the riots while I was at a Federation meeting,' she says, pulling the net curtain back a fraction with a curl of her finger. 'You should see it out there. The whole of the East End is ablaze. I had to see you were safe. I couldn't bear the thought of you being here alone and scared.'

'Gillian, there was really no need, I . . .' Suddenly the room starts to spin. I reach for the bedpost, try to steady myself.

'Darling, you're in shock,' says Gillian, rushing to my side and placing her hand on the small of my back, a gesture that sends a fizz of electricity up my spine. 'You were always prone to fainting fits. Now, sit down on the bed a moment and breathe slowly.'

I reluctantly do as she says, but all the while I am willing her to go. Just being near her makes me feel tense.

'You can't possibly stay here,' she says, crouching next to me, her boots making a crunching sound on the broken glass. 'Sylvia says this is just the beginning. They're baying for blood after what happened to the *Lusitania*.'

Sylvia. A name I hoped I wouldn't hear again.

'You're still working with her,' I murmur, half to myself, as my head begins to clear.

'Yes, I am still part of the Federation,' she replies brusquely. 'Our work is needed now more than ever. Do you know how many women are living in poverty in the East End as a direct result of this blasted war? I've seen sights I wouldn't wish on anyone. Mothers surviving on vegetable peelings scavenged from dustbins, babies suffering with rickets and malnutrition. We're heading back to the worst of the Victorian era yet it's all being swept under the carpet. God forbid, we lower morale by speaking the truth while our boys are out there fighting.'

Her eyes blaze with indignation and a smile escapes me. She is still the same old Gillian. Still making a noise about the injustices of the world. Still trying to save everyone. She catches me and her face softens.

'I've missed you,' she says, lightly resting her fingers on my cheek. 'I wish I could go back and relive our time together. I would do everything differently. I know you weren't thinking straight when we last saw each other, that you were scared about us being found out. And I understand that, I really do. I heard what happened with Otto too, you must feel—'

At that, there is an almighty crash on the street outside. The sound of horses' hooves and drunken men shouting. Gillian leaps to her feet and rushes to the window.

'We have to get out of here,' she says, turning to me, the colour drained from her face. 'It's not safe.'

'I'm not going to let a few idiots force me out of my home,' I cry, stumbling to my feet. 'This whole thing will blow over in a few hours. It always does.'

'I'm not sure about that,' says Gillian. 'Come and see.'

I join her at the window and look out onto the street where crowds of men, women and children line the cobbles, their faces riven with anger and hatred.

'They're baying for blood,' says Gillian again, letting the lace curtain drop. 'You have no choice but to leave. Now, why don't you pack a bag and I'll wait for you downstairs to escort you safely out of here.'

'There will be no need for that,' I say. 'I have no intention of showing these thugs that I'm afraid.'

'There are dozens of them out there,' says Gillian. 'And, like that brute earlier, they'll more than likely take you for a chap and try to fight you like one.'

'All right, all right,' I cry, a dull feeling of dread creeping through my bones. 'You can accompany me if it makes you feel better. I shall book into a hotel until this blows over. But don't think everything is back to the way it was between us. We're not friends, Gillian.'

'I never claimed we were,' she says, a note of sadness creeping into her voice. 'I'll be downstairs when you're ready.'

She nods her head, then swiftly leaves the room.

'Courage,' I whisper to myself, as I take the small leather suitcase down from the top of my father's wardrobe. I lay it on the floor and then, pushing the bed aside further – a task that takes me several attempts – prise open the loose floorboard. I lift out the metal takings box first and scrutinize the contents. Six pounds, eight shillings and fivepence. I had been sure there was more than that but with Violet's wages and suppliers to pay on top of the dwindling custom these last few months, our income has shrunk considerably. I recall how Otto used to help my father bank the takings before the war forced us all to be suspicious of everyone and everything, before we had to hide money under the bed.

And then a terrible thought comes to me. What if he comes back and I'm not here? What if he goes away again? I couldn't bear the thought of him returning to an empty house. I could write him a note, I think to myself, tell him the name of the hotel I am staying in, but then I think of the mob, the hatred etched on their faces. What if one of those men found the note?

Just a couple of days in a hotel, then you can come back and reopen the bakery, I tell myself, putting the floorboard back in place. And I'm sure Violet can be persuaded to return. She is a sensible girl with a bright future ahead of her. Surely she knows better than to follow the demands of her drunken brute of a father.

Once I have put the bed back in place, I take the boxes and pack them into the suitcase. Then I grab a couple of shirts and trousers, underwear and socks from the chest of drawers in my bedroom and add them too. Just enough for a couple of days, I tell myself, as I walk down the stairs, no need to bulk myself up with unnecessary luggage.

But as I step inside what was once the bakery my stomach lurches.

The front windows have been smashed entirely; fragments of broken glass cover the floorboards and crunch underfoot as I make my way over to what used to be the counter.

'What have they done?' A hoarse whisper escapes my lips, my body trembling.

The magnificent teak counter, my father's pride and joy, has been hacked to pieces. The pretty glass display cabinets, where Violet had earlier placed our bestselling apple strudels and warm breakfast rolls, lie in pieces on the floor. The framed portrait of my parents that hung above the counter all these years has been defaced, 'Murderers' written in black ink across their faces.

'I have no words. I'm so sorry, Kat.'

I look up and see Gillian standing by the door, her hands gripping the lock chain.

'They've taken the till,' I say, noticing the gap where the

ornate metal cash register once stood. 'So money earned by Germans is good enough for them but not decent, hard-working German people.'

My voice trembles with rage.

'Come on,' says Gillian, gesturing to me. 'Let's get this over with.'

She opens the door and as we step out onto the street a cry rises up from a group of men standing on the pavement opposite.

'German scum! Get the hell out.'

'We are not German, we are Englishwomen,' retorts Gillian, as I march on ahead. 'I am the owner of this building and I demand you remove yourselves from here at once.'

'Go to hell, Lady Muck!'

'Stuck-up tart!'

As I walk down the street, with Gillian rushing to keep up behind me, I look down at my feet. My hobnail boots are coated in a thick layer of glass, plaster dust and sugary grime. I grip the metal bar, fully prepared to use it if I have to.

But as I turn the corner, all hope drains away. The mob that had stormed the Mile End Road looks pitiful in comparison to the veritable army now terrorizing the occupants of Stepney Green. There must be two hundred people, mostly men and boys, assembled outside a row of shops. I notice, with horror, that some of them are armed with knives and hatchets.

'Cover your face,' hisses Gillian behind me, as we approach. 'And don't speak. If they catch your accent, we're done for.'

Reluctantly, I do as she says and pull down my cap so that my peripheral vision is obscured. Staring straight ahead, I navigate my way through the baying crowd.

As we draw level with the first shop, I hear cheers. Looking up, I see two men in shirtsleeves and braces lowering a piano from the top window of Schumacher's, the chemist's.

'Easy does it, lads,' cries an older man on the street below. 'Won't be worth anything if you smash it.'

'This is for those poor babies, you murdering filth!'

My body stiffens as we head deeper into the crowd where an elderly man is standing, barely clothed.

'Herr Schumacher,' I gasp, as I recognize the kindly pharmacist who provided my father with his medicine right until the end. Though he looks so different without his round wire spectacles, immaculate suit and always-pristine white coat.

Behind me Gillian prods me in the back.

'Shh, Kat,' she whispers. 'Not a word.'

Two men, armed with hammers, are stripping the last of the old man's clothes from his frail body, while a group of boys, no older than ten, drag a trough of water into the centre of the pavement.

'Dunk him in. See how he feels to drown!'

'I have to stop them,' I mutter, under my breath. 'He is an elderly man. A good man. This is barbaric.'

I rush forward, holding the metal bar aloft.

Stop!' I cry. 'Stop it at once.'

'You can't help him,' snaps Gillian, pulling me back. 'They'll kill you.'

Swallowing down my anger, I walk away from the

terrible sight, but the screams of the mob and the splashing of water barrage my conscience. I shall never forget this, I think to myself as we pass Verner's, the grocer's, where two policemen are emerging from the broken glass, their arms laden with tins of corned beef.

When we reach the Cambridge Hotel in Bethnal Green, the place where Father, Otto and I had stayed on our first night in England, I stop and turn to Gillian.

'This is the place,' I say dispassionately. 'You can leave me now.'

'Are you sure you don't want me to come in with you?' she says, placing her hand on my arm. 'Make sure you're all right.'

'I'm quite sure,' I say, firmly moving my arm away. 'Goodbye, Gillian.'

I turn and make my way up the stairs, glancing down at my filthy boots. I remember this place as the height of sophistication and grandeur from when I stayed here as a child, though with its peeling paint and grubby windows, it looks to have gone a little downhill in the intervening years. All the better, I think as I enter the lobby, at least I won't be turned away for looking a mess.

There is a small desk just inside the entrance with a bell placed on top. There is no sign of any concierge, so I place my bag by my feet and ring the bell. After a couple of moments, a man in a navy suit and tie appears from a room to the left. He smiles warmly at me as he makes his way to the desk.

'Good evening, sir, and welcome to the Cambridge,' he says, opening a large leather book and flicking through the pages. 'You have a room booked?'

'Er, no. I was hoping to book one now.' I remove my cap and let my messy hair fall free. 'And it's miss.'

'My apologies, miss. Well, you're in luck. We have a few vacancies,' he says, his finger poised on the page. 'Will you be requiring a single room?'

'Yes,' I reply. 'For two nights.'

'May I have your name?' he enquires.

'It's Drechsler,' I reply. 'Miss Katerina Drechsler.'

He looks at me then, his eyes narrowing, the smile fading.

'I'm afraid we have no rooms,' he barks, slamming the ledger shut. 'We are fully booked.'

'But you just said you have vacancies. I don't understand.'

'Miss, I think it is in your best interests if you leave. Now.'

It is only then that it dawns on me. He is turning me away because I am German. This hotel, this haven where my father, brother and I were greeted with such warmth all those years ago, has now deemed me an enemy of the state. I want to shout at this man, demand to see his superior, kick up a fuss. But I know that such a response would be futile. In the space of twenty-four hours, London as I knew it has changed, perhaps irreparably.

'I understand,' I say stiffly, grabbing my bag. 'I am sorry to have troubled you.'

Tears blur my vision as I hurry out of the doors. I might have said so, but I don't understand. I don't understand any of it.

'Kat?'

Wiping my eyes with the back of my sleeve, I see Gillian sitting on the steps. She gets to her feet and rushes towards me.

'What happened?' she says. 'Were there no rooms?'

'There were rooms,' I say. 'Just not for me.'

'Oh, darling.'

'There's nothing else for it,' I say, in no mood for her pity. 'I shall have to return to the bakery. Hide upstairs until all this blows over.'

'It's not going to blow over,' she says gently. 'It's going to get worse. Now come with me.'

She cocks her head and scurries down the steps.

'Come where with you?' I say, following her reluctantly.

'You'll see soon enough,' she says, taking my arm. 'Now, come on, Kat. Trust me.'

6

EDIE

Cornwall

Present Day

'Call Ned. He'll have this sorted in no time.'

Alexander is standing looking up at the ceiling which now features a large tea-coloured stain. It is only 9 a.m. and I have already emptied five buckets of grimy water down the kitchen sink.

'Ned?' I say, handing Alexander a steaming mug of tea, then perching myself on the edge of the sofa, my feet damp from treading across the sodden carpet which no amount of towels and blankets spread across it has helped to prevent. Alexander stands amid the detritus, the edges of his cream sweatpants turning grey from the filthy water. He had called round first thing, after receiving my voice message, confessing to drifting off after the half-bottle of red that had accompanied his dinner and apologizing profusely for missing my call.

'Ned Kendal,' says Alexander, coming to join me on the sofa. 'Local handyman. Looks about ninety but don't let that put you off. He rewired the cottage for me single-handedly and at such a reasonable rate I actually thought he was joking. Here's his number.'

He takes out his phone and texts me the number, then gestures to the hole in the wall.

'He could probably help you with that too,' he says with a smirk. 'What on earth happened?'

'It's a long story,' I sigh, as the events of the earlier part of the previous evening come back to me in fragments. The strange box, the sinister inscription. Alexander looks at me expectantly, but I am aware of time running away with me and the seventy-eight Tarot designs that I haven't even started working on. 'I tell you what, why don't you come over for coffee when I've finished work later and I'll tell you all about it. About fourish?'

'Sure,' says Alexander, getting to his feet. 'I'll pop into the village and pick up some cakes.'

'That would be lovely,' I say, walking him to the door. 'I'll see you then.'

'You will,' he says, pulling his hood up as he steps out into the rain. 'And don't forget to call Ned.'

I try to put the events of the previous evening to the back of my mind as I sit down to draw. My work table is wedged in the bay window of the tiny box room overlooking the front garden where I can see right out towards the cove and the sea. As I sit here looking at the rain, which has now slowed to a steady drizzle, the violence of last night's storm and the strange figure seem like a half-remembered dream. If it hadn't been for the roof slate, I would have found it all entertaining. A bit of drama amid the peace and quiet. I know what real drama feels like, the skin-prickling terror, the sickening knot in the stomach when the sirens that normally screech past your door now stop immediately outside it. A familiar dread begins to rise through my body, making its way from the pit of my stomach right up to my throat. 'Stop it, Edie,' I tell myself, taking a sip of water from the glass next to me, trying to gulp down whatever fear is threatening to explode inside me. 'Focus on the work.'

So I breathe in and out slowly and begin to read through Rebecca's notes. The only sound I can hear is the cooing of the turtle doves on the silver birch tree outside my window, the soft exhalation of my breath and the steady drip, drip of water.

'Shit,' I exclaim, remembering the leaking ceiling and grabbing my phone. I call Ned Kendal as I run downstairs, just in time to retrieve and replace a close-to-overflowing bucket. He doesn't answer so I leave a message, explaining who I am and what the problem is. As I click off and head back upstairs, I catch a glimpse of myself in the landing mirror. They say grief alters you, but I was unprepared for just how much it would affect my appearance. My once bright blue eyes are dulled and purple half-moons sit underneath them, a legacy of eighteen months' crying and sleeplessness. My hair has grown out of the sharp blonde pixie cut that had been my trademark since my student days and now hangs limply on my shoulders. Grey roots that I once attacked with boxes of hair dye at the first sign have now won the war and there is little sign of blonde left, save for a few wisps around the ends. The insipid shade gives my pale skin a sallow and lifeless hue. My linen shirt and ripped jeans hang wide and loose off my body, the jagged edges of my collarbone jutting beneath the folds of linen. Even my breasts have shrivelled and lie flat underneath an old off-white unpadded bra. I am no longer a sensual being, I think to myself, as I pad back into the workroom. I am a shrivelled crone, a shell bearing the name Edie and carrying out her tasks like an automaton; all trace of the woman I used to be was cleaned and swept away that night, never to be seen again.

So vivid is this realization, I wonder whether the figure I thought I saw last night was some sort of out-of-body experience, simply a projection of what I have become.

A shiver flutters through me as I sit back at the desk and open Rebecca's notes again, willing my brain to focus on the words on the screen in front of me and not on the niggling dread that seems to be infiltrating every fibre of me.

In the brief, Rebecca has provided a description of each Tarot card as well as its place in the order of the deck and, as I read, I find myself relaxing into the words.

The Tarot is fundamentally the story of the Fool's journey, she writes. *Which is rather like the story of life: from the innocent optimism of the infant right through to the wisdom of old age and the ultimate cessation of earthly life which makes way for the glorious entrance into the spiritual realm.*

The story of life, I mutter to myself, as I take out a fresh sheet from my sketchbook and sharpen my pencil with my trusty Stanley knife. I suppose only the very lucky get to enjoy the wisdom of old age. Fifty-four summers was all David got. And yet he *was* wise, he was the wisest person I have ever known.

Come now, Edie. I hear his velvet-rich voice in my head. Enough of this maudlin talk, you've got a Fool to draw.

I smile to myself as I lay out the paper and set to work. The hours fall away and before I know it, the alarm on my watch is alerting me to the fact that it is four o'clock. Where has the time gone?

'Edie! I'm here!'

A voice flutters up from the garden. Laying down my pencil, I lean out of the open sash window. The rain has stopped, and the garden is drenched in brilliant sunshine. Alexander is standing in the little strip of pathway between the primroses and bluebells, looking just as jumbled as my mismatched cottage garden plants. He has changed out of his fleece and sweatpants and is dressed in a rather smart cream linen shirt and jeans. His dark hair, peppered with grey, falls over one eye as he peers up at the window, a hessian jute bag clutched in his hand.

'I have cakes,' he exclaims, with an air of childish excitement. 'Now how about you tell me all about that hole in the wall.'

Later, sitting at the kitchen table, I watch as Alexander wedges the box open, after treating the latch with a liberal dose of WD-40.

'Just a bit of rust,' he says. 'And no wonder, after being hidden behind a wall all these years. Or at least, we have to assume it's been in there for a long time.'

'It certainly looks like it has,' I say, pulling the box towards me.

Peering inside, I see a package wrapped in purple silk and a stubby, cylindrical box, rather like a poster tube. Relieved that there don't appear to be any mortal remains, I take out the items and place them on the table in front of us. The tube has a label on the side that recalls the ones on old Victorian medicine bottles, extolling the virtues of camphor or cocaine for the common cold. The paper has yellowed round the edges and the words, printed in thick black lettering, appear to be in German:

HERR PROFESSOR JOSEF GARN. STIMME PROJEKT 30

Turning the tube over, I see that someone has written, in neat capitals in the left-hand corner, *DÄNHOLM STAMMLAGER 1918*. I put the tube aside and take the package in my hands. As I slowly unravel the purple silk, I see a figure hanging from a tree, a golden light surrounding him. The Hanged Man. Peeling away the rest of the silk wrapping, I am astonished to see a deck of beautifully painted Tarot cards.

'How extraordinary,' says Alexander, leaning across to get a closer look.

I flick through the deck, marvelling at the beauty of the illustrations, their jagged lines, muted autumnal colours of burnt sienna, ochre and cobalt, and folktale figures recalling the work of my favourite artist, Arthur Rackham, subject of my art school dissertation and something of a hero to me. As I do, something falls out from between the cards and drops to the floor.

Alexander reaches down to retrieve it.

'It's a photograph,' he says, placing the picture on the table in front of me.

The image is black and white, and badly faded, but I can just make out two people. In the foreground, a fair-haired man dressed in prison uniform stands in front of a desk behind which sits a young woman with glossy dark hair, pinned back into a neat chignon. The woman is smiling at the man, while he stares back at her with bruised, expressionless eyes. Something about their body language, his blank eyes, her uneasy smile, unsettles me. With his striped uniform tattered and torn, the shadows under his eyes, the sense of hopelessness and resignation, he looks like a condemned man facing his executioner. Trying not to think of the ambulance sirens, the courtroom, the look on those men's faces as the judge sent them down, I turn the photo over. To my surprise, I see that someone has written, in the same neat handwriting as on the tube, two words:

For Kitty.

7

MIRIAM

Dänholm Prisoner-of-War Camp

October 1918

When I am not assisting Herr Garn with the recordings, I am expected to continue with my nursing duties and today I have been tasked with administering vaccinations to the new arrivals. After the typhus outbreak of 1915 that almost wiped out the entire camp, the commandant has decreed that all prisoners must be inoculated. They may be captives, he announced to the medical team, but we still require them to be fit to work. He did not want to admit it, but it's easy to guess that the German war economy must be on its knees and, going forward, we must depend upon captive labour in order to survive.

Though it is still early, barely six in the morning, a group of emaciated men are already ensconced in the breaker's yard, hauling pickaxes that probably weigh more than they do at a mountain of stones.

As I walk, I feel a dozen pairs of eyes upon me. Watchtowers are placed at every angle of the camp so that no matter where you are, or what you are doing, your movements can be seen by the armed sentries. Herr

Garn compares the architecture of the camp to Jeremy Bentham's 'Panopticon', where the whole is visible at all times, and therefore able to be controlled. As I round the corner near the huts that house the officer-class POWs, I almost collide with a camp guard, the blade of his bayonet coming perilously close to my face.

It is Dieter.

'*Vorsichtig!*' he yells instinctively. Then, recognizing me, his expression softens.

'*Entschuldigung, schöne Frau.*'

I nod politely, accepting his apology.

He turns and barks an order to a group of men trailing behind him. With their ill-fitting prison uniforms and emaciated frames, they are a sorry sight as they stagger in his wake, like stray dogs on their way to the pound. As I stand aside to let them pass, the men at the back of the group elbow me out of the way.

'German whore,' one of them mutters, slamming his fist down onto the book I am holding as he walks by.

Dieter, oblivious at the head of the pack, marches on, the metal insignia on his uniform glinting in the sun.

I crouch to retrieve my book which has landed face down on the damp grass but, as I do, a hand with thick grazed knuckles and dirty fingernails intercepts mine and grabs it.

I look up, shielding my eyes from the glare of the autumnal light, and see a broad figure standing over me.

Prisoner X. His already short hair has been shaved completely now and he is wearing a new prison-issue uniform, but I recognize the broad shoulders, the large, doe-like blue eyes and the deafening silence.

Wiping the cover with the back of his sleeve, he fixes me with a long stare, then looks down at the book and runs his fingers round the gold embossed lettering. I watch mesmerized as he traces the author's name, Herman Hesse, and the title, *Gertrud*. The book had been given to me as a birthday present from my dear friend, Nonny, with whom I shared a dorm at Freiburg. I had never read Hesse before, but Nonny felt that, as a German who had grown up in India, I would find some common ground in his work. And she was right. I had started reading it the previous evening and had already fallen for the author's sharp yet mystical voice.

Prisoner X's eyes seem altered when he looks up and returns the book to my hands. It is as though he is seeing me for the first time.

'Thank you,' I say, making sure to speak in English so he understands. 'Kind of you to clean it. Have you read any Hesse?'

He lets out a sigh that sounds like exasperation, then, with a shake of his head, rushes off to retake his place at the back of Dieter's miserable little band of men, leaving me standing there on the grass, the sound of dance-hall music trickling out of the British officers' huts behind me. Unlike the regular prisoners, the officers are exempt from work. They still receive their allotted pay and can buy good food and cigarettes. Most days, it is usual to see parcels arriving from Harrods and Fortnum & Mason, British luxury stores, and delivered to the officers' doors. It is galling for us nurses to witness this when we spend most days treating their fellow countrymen for malnutrition. War is a strange concept. For all the talk of patriotism and pulling together on the battlefield, the divisions that exist in peacetime still prevail.

One of the officers, a raffish-looking man with oiled black hair and a pencil moustache, steps outside and lights a cigarette. He winks at me as I walk past. I ignore him but I hear the expletive he mutters in my wake. What is it about men? Why do they feel we women ought to pander to their every lewd whim, that we should be grateful to be harassed?

When I arrive at the sanatorium hut, there is already a long queue of prisoners snaking round the building. Most of them will be expected to show up for work at eight, some staying in the camp, others being bussed off to the nearby mines to undertake a twelve-hour shift. We have warned the commandant that the vaccination can cause some swelling and, in some cases, fever, and therefore it is wise for the men to be excluded from work for at least a portion of the day, but our request fell on deaf ears. The men are lucky enough to be getting such medical treatment, he bellowed, and it is given to them so that they can work, not laze about in bed.

As I make my way through the line of men, my heart sinks. They are thin enough already and they have only been in camp a couple of days. Back-breaking manual labour and a diet of gruel and stale bread is only going to deplete them further. What is the point of our inoculation programme in the face of this? One cannot vaccinate against hunger and exhaustion.

'Good morning, Miriam,' says Frida, the elderly matron, when I arrive at the hut. 'We have a new girl starting today. May I introduce you to Julia.'

She gestures to the young woman standing beside her, a

small, fine-boned girl with conker-brown hair and piercing blue eyes framed by perfectly shaped dark eyebrows. She is quite a beauty, but beauty comes at a cost in this place of sex-starved men. She will have to be careful.

'Pleased to meet you, Fräulein Ziegler,' says Julia, smiling warmly. 'I have prepped the syringes for you. Please let me know if there is anything else I can help you with.'

'Thank you,' I say, noticing, sadly, how immaculate and starched her uniform is. It will not stay like that for long.

'You can let in the first six now,' I tell her, as the clock above the examining station strikes the hour. 'And please, call me Miriam.'

As the men file in, a shiver flutters down my spine. Though I have been working in camps since the beginning of the war, the sight of full-grown men, hardened soldiers, shorn of their hair, starved to the point of emaciation, still unsettles me.

'Mornin', darlin',' says the first man as Julia leads him over. 'Don't you recognize me?'

'Mr Boscombe,' I say, remembering his voice. 'How could I forget you?'

'You don't want me reciting no Bible nonsense, do you?' he says, rolling up his sleeve to reveal a painfully thin arm.

'Not today, no,' I say, taking the syringe. 'Now, try to relax your arm. You'll feel a little prick, then it will be all done.'

'Oh, I'm used to feeling like a little prick,' he laughs, turning his head to get the approval of the other men. 'Isn't that what they called me back at the barracks, Lumley?'

Beside him, Julia's cheeks flush though I see she is trying to suppress a smile. I decide then and there that I like her.

The last auxiliary had been a dour young woman called Hildegard, who believed in the biological superiority of the German race. Even Frida, a proud German, was left shaken by her rantings, and we all breathed a sigh of relief when she was redeployed to another camp.

'You liked that joke, didn't you?' says Boscombe, nudging me. 'Not as straight-laced as you look.'

'Try to keep your head still,' I say, biting back a grin as I press the needle into his arm. 'Right, we're all done. Now, take this and keep it on the area briefly. And I recommend you rest here quietly for a couple of minutes before leaving as you might feel light-headed.'

I hand him a tiny square of paper bandage. With supplies low, we have to ration what is left.

'There'll be no need for that,' he says, with a gappy smile. 'I'm an Essex boy who's been in the trenches. Some daft needle's not going to beat me. Besides, I got to be on the bus for the mines at seven forty-five sharp.'

'I know but I would still recommend you take a couple of moments,' I say. 'Now, you may feel some swelling in the arm as the day goes on. That is perfectly normal but if you develop a fever or feel sick you must come back here as soon as you can. Do you understand?'

He nods his head.

'I'll be fine,' he says, jumping from the chair and rolling his sleeve down. 'Like I said, an injection's not gonna floor me.'

'I'm sure it won't,' I say, admiring his bravado in the face of such hardship. 'Nonetheless, try to have a good breakfast and pace yourself when you're at the mines.'

'Oh, I shall do that, m'dear,' he says. 'I shall order a Full

English from our Jerry hosts and wash it down with a cup of milky cocoa, then I shall ask the kindly chap at the mines if he wouldn't mind awfully if I have a bit of a nap.'

His speech is for the benefit of his friends, not for me, and they cheer and pat him on the back as he makes his way out.

'You meant well,' says Frida, as I hand her the needle to be sterilized. 'And he'll be eating his words if he has to come back here with a raging fever.'

I smile. She is trying to make me feel better, but Boscombe was right. How can we advise good health when these men are surviving on the bare minimum? What use is a typhus vaccination when they are half-starved? Filling up a new syringe, I return to my station with a heavy heart.

'Who's next?'

I look up and see Prisoner X, accompanied by Dieter.

'Get moving,' snaps the guard, pushing his prisoner towards me.

'Please, take a seat,' I say gently. 'This won't take long.'

He sits on the chair while, behind us, Dieter turns his attention to Julia.

'Ah, you're new,' he exclaims. 'And, may I say, what an improvement you are on that last one. What a beast she was.'

In the chair, Prisoner X keeps his eyes on me as he rolls up his sleeve and, to my shame, I find my hands are trembling as I wipe the top of his arm with antiseptic. He has a tattoo on the very spot where I am about to administer the injection. It looks like the number 8, on its side. Beneath it, in swirly blue ink, are written the words *For Eternity*. A reference to the 'darling wife' from the photograph, presumably. I inject the vaccine into him without a word.

'Where are you from?' Dieter asks Julia. 'You have such a wholesome German look. Those eyes. As my father used to say, a purebred.'

He pats Julia's behind, a gesture that makes me gasp with indignation. Prisoner X looks up at me and raises his eyebrows. It is a fleeting gesture but loaded with meaning. He disapproves of Dieter's boorish behaviour just as much as I do.

'I am actually part Spanish,' replies Julia brightly. 'With a little Swiss in the mix too. More mongrel than purebred. As *my* father would say.'

She holds out the sterilizing bowl and, as I pop the syringe into it, she catches my eye and winks.

'All done?' barks Dieter, clearly annoyed that Julia has not fallen for his advances. 'Right, out of that chair and into the labour yard. You have work to do.'

He grabs Prisoner X by the arm and bundles him out of the room.

'Are you all right?' asks Frida, as I wash my hands a few moments later. 'You've broken out in a sweat.'

'What do you mean? I'm perfectly fine.'

But as I look down, I am shocked to see that my pale blue uniform is covered in wet patches. Frida puts her hand to my forehead.

'Feels a bit clammy,' she says, with a frown. 'I hope you're not coming down with the Spanish Influenza. I hear it is sweeping Upper Dänholm, though I prayed we'd be safe here on the other side of the bridge. Listen, Julia and I can dispense the rest of this. I think you should go and lie down.'

'That won't be necessary,' I say, as another set of men files in. 'I just got a bit overheated, that's all.'

'Miriam, that is not a request – it is an order,' says Frida sternly. 'I need you healthy. Now go. I shall drop in some broth when I have finished here.'

I have a feeling that the hot flush is not Spanish Influenza but rather a result of my being up close with Prisoner X, but I realize there is no point arguing with her. As matron, whatever she says goes. Handing my apron to Julia, we catch each other's eyes and I see something in her face that reassures me. She is a good person, I think to myself, as I make my way out. And that is a rarity in this place.

As I cross the quadrant, relieved to feel the cool sea air on my face, I hear a dog barking. I look up and see two guards with Dobermanns at their heels escorting a group of prisoners from the labour yard to the dining huts.

The prisoners appear to be in good spirits, laughing and joking with one another. I spot Harry Boscombe, the chipper young man from Essex, gesticulating behind the guard's back, mocking the German's stiff gait to the delight of the other prisoners. I stand back to let them pass. Boscombe notices me and waves his hand. 'Enough of that,' snaps the tall man who is walking alongside him. The bristles on his scalp have a red tinge to them. He smacks the back of Harry's head, then fixes me with a stare that is intended to intimidate. 'German whore,' he spits, as he draws level, in an accent I recognize as Scottish. Beside him, Boscombe meekly withdraws his hand.

'Get a move on, you dumb shit.'

I turn to see Dieter. He is walking behind a prisoner,

pressing his rifle to the small of the man's back. The victim's head is bowed, his khaki cap pulled down over his face. But as they draw level with me, I see that it is Prisoner X. He looks up and the expression on his face makes me start.

This man, this silent enigma, whose very presence here appears to elicit fear and suspicion from both the prisoners and the guards, locks his pale blue eyes on mine, and I see, for just a fleeting moment, not an enemy, not a dangerous prisoner but a scared little boy pleading for help.

8

KATERINA

London

May 1915

As Gillian and I weave our way through the labyrinthine streets of Soho, I am struck by how much has changed in the last year. Following the Lighting Orders under the Defence of the Realm Act last year, the oil lamps have been partially dulled with black paint halfway down the glass, plunging the streets into a thick soup of semi-darkness, making it impossible to see more than a few paces ahead. The shop windows of Piccadilly, once a riot of colour and lights, are now shuttered and subdued. Khaki-clad figures of both sexes walk gingerly along the pavement, casting furtive glances left and right as if anticipating a German ambush from the opulent doorway of Fortnum & Mason. Sporadic searchlights, sweeping the skies for enemy airships, provide the only light in this subdued and cowed city. The air smells of petroleum and despair.

And yet it is not just the shuttered shops and the dimmed lights that disquiet me. Some intrinsic element has also disappeared. It is that the voice of the city, the strange hulking baritone that I could feel in my core from the moment I arrived here as a child, the distinct London roar, has now fallen silent and in its place is something that sounds like a muffled cry.

As we pass by restaurants once famed for their Italian, Greek or German fare, now forced to modify their menus and serve pork chops and baked potatoes in place of leberwurst and spaghetti so as not to offend the boys off fighting in the war and their loved ones left behind, it seems as though the city's soul has been sucked out and is floating in the half-lit sky above our heads, still close but tantalizingly out of reach.

'It's the lack of light that I find so disorientating,' says Gillian, as we cross a sombre Shaftesbury Avenue. 'A year ago, no one could have conceived of a West End without its neon. How life can change in such a short space of time.'

I do not answer. My thoughts return to that evening: my grief at what I had done, at the fact that I was too scared to be truly myself, that I had broken Gillian's heart. I watch her striding ahead of me and, with a pang of longing, recall those heady early days when we would huddle together in the back of a hansom cab after attending our Divine Order meetings in Soho Square, the driver oblivious to Gillian's hand working its way up my thigh, her delicious orange blossom scent filling the cab and my heart. Strange to think that it was just four years ago that we first met. 1911 feels like another world now, a world of light and promise and hope.

'Here we are at last,' says Gillian, taking a sharp right turn and stopping outside a rather run-down three-storey building. The ground floor has a curved window and traces of lettering visible above the door. In the gloom, I can just about make out the word *sons*. A family business, perhaps, its sons now lost to the war.

'It's no palace, I'm afraid,' says Gillian, wrinkling her nose. 'But it's warm and clean. And it's home for you for as long as you need it.'

She looks up at me, and for a moment we are back in Soho Square that first time. The guest speaker, W. B. Yeats, is reciting his latest poem, and I am seated next to the most beautiful being I have ever encountered. Beautiful, that is, not in the physical sense – though Gillian's handsome face has always attracted admirers – but, rather, spiritual. Gillian's courage, her vitality, her curiosity, her willingness to defend and protect the persecuted, shone from her that evening like the rays of the midday sun. When Yeats had finished his poem, a haunting ode to the infinity of love, she had glanced at me just as she is now, and what I saw in her eyes told me that this woman would always be part of me, whether we were together or not.

'Kat?' she whispers, her soft voice snapping me out of my reverie. 'Are you all right? I know it's not what you're used to, and this part of town is rather grim, but it's just until things blow over and—'

'I'm fine,' I say, trying not to return her gaze, trying to shield my heart. Don't let her do it, I tell myself, don't let her reel you back in. 'And I have no problem with the place. It's good of you to put me up. But, like you said, it's not going to be for long. As soon as it's safe to do so I shall return to Mile End.'

'Of course,' says Gillian, her smile fading. 'Now, let's get inside. I don't know about you, but I could kill for a mug of cocoa.'

She opens the front door, and we step into a dank, narrow hallway, the walls covered in sickly red-and-gold flock wallpaper. The air smells of laundry that's been left to sit in dirty water, a damp, earthy scent that sticks in my throat as I follow Gillian up a flight of steep wooden stairs.

'Are there any other occupants in this building?' I ask, when we reach the landing, which has three doors leading off it.

'Just me as far as I know,' replies Gillian, heading towards the door at the far end of the landing. 'Unless you count the mice and cockroaches. Not the nicest of bedfellows.'

I wait for her to tell me she is joking but she just raises her eyebrow and shrugs. I cannot believe that the Gillian Huffingham Barnes, daughter of a wealthy shipping magnate, who had spent most of her life floating between her family houses in Kensington and Oxfordshire, now calls this her home. As she opens the door, Sylvia's face looms in my mind's eye. It is she who put Gillian up to this, I am sure of it. All her talk about the evils of inherited wealth and the monster that is Capitalism. Gillian has always idolized Sylvia, felt she had to prove herself to her. Is living like this, I ask myself, as I follow her into the room, the ultimate test of her faith, the ultimate show of devotion?

'Make yourself comfortable,' she says, taking my coat and placing it on the back of the threadbare sofa. 'I'll get a fire going. It can be rather chilly in these rooms right up until summer.'

She lights an oil lamp and in its soft glare I have the chance to see her and the room properly. Despite the shabby clothing – she has acquired Sylvia's 'uniform' of sturdy shoes, sensible skirt and high-necked blouse in various shades of moss and mud – Gillian cannot shake off her aristocratic bearing. She still carries herself as she did when I first met her, draped in silk and smoking a cigarette in an ornate, ruby-encrusted holder, with her straight back and her snub nose raised in the air. Here among the peeling yellow wallpaper, stained carpet and threadbare furniture, as she kneels in front of the rusted fire grate, it is like watching an actress play a role.

'We have fire,' she cries triumphantly, getting up from her haunches and looking to me for validation like a child who has just spoken its first words. 'Now for that cocoa.'

'Gillian, how . . . how did you end up here?' I ask, when she returns with two cracked beakers of cocoa from the thin strip of countertop at the far end of the room that constitutes a kitchen.

'Sylvia found it,' she says, handing me the warm drink.

Of course she did, I think to myself. Just as I suspected. This place has Sylvia written all over it.

'It's so good to see you,' she says, perching herself on the sofa next to me. 'Walking through the West End with you just now brought back so many memories. Cocktails at Café Royale, those matinees at the Opera House with the usher who insisted on calling you sir and you told him you were a Hungarian count. Happy days. Heady days.'

'All in the past now,' I say, bristling at Gillian's whimsical and selective memory. 'Along with the Divine Order.'

'The Divine Order,' sighs Gillian. 'You know my mother never approved of my involvement, said it was a satanic cult and yet, oddly enough, she would rather I be part of that than the Federation. Rather Satan than Sylvia, that's what my mother thinks.'

For once I agree with Gillian's mother.

'So, how is Lady H B?' I ask, taking a sip of cocoa.

'I have no idea,' says Gillian. 'I haven't seen her since the war began.'

'Really?' I exclaim, recalling how much power Henrietta Huffingham Barnes exerted over her daughter. 'What happened?'

'Oh, you know Mother. I couldn't breathe without her taking offence. She's disapproved of me from birth. Anyway, we had a frightful row – I won't bore you with the details – and I gave her a few home truths. The upshot was she told me I was dead to her, and we haven't spoken since.'

'Oh, Gillian, I'm sorry. Was it . . . was it because of us?'

I flinch as I recall the expression on Henrietta's face when she walked in on us mid-embrace. It was then I decided I had to end it. We were taking too many risks.

'Not directly,' she says, flicking her hand dismissively. 'Though she made her feelings pretty clear after you'd left that night that I was a disgrace, a deviant who was bound for the fires of hell. Ironic, really, because if rumours are to be believed she had a few sapphic dalliances herself in her younger days. Anyway, I told her I was leaving, said that I couldn't be under the same roof as her a moment longer. She must have racked her brains to find a way to stop me and it came in the form of emotional blackmail, some-thing Mother is quite the expert at. She spent the evening wailing and crying, told me she was seriously ill, that she wasn't long for this world. And because I am soft-hearted, I fell for it and ended up nursing her for three interminable months, until, suddenly, she made a miraculous recovery. It seems she wasn't dying after all. Funny, that. Once again, I'd fallen for Mother's treachery but, for me, the end finally came a few days later. In a fit of fury, she had dismissed a housemaid, Molly Nairn, who had been with us since she was fourteen and was an exemplary worker. Poor girl was pregnant and facing destitution. She begged and pleaded to be kept on but Mother wouldn't budge. I knew then that I couldn't continue tolerating her. It felt like, in being the dutiful daughter, I was condoning her appalling behaviour. First with you and now with Molly.'

'That must have been hard for you, though,' I say, feeling rather shameful at my own cowardice. 'To just walk away like that.'

'On the contrary,' says Gillian, not meeting my eye. 'When something is dead, done and over with, one knows. In a way, I should be grateful to Mother. If it wasn't for her, I wouldn't be here.'

'How so?'

'Well, at the time of the almighty row, I'd just taken over the Federation's operations in the West End though I'd been staying with friends in Whitechapel. I realized with so much work to do – I'm pretty much on call round the clock – that I needed to be closer. That's when Sylvia stepped in.'

'Sylvia.' The name slips from my lips like a piece of gristle.

'Yes,' says Gillian, oblivious to my distaste. 'She'd been helping a family who had lived upstairs, and they had been rehoused. I spoke to the landlord, who couldn't quite believe anyone would want to live here, and I was in the

82

next day. To be honest, I'm not here much. What with house visits and my afternoon drop-in sessions in Soho, I'm kept on my feet until late into the evening. Honestly, you wouldn't believe the hardships this war has placed on women and children. If it wasn't for Sylvia and her indomitable spirit, these poor people would be left to die.'

'Three cheers for Sylvia,' I say, my barely concealed envy bubbling to the surface. 'Where would we all be without her?'

'Kat, darling?' says Gillian, affronted. 'Whatever do you mean? Sylvia was always kind to you, which is more than can be said for you. She's a good person. You'd probably like her if you gave her a chance.'

'Gave her a chance?' I cry, almost spilling my cocoa on the grimy carpet. 'Everything is so simple for you, isn't it?'

'What do you mean?' says Gillian, her eyes blazing.

'Gillian, I thought your mother was going to expose us after she walked in that night,' I say, recalling the horror of it all. 'I was terrified. You say give Sylvia a chance but when it came to me . . . Oh, it doesn't matter. Gillian, do you have any idea what the last year has been like for me? Being torn apart from the two people I loved most in this world?'

'I'm sorry, Kat,' she says softly. 'I should have come after you that night, should have fought for us more. But I suppose I felt you needed space, needed time to think, and I didn't want to pressurize you. I know how much you have always guarded your privacy, especially after what happened to you as a child. And I know you must have thought it was all going to happen again if Mother blabbed to all and sundry. Despite that, I should have come to find you, should have tried to put your mind at ease, at least, but I was a different person back then. I didn't think that I had rights until Sylvia taught me—'

'Sylvia again,' I sigh, edging out of my seat. 'I'm sorry, Gillian, but this isn't going to work. I can't stay here. I'm going to go back home.'

'Don't be so ridiculous,' cries Gillian. 'It's the middle of the night and the streets are full of mob-handed yobs. Why don't you get some rest? I've made up a bed for you in the spare room. A proper night's sleep will do you good. And if you still want to go back to Mile End in the morning then I won't stop you.'

The bed is narrow and stiff. Its wooden sides press against me. As I lie here, watching the moon cast translucent orbs on the chipped ceiling, a cacophony of voices and images weaves in and out of my consciousness. I hear my father, his soft German lilt fraught with emotion, urging me to return to the bakery:

'The people need their bread, Katerina, we cannot let them down.'

I see him standing in the detritus of the shop, his apron matted with dust and flour, his face riven with fear. As the moon disappears behind a cloud, his image fades into the shadows and is replaced with that of Otto, the last time I saw him, on the platform at Victoria station.

'I was your greatest defender, Katerina,' he hisses, the smoke from the train rising in tendrils around his body, as though swallowing him up. *'All your life, I protected you, shielded you from those who wanted to lock you away. I believed in your gift, but now? Now I think they were right. You are cursed and you have used that curse to destroy my life. You are dead to me now, Katerina, you hear? Dead.'*

I hear a train guard's whistle, its shrill sound rattling my bones, then Otto disappears into the smoke and a woman steps forward and sits down on the bed.

'*You know you weren't enough for her,*' says Sylvia, the metallic green and purple of her pin button glinting in the pale moonlight. '*That's why she said her mother was going to expose the relationship. It was her way of getting rid of you. After all, what are you? A fortune teller who bakes cakes. Gillian needs more than that, she needs mental stimulation. She needs to be with someone who inspires her, who she respects.*'

'Leave me alone,' I cry now, leaping from the bed. 'Please, leave me.'

I stand in the centre of the room, the heavy wooden wardrobe and chest of drawers looming from either side, like armoured medieval soldiers facing each other down on the battlefield. Glancing back towards the bed, I am relieved to see just a bundle of blankets. She wasn't here, none of them were.

I light the oil lamp and begin to dress. Otto had not said that to me at the station – in fact, there hadn't even been a farewell, he had simply left home that morning without a goodbye. He didn't need to tell me that I had betrayed him and that I was dead to him, I had known it, just as I know it now.

As I slip on my boots, I notice my suitcase tucked next to the chest of drawers and momentarily entertain the idea of taking out my cards. They could tell me what this is all about, offer wise counsel. But as I tie my laces with trembling fingers, I realize I am too restless to channel whatever messages the cards may have. Instead, I take the oil lamp and, remembering the faded sign above the front door, set out to explore the rest of the building.

I hear Gillian softly snoring as I pass her room and tiptoe out of the flat. She was always a deep sleeper and I remember, as I gently close the door, her lying next to me in Kensington Gardens all those years ago, her straw hat lopsided, the sun pouring onto her face casting it in gold like a pharoah's mask, her chest rising and falling as she slept, her hand folded around mine.

'*You weren't enough for her.*'

Sylvia's phantom voice invades my mind as I walk down the narrow staircase, the oil lamp held in front of me to light the way. My chest feels tight as I reach the hallway. I need to silence these voices, need to put my fears to rest for just a few hours, yet it feels impossible. They follow me wherever I go.

Moving the lamp from side to side, I try to get my bearings. The hallway is empty save for a stubby wooden sideboard. As I edge closer, I see a thick, vertical gouge in the wall above it. Flakes of plaster have fallen onto the sideboard, smattering like snow across its surface. I wonder who could have inflicted this wound upon the wall, what weapon they had used. I see a man, shirtsleeves rolled up, face reddened with exertion, taking a mallet and raising it above his head. As it impacts the wall with a thud, I see the mob assembled outside my bakery, hear the hatred in their voices, wince as the glass smashes and I hurtle up the stairs.

Gathering myself, I turn away from the damaged wall and make my way further along the hallway. Up ahead, on the right, I see a doorway. I know I shouldn't go through it, but curiosity gets the better of me and before I can help myself, I am turning the handle and stepping inside a darkened room.

Holding the lamp aloft, my eyes adjusting to the new-found light, I gasp at the incredible sight in front of me. Then, somewhere on the periphery of my consciousness, I hear a gentle voice whisper, '*Here it is. A gift for you, my dear.*'

9

EDIE

Cornwall

Present Day

'I wonder who Kitty is,' says Alexander, as I pour us both a cup of tea, the box still open on the table in front of us. 'It's all so intriguing. Now, are you sure I can't tempt you with one of these madeleines? They really are delicious.'

'I'm fine with just the tea, thank you,' I say. 'Though they do look rather lovely. I haven't seen proper madeleines like that in years. My father used to make them when I was a kid.'

'They're particularly good,' says Alexander, already on to his second. 'We had a tea room in the village when I was at prep school in Wiltshire that used to serve something similar. A taste of the past, eh? Gosh, hark at me, coming over all Proust.'

He laughs, then blushes crimson. In my old life, I used to avoid old public school boys like the plague, but I find Alexander, with his strange combination of razor-sharp mathematical brain and slightly off-kilter humour, rather endearing.

'Do excuse me,' he says, reaching for his large polka-dot

handkerchief to wipe his mouth. 'Anyway, now we've had our sugar hit, let's get back to the mystery of Kitty. I remember Susan, the lady who runs the bakery in the village, telling me that it was founded back in the twenties, by a woman who used to live in this cottage. Could that be Kitty?'

'I don't think so,' I say. 'This cottage was left to my dad by his grandmother back in the seventies. I don't think she had anything to do with the village bakery but then I'm afraid I don't know much about her. All I know is her name and it definitely wasn't Kitty. It was Jane.'

'I wonder if Jane is the woman in the photograph,' says Alexander, taking a sip of tea. 'With the prisoner.'

'Possibly,' I reply. 'But then, the box might not even belong to her. The cottage was rented out to various tenants for years. Though why would anyone hide such a thing in the wall?'

'Perhaps it was a safe of some sort,' says Alexander, leaning back in his chair, his hands clasped round his middle. 'One of my early clients, an old Etonian chap, told me how his grandmother had kept her life savings in a household safe. After the crash of twenty-nine, no one trusted the banks. I think that was rather common back then.'

'Perhaps,' I say, recalling my father's stories about people in the East End keeping suitcases full of cash under their beds even as late as the sixties. 'Yet there was no sign of a safe door or a combination lock, it was just a big, gaping hole.'

'I read that this area got badly bombed during World War Two,' says Alexander, leaning forward to refill our cups. 'Most of these cottages will have suffered some sort of damage. I imagine in the following years that wall will have been replastered countless times. Perhaps Jane, or the tenant, forgot they'd even put the box in there.'

'And yet the box, and its contents, remained intact,' I say, a shiver fluttering through me despite the heat of the sun, as I think about the strange carvings on the box and those words: *Mystic. Medium. Messenger.* 'It's all rather unsettling really. Particularly the Tarot cards. And just when I've been commissioned to design a deck too.'

'You have?' exclaims Alexander, his face brightening. 'How wonderful. We had someone come and do a reading at the company Christmas bash last year. I was a bit dubious when the idea was first mooted but according to my CEO, who is far more clued up on these sorts of things, Tarot is the new mindfulness. It's a big thing.'

'So I keep hearing,' I say. 'Though I've never seen the appeal, myself. My mother used to say that some things are best left alone, and I've always been inclined to agree with her.'

'I suppose,' shrugs Alexander. 'But if it pays the bills, who are we to complain? Anyway, back to the box. It's the prisoner-of-war camp reference that really intrigues me. I wonder what that could be.'

'That thing like a giant crayon that we found inside the cardboard tube?' I say, sipping my tea. 'I have no idea. My husb— David would have likely known what it was. He was an authority on the Great War poets.'

I pause, the unspoken grief hanging in the space between my Cornish kitchen and a London where I am newly married, lying on a shabby, second-hand sofa in our bedsit and listening while David reads from Wilfrid Owen's

'*Dulce et Decorum est*' in preparation for his first seminar as a newly qualified lecturer. That image of men marching asleep, limping on bloodied, shoeless feet, haunted me. It returns now, mingling with the memory of David's warm hand on my shoulder, the other clasping his notes, the smell of cigarette smoke, cheap red wine and dry roasted peanuts – our staples in those lean, early years – and the staccato thud of the Jam, the band David had discovered and fallen in love with as a boy, coming from the record player. He always played loud music while he worked, said it helped him focus. So much so that now, when I think of those young poets who lost their lives in the Great War, I don't think of Edwardian men with neat moustaches and side partings, I see angry young punks with spiky hair and drainpipe trousers. '*Paul Weller and Wilfred Owen aren't that different when you come to think of it, Edes,*' David used to say when I asked how he could concentrate with music blasting out like that. '*They were both angry at the same thing, the thing that people will still be angry at long after I'm dead. The bloody English Establishment.*'

'I think it's a wax cylinder,' says Alexander, jolting me back to the present.

'Sorry?'

'Inside the tube with the German writing on it. If I'm not mistaken, it's a wax cylinder.'

'Is that something specific?' I say, draining the last of my tea and hoping the caffeine will bring me to my senses. 'If it isn't a large crayon, I thought it could be a candle of some sort.'

'Pass the box over,' he says, clearing a space in front of him. 'I just want to have another look at it.'

I do as he says, then take the dishes to the sink to rinse.

'As I thought,' he says, looking up at me over his black-rimmed glasses as I return to the table. 'It *is* a wax cylinder.'

'What is it used for?' I say, sitting down next to him, the woody scent of his cologne filling the air between us.

'It's an early form of record,' he says, examining the object carefully. 'I think it was Thomas Edison who invented it.'

'How do you know all this?'

'Oh, my grandfather had loads of them in his study with all his favourite music-hall tunes on them,' he says, his eyes lighting up as he speaks. 'I used to love playing them when I was a boy. It sparked my passion for collecting vintage records. I have hundreds of them back at my flat in London. I really should bring them down here, but I'd have to find the space.'

'Do you think there could be something on that thing?' I say, taking the cylinder from him and turning it over in my hands. 'A recording?'

'Most likely,' he says. 'Now, employing my A-level German, I can see that this label refers to a *"Stimme Projekt"* which roughly translates as Voice Project. And *"Stammlager"* is German for prisoner-of-war camp. I know that Dänholm is an island off the coast of Germany. Being cut off from the mainland, it would make sense to have had a POW camp there. But who is Josef Garn? Could he be the man in the photo?'

'Is there any way we could play it?' I ask, wondering how anything as strange as this waxy lump could ever have been used to play music. 'Perhaps the answers to those questions are on the recording.'

'We'd need an old phonograph,' says Alexander. 'And they're as rare as hen's teeth nowadays. It seems this recording and whatever was going on in that camp will have to remain a mystery. You should keep it all safe though, nonetheless, particularly that box. Right, I'd better be off.'

As I see him out, he says, 'Listen. Would it be an absolute bore if I asked you to pop in and feed Jupiter tomorrow morning? I have to drive up to London this evening. I've got a meeting first thing and won't be back till late.'

'Of course,' I say, with some reluctance, remembering that the last time I fed the cat, he had bitten my finger when I tried to stroke him.

'Thanks, Edie,' Alexander beams. 'I'll leave the food out on the kitchen counter. Bye now.'

'Bye, Alexander.'

Back in the cottage, I am about to head upstairs to get back to work when my phone rings.

'Hi, Mum, it's Dora. Just calling to see how you are?'

'Hi, darling,' I say, bending to retrieve the overflowing bucket from the living room. 'You sound tired. Long day?'

While Dora fills me in on the bookcase she's bought for the new flat, the jollof rice she cooked for dinner last night, which was 'nice but not as good as Dad's' and the new period drama she's got into on Netflix, I feel a pang of sadness and guilt. Though it is lovely to chat to my daughter just like we did when she was a teenager, I don't want her to feel as though she has a duty to call me every evening. I don't want her to think of me as a burden.

'Well, I've had an interesting couple of days,' I say, emptying the bucket down the sink as quietly as possible. I don't want Dora to know about the leaking roof. I want to reassure her that all is well down here, and that I'm not spending every evening sobbing into my pillow. 'I found this box.'

I tell her about the box with its mysterious carvings and equally enigmatic contents.

'My neighbour reckons the tube is something called a wax cylinder,' I say, omitting to mention Alexander by name. It's silly but I don't want Dora to think that I'm getting friendly with a younger, single man. 'Apparently, they're a precursor to vinyl discs. Recordings were made on them back in the early nineteen-hundreds. And it had a label on it with the name of a German prisoner-of-war camp and the words "Voice Project" written on it.'

Dora is silent for a moment, and I fear I may have bored her to death.

'It's all a bit silly really,' I say. 'And probably nothing but a load of old junk.'

'No, I was just thinking,' she says, her voice calm and steady, so like David's. 'I've read about that before somewhere. That's right, it was when I did that evening course on the Edwardian language at the Bishopsgate Institute when I was seventeen. It was with Dad's friend the linguist, remember?'

'Vaguely,' I say, though in truth I have no recollection. Dora and David were as thick as thieves when it came to their academic interests. It was lovely to see, though most of their conversations went right over my head.

'He told us about these projects that were conducted during the First World War where they recorded soldiers' voices,' she continues. 'A team of linguists from the university came up with them. The aim was to collect the voices of British soldiers to create an archive of regional dialects, many of which were already dying out. With so many British soldiers being herded into one place, the German prisoner-of-war camps were the ideal environment to conduct this research. There's an archive in the British Library, I'm sure of it. It might be worth contacting them, see if they can shed some light on it.'

'Oh, I don't know. It sounds like an awful lot of fuss over nothing.'

'Maybe,' she says. 'Listen, Mum, I'd better go. I have a pile of reading to get through. Have a good evening.'

'You too, darling.'

She clicks off and I feel as though I've offended her by saying it's all a fuss over nothing. I know how she misses her chats with David, how they were kindred spirits in their love of literature and words. Whereas I'm the one she worries about, the one she checks up on to make sure I haven't fallen apart. I need to show her that I'm OK, that she doesn't need to worry. Maybe the first step could be solving the puzzle of the box.

After returning the empty bucket to its spot on the sodden carpet, I take my laptop into the kitchen and type in the words *British Library archive WW1*. It brings up a name. Stephen Mountjoy. Senior Curator. Clicking on it, I am then directed to a page with an email address. Do I have the time to pursue this? I wonder to myself as my hand hovers over the 'contact' button. I have seventy-eight Tarot cards to design and finish by the end of the summer, a leaking roof and a ruddy great hole in my wall. Do I really need to be pursuing this? Yet before I know it, I have typed out a lengthy message, telling Stephen Mountjoy all about the box, its contents and, most importantly, the wax cylinder.

As I press Send I hear David's voice in my head: '*Oh, Edie. What have you started now?*'

Just then I hear a noise outside, a scratching noise. Closing the laptop, I look out of the kitchen window onto the front garden. It is still light though a dark, deep blue sky grows heavy on the horizon. I hear the noise again. It seems to be coming from the front of the house. Aware that Alexander is in London and with the memory of that shadowy figure disappearing up the road last night, I take the long metal doorstop from the kitchen and slowly make my way towards the door. They say the body has a second sense when another human being is close by, and I just know as I put my hand on the latch that there is someone standing on the doorstep.

'Who is it?' I cry, trying to sound assertive and in control. 'Who's there?'

There is no answer but as I lift the latch, I feel the door push open from the other side and as I stumble backwards a strange voice calls out my name.

10

MIRIAM

Dänholm Prisoner-of-War Camp

October 1918

The man standing in front of the phonograph has rejected the Bible proffered by Herr Garn, laid open at the Parable of the Prodigal Son, and has, instead, opted to recite a piece from his own holy book.

It is the last session of the day and with just two soldiers left to record, Herr Garn relents and reluctantly closes his Bible as Private Ranvir Singh of the 36th Sikh Regiment begins to speak the words of the Guru Granth Sahib.

Though the influence of the British occupiers of his homeland can be heard in his clipped vowels and overly formal diction, Private Singh's voice is infused with a cadence as smooth as velvet. It is a sound I have not heard since childhood and, as he speaks of higher truths and worldly love, of Dharma and grace, I am transported to the spice gardens of Kerala where I was sent at the age of six to stay with my wealthy aunt and uncle while my father stayed in Germany to grieve the loss of my mother.

As Private Singh continues, I close my eyes and find myself falling down a rabbit hole of memory. I can taste the ripe mango, freshly plucked from the tree and cut into thin slices with a scimitar, the juices trickling down my chin as I greedily devour it, feel the midday sun burning through my linen dress as a holy man bedecked in robes the colour of the clay earth parades past the veranda, chanting words I do not understand but which I feel piercing my soul, and leaving the scent of tobacco and incense trailing in his wake. I smell the bittersweet scent of chai stewing in a tall glass pot, its leaves freshly plucked from the plantation up the hill, and hear the polite chat of my aunt's friends: the melodious tenor of Tommy Flynn, the red-haired Irishman who managed the local gold mine, the staccato baritone of Major Wolsey, born in Kent but sent out to '*Indyar*' as a young soldier to '*keep the natives in line*', a sentiment that much amused Chellam, my beloved Tamil nanny. '*Thousands of years of civilization and we have to be brought in line by a fat old white man like him*,' she would whisper to me as we sat threading daisies into a chain while Wolsey helped himself to a generous portion of poppyseed cake. '*But my dear girl*,' I would cry to Chellam, puffing out my chest just like the major. '*Whatever would you lot do without us Brits.*' '*You have the gift, Mir*,' Chellam would tell me as I mimicked each of the house guests in turn. '*In Tamil we would say it is the gods speaking through you.*'

I am so happily ensconced in the Keralan sunshine I do not realize that the soldier has finished speaking until I hear Herr Garn clear his throat. Opening my eyes, I feel his gaze and that of the two soldiers fixed firmly on me.

'Thank you, Private Singh,' says Herr Garn, casting a stern glance in my direction. 'That will be all. Now, Fräulein Ziegler, if you could check the sound levels before the next recording.'

My cheeks flush as I get up from my chair. Private Singh gives me a smile that seems part sympathy, part understanding. His recitation had taken me somewhere else, back to a land and a time when I had felt truly free and where my interest in voices – their cadences, their diversity, the culture and history attached to each and every one – had taken shape. As Singh nods his head and turns to leave, I feel a frisson of sadness, a sudden realization that I will never return to that moment in time, the India of my youth, and that in this desolate place, locked in on every side by the sea, we are all prisoners.

But then something comes to me, an idea. Leaving the sound levels for a moment, I walk across to Herr Garn, who is flicking through the pages of the Bible while the last man waits patiently, and ask if he can spare a moment.

'What is it, Fräulein Ziegler?' he says, holding the page with the bookmarking ribbon.

'Herr Professor, I have had an idea,' I say, lowering my voice, aware of the man's eyes on us. 'I hope you do not think me impertinent, but I couldn't help but notice that when the men recite, whether that be from the Bible or, in Singh's case, the Guru Granth Sahib, they tend to . . . how can I put it? Alter their voices.'

'Alter their voices?' says Garn impatiently.

'They are approaching it as though it is a performance,' I say, trying not to buckle under Garn's stern gaze. 'Rather like being at school, I suppose. And as a result, they are masking their true accents.'

'Nonsense,' cries Garn, shaking his head dismissively. 'You mean to tell me you can't hear Boscombe's Essex drawl when he reads the Parable of the Prodigal Son?'

'Of course not,' I say, steeling myself. 'But what if the men were more relaxed? What if, as well as reading from the Bible or a holy book, we ask them to tell us about their lives?'

'About their lives? My dear girl, this is a serious research project, not some cosy tea party with idle chatter. And may I also remind you, these men are not only prisoners, but they are also the enemy. What would the commandant say if he thought we were inviting them to relax and speak lovingly of home? Home being England, the place we Germans are currently at war with.'

'You are quite right, Herr Garn,' I reply. 'But what about when the war is over? When you return to Berlin with your recordings and begin the real task of analysis. Wouldn't you feel you had missed a golden opportunity of hearing myriad dialects spoken freely, not constrained by Bible verses?'

He goes to speak, then pauses. I watch as he places his finger on his top lip, his eyes narrowing.

'As I said, Herr Professor, it was just a thought. We can stick with the verses if you wish.'

'No, what you say is true, Fräulein Ziegler,' he says, his frown softening. 'It would be beneficial to hear the men speak freely. From now on, we shall give them a choice. They may recite a verse or tell us their . . . how would you put it?'

'Their story.'

'Their story. Indeed. Right, let us get on with the session. Who is next, please?'

'Kept us waiting long enough, you Kraut bastards. Now what do ye want me to do?'

I look up, shocked at both the expletive and the appearance of the man approaching the recording platform. It is the man I last saw crossing the labour yard with the rest of the prisoners, the one who had spat obscenities at me.

I look down at my list and see that his name is Private Douglas Reid of the Royal Scots Dragoons.

His narrow grey eyes fix on me as I shakily check the sound levels. Beside me, I hear Herr Garn clear his throat.

'Private Reid,' he says, his steely eyes fixed firmly on the man. 'You have a choice. You may read a verse from the Bible, or you can tell us about yourself. Something interesting.'

'Well, I'm not reciting from that in front of you heathens,' spits Reid, flashing Herr Garn a ferocious stare. 'And I'll be damned if I'm telling you anything about myself, interesting or not. Wouldn't trust you bastards as far as I can throw you. Nah, if that coloured fella could read from his book of nonsense, then I'm gonna read what I want and all. All right?'

'As you wish,' says Herr Garn, his moustache twitching with indignation. 'Fräulein Ziegler, are we ready to record?'

I nod my head and bring down the lever. On the platform in front of me, Reid takes a theatrical inhalation of breath.

'This masterpiece is from our man Rabbie Burns, God rest his soul,' he blusters, spraying bursts of spittle onto the horn. 'My pa used to holler it at my ma after a few drams. It's called "Wad Ye Dae That?"'

From his position by the window, I hear Herr Garn mutter something under his breath as Reid begins to recite a garbled verse, the only intelligible part being the last line where the subject informs the speaker that she has been fucked five times a night. This, Reid bellows loudly into the microphone once, twice, three times, while staring directly at me. I instinctively step back from him, gooseflesh prickling my skin. He winks at me, then takes a deep breath to deliver the line one more time, but before he can get the words out, Herr Garn steps away from the window and gestures to me to end the recording.

'Thank you, Private Reid,' he says, placing a hand on the man's shoulder. 'That was . . . enlightening. You are free to go now.'

With those words, Reid spins on his heels, his face just inches from Garn's.

'Free to go,' he hisses, balling his hands into tight fists. 'You mean home? Or back to the stinking trenches to kill some more of you lot? You verminous bastards.'

Herr Garn's face flushes purple. He takes a step back, but Reid maintains his stance.

'Ah,' says Reid, an ugly smile appearing on his face. 'You mean back to ma room? Back to ma cell? My mistake. For one minute I thought that was what this was all about. We poor bastards come and talk shite and in exchange you let us go but nah, you're still our gaolers, despite your Bible. That piece of skirt over there might be a beaut with her bonny face and her big bosom but she's still a filthy German, still evil to the core.'

He flashes me a look that seems to pierce my whole body. I place my hand on the back of the chair to stop myself from shaking. It is then I realize how vulnerable Herr Garn and I are, holed up in this forgotten room at the far end of the camp, away from the guards, at the mercy of men like Reid whose bristling anger may at any moment turn into violence.

'Private Reid, I said that will be all,' says Herr Garn. He pushes out his chest but even standing straight he is still at least a foot shorter than the formidable Scot.

Reid opens his mouth to speak but before he can do so the door opens, and Private Singh enters.

'Apologies,' he says, nodding to us all in turn. 'I left my overcoat behind.'

He gestures to a threadbare khaki garment folded over a chair at the back of the room.

Reid falters. His moment has passed. As Private Singh collects his coat, the Scot gives Herr Garn one final death stare, then storms out of the room.

As he slams the door behind him, I feel my body loosen.

'I . . . I will erase the recording,' I say to Herr Garn, scrambling to remove the wax cylinder with trembling fingers. 'That poem he recited . . . it was not suitable. Not suitable at all.'

At the back of the room, Private Singh drapes his coat over his shoulders and bids us a polite farewell. I watch him depart, uttering a wordless prayer of thanks that he arrived when he did.

'That will not be necessary,' says Herr Garn, as Singh closes the door behind him. 'I actually found it extremely interesting, from a linguistic perspective. This is what I am trying to impart to you, Miriam, the importance of remaining objective. We may find that man to be offensive and crude, but it is not his character we are interested in but his voice. Had he told us a story, as you had suggested, it might have been just as lewd yet still a rich source of linguistic information for us. What I am saying is that if we let our emotions and biases influence our work, then the validity of this project, its academic rigorousness, will be destroyed. Do you understand?'

'Yes, Herr Professor,' I say, my cheeks flushing at the admonishment.

'Good,' he says brusquely. 'Now leave the phonograph switched on, will you? I am going to spend a few hours listening to what we recorded today. That will be all for tonight, Miriam. You may go.'

'Thank you, Herr Garn,' I say, taking my coat from the hook by the door. 'I shall see you in the morning.'

He waves a hand dismissively before turning his attention to the phonograph.

Outside, the air is warm and still. The leaves on the trees that line the exterior of the camp are turning golden, though their beauty is tainted somewhat by the thick barbed-wire fence that intersects them.

I hear a dog bark and look across the quadrant to where two guards are smoking a cigarette, a thickset Dobermann snapping at its leash beside them. The four watchtowers bear down upon me as I take a left turn towards the latrine block which marks the halfway spot between the recording studio and my room. I feel the eyes of the guards on me as I always do when I am walking this way but tonight, I feel something else. A presence closer than the men in the watchtowers. As though someone is following me. I quicken my gait but as I reach the corner of the latrine block something catches on the back of my coat. I turn and see Reid, his hand clasping my collar.

'Fancy a private reading, darling?' he says, pressing his cracked lips to my cheeks. 'Show you how a Scotsman likes to fuck.'

'Let me go, please,' I say sternly, Garn's speech echoing in my head, determined not to let my emotions get the better of me. Not to betray my fear. 'Or I shall have to summon a guard.'

'You do that, lovey,' he sneers. 'I bet most of that lot would like to join in. Have a piece of you. Still, I don't mind sharing.'

He pulls me closer towards him and I can feel, to my disgust, the bulge in his trousers pressing against my leg. I need to scream, to run, but my mouth is dry with fear and my feet are rooted to the ground.

'Please,' I whisper, pulling my body away from him. 'You will get into serious trouble if you are found doing this. They will put you in solitary. Is that what you want?'

'Don't patronize me, you German bitch,' he spits, spinning me around and pressing my face against the wall of the latrine block. 'Now, shut your mouth and take what's coming.'

My body freezes with terror as I hear him unbuttoning his trousers. I close my eyes, my mind taking me, perversely, back to the garden in Kerala, to Chellam and the daisies. Behind me, Reid's body suddenly grows heavier. I hear a shout. Reid's voice. Turning, I see him lying on the floor. A shadow bears down over the prone man. I look up to see Prisoner X standing there, his foot on Reid's back.

'I . . . I didn't know what to do,' I say, my voice trembling with shock and fear. 'He grabbed me and I . . .'

Prisoner X puts a finger to his lips and holds out his

hand. Taking it, I step over Reid, who is spitting out threats and expletives, and, with Prisoner X watching me, I walk back unsteadily in a daze to the safety of my room.

Later, as I am sitting by the fire, cradling a cup of thin soup, and attempting to read the next chapter of Hesse, hoping to erase the image of Reid from my mind, I hear footsteps outside. My heart pounding, I place the book and cup on the floor, take up the iron poker from by the fire, and edge my way towards the window to look out. I see the outline of a man standing on the wooden veranda, though I can tell from his posture and haircut that it is not Reid. I wait, my body growing limp with exhaustion and relief, then hear a faint tapping. Once, twice, three times. Keeping the poker in my hands, I creep towards the door.

With shaking hands, I unhook the latch, praying that whoever is out there does not wish me harm. But as I open the door, I am greeted with a sight so horrifying I almost lose my breath.

11

KATERINA

Seven Dials

May 1915

I smile to myself as I place the oil lamp down and take in my surroundings. Who could have thought it? A fully functioning kitchen, complete with stove and ovens.

The countertops are thick with dust and grime and as I run my finger along them, I accidentally send a pile of papers scattering to the floor. Picking them up, I see that they are old menus. This place had once been a pie shop called Maxi's and had sold a variety of hot and cold meat pies as well as sausages and bratwurst. My heart aches as I read that last word, the delicacy of my homeland, then glance up at the small type at the top of the menu: *Proprietor: Max Kircher.*

A German who, by the look of this place, had gathered his belongings and abandoned his life and his business. I can hear the cries of the mob as I place the menus back on the counter, feel the racing of Max Kircher's heart as he hastily gathered his belongings. I see the pale, terrified faces of his children, the wretched resignation of his wife, as they fled into the back alley while the mob stormed the building. I hear his wife whisper, '*Where will we go? What will we do?*' And Max's reply: '*We will get as far away from here as possible, my love. We will start again.*'

As the image fades and the voices fall silent, my attention turns to the shop. Though it has been trashed by the mob, the stove and ovens appear to be in working order and the display cabinets at the front of the counter, where Max would have placed his steaming hot pies and pasties, have remained unscathed. The graffiti and dirt can be easily cleaned away and it will do me good to have a few hours' distraction. Within a few minutes, after locating a bucket and mop from the store cupboard, I set to work.

The sun is just coming up when I hear footsteps coming down the stairs. Gillian. I wonder if she has noticed I am not in my bed. But then I hear the front door slam shut. She has gone. Off to begin her day's work at the Federation, off to impress her precious Sylvia. I feel hurt that she left without saying goodbye and then I chastise myself for caring. We are not a couple. She is free to do as she pleases.

Squeezing the excess water from the mop, I prop it up against the counter and take the bucket into the kitchen. As I pour the dirty water down the sink, I hear my father's voice in my head: '*The Devil makes work for idle hands, Katerina. Now fetch some eggs, sugar and flour and let's get started. There are hungry mouths to feed.*'

'Yes, Father,' I exclaim now, a warm feeling of industriousness stirring inside me. 'Let's get started.'

I locate flour and sugar in the stock cupboard at the back of the kitchen, dabbing my finger in each to check they have not spoiled. Both taste agreeable and as I dash upstairs in search of eggs, I see Max Kircher's wife standing at the store cupboard while her husband packs their belongings into a battered old case. *'But what about the flour and sugar? It seems a waste to leave them when they have only just been bought.'* 'Close the door, my love,' he replies, standing in the doorway with the children behind him. *'The less baggage we have the better. Come, leave the flour and sugar for the mice. It seems the vermin have the keys to the city now.'*

The flat smells of Gillian's perfume and I am momentarily struck by a deep sense of longing as I make my way to the tiny kitchenette. She has left a half-drunk cup of tea on the draining board, her pink lipstick stained round the rim. I pick it up and press it to my lips, remembering the summer of 1912, Hampstead Heath, the two of us stripping to our swimsuits and running down to the ponds. Then I recall the soft press of her mouth, the scent of her damp skin.

Enough now, Katerina, I tell myself, spotting a crate of brown eggs on the shelf, don't do it, don't let her back in. Placing the cup in the sink, I take the eggs and hurry back to the pie shop. There is work to be done.

By the time the clock strikes noon, I have baked three batches of syrup cakes. The decision to bake these particular cakes came partly from nostalgia, as these were the first confections Papa taught me to bake when I was six years old, and partly from necessity, as they only require the most basic of ingredients. Taking the cakes from their metal baking trays, I place them carefully into the display cabinets to cool. I have baked far too many but perhaps Gillian can take some of them to the Federation tomorrow and share them out amongst the women and children.

I am just cleaning down the surfaces with a damp cloth when the door opens and a woman enters. She is middle-aged, plump and rosy-cheeked, and is dressed smartly in sage-green silk and fur-trimmed hat.

'Good afternoon,' I say, putting down my cloth. 'Can I help you?'

'Oh, I just saw the light on and wondered if the pie shop had reopened,' she says, her eyes fixed on the tray of cakes. 'But it looks like it's a bakery now. I say, how much are those cakes? They look delightful.'

'I'm afraid they aren't for sale,' I say, suddenly aware of my dishevelled appearance. 'I'm just cleaning the place up. The cakes were a little distraction. But you're welcome to sample one if you like. I've made far too many as usual.'

The woman glances at the cloth in my hands and grimaces slightly.

'Oh, what a shame,' she says. 'Our friends, the Anstruther-Walkers, own several buildings on this street, and it's been terrible to see so many businesses close. The pie shop was very popular but then one can't expect decent people to be tolerating Germans at a time like this. I hear they simply fled in the night leaving all this mess. But then they are not a civilized race, are they?'

My heart starts to palpitate as she speaks, remembering the baying crowds as I fled Mile End, the look on the concierge's face when I told him my name.

'Anyway, you've twisted my arm,' says the woman, her plummy voice cutting into my thoughts. 'Those cakes look far too scrumptious to turn down.'

With trembling hands, I take a set of metal tongs, select the plumpest cake and hand it to the woman.

'I'm afraid I haven't any napkins,' I say, shocked as I hear Gillian's mannered English accent come out of my mouth.

'Oh, don't worry,' says the woman, removing her gloves and taking the cake with her thumb and forefinger. 'It's all rather fun.'

I watch as she takes a bite, recalling my father's steady patience as he guided me through each stage of the baking process. As a proud German who had taken great joy in feeding the people of the East End with his delicious confections, he would have been shamed and hurt to hear this woman's sentiments regarding his countrymen and women. I can hear his voice in my head as I watch the woman eat the cake. *An uncivilized race, Katerina?* he whispers, sorrowfully. *Is that what they think of us now?*

'My dear, that was exquisite,' gasps the woman, as my father's voice retreats. 'And I have taken tea in some of the finest dining establishments in the world. I say, you're wasting your talents being a char woman. If I were you, I'd look to find some work in a bakery or perhaps in the kitchen of a fine house.'

She smiles condescendingly and I am cheered to see that she has syrup on her chin.

'Perhaps you could even come and work for me,' she says, brushing stray crumbs from her fox-fur stole. 'What is your name?'

I am about to blurt it out when something makes me pause. Taking a deep breath to compose myself, I smile politely and reply.

'My name is . . . Kitty. Kitty Dexter.'

'Ah, splendid,' says the woman, taking a card from her handbag and handing it to me. 'Well, Kitty, if you would like to come and bake some of those marvellous cakes for my friends – and we're talking about the wives of admirals and lords here – then do drop me a line.'

I thank her politely but after she has left, I look down at the card with the words *Dorothy, Lady Jamison* printed in gold cursive script, and know exactly what I am going to do. I will not be getting in touch with Lady Dorothy and baking cakes for her bigoted friends because the moment she tasted that cake I made my decision.

I am going to reopen this place as a bakery but, unlike in Mile End, it will not be Katerina Drechsler serving the local community with delicious delicacies, it will be Kitty Dexter, an Englishwoman born and bred. If I am to survive in this strange new climate then all trace of my German identity must be as the crumbs on this floor, completely swept away.

12

EDIE

Cornwall

Present Day

At first, I think that the person pushing his way through the door is Alexander, back from London and in a rush to get out of the cold. But it is a warm night and the elderly man standing in front of me is not my affable neighbour. He is tall and lean with broad shoulders squeezed into faded blue overalls. His hair, half-concealed by a white fisherman's hat, is straggly and grey and his face is criss-crossed with deep wrinkles that become more pronounced as he scowls at me over the top of his thick-rimmed spectacles.

'You said you 'ad some work as needs doing,' he says, barging past me into the hallway.

'Excuse me, who are . . .' I begin, as I hurry after him. Then I notice he is carrying a toolbox and I realize this must be Alexander's 'eccentric' workman.

'Ned Kendal?' I say, extending my hand. 'I'm Edie. Pleased to meet you.'

'Aye,' he says, with a brisk nod, ignoring my hand. 'Got a leaking roof hole, eh? That'll be the storm the other night.

Shook the whole cove up, it did. If you show me where it is, I'll get on to fixing it.'

'Now? But it's almost seven o'clock.'

He looks at me blankly.

'Rather late to start work, isn't it?'

'Do you want it fixing or not?' he says, glancing round the room.

'Of course,' I say, padding after him across the sodden towels. 'It's just, won't you have to go up on the roof to replace the tile? It'll be dark soon and I don't want you to fall.'

'Don't worry about me,' he says, glancing round again with narrowed eyes. 'I've never fallen from a roof in fifty years. Don't intend to now. Blimey, what's happened there? More storm damage?'

He points to the hole in the wall.

'No, I'm afraid that was me,' I say, feeling rather foolish. 'I'm renovating the cottage and I was taking off the plaster-board when that hole revealed itself.'

He crouches beside the hole and starts pulling out bits of plaster, groaning and clutching the small of his back as he goes. Once again, I am questioning whether he is up to the job. He must be almost eighty.

'Faffing about with this wainscot, eh?' he says, turning to me, his face flushed.

I nod my head like a schoolgirl being admonished for vandalizing my books.

'Thought as much,' he replies, shaking his head. 'Down from London, are you? Like him next door?'

'I am from London, yes,' I say impatiently. 'Though I have moved here permanently. This isn't a holiday home. In fact, it once belonged to my great-grandmother and—'

I stop. Why do I feel the need to explain myself to this man? He is here to do a job, not lecture me on my life choices.

'Great-grandmother?' he says, his expression hardening. 'What was her name?'

'Jane,' I say, glancing at the clock on the wall behind him. I have a feeling we're going to be here all night.

He goes quiet then and turns back to the hole in the wall.

'Like I said, this is my home,' I say, aware that I am blathering. 'I intend to stay here long term.'

'That's what they all say,' he says with a sigh. 'It's all very well in the summer when the sun's out and they can lie on the beach. But once they've endured their first Cornish winter, they up and leave, back to the smoke, without so much as a goodbye or a care for the folk left behind. I've seen it countless times over the years.'

'Do you think you can fix the hole?' I say, refusing to get into a debate about cowardly Londoners. 'If not, I can call a firm in.'

He turns and looks at me quizzically. Then he starts to chuckle.

'A firm,' he chortles, shaking his head. 'There'll be no need for that. I've spent my life patching up these cottages. I could do it blindfold.'

'And what about the leak?' I say, in my best stern voice.

'I can stem it tonight,' he says, looking up at the ceiling.. 'Patch it up, then come back tomorrow and fix the slate. You say it was broken?'

Clearly news in this part of the world spreads fast. 'The tile was cracked in two,' I say, stepping aside as he brings his large toolkit in from the hallway. 'It's in the kitchen. I can get it for you if you think it's fixable.'

'No need,' he says, his back to me. 'I've got some at home I can bring with me tomorrow.'

He takes a dust sheet out of his toolbag and lays it on the floor.

'Right, you can leave me to it,' he says, pulling out various tools from the bag. 'But a cup of tea wouldn't go amiss. Mine's white with two sugars.'

'Of course,' I reply, then shuffle off to the kitchen in stunned silence.

As I wait for the kettle to boil, I hear him banging and crashing, letting rip a stream of expletives as he goes. I think of what Ronke would say if she were here: '*Edie, girl, what the hell are you doing, letting some old geezer trash your place? Have you even checked his references? He could be anyone.*'

Oh dear, I think to myself, as I pour the tea. Wrong call again, Edie.

A cloud of plaster dust swirls through the air as I walk into the living room, so thick I can barely see Ned. Placing the tea on the side table next to the hole, I notice the box sitting on the sideboard. Perhaps Ned can shed some light on it.

But when I tell him, the colour fades from his face.

'Let me show you what's inside,' I say, unclipping the latch. 'It's most curious but as you've lived round here all these years, I thought you might know what it is or who put it there.'

'I don't wish to see it,' he says, his face still ashen. 'Folk shouldn't go digging around in places that don't concern them.'

'I was renovating,' I exclaim. 'And it's my wall. I can do as I please with it.'

'Just saying there are some things best left alone,' he says, placing his cup of tea down.

'Sorry for snapping,' I say, hoping I haven't offended him so much that he packs up and leaves without finishing the job. 'That was rude of me.'

'Water off a duck's back,' he replies. 'Just saying what I think, that's all. We talk straight, us Holton folk. Now, you go and get on with your evening and leave me to it.'

'Of course,' I say.

'May I ask, miss,' he says, as I reach the door, 'do you believe in the Devil?'

'I beg your pardon?' I say, rather theatrically as I truly cannot believe what I am hearing.

'I said, do you believe in the Devil?'

He stares back at me, his eyes enlarged by the thick lenses of his glasses, and the temperature in the room seems to plummet.

'I . . . I suppose I've never thought about it,' I say, my voice trembling.

'You said this cottage belonged to your great-grandmother?' he continues.

'That's right,' I say, feeling confused. One minute he wants to be left alone, the next he wants to talk about the Devil, and now Jane. 'My father's grandmother.'

'Hmm, that makes sense,' he says, shaking his head. 'Terrible, the kind of people that ended up in the cottage.'

'I don't quite understand what you mean.'

'I'm talking about the tenants of this place,' he says, lowering his voice as though those very tenants were hiding in the corner eavesdropping. 'There's been a fair few over the years and they all had the same thing in common.'

'What's that?' I say wearily.

'Devil worship,' he says.

I cannot help it, but I find myself laughing. It is so preposterous, the whole thing.

'It's not a laughing matter,' he says, clearly affronted. 'Playing around with the occult. It's dangerous. And the strange thing is, they all seemed perfectly nice when they moved in. Just like you. Makes you think if there's not something about this cottage that, well, I don't know, tips them over the edge. But then that wouldn't surprise me, knowing what went on here when I was a nipper. The last one was the worst, mind, the things he got up to. Made my blood run cold.'

My thoughts turn to the box. Its strange carvings, the mysterious inscription hinting at some supernatural connection. Yet despite all of that, I feel perfectly safe here. It's my home, my haven, and I feel angry at Ned Kendal for smearing it like this.

'I'm afraid I don't believe in such things,' I say, smiling politely.

'And yet finding that has unsettled you,' he says, gesturing to the box which is sitting ominously on the sideboard. 'I can tell it has. And I don't blame you. I'll leave it at that, but I just thought you might like to be informed as to what has gone on in this place, the kind of people it attracts.'

'I'll let you get on with your work,' I say.

But as I go to leave the room, he says something that makes my own blood run cold.

'That last tenant. He really was the worst of them. Evil through and through. Name was David. David Hart.'

13

MIRIAM

Dänholm Prisoner-of-War Camp

October 1918

Prisoner X stands on the step, his lip swollen and bloodied.

'Come inside,' I say. 'I will tidy those wounds.'

He shakes his head and I realize how foolish I am being. Invite a prisoner into your room? What are you thinking, Miriam?

'Wait here,' I say, taking a cursory glance across the darkened quad to check that we are not being watched. 'I will fetch my first-aid box. You don't want to risk that wound becoming infected.'

When I return he is standing on the porch, his eyes lowered to the ground, his body trembling from head to foot. His posture is the same as when I last saw him, bearing down over my attacker, his foot pressed to the man's shoulder blades.

'Reid did this to you, didn't he?' I say, taking care to pronounce the English words carefully as I take a bottle of antiseptic and a couple of cotton squares from my bag.

He looks up at me and his eyes tell me I am right. My head is a ball of confusion. On the one hand I am thankful that Reid got what he deserved but on the other, with a terrible sense of foreboding, I feel that Prisoner X may just have made things worse.

'I apologize for the makeshift dressings,' I say, soaking the edge of the square in antiseptic before dabbing his cheek. 'I'm afraid they've started rationing bandages and cloth now.'

He raises his eyebrows, then winces in pain. One of the cuts, just above his left eye, is deeper than the others and has tiny fragments of glass embedded in it, making me wonder if he has been attacked with a bottle.

'This may need stitches,' I say, taking a pair of sterilized tweezers from the bag and carefully removing the glass. 'It's very deep. For that we would need to go to the sanatorium as I do not have the right equipment here.'

His eyes change as I say this, the soft expression giving way to something I saw the other day: a raw, almost child-like fear.

'Wait here a moment,' I say, when I have removed the last of the glass. 'I'll just take this to the kitchen and fetch my coat.'

Leaving him on the step, I place the cotton squares in the sink and leave them to soak.

'If we leave now, we may just avoid being seen,' I call out as I dry my hands on a cloth. 'I know the guards nearest the sanatorium like to play cards at this hour. With a bit of luck, they will be distracted.'

But there is no reply as I head to the door. And I know, from the heavy silence that hangs over the night air like a winter blanket, that X has fled.

*

At the recording session the following day, I feel conspicuous. When Herr Garn issues his usual instructions, I feel his words are weighted with innuendo, as though he knows what happened last night. So, when he says, 'Miriam, could you check the sound levels?' I hear, '*Greeting a prisoner at the door of your living quarters? An enemy prisoner? And a dangerous man at that. What were you thinking?*'

'Penny for them?'

I snap out of my paranoia and look at the young man standing in front of the horn.

'You were off on a sunbeam just now, pet,' he says, in a voice that rises up and down like the horses on a carousel, an accent that Herr Garn informed me at the beginning of the session is known as 'Geordie' and is native to Newcastle, a city in the north-east of England.

'I'm sorry,' I say, flinching at the young man, a painfully thin youth with dun-coloured hair, sunken cheeks and grey teeth, the memory of Reid's voice in my ear as he pressed me to the wall still fresh in my mind. 'Ready when you are.'

'Well, I dunno if mine is much of a story,' begins the young man, his cheeks flushing with embarrassment. 'But here goes. My name is Geoffrey Routledge, though everyone calls me Geoff, and I was born in the countryside in a place called Hexham, though we moved to Newcastle when I were a bairn so as my father could find work as a shipbuilder. Is this the kind of thing you were wanting, Professor?'

Herr Garn looks up from the notes he has been writing.

'It's perfect, Routledge,' he says, waving his hand. 'Do go on. Tell me about the ships?'

As the boy continues, his North Country accent turning 'father' to 'fatha' and 'country' to 'cunry', I hear a murmuring coming from the young men behind him.

'We'll meet at midnight. Tom's on kitchen duty. He'll sort us out.'

'Are you sure, Harris? I hear there's Huns covering every base of the kitchen wing.'

'I'm sure as the eyes on my head, you chicken. Tom's a good 'un and he says those Huns as guard the kitchens are not up to snuff. Likely they'll be goosed by midnight.'

'What's for the taking?'

'Tom's gonna sort us some mucking and leftover bread, maybe some of that sausage the Huns like. Bit disloyal of us to eat that stuff but needs must, eh? You in?'

'I'm in, Harris.'

Listening to them, I am reminded of X's emaciated frame as he stood at the door. We all know that the men are being half-starved but as they are prisoners and the enemy we are supposed not to care. We are supposed to turn a blind eye.

Herr Garn has heard them too. He glances in my direction and shakes his head in disapproval. Will he turn them in? Will he make use of their voices but deny them their sustenance? As always with Herr Garn, I am never quite sure what his intentions are. I know that he is committed to his academic work, but I also know that he is equally committed to the German cause, and he would do nothing to aid the enemy.

Those young boys are on my mind later as I lie in bed listening to the clock strike midnight. They will be gathering in the kitchens now. Somewhere in the distance, I hear dogs barking and the sound of a gunshot and I do something I haven't done since my mother died. I pray. I ask God to protect those young men, to turn a blind eye as they take their meagre stash of food and to protect them from the wrath of the guards.

As I finish the prayer, I turn to face the wall and close my eyes but as I am drifting off, I hear a soft tapping at the door. There is no moon tonight and the room is in darkness. With a pounding heart, I stumble out of the bed and try to locate my matches to light the oil lamp. The tapping comes again, louder this time, and I stub my toe on the table. When I finally locate the matches, I light the lamp and bring it with me to the door.

'Who is it?' I whisper.

There is no reply.

My first thought is Reid. What if it is him? What if he has come to seek his vengeance on me for what happened last night? But then if it were Reid he would respond with some expletive-laden filth and try to force his way inside. No, the silence can mean only one person.

Opening the door a fraction, I peep out and see a flash of blonde hair and a thick white cotton square.

X.

'Hello,' I say, suddenly aware of my state of undress. I am standing here in only my nightgown. 'What is it? Is everything all right?'

He doesn't respond.

'Would you like to come in?' I ask, as a white searchlight spans across the grass behind him.

He nods his head and comes inside.

'It is rather late,' I say, closing the door and fetching my dressing gown from the end of the bed. 'And I know I really shouldn't be letting you in at this hour.'

Buttoning my gown right up to the top, I ask if he would like something to eat. He nods his head and hesitantly moves to sit in the chair by the dying embers of the fire.

'There's not much heat left in the fire, I'm afraid,' I say, taking the pink candlewick bedspread from the end of the bed.

I wrap it round his shoulders. He lifts his hand to pull it closer and momentarily our fingers meet. He looks up at me and I see that he is trembling not from fear but something else, something darker. A silent rage. I remove my hand from his and go to the hob to heat up a can of leek and potato soup.

While it simmers I watch him, realizing that this is the first time I have been alone in my room with anyone, let alone a British prisoner. And after what happened with Reid, I really ought to be careful. Yet there is something about X that elicits trust and safety. In fact, he seems to pose more of a threat to himself than to me. His hands tremble as I pass him the bowl of soup and I notice as he takes the spoon to his mouth that his lips are cracked and dry.

'Would you like some water?'

He nods his head and when I return with the cup, I see that he has polished off the soup, the empty dish lying on his lap like a begging bowl.

'You must have been hungry,' I say, taking the bowl and placing it on the floor. 'But then I hear that the rations they give you are pretty mean.'

He stares at me as he drinks the water, his pale blue eyes

swollen and bloodshot. When he has finished, he sits back in the chair and closes his eyes.

I want to ask him why he is here, what exactly happened with Reid, why he has been assigned an armed guard in the day yet appears to be at liberty to roam the camp at night and, more pertinently, why he has lost his voice. But I know it would be futile. He will not answer. He will simply stare at me with those strange milky blue eyes. Besides, it is late and though I know I should report him for being here, that I am breaking the rules of the camp by being alone in my hut with him, that I would be punished severely if he were caught here, I find his presence strangely reassuring.

'Rest, if you like,' I say, climbing into bed and pulling the covers up to my chin. 'You must be very tired.'

With his eyes still closed, he pulls the bedspread up in the same way and settles into the folds of the chair.

'When I was a little girl, I used to make such a fuss at bedtime,' I say, keeping my voice low. These walls are very thin.

X's eyes flutter open and he turns to me.

'My father used to despair,' I continue. 'But what he didn't realize was that I couldn't go to sleep without my favourite lullaby. It was the one my mother used to sing to me before she died. "*Guten Abend und gute Nacht*."'

With those words, X flinches as though he has been struck. And I realize that, as a British soldier, the German language may seem offensive. I do not want to scare him away, so I sing the lullaby in his language.

Good evening, goodnight,
Covered with roses

Adorned with thorns
Slip under the covers
Tomorrow, if it is God's will,
Will you wake again
Tomorrow, if it is God's will
You will wake again.

As the verse comes to an end, I hear a noise, a low, guttural sound like an animal in pain. Looking up, I see something that makes my heart ache. X, his head in his hands, is weeping.

14

KITTY

Seven Dials

June 1915

What a difference a name makes, I think to myself as I stand in line at the grocer's stall in Covent Garden, along-side the Smiths and the Robinsons, the Jessops and the Woods, exchanging smiles and pleasantries. To them, I am just another patriotic Englishwoman, keeping the home fires burning while our men fight the murderous Germans in the sodden fields of Flanders. I nod politely and offer my condolences as they tell me about a friend of a friend whose son was killed at Ypres in April, listen as they shake their heads and say that '*he died fighting for his country and what better death could there be than that?*' and how they hoped his comrades avenged his death by bayoneting a dirty Kraut. Katerina would have railed at such talk, her thoughts would have turned to her brother, one of the 'dirty Krauts' of whom these women speak; she would have told these women a few home truths, asked them what right they had to speak of fellow human beings this way.

But that was Katerina Drechsler, the woman I had been right up until Lady Dorothy tasted that cake. The following morning, I had woken up as Kitty Dexter, a young woman newly arrived in London from the English provinces, a keen baker who had come to help her friend, Gillian, in her work at the Federation but who, upon discovering an abandoned pie shop and testing a batch of cakes on the discerning palate of a titled woman, had come up with the idea of opening a bakery. It would be just what this neglected corner of the West End needed, a little bit of sweetness amid the bitter taste of war.

I had stayed up half the night concocting the story. In fact, so vivid was Kitty's biography, I could see it stretched out in front of me in bright colours, as clear as one of my visions. And yet, Kitty was no spirit, she was a living, breathing woman, a woman who had lived parallel to me all these years; she was the other side of me, the light to my dark. Hers was the life I could have lived if fate had delivered me to an English family instead of my German one. Only the thinnest of threads separated her identity from mine, I realized, as I stood in front of the mirror, dressed in Gillian's ankle-length linen skirt and high-necked navy blouse, shaping my mouth around the English words with my new English voice.

'Good afternoon, sir. My name is Kitty Dexter.'

'Well, hello there, Miss Dexter,' says the cheery young grocer standing behind the counter. 'What can I get you?'

'Oh, I'm not quite sure,' I say, laughing coquettishly. 'You have so much on offer. Those pears look particularly good. So ripe and plump. I'll take a dozen.'

The young man's cheeks flush as he places the fruit into a large paper bag. He has no idea that he is playing a part in this game of mine and I feel a surge of energy as I dart around the shop, placing various items into my shopping basket, aware that the young man is watching me, desiring me.

I leave the shop laden with bags of flour, sugar, dried fruit, yeast and butter as well as a bag of liquorice toffee the grocer slipped into my basket. 'Nice to make your acquaintance, Kitty,' he says with a wink as I make my way out. 'Hope to see you again soon.' 'I'm sure you will,' I reply, flashing him a smile. And I can't quite believe what I have just done. Openly flirting with a man. Me, Katerina Drechsler. Who would have thought I had it in me? Still, I think to myself, as I twirl my skirts and make my way out into a bustling Covent Garden, better to be thought of as a man-loving woman than a German one. If I am to survive in this city, then I must keep the likes of the grocer and his customers on side. Whatever they want me to be is what I will give them.

At the corner of Neal Street, I notice a hardware shop with pots of brightly coloured paint outside. A handwritten sign proclaims, *Three pots for a penny. Reduced to clear.* On closer inspection I can see why the price is so low. After all, who in their right mind would have use for such shades as *Sunset Orange*, *Shocking Pink* and *Nightshade Black*? But I have never been in anything close to a 'right' mind and before I know it I am bundling up the narrow staircase to Gillian's flat, my arms laden with pots of black and pink paint.

'My goodness, what's all that?' says Gillian, looking up from her typewriter which she has wedged on the table by the wall. 'Fancied a spot of decorating, did you?'

'Better than that,' I tell her, dropping my parcels onto the floor. 'I'm going to open up the shop downstairs as a bakery.'

She watches me as I unwrap the paint.

'The abandoned pie shop? Won't you need a licence for that sort of thing?'

'Possibly. Though I very much doubt Westminster Council will grant a licence or lease to a German woman in the current climate.'

'So, what do you intend to do?' says Gillian, exhaling a cloud of smoke. 'Squat?'

'Exactly that,' I say boldly. 'And if the council do come calling then . . . well, I'll work that out as and when.'

'Good to see you've lost none of that rebellious spirit,' says Gillian, with a smile. 'Though I could talk to Sylvia about it. She's had tons of experience in setting up commercial premises. Perhaps she could have a word with the council on your behalf, tell them that you're a pillar of the community or some such, albeit a German one.'

'There's no need to involve Sylvia,' I snap, feeling my excitement draining away.

'Fine,' says Gillian, with a shrug. 'But I ask again, what will you do when the council come knocking?'

'Like I said, I shall cross that bridge when I come to it.'

'And the clothes?'

'What about them?'

'Look, darling,' says Gillian, leaning back in her chair and lighting another cigarette. 'I'm all for you being careful in this hostile climate, being discreet about your German heritage, but does this subterfuge have to involve you dressing like that? Isn't the name change enough? You remind me of my Aunt Marie. All you need to do is douse yourself in copious amounts of lavender oil.'

'I shall take that as a compliment,' I say, unbuttoning my coat and throwing it onto the couch.

'Seriously though, Kat,' says Gillian, taking a drag of her cigarette. 'That costume makes me feel queasy. It's like you've become someone else.'

'Which is exactly the point,' I say, scrunching the brown wrapping paper into a tight ball. 'And please, call me Kitty. Look, Gillian, I have to present a completely different persona if I am to survive here. What if someone comes into the bakery and recognizes me from Mile End? We'd have that mob on the doorstep in minutes. You were there that day. You saw how venomous those people were. If they'd had their chance, they would have killed me.'

'I know, darling,' she sighs. 'And I do understand, really I do, it's just would it be too much to ask for you to dispense with the skirts and rouge behind closed doors? The way you fashioned yourself with no care for what was expected of you was one of the reasons I was so drawn to you, it *is* you. And besides, I've had enough bland, upper-class English gals to last me a lifetime.'

I do not press as to how many of these English gals she has had and nor do I respond to her request for me to dress as she wants me to behind closed doors. For as far as Gillian and I are concerned, there is no 'behind closed doors'. Our relationship is strictly platonic, two friends sharing an apartment, nothing more. It is the only way it can be.

'Let's just pretend I'm an actress,' I tell her as I load the paint pots into a basket to take downstairs. 'And I'm playing a role. Think what a good deal that is – you get to watch a character unfold from the privacy of your own home and you don't even have to pay for a ticket.'

'Whatever you think is best . . . Kitty,' says Gillian wearily, turning back to the typewriter. And with that I leave her to get on with her writing.

We spend the next few days getting the shop ready. After her initial shock, as well as a few grumbles that I have interrupted her work on a special edition of the *Dreadnought*, Sylvia's suffragette newspaper, Gillian soon came round to the idea of the bakery. 'I suppose, if nothing else, it will keep you busy,' she says, holding the ladder as I carefully trace the lettering onto the signage. 'I was telling Sylvia just the other day, if you're not able to commune with the spirits or bake pumpernickel bread then you fall into a terrible funk.'

Ignoring her reference to Sylvia and the rather dismissive remark about my gift, I step down from the ladder and stand back to take a look at my handiwork.

'Well, I say it's glorious,' says Gillian, looping her arm through mine. 'Just perfect.'

She kisses my cheek, a gesture that makes me wince. Yet I cannot help but smile as I look at the words on the sign, emblazoned in bright pink lettering:

KITTY KAT'S BAKERY

The following day I wake at dawn to the sound of animated voices. Wiping the sleep from my eyes, my thoughts immediately turn to the mob. Have they discovered me? Have they come armed with clubs and knives to drive me out like they did in Mile End?

But as I open the curtains, the sight that greets me in the pale morning mist lifts my soul. A queue of women armed with shopping baskets and recalcitrant children is snaking its way up the street.

'Gillian,' I hiss, as I run to gather my dress and pinafore from the chair by the bed. 'Quickly.'

I run into her bedroom and pull open the curtains.

'Gillian, look.'

'What is it?' she groans, her pale hand shielding her eyes from the sunlight pouring into the room. 'What's all that noise?'

'That noise,' I say, dabbing a tot of rouge on my cheeks as I run for the door, 'is the sound of our future. Our customers. They have come.'

15

EDIE

Cornwall

Present Day

'David Hart?' I repeat. 'That was the tenant's name?'

'It was,' says Ned, returning to his toolbox from which he extracts a tub of plaster. 'Though I don't like to say it out loud. Never believed in cursed individuals until I met that fella. Evil to the core he was. Pure evil.'

I know it is just a coincidence that the tenant and my late husband share a name, but I need to reassure myself, need to settle this churning feeling that Ned's revelation has stirred up inside me.

'Can you tell me more about this man?' I say, as Ned unfolds his stepladder and places it underneath the damp ceiling. 'What was he like?'

'I told you – I don't want to speak of him,' says Ned, climbing onto the ladder. 'I just wanted to let you know the sort of folk this cottage has attracted. Alls I'll say is that he wasn't from here, he was a foreigner. Not one of us. And if I were you, I'd take that box and throw it in the sea. No good will come from having it lying around if that man had anything to do with it.'

It is almost midnight by the time Ned has finished patching up the hole and, having refused my suggestion of paying him via BACS as he doesn't have a bank account – 'Don't trust those bankers. Never have, never will!' – we agree that I will drop off some cash at his house the following day.

'There's a machine in the village, so I'm told,' he says, folding up the paint-spattered dust sheet and placing it in his bag. 'In the general stores, by the delicatessen.'

I thank him, while trying to get my head round the fact that someone can function in the twenty-first century without a bank account or debit card.

'Oh, I'll also need your address,' I say, as I see him out. 'What number are you?'

'Don't have a number,' he says, placing his cap on his head, the peak obscuring his face. 'Mine's the last one on Main Street, just after the pub and before the road forks out to the coastal path.'

'I'm sure I'll find it,' I say, unlatching the door and letting in a wave of salty night air. 'Thanks for all your help, Ned. Drive safely.'

He mutters something about Londoners as he shuffles down the path, his metal toolbox glinting in the glow of the gibbous moon.

Returning to the living room, I exhale slowly, thankful that Ned is gone. He appears to have made a good job of the ceiling and the hole in the wall, but his strange comments have left me feeling shaken.

David Hart. It has to be a coincidence, of course it has. David lived with me in East London. He came home every night at six o'clock and started cooking. I think I would have noticed if he'd been slipping off to lead a double life as a satanist in my great-grandmother's cottage. The idea is beyond preposterous. And yet Ned's insistence has made me question everything. There has always been something about that night, David's last, that I didn't understand. The way those men just appeared, the sneer of their faces when they saw David approach. Was there something more to it, something I am not seeing? Then I think about those trips David made to Europe and the States, the academic conferences, the literary festivals. What if he was doing something else instead?

Pull yourself together, Edie, for God's sake, I tell myself, as I close the curtains. You're questioning your husband of thirty years on the word of a shambolic man who is so paranoid he doesn't even have a bank account. Come on.

I'm about to turn out the lights and head up to bed when I notice the box on the sideboard. Its lid is wedged open. Has Ned been snooping? Most likely. Stepping towards it, my eye is drawn to the silk-wrapped Tarot cards. Though the box and Ned's reaction to it spooked me, I am intrigued to explore the drawings on the deck in more detail. How can anything so beautiful, so perfectly crafted, be evil? I feel cross with myself for falling for the silly superstition of an old man who probably hasn't strayed too far from the confines of the village his whole life and who, quite clearly, views those he doesn't know as enemies. I cannot let it affect my judgement, particularly now. After all, I have a commission to complete and here is an exquisitely illustrated, original set fallen straight into my lap. It makes sense to do a little research.

Sitting down on the armchair, I unwrap the purple silk

and place the deck on my lap. Instinctively, I start to shuffle them. Immediately my mind conjures Dora as a child, her inquisitive mind and how she loved nothing better than playing card games with me and David on rainy Sunday afternoons. I see her now, thick dark curls falling in her face, her hand poised over the cards, waiting to shout out 'Snap!' Then something strange happens. All the tension I have felt these last couple of days starts to fall away. My hands loosen, my breathing slows down, I feel an immense sense of calm, a warm feeling of peace bathes me from head to toe and then, out of nowhere, a card jumps out of the deck and lands on the floor at my feet.

I reach down to retrieve it and see *The Tower* written in gold ink across the top of the card. I am still a novice when it comes to the Tarot but from my own brief research and Rebecca's notes, I can see that the illustration deviates from the traditional imagery associated with this card. Instead of a stone tower collapsing, the artist has drawn a hot air balloon, with claret and mustard stripes, plummeting from the sky with terrified figures leaping from it to the ground.

I stare at the card and suddenly the figures seem to become animated, their arms and legs flailing as they tumble through the air. My mind returns again to that night, the noise downstairs, the two hooded figures, the fact that they had known David's name. Though I had seen the taller of the two pick up the envelope addressed to David, heard the hatred in his voice as he looked up and said, 'Dr David Hart,' what if it was all part of something bigger, something darker? What if they already knew who he was? I think of Ned's comment about David Hart, the tenant, being 'pure evil' and a shiver ripples through my body.

'Enough of this, Edie,' I tell myself firmly, as I place the card back into the deck and wrap the purple silk round it, holding whatever it is I have just released tightly in place. 'Time for bed.'

After an unsettled sleep plagued by dreams of the events of that October night interwoven with faceless figures leaping from a burning hot air balloon, I head to Alexander's cottage to feed Jupiter. Locating the spare key that Alexander keeps underneath the pot with the olive tree by the front door, I let myself in. The cat is nowhere to be seen but there is a pile of post on the mat. I take it into the kitchen and place it on the table. While I scrape a tin of foul-smelling cat food into Jupiter's metal bowl, my eye is drawn to an opened letter propped up against the teapot on the counter. It has a stamped letterhead bearing the name Benson & Weir Property Services below which is written: *SUBJECT: PLANNING APPLICATION FOR TWO-STOREY BUILDING.* Strange, I think to myself, taking the bowl and placing it on Jupiter's plastic feeding mat, Alexander has never mentioned anything about extending his cottage and surely he can't do it anyway because the only area to extend into is the plot occupied by Moonstone Cottage. But then perhaps the letter is referring to his London flat or another property entirely. I shouldn't be looking at his private post anyway, I tell myself, as Jupiter slinks into the kitchen and throws me a disdainful look, reminding me why I have never liked cats.

Five minutes later I am power-walking through the village in search of Ned's house. According to him, it is the last one before the coastal path but as I reach the end of the village, the signs for the beach up ahead of me, all I can see to the left is a mass of overgrown gorse. Spotting a woman heading for the coastal path with her dog, I flag her down and ask for directions.

'Ned's place?' she says, with a wry smile. 'You're here. His is the caravan on the left there. It's hidden by all those bushes. But then, knowing Ned, that's how he prefers to be.

'Good luck,' she says as I make my way through the bushes. The wilderness soon opens up into a small, concreted area, at the centre of which is a squat white caravan. Ned must have seen me walking up as, before I get the chance to knock, he appears at the door, the local newspaper folded under his arm.

'Now then,' he says, with a nod. 'Cuppa?'

I really should get back and make a start on my morning's work, but curiosity gets the better of me and before I know it I am sitting at Ned's pull-out table nursing a mug of strong tea and nibbling a ginger biscuit.

'I was thinking about what you said about the tenant,' I say, watching as Ned places the cash I have given him into a used envelope and locks it in a metal tin. 'That he was called David Hart. This may sound crazy but that was my late husband's name. Are you quite sure that was the name of the tenant?'

Ned looks at me blankly.

'I'm not saying you were mistaken,' I say, tripping over my words. 'It just . . . it just gave me quite a start to hear my husband's name. You can understand.'

'Like I said, that man was not a good sort.'

Ned sits down opposite me, his face inscrutable.

'And I can see from looking at you that you wouldn't be married to someone like that,' he says. 'You seem a decent, respectable person. David Hart was the opposite of that.'

'And you think it was him who put that box in the wall?' I say, feeling, like I did last night, a deep sense of discomfort.

'Could have been,' he says, taking a sip of tea. 'Or it could have been Kitty.'

'Kitty?' I say, remembering the name on the photograph. 'Who's that?'

'She was the owner of the cottage when I was a lad,' he says.

He looks off into the middle distance, as though in a trance. I am beginning to wonder if he might be suffering from some sort of senility. His advanced age and the disordered state of the caravan certainly point to it.

'No, you're mistaken,' I say, glancing at my watch. I really should get going. 'My great-grandmother owned the cottage going way back to the twenties, I'm sure.'

'I think it's you that's mistaken,' he says, getting up from the table. He walks over to the other end of the caravan and opens a cupboard above the bed. I glance at the door which is just inches from the table. If he tries anything funny, I can make a run for it.

'Have a look at this,' he says, returning to the table with a faded brown envelope. He takes a photograph out of it and hands it to me.

The photo is black-and-white and shows a woman with wavy shoulder-length dark hair, holding a plump-faced baby. They are standing outside a cottage, the name clearly visible on the sign behind them.

'This is Moonstone Cottage,' I say. 'But who are these people?'

'That lady is my dear old grandmother,' he says, taking the photo from me. 'And the little fatty she's holding is me.'

'You lived at the cottage?'

'No,' he says brusquely. 'Gran used to do a bit of cleaning work for the lady who owned it. And that lady's name was not Jane. I can tell you that for certain. Her name was Kitty.'

'But I can assure you, my great-grandmother's name was Jane,' I say, feeling rather hot in the stuffy caravan. 'And she definitely owned Moonstone Cottage. Perhaps this Kitty person was a tenant or a previous owner.'

'Listen, dear,' he says, leaning forward so I can smell the milky tea on his breath. 'It can't be easy to hear that you've got it wrong. Lots of London folk turn up here thinking they've got some family claim on some place or other, but I have lived here all my life and I can tell you that it was Kitty who owned Moonstone Cottage. She had the bakery too and she lived there up until her death in the fifties. Strange woman she was, though my grandmother fell under her spell.'

He starts to laugh then. I want to protest that the cottage was left to my father in a legal will, that I have every right to be living there, but then I wonder, again, whether there may be a little confusion at play in his recollections and, not wanting to press him further, I thank him for the tea and tell him I must be going.

Heading home through the village, I stop outside the bakery. *K's Stores* is written in deep pink lettering across a pale pink-and-white hoarding. Though I have walked past the bakery often since moving here, today, for the first time, I notice the swing sign hanging from a cast-iron bracket just above the door. A light breeze blows it back and forth making it hard for me to get a good look at it. Once it settles, however, I see something that causes me to start. The image on the sign is a beautifully painted hot air balloon with claret and mustard stripes. It is strangely familiar.

And then it hits me. Though there are no falling figures, and the balloon is rising gracefully into the sky rather than tumbling to the ground, I now realize where I have seen this image and this drawing style before.

The illustrations on the Tarot cards in the box. They were made by the same woman.

Kitty.

16

KITTY

Seven Dials

June 1915

The next few weeks pass in a whirl of activity with customers flocking from far and wide to sample the cakes and pastries. Gillian has pitched in to help, combining her work at the Federation with numerous shifts behind the counter, where she has brought her ribbon-curling skills to the fore in the shape of beautifully presented cake parcels that have gone down a storm with the customers. 'All those years of watching Mother fussing over table decorations were not wasted after all,' she had laughed, when I commented on her new-found skill. This morning, I have left her attending to the shop while I prepare myself for a rather important appointment.

When the interview request arrived from the *London Evening Standard* last week, I had panicked. It was one thing giving myself a new name and talking with an English accent but to have my photograph plastered all over the newspapers where I would be seen by thousands of people was quite another. 'I can't do it,' I said to Gillian, when she read me the letter that had been posted to the shop that morning.

'What if they suspect something? What if someone from Mile End recognizes me?' Gillian had tried to reassure me, telling me that publicity like this was gold dust for a fledgling business like ours. Though I knew she was right, I still had a niggling fear in the pit of my stomach. Reporters were like bloodhounds, attuned to sniffing out a story, and a German masquerading as an Englishwoman was the kind of scoop they have a nose for. I couldn't take any chances so, with the aid of a sharp pair of scissors and some vegetable dye, I had set about the final stage of my transformation.

'Kitty, he's here.'

Gillian's voice trickles from the shop to the back kitchen where I stand regarding myself in the small smudged mirror. I barely recognize the woman staring back at me with her jaw-length glossy hair and perfectly made-up face and yet I am thankful for that.

As I tie a fresh white apron round my waist and make my way into the bakery, I am an actress taking to her stage. I just hope that my audience will believe what he sees.

'Ah, Miss Dexter.'

The reporter, Maurice Newton, an elderly chap with a drinker's red nose and a heavy paunch, is sitting at the table in the anteroom, a plate of freshly baked pastries in front of him. He stands to greet me, brushing a crumb from his bushy grey moustache.

'I must say, you have caused quite a stir,' he remarks, regarding me thoughtfully over the half-moon lenses of his spectacles as we take our seats. 'Housewives, mine included, seem to have fallen under your spell. My wife cannot get enough of those Victoria sponges. And judging by these delicious pastries, I have to concede that she is right. Ah, thank heavens for people like you, dear, women who can actually do what the fairer sex were sent to this earth for. How I wish I could say the same about my wife but, unfortunately, she favours her games of bridge with her lady friends over baking. I fear it is a sign of the times and that many poor husbands will find themselves going hungry. How delightful, then, that we have ladies like you, Miss Dexter, who keep those home fires burning.'

I smile politely, but as he lowers his head to scribble into his notebook, I allow myself a little sigh of satisfaction. For at the mention of his wife my clairvoyance, dormant these last few weeks, sprang into life and I saw a buxom red-haired woman, locked in a passionate embrace with a handsome young man who appeared to be dressed in a post office uniform.

I haven't the heart to tell him that his wife is more interested in sex than sponges or that her games of bridge are far more exerting than he realizes.

To my relief, the rest of the interview flows seamlessly and it is all over within an hour. So buoyed am I that my cover has remained intact that I enthusiastically agree to join Gillian later that evening for a stroll through Covent Garden to catch the last of the summer light.

'See, I told you it would be fine. Honestly, Kitty, you worry far too much.'

She is right, the interview was painless. Still, I think I managed to convince him that I am indeed a young Englishwoman named Kitty and he seemed happy enough as I sent him on his way with a bag full of baked treats for his 'domestically challenged' wife. Instead of a bloodhound, I was sent an old Labrador. I was safe, it seemed, for now.

'Oh, look, there you are! Ah, how marvellous.'

Gillian has stopped by the news-stand outside the Tube station, the front-page headline of the evening edition of the paper declaring in bold font: LITTLE SHOP OF WONDERS CASTS A SPELL ON LONDON'S HOUSEWIVES.

'It's you, darling,' says Gillian, pointing to the (thankfully) rather blurred image of me standing outside the shop, my hands folded in front of me. 'Fame at last, eh?'

'It's all rather embarrassing really,' I say, as Gillian slips a halfpenny into the paper seller's tin. 'I can't imagine what poor Father would say if he . . .'

As I speak, a strange darkness settles on the stall, like the prelude to a thunderstorm.

'Oh, 'eck, here we go,' says the stallholder, glancing at the sky. 'Let's hope this don't mean trouble.'

Following his gaze, I look up and see a shape hovering in the sky above Leicester Square. Like the hot air balloon of my childhood, there is something otherworldly about the Zeppelin, something ghostlike and foreboding. Gillian and the stallholder stand, open-mouthed, mesmerized by the sight but I do not like it one bit. Watching it hovering there suspended in the air, I am reminded of the Hanged Man in the Tarot, stuck in an eternal limbo, unable to escape.

Clutching the newspaper to my chest, my blurred image folded into the drapes of my coat, I give Gillian a nudge, snapping her out of the reverie.

'Come now,' I say, taking a final glance at the strange orb suspended above us. 'Time to go home.'

17

MIRIAM

Dänholm Prisoner-of-War Camp

October 1918

I wake the next morning to violent hammering on the door. Leaping from the bed, my legs trembling in fear, I see the candlewick bedspread neatly folded on the chair and memories of the previous evening trickle down my consciousness.

I had sung him to sleep. He had wept. Now he has gone.

The door pounds again and I stand halfway between it and the bed, not daring to move, my brain fizzing with questions. What if someone saw him leave? What if it is the commandant himself come to reprimand me?

'Miriam? Are you in there?'

Relief floods through my body at the sound of Frida's voice. Slipping my robe over my shoulders, I open the door.

'Oh, thank goodness you're awake,' says Frida, bustling into the room, her face flushed, the smell of camphor emanating from her hair, her skin, her clothes. 'We need you at the sanatorium, urgently.'

'What is it? What has happened?' I say, glancing at the clock. It is not yet five o'clock.

'A group of prisoners received a beating overnight,' says Frida, taking my uniform from the wardrobe and handing it to me. 'Some of them in a very bad way, bleeding all over their bunks, making a mighty racket too, so the guards brought them in to us. Now, get ready and I'll explain more on the way.'

The sun is just rising as we reach the sanatorium. While Frida strides ahead of me, I cast a glance across the camp. In the distance, I see the silhouettes of the guards in the watchtowers, see the smoke rising from the kitchen chimneys, and a queue of men lining up to be taken to the mines where they will work until sunset. An ordinary morning in the camp and yet I feel something is not right, something has shifted.

'Miriam, hurry along.'

Frida beckons me into the sanatorium where Julia is flitting about the room, clutching bowls of water clouded red with the blood of the young men who wince and recoil in agony on their makeshift beds.

'If you could start over there,' says Frida, gesturing to a line of occupied beds on the far side of the room. 'There's iodine and dressings on the trolley, though be sparing with the latter, dear. We have very little left.'

'Yes, Matron,' I say wearily, as I wash my hands and place my apron around my waist.

I hurry over to the first bed where a young man is lying on his back, his face swollen and bruised. A livid red cut runs from the edge of his eye socket right down to his jaw. I am deliberating whether the wound will need stitching when the young man opens his eyes and leaps unsteadily to his feet.

'Get away from me, you German bitch,' he screams, holding out a hand defensively. 'Look, lads, it's her. The snitch.'

He glares at me, then spits on the floor, the pinkish fluid coming to rest by my feet. It is then I realize who he is. Harris, the young man who organized the raid on the kitchen.

'Mr Harris,' I say, taking his arm to guide him back onto the bed. 'Calm yourself now. I am here to dress your wounds, that is all.'

'Dress the wounds that you were responsible for,' cries a young man from the next bed along. 'You and that old duffer. Telling us you're neutral, that you're only here for academic purposes. Load of rot. You're as neutral as the Kaiser.'

He glares at me with contempt. I avert my gaze and try to focus on stitching up Harris's wounds but I think of Garn's expression yesterday when he overheard the men plotting. It was one of utter disapproval, almost disgust. Would he go so far as to report them?

'Snitch!' whispers Harris as I get up from the bed, his bloodshot eyes boring into me.

'Snitch!'

The other men take up the cry, thudding their hands against the wall in a sinister beat.

Harris jumps from the bed, grabs a metal bowl from the floor and starts pounding it with his fists.

'Snitch.'

'Snitch.'

'What on earth is going on here?' Frida booms as she appears beside me. 'Young man, you will get back onto that bed at once. As for the rest of you, cease this non-sense this minute. Nurse Ziegler is here to attend to your wounds, and you will let her go about her work. Do you understand?'

The men fall silent while Harris, suitably chastened, clambers back onto the bed.

'Deep breath now,' whispers Frida, taking my arm which is trembling uncontrollably. 'Pay no heed to them. They should be grateful we have agreed to look after them and that all they sustained were a few cuts and bruises and not a firing squad. The guards were lenient this time, but they won't be the next. This lot will think twice before they try to steal food from our kitchens again.'

She clicks her tongue, then releases my arm. As she walks away, a sick feeling settles in my stomach as I recall the conversation Harris and the others had in the recording studio the day before. They think I informed the guards.

'Mr Harris,' I say, pouring a cup of water and bringing it over to his bed. 'I swear to you, it wasn't me. I would never do such a thing. I know how hungry you men are, you're skin and bone.'

'You and that four-eyed professor were the only people in the room that weren't a prisoner,' he says, his voice dripping with hatred as he snatches the cup from my hands. 'And the guards knew every detail of our plan, right down to the exit route. Now, either you snitched, or the old man did. Either way, it don't matter. You can flounce around with your fancy recording equipment and your flowery poetry and shit but at the end of the day, you're nothing but Kraut scum. Now do your job, then leave me alone.'

When the shift has ended and I arrive for my duties at

151

the recording studio, I am so physically shaken I sit with my head in my hands for fear that I will faint. I feel sickened that those young men, who just yesterday were laughing and joking with me, think that I was responsible for their ferocious beating.

'Fräulein Ziegler, what is the matter?'

I look up and see Herr Garn standing in the doorway, clutching the Bible to his chest.

I wipe the tears from my eyes and try to gather myself, ashamed that the professor I have spent these last few months trying to impress with my linguistic abilities is seeing me in this state.

'It is nothing, Herr Professor,' I say, going to the platform and busying myself with the phonograph. 'Some of the young men who we recorded yesterday were badly beaten by the guards for stealing food. It upset me, that is all.'

'Why would that upset you?' he says, narrowing his eyes.

'Well, they are our subjects first of all,' I say, my voice trembling. 'Who volunteered their time so graciously for our project and—'

'Subjects?' says Herr Garn, placing the Bible down on the table with a thud. 'These men are not subjects, they are prisoners. British prisoners. The enemy of our people. And I'll remind you, Fräulein Ziegler, it is not "our" project, it is mine and mine alone. An academically rigorous project that requires strict impartiality. These men are to me as an amoeba under a microscope is to a biologist – they are objects to be studied. Your tears disturb me greatly for I fear you are letting emotions cloud your judgement.'

'Herr Garn, these men are starving,' I cry. 'They are skin

and bone, you can see that for yourself. Is it any wonder that they stole some food?'

'Ah, so they are thieves,' he says, with a smirk. 'They were caught, and they were rightly punished. That is the end of the matter, Fräulein Ziegler. Now pull yourself together or else I will have to surmise that you are not mentally equipped to continue in your role as assistant and therefore release you from your duties. Do I make myself clear?'

'Yes, Herr Professor,' I say.

'Good, now set up the phonograph at once. We have work to do.'

Later, as I lie in bed, watching the hands of the clock creep towards midnight, I run over Herr Garn's words in my head: '*These men are to me as an amoeba under a microscope is to a biologist.*' It was a side of the professor I had never seen before, an iciness he had so far kept hidden.

When the knock arrives a few moments later, I am half-expecting it, though what I don't anticipate is how relieved I feel at the sight of him standing on the doorstep, his pale, sad eyes gleaming in the moonlight. The men's accusations have left me feeling wretched, as though I am a bad person, when I came to this camp only to do good, to help and heal.

X steps into the hut, then turns to face me, and as he does something odd happens. It is as though the rational side of me has removed itself from my being, leaving only sensation and an animal urge so strong I feel I will die unless I follow it.

'I want you,' I say, pulling him to me and pressing my face into the warmth of his neck. 'I want you so badly.'

I feel his body go rigid. Instead of yielding to me, he

is resisting. I extricate myself and immediately regret my actions. I have terrified him. The poor man comes here only to warm himself by the fire and avail of a hot cup of tea and I have thrown myself at him like a drowning woman at a life raft.

'I am sorry,' I say, composing myself. 'I don't know what came over me, I . . .'

He comes towards me, his eyes full of longing, and my words dissolve into the warmth of his lips. Herr Garn's voice inside my head screams at me to stop, that this man is a prisoner, an enemy of our people, but his soft hands pressing against my skin are a comfort in a cold and cruel world. As his tongue touches mine, the voices clamouring to be heard – Garn and Frida, the prisoners and the guards – fall silent. Then something astonishing happens. He presses his mouth to my ear and whispers in a soft English-sounding voice:

'I want you too.'

18

KITTY

Kitty Kat's Bakery

Winter 1915

The woman who walks into the bakery a few moments before closing time looks as though she hasn't had a proper meal in weeks. If despair could manifest itself in human form, then this waif with her sunken cheeks, grey pallor and threadbare clothes would be it. I watch as she takes out a purse from her handbag and counts the coins inside, her face clouded with anxiety and hunger.

'How much are they?' she says, pointing to the two iced fruit buns sitting under the bell jar on the counter, the only two items left.

Her face seems to shrivel as she awaits my reply, like a pugilist preparing to receive a fresh blow.

'Free of charge,' I say, removing the buns with a set of silver tongs.

'I don't need charity,' says the woman, her mouth tightening indignantly. 'I got money here.'

'It's not charity,' I say, placing the buns into a cardboard box. 'They're a little stale from being out on the counter all day. You'd be doing me a favour taking them. Otherwise I'd have to throw them out.'

'Well, if that's the case, thank you,' she says, flashing the merest hint of a smile as she closes her purse and puts it back into her handbag.

'You're welcome,' I say, snipping a length of pink ribbon from the roll. 'Nothing better than an iced bun with a cup of tea, eh? Make sure you eat them today, though, as they'll be hard as rocks by tomorrow.'

'I'll do that,' she says, her bottom lip quivering. 'Though it'll be my girl that eats them. She's like her pa, got a right sweet tooth on her.'

With that the heavens open outside. I look up from wrapping the box as the rain beats down on the window and see a young man huddled in a trench, torrential rain beating down on him. He is repeating a name, over and over: '*Connie. Connie.*'

I know, deep within me, that it is a message for this young woman.

'There we are,' I say, handing her the finished box. 'I do hope you enjoy them.'

'Connie certainly will, that's for sure,' she says, her eyes lightening. 'She loves sweet things, likes to bake them too, or at least she did in the days when we could afford the ingredients. Stuff's become so expensive these days.'

'Connie is your daughter?' I say, my heart palpitating as it always does when messages start coming through.

The woman nods her head and smiles.

'And Connie's father?' I say. 'The man with the sweet tooth. Is he away fighting?'

'He is,' she says, her smile fading. 'But we've had no

word from him in months. I can't sleep with worry. I wrote to him half a dozen times telling him that he has to help us sort out the Separation Allowance. The woman from the Families Association told me I had to get him to write to them to have it released. Can you believe it? As if he hasn't enough to do dodging bullets and mustard gas. And you see we've had no money, not a penny since last month. I've had to sell my furniture and some of his tools just to get through. If I get a telegram telling me he's been killed I don't know what I'll do. It's the thought of him coming back to us that's keeping me going.'

The words tumble from her in a torrent, as though she has been storing them inside her for so long, they are forced to break out, like water through a dam. I feel such pity for her that I am compelled to do something I swore to myself I would never do again.

'My dear, I might be able to help you,' I say, gesturing to the side door that leads to the back room. 'Would you like to step this way?'

The reading confirms what the woman spoke of earlier. As I lay out the cards in a Celtic cross on the table in front of me, the woman shakes her head and sighs.

'That doesn't look too promising,' she says, pointing to the card nearest to her. 'Folk in rags. I'm not going to end up homeless, am I?'

I look down at the card. It is the Five of Pentacles. The card of lack and want, of abandonment, of being cast out into the cold, rejected by society, an alarming card in any reading, and yet seeing it in this position I have hope.

'This part of the cross highlights where you have come from,' I say, taking the card and rubbing it between my finger and thumb, drawing out its energy. 'The decisions you have made in the past, the external circumstances that shaped your destiny. You have experienced much hardship in your life, haven't you?'

The woman nods her head.

'I was born in the workhouse in Bow,' she says, her voice trembling. 'Mother died of polio in there when I was three and I stayed there until the age of twelve when I got placed in the home of a doctor and his family, working in the kitchens. It was there I learned to bake. The cook was a wonderful woman. Big old country girl from Somerset. She taught me how to bake pretty much everything, pies, suet puddings, sponges, fruit loaves, the softest bread rolls.'

Her eyes light up as she talks, the pain and anxiety seem to lift, and for a moment she looks like a young girl again, fresh and hopeful, unencumbered by the stresses and strains of life.

'But then, when I was sixteen, the doctor died, and his wife went off to live with her sister in the countryside,' she says, her smile fading. 'I had nowhere to go, no job. Ended up getting a bit of work at Billingsgate Market but it wasn't enough to secure lodgings and I ended up . . . well, I'm ashamed to say I ended up sleeping in doorways. Would still be there now if it wasn't for Phillip. He came to the stall on an errand for his uncle: "A pound of your best haddock, if you please." That was the first thing he said to me. Romantic, eh?'

'Phillip's your husband?'

'That's right,' she says wistfully. 'Love of my life, he is. Took me for a fish supper of all things later that day and we've been inseparable ever since. The day we got married and moved into our little rented terraced house was one of the happiest of my life. I was pregnant with Connie too, though I didn't tell you that.'

'Your secret's safe with me,' I say, smiling. 'It sounds like you were very happy.'

'We were,' she says, her eyes filling with tears. 'Before this bloody war started. Do excuse my language. Get home in one piece, that's what I said to him when he left for the Front. Never mind heroics, I just want you back in our lovely little home. All three of us.'

'You'll be together again,' I tell her, as she takes out a greying handkerchief to wipe her eyes. 'I felt it when we spoke earlier, and I can see it here in the reading. You see, the Five of Pentacles, as I told you, is in your past. Though I know you are feeling hardship now, I promise you it will pass. It is these cards that show us the way forward, that point to joy and celebration up ahead.'

I pick up the two future cards and show them to the woman.

'First, in the near future, we have the Three of Cups. I see friendship and collaboration for you with like-minded people. There'll be much to celebrate and the loneliness and scarcity you've been feeling will slowly fade away.'

'Oh, do you think so?' she says, her voice full of hope.

'It is what the cards indicate,' I reply.

'What about this one?' she asks, pointing to the second future card, the Ten of Cups, which shows a family standing joyously, hand in hand, in front of a dazzling rainbow and a warm and welcoming home. 'What does this mean?'

'This is your outcome,' I tell her, closing my eyes and wrapping my hands around the card. Heat sears through my palms and I hear a man's voice reciting a nursery rhyme: '*Jack be nimble, Jack be quick, Jack jump over the candlestick.*'

I open my eyes and see that the woman has clasped her hand to her mouth.

'How did you know?' she says, shaking her head incredulously.

'Know what?'

'That nursery rhyme. It was Connie's favourite when she was a tiny girl. Phillip used to sing it to her at bedtime.'

I hadn't noticed I had spoken the words aloud, but I am suddenly gripped with an icy cold feeling throughout my body. If I have just channelled Phillip then he must be . . . No, I say to myself as the woman waits for me to continue, I cannot tell her this. After all, I cannot be sure that he has passed over. Perhaps it was his higher self that I was channelling. And besides, here is the Ten of Cups, the card of happy ever after, of families reuniting. No, I am mistaken, Phillip is safe and well and will return home soon.

As I recount the meaning of the card to the woman, I am distracted by a shuffling noise. Turning, I see that the long velvet curtain that separates the bakery from this room is moving. Not wishing to alarm the woman, I get up from the seat and go to investigate, hoping that I have not raised any unwanted spirits. I saw this happen once at a seance organized by the Divine Order. The reader had fallen into a trance and unleashed an entity that appeared to take form and set about wreaking havoc, throwing furniture round the room and smashing the windows. It was the most disturbing thing I have ever experienced.

But as I draw closer to the curtain, I see that my fears are unfounded. A pair of scuffed brown lace-up shoes peep out from beneath the velvet drape and a child's hand grips the edge. Drawing it back, I see a young girl aged about twelve. She is painfully thin with long black ringletted hair and deep-set green eyes that are strangely familiar.

'Connie,' cries the woman, pushing her chair back and rushing over to the curtain. 'I told you to wait outside with my shopping basket. What are you playing at, snooping like this?'

'I didn't know you were born in a workhouse, Ma,' says the girl, stepping out into the room, the light from the oil lamp illuminating her gaunt but pretty face. 'Or that you slept in doorways.'

The poor woman, looking mortified, grabs the girl's hands and escorts her out, turning to me at the door with a wide smile.

'Apologies for the interruption,' she says. 'And thank you for the reading. It's lifted my spirits no end.'

'Mine too,' I say. 'Good luck, my dear.'

'Separation Allowances,' says Gillian, as we sit sharing a pot of vegetable stew later that evening. 'Benefits given to the families of soldiers called up at a moment's notice. It's the bane of our lives at the Federation. The payments are so slow in coming, if they come at all, that most women are forced to sell their worldly goods or themselves just to keep the wolf from the door.'

'Prostitution?' I say, thinking of that poor young woman's frail body, her sad eyes. 'When their men are fighting for this country. That is a disgrace.'

'Welcome to my world,' says Gillian, raising her eyebrows and dipping a crust of pumpernickel bread into the thick sauce. 'That's one of the reasons Sylvia broke away from her mother and sister. Their focus has always been on securing the vote for women like them, the middle-class daughters of gentlemen. That's all well and good but Sylvia knew there were thousands of women like the one you met today, ordinary women struggling to survive, who need our support. Yes, the suffrage movement is important but if most of the electorate are dead or starving what use is the vote?'

'I had no idea,' I say, recalling the look of hope on the woman's face when I led her to the anteroom. 'It is a sobering discovery.'

When I wake the following morning, Gillian is standing above my bed, arms folded, a puzzled expression on her face.

'Why didn't you tell me?' she says, grabbing her coat from the hook by the door.

'Tell you what?' I say, climbing out of bed, my bare foot catching on the iron frame.

'That you were doing readings again.'

'How do you know about that?'

'Oh, look, it's really none of my business,' she says, flinging the door open. 'And I don't have time to hear what you've been up to. However, the women downstairs might.'

'Women?' I say, rubbing my injured toe which has turned an alarming purple. 'What women?'

'Go down and see for yourself,' she says, wrapping a cherry red wool scarf around her neck. 'I've never seen such a crowd. Now I must go, or I'll be late for work.'

And with that she is gone. Ten minutes later, after

hurriedly dressing, I limp into the shop and see a queue of women, at least thirty, lined up on the street outside.

'I'm afraid you're rather early,' I say, opening the door and raising my voice so the women at the end of the queue, which is snaking right up towards Shaftesbury Avenue, can hear. 'We don't open until seven and I haven't made the first batch of buns yet.'

'Oh, we're not after buns,' says the woman nearest to me, a tiny, birdlike waif with large brown eyes that seem too big for her face. 'We've heard you offer . . . extras.'

'I'm sorry, I don't know what you mean,' I say, feeling the blood rushing to my head. A policeman patrolling the street opposite pauses to regard the queue then, to my relief, seems to conclude that these are simply women in desperate need of baked goods and walks on.

'Oh, stop being so coy,' says another woman, a matronly figure with fuzzy grey hair spilling out of her bright green cloche hat. She pushes her way to the front and stands inches from me, thickset arms folded across her chest. 'Jean told us what you did for her. Said it was life-changing.'

Jean, I think to myself. So that was her name. It seems she has informed the entire neighbourhood.

'Look, love,' says the woman in the green hat. 'Just tell us straight. Are you going to give us a Tarot reading or not?'

In the end, the decision is taken out of my hands. As I stand at the door of the bakery, watching as the line grows longer, the voices of these women's loved ones begin to strike up in my head, a ceaseless cacophony of messages bursting to come through.

'I'm sorry about all this,' says a familiar voice.

I turn to see Jean, the woman from yesterday's reading.

She has made her way to the front of the queue. Connie peers from behind her.

'I only mentioned it to Hilda when she dropped by last night and now it seems she's told the whole district. I'm ever so sorry.'

'You don't need to apologize,' I say, casting a furtive glance up the street as the policeman turns left onto Shaftesbury Avenue. 'I'm just rather overwhelmed, that's all. I don't really have the time to give readings just now as I must open the bakery. I don't have any help at the moment, you see.' And it is true. With Gillian having to commit fully to the Federation these last few months, I have found myself baking into the night just to meet demand.

With that, Connie looks up at her mother, her grey eyes sparkling.

'I know what you're thinking,' says Jean, shaking her head. 'But we'll have to ask the lady.'

'Ask me what?' I say, my head buzzing with the voices within and without.

'Well, it's just as I told you yesterday, Connie loves to bake,' says Jean tentatively. 'Before the war, when Connie was tiny, I had a little job in a tea room in Covent Garden. Rock buns were my speciality and I've passed on my skills to my daughter.'

'That's very nice,' I say distractedly.

'What I'm trying to say, miss,' she continues, 'is that we – that is, Connie and I – can help in the bakery while you give the readings. Only if you wish, though. I know I'm being bold in asking you, but I am a decent person, you can trust me with providing you with exemplary service and . . .'

'Of course,' I say, noticing that her voice is shaking with nerves. 'That would be an enormous help. Do go in, both of you. You'll find aprons behind the counter and there's a batch of rolls that need putting in the oven if you'd be so kind. If it goes well then, yes, I'd be happy to offer you a job.'

It's the least I can do, just in case the voice I heard yesterday does turn out to be from the other side. Jean's face brightens instantly, and she grabs my hand and shakes it.

'Thank you, miss,' she says. 'Thank you ever so much.'

With Jean set up behind the counter and Connie primed to usher the women in, one at a time, I sit down at the table in the back room, take a deep breath and close my eyes.

'Let this be a space of safety and hope,' I whisper. 'Negative spirits take your leave. Those who wish to impart love and truth, my heart is open. Give me the strength to pass on your messages with clarity and sincerity. Blessed be.'

And with that, I gesture to Connie to let the first of the women in.

Over the course of two hours, I sit, rigid on my wooden chair, and tell these careworn and desperate women what they need to know. Some of the messages are positive, such as the one from a sprightly old man called Kenneth who recently passed and has come through to reassure his wife Hilda, she of the green cloche hat, that their son, Billy, is safe and alive and in Kenneth's words *will be back home raiding the larder before you know it*. He also tells his wife to check a forgotten post office savings account he set up when they were first married, reassuring her that *there's enough in there to see you through a good few years*. Hilda leaves with a bag of iced buns and a spring in her step.

The same cannot be said for the timid young lady who comes in just as the clock on the wall in front of me is striking ten. Her hands tremble as she sits down opposite me, and I notice a vivid yellow bruise on her right cheekbone. Her coat is thin and fraying and the skin on her bare legs is goosy and blue. She looks like she hasn't had a wash or a hot meal in ages. But there is something else about this young woman, who cannot be much older than seventeen or eighteen, that unsettles me, something haunted about her expression. It is as though the light and the life have been sucked out of her, leaving behind a husk, a hollow shell where an innocent girl had once been. '*Why did you do it, Aggie?*' The voice in my head is a young man's, very youthful with a South London burr. When I impart these words, Aggie grows rigid, then tears fill her hollow eyes and she puts her head in her hands. 'I didn't have any choice,' she cries, her voice shaking like a terrified child's. 'The landlord's been at me for the rent, and they turned the water off. That old harridan in Bracken's said she couldn't give me no more credit, so I had no food, lived off potato peelings from next door's compost. He said it would be a one-off, that no one would ever find out, that he had to make sure he got his rent, one way or another. Oh, Mick, I'm sorry. Please can you forgive me.'

Mick grows silent. I wait, hoping that this young man might find it in his recently departed heart to forgive his terrified young widow, but there is nothing. Instead, I do something that may not be right but which I feel needs to be done. 'He forgives you, Aggie,' I say, placing my hand on hers. Her skin is freezing to the touch. 'But you're to find help, do you understand?' She nods her head and I send her away with a loaf of pumpernickel bread, which Jean carefully wraps in parchment paper, and the address of the Federation. 'Ask for Gillian,' I tell her, placing the scribbled note in her hands. 'She will help you.'

After that, I return to the table and slump down into my chair, feeling as though I have lived a hundred lifetimes in the space of a couple of hours.

19

EDIE

Cornwall

Present Day

The smell that hits me when I step into the bakery sends me right back to my childhood, sitting at the kitchen table, my stomach rumbling, as Dad brought out a fresh batch of soft bread rolls from the oven. If heaven had a scent, then my parents' kitchen on Saturday afternoons in the 1970s would be it.

The floor is covered in old-fashioned lino patterned with red and yellow squares, another burst of nostalgia that reminds me of the cafés I used to frequent as a child on Bethnal Green Road. There are little rickety wooden tables and chairs dotted around with milk-bottle vases full of wildflowers, glass salt, pepper and vinegar pots, and handwritten paper menus. There is a vinyl-topped counter with glass display cabinets underneath groaning with the sweet delights of my childhood: fresh cream horns, vanilla slices, peach melbas, glazed ring doughnuts and flaky apple strudels. If I close my eyes and inhale, I could be back in Dad's cake shop *circa* 1982, home from school and dying for a sugar kick before settling down to do my homework to the sound of Gary Davies, my favourite DJ, on Radio 1.

It is for these reasons that I have thus far avoided setting foot in this bakery. Though I have lived in the village for just over a year and have heard nothing but praise, courtesy of Alexander, for the delicious confections created in K's Stores, the idea of visiting it made me feel sick to my stomach, fearful of being confronted with memories too painful to bear. For me, a bakery, with its attendant scents of sugar and spice, represents the happiest moments of my life.

Growing up, my dad's cake shop was my second home, its produce my daily fare. It was the heart of everything. When I met David, he became part of that too. Every birthday, every anniversary, every milestone, was marked and celebrated with a glorious confection lovingly created by my father. And just as I haven't been able to cook dinner and sit at the table to eat it without David, so, since his death, I have not been able to entertain the idea of buying cake. Safer to drive the short distance to the local soulless supermarket, and buy a loaf of processed sliced bread to consume standing up, not tasting, just gulping, eating for energy not emotion, than venture to a bakery and risk falling down a rabbit hole of memory. That is what I have told myself this last year.

I take a seat by the window and cast my eyes around the wood-panelled walls. They are crammed with framed pictures: sketches of Cornish seascapes, garish prints of multicoloured beach huts, moody black-and-white photos of thunderous waves, and a cluster of photos of the bakery through the years. I crane my neck to get a closer look, wondering if any of the sketches are Kitty's, though none of them appear to have her style or flair.

'Hello, love. What can I get you?'

I look up and see a petite, rather elderly, woman with bobbed grey hair standing by the table with a notepad and pen. She is wearing a candy pink-and-white striped apron with the letter '*K*' printed in bold pink across the top.

'Oh, I recognize you. You're the lady who's moved into Moonstone Cottage,' she says, her rather stern expression softening. 'I've seen you striding down to the beach a few times and wondered when you might pop in. Ned said you've been having problems with your walls.'

How quickly word spreads of one's inadequacies. I suddenly feel rather foolish.

'Yes,' I say, rolling my eyes. 'I'm the daft woman who thought it would be a good idea to pull down an entire plasterboard wall by myself.'

'Ah, you don't want to be doing that, dear,' says the woman with a sigh. 'You'll give yourself an injury. Best leaving that kind of thing to Ned. He's the expert round here. He refitted this shop when my mother bought it back in the fifties, had it shipshape and ready to go within three weeks. Did the same for me when I renovated it a few years ago. I honestly don't know how he does it. I'm Susan, by the way, though everyone round here calls me Sue.'

'Pleased to meet you, Sue,' I say, extending my hand. 'I'm Edie.'

'Short for Edith?' she says, shaking my hand briskly.

'That's right,' I say. 'Named after my mother's favourite aunt.'

'Well, Edie,' she says. 'What can I get you?'

I pick up the paper menu that is wedged between the salt and pepper pots and cast my eye across it. There's a choice of tea, coffee or hot chocolate, toasted tea cakes with butter and jam, the 'cake of the day' or something called a 'Cornish Breakfast' which sounds suspiciously like an English breakfast, though the eggs are described as 'locally laid'.

'I'll just have a pot of tea, please,' I say, slotting the menu back into place.

'Is that all?' says Sue, looking up from her notepad. 'Sure I can't tempt you with a vanilla slice? I made them fresh this morning and the pastry is so soft and flaky it melts in the mouth.'

Though I don't have much of an appetite, I'm sure Alexander, with his sweet tooth, will appreciate a treat when he gets back from London, so I order two to take away. I shall pop them in his fridge when I give Jupiter his evening meal later.

While Sue fetches my tea, the trepidation I had felt at coming to the bakery starts to fade away. Rather than bring back painful memories, the sights and scents of the bakery are making me feel as calm as I did when I was a child, sitting on my father's counter with my colouring pencils, drawing pictures on his notepad of the customers coming in and out. Almost instinctively, I take out my sketchbook and begin to draw the scene unfolding before me. As I do, I think about what Rebecca had said about the Tarot deck featuring ordinary people and an idea comes to me. I am just turning to a fresh page when Sue returns with the pot of tea and a white cardboard box.

'That'll keep your vanilla slices fresh,' she says, handing it to me. 'Oh, you're drawing. Ned said you were an artistic type.'

'That's right,' I say, placing the sketchbook on my lap

while I pour the tea. 'And I was wondering if you would like to pose for a drawing for me. I'm working on a project and wanted to sketch some of the villagers.'

'Well, I don't know why you'd want to draw an old biddy like me,' says Sue, her cheeks flushing pink. 'But anything to help an artist. When would you like to do it?'

'No time like the present,' I say, taking my sketchbook.

'What, now?' exclaims Sue, patting down her hair. 'I'm in my old work rags and haven't got my make-up on.'

'That's perfect for me,' I say, beginning to outline Sue's face with my pencil. 'I want to capture people as they are in the moment.'

'Well, if you're sure,' she says, sitting down opposite me and folding her hands on the table. 'How exciting. I've never been sketched before.'

'Tell me about the woman who founded this place,' I say, my eyes darting between Sue and the page.

'That will be Kitty,' says Sue. 'She owned this place and your cottage.'

'That can't be right,' I say, looking up. 'It was my great-grandmother, Jane, who owned Moonstone Cottage.'

'Are you sure, dear?' she says, looking back at me quizzically. 'Because as far as I know, Kitty moved into the cottage in nineteen eighteen and lived there until she died in the fifties.'

'Could Kitty have been a tenant?' I say. 'She might have rented the cottage from Jane.'

'No, she definitely owned the cottage,' says Sue, waving her hand at someone walking past the window behind me. 'As well as this place. My mother used to pop in and see her there. Now the name Jane does ring a bell, but I'm afraid my knowledge is sketchy as it was long before my time. I do remember the various tenants that have lived there over the years, though I must say, the less said about them the better.'

I think of David Hart, my husband's namesake, and feel an urge to ask Sue about him but something makes me stop. Though I know it is preposterous that my sensible husband could have been living a double life down here while dabbling in the occult, there is still a niggling doubt in the pit of my stomach. After that fateful October night, I don't take anything for granted. I thought my life was perfect before that night, thought that nothing could shake its foundations. And yet, despite my doubts, I am not ready for what would happen to me if they were confirmed. I am just about coping as it is.

'Going back to Kitty,' I say. 'What was she like?'

'Like I said, I didn't know her, but my mother did,' says Sue. 'Kitty took her on as a Saturday girl here just after the Second World War. She trained her in all kinds of baking, then left her this place in her will when she died.'

She gets up and goes behind the counter, taking a photo from the wall.

'Here she is,' she says, returning to her seat and placing the photo on the table between us. 'Pictured with my mother in nineteen forty-seven.'

I look at it in astonishment.

'This is Kitty?'

'Yes. That's her,' says Sue. 'Interesting style, wouldn't you say?'

'Absolutely. Particularly for nineteen forty-seven.'

In the photo, Kitty stands arm in arm with Sue's mum, a

short, rather plump young girl with dark curled hair pinned to the side and a gappy-toothed grin. Next to her, Kitty looks like a time-traveller from 1990s Hoxton. In fact, she looks exactly like I did back then. Her blonde hair is cut in a choppy fringed bob around which she has tied a patterned scarf. Her wrists are bedecked with beaded bracelets that wouldn't look out of place at Glastonbury. She is wearing a pair of men's overalls unbuttoned to her chest bone and a pair of chunky hobnail boots. If I had met her at art school, we would have been best friends.

'Wow,' I exclaim, handing the photo back to Sue. 'I had no idea Kitty was so . . . ahead of her time.'

'My mum had another word for it,' she replies, with a smirk. 'Oddball. That was it. Kitty was a lovable oddball.'

At those words, I am filled with an overwhelming urge to defend Kitty. I never knew the woman and yet I feel a deep sense of kinship with her.

'Though if it weren't for Kitty, I wouldn't have this business,' says Sue, wiping the glass of the picture with the back of her sleeve. 'And for that I am eternally grateful, oddball or not.'

Just then the door opens, and a group of tourists, laden with rucksacks, maps and several small children, enters.

'Oh, here comes the lunch rush. I'd better jump back behind the counter,' says Sue, getting up from her seat. 'Pop back any time, dear, to finish your drawing.'

I look down at the sketchbook, see the heart-shaped face framed by silvery hair, one hand clutching a photo of yesteryear, the other a cup of steaming tea, and I feel content that, with a few more tweaks, it will be perfect for what I have in mind.

'Thanks, Sue,' I say, grabbing my coat from the back of the chair. 'But I think I've got what I need.'

After feeding Jupiter and leaving the vanilla slices in the fridge for Alexander, I make my way down the coastal path. A memory stirred in me when I was sketching Sue of the time we brought Dora down here for a little holiday when she was six months old. That summer was a scorcher and, eager to escape the heat of London and our tiny, top-floor flat, we had bundled all our baby paraphernalia into the car and driven down to Cornwall where we booked into a B & B in St Ives. The town had been bustling with tourists that week, so we were happy to escape to the tranquillity of Lytton Cove for the day. We parked up in Holton and walked to the beach. David was in a great mood that day. He had just completed his PhD and looked as though the weight of the world had been lifted from his shoulders. I can see him now, as I crest the coastal pathway, marching along ahead of me with Dora strapped to his chest, hear his soft, reassuring voice describing every sight and sound to his beloved child.

'Look at those pretty shells, Dora, see how they sparkle in the sun. Now, let's see who can spot the sea first. A few more steps and it will be there. Ready? There it is! Isn't it beautiful, baby girl?'

But now there is just silence and a vast stretch of empty beach ahead of me. The temptation to cry out, 'I can see the sea, David! I can see it too,' as I did whenever we reached this point is overwhelming but there is no one to hear me.

Come on, Edie, I tell myself, as my feet sink into the soft sand. Don't go there. Stay focused on your work.

Setting up my camping chair at a spot where the light is good, I close my inner box of memories and turn my attention to today's Tarot card, the Ten of Cups, running over Rebecca's notes in my head.

This is the card of utter joy, of wish fulfilment, happy ever after and a life well lived. It is the attainment of a perfect life, a contented heart, love, warmth, and a happy home. It is the card of family, of being with the ones we love the most.

As I start to make my initial sketch, a pencil drawing of a baby girl in a frilly swimsuit building sandcastles on the beach, a shadow appears on the page. It feels as though someone is standing behind me looking over my shoulder at the drawing. I sense a warm breath on my neck which causes me to turn sharply but there is nothing there.

It was just the sun dipping in the sky, I tell myself, remembering how this Cornish coastal light casts strange shapes and shadows at certain times of the day. Returning to my sketch, I begin to create the outlines of the baby's mother and father, who are kneeling beside her as though in worship.

I can hear David's voice in my head as my pencil darts across the page, as clear as it was all those years ago.

'If I could freeze this moment, Edie,' he had said, as Dora took her nap on the blanket, exhausted from sand-castle building, and we sat beside her drinking coffee from a flask, 'and keep us all together, just as we are right now, I would. This is everything I have ever wished for. This is my world, just the three of us.'

I look up from the sketchbook as the sea and sky merge into a milky blue haze and wonder where David is now. Is he at peace? I don't know the answer. All I know is that

I have never felt as lonely as I do right now. And then it comes again, that niggling doubt. The name of the strange tenant, the man who dabbled with the Devil. It couldn't be David, could it?

Putting down my sketchbook, I take my phone from my bag. I need to call Dora, need to hear her voice. After all, as the third piece of our little family trinity, she is the only person who can remember those moments, the only one who understands, the only one who could put these ridiculous doubts to rest.

I am about to call her when my phone buzzes. It is a text from Alexander.

> Hi Edie. Thanks for feeding Jupiter. Make sure he doesn't trick you into giving him double portions. He can be very convincing when he flashes those big blue eyes of his. Listen, I'm still in London but I've been chatting to a mate of mine, Tony George, a fellow vintage record aficionado, and he reckons he might be able to digitalize that wax cylinder of yours. Said he'd do it gratis as a favour to me. He's based in Stepney Green and has a free afternoon tomorrow. I know it's short notice, but do you fancy a day trip up here? If so, lunch is on me. A x

Of course I should go. Alexander has gone out of his way to help me solve the riddle of the wax cylinder. It would be rude to turn him down. But as I type out my acceptance, I feel a deep sense of unease. Stepney Green. Just a stone's throw from our old flat. An area I have spent the last twelve months avoiding. Of all the places in London, why did Tony George have to be there?

20

KITTY

Seven Dials

September 1916

As the brutal winter of 1915 gave way to the spring of 1916, the war showed no sign of abating, indeed if the horrific reports coming through from the Somme were to be believed, it appeared it was growing even bloodier and more deadly. And as the fatalities increased so did the demand for readings. I soon found myself holed up most days in the back room while Jean and Connie, who thanks to the thriving success of the bakery I was able to employ on a full-time basis, served and baked out front. Jean proved herself to be a diligent and loyal worker, and Connie every inch the willing apprentice, carrying her notebook with her at all times while I talked her through the rudiments of bread proving, pastry making, the artistry of icing a cake and, her favourite one, the traditional sugar loaf. 'They look like church candles,' she remarked when we had finished our first batch, the simple blending of water and sugar moulded into festive conical shapes appearing to be an act of sorcery. 'But that is what baking is really,' I told her as we cleaned the kitchen afterwards. 'A form of alchemy that turns simple ingredients into something truly magical.'

Gillian, despite her initial bemusement that I had returned to my clairvoyance, came to see the impact my readings had on the clients, the hope it gave them, and soon we found that there was a steady stream of women making their way to the Federation straight from a reading, seeking out help that they hadn't known was available.

'Have you got a moment, Kat? We've something we want to run by you?'

I look up from the reading table. Gillian is standing in the doorway. Beside her, dressed in a stiff brown corduroy skirt and oversized wool coat, is Sylvia.

'Good afternoon, Kat ... er, Kitty,' says Sylvia, a smile appearing briefly then fading from her moonish face. 'How are you?'

Immediately, the energy in the room shifts. It feels airless, suffocating, even though there is a crisp draught blowing in from the shop. I glance at my sage brush, feel an overwhelming urge to light it and cast it round the room to clear the toxicity of Sylvia's presence. But I resist, aware that, even for me, that would be the height of bad manners.

'I am well, thank you, Ms Pankhurst,' I say brusquely.

'Please,' she says, smiling warmly despite my frostiness. 'Do call me Sylvia. I can't bear formalities.'

'As you wish,' I say, blowing out the candle and wrapping a silk scarf around my cards. 'What is it you wanted to run by me? I'm in rather a rush, you see.'

'Oh, Kitty,' sighs Gillian, casting an apologetic shrug towards Sylvia. 'Don't talk nonsense, you've quite clearly finished for the day.'

'I must say I'm intrigued,' says Sylvia, coming over to the table where the ancestors of Nora, the young mother whose cards I've just read, still linger amid the candle smoke. 'The young woman we saw leaving just now as we came in, what was her story?'

'Well, she hadn't eaten for a week,' I say, deciding this is the perfect moment to light my sage brush and clear the energy from the room. Sylvia coughs, then smiles, oblivious as I wave the brush around her. 'Said she'd resorted to raiding the neighbours' bins after dark. It's a disgrace, it really is. How can this happen to people in a so-called civilized society? She said her husband was a builder who earned a good wage before the war but when the call-up came he thought he was doing the right thing, serving his country. And yet the country has let his wife starve. Just like poor Jean, and countless others. Anyway, I sent her away with a bag of broken biscuits and a heartening message from her late grandmother. I thought it the least I could do.'

'This is what we wanted to talk to you about, Kitty,' says Gillian. 'Much as we'd like to keep giving away food it's not sustainable and we'd be no help to those women if we went under. I was talking to Sylvia about it, and she's come up with an excellent plan.'

'Of course she has,' I mutter, placing the cards back into my wooden box.

'I know you're frightfully busy,' says Sylvia, either oblivious to, or choosing to ignore, my rudeness. 'But I think between us – and I will give you credit, darling Gill, because it was you who drew my attention to these women who've been coming back and forth between here and the Federation – yes, between us we have an offer to make you.'

'And I think you're going to like it,' adds Gillian excitedly. 'Hear us out, Kitty. It won't take a minute.'

'All right,' I snap, irritated at Sylvia's familiarity with 'darling Gill' and bone-tired from a day channelling the other side. 'I'm all ears. But first I need to lock up, otherwise we'll have late-night shoppers thinking we're open for business.'

'We'll come with you,' says Gillian, following me into the shop, Sylvia trailing behind dourly. They stand side by side, watching as I pull down the metal shutters with a long hooked rod.

'Go on then,' I say, turning the door sign to *Closed*. 'Tell me about this plan.'

'Well,' says Gillian, glancing at the older woman like a child asking its mother for permission to speak. 'Last year, Sylvia introduced a cost-price restaurant in the Women's Hall at the Federation's headquarters in Old Ford Road, to provide meals for the poor families of the district.'

'Like you,' interjects Sylvia, 'we were hearing horror stories every day from women who couldn't afford to feed themselves or their children. A lot of these women were working in the factories, taking on the jobs of the men who have left to fight, but they get paid such low wages they can barely survive. The restaurant allows them to get at least one decent meal a day for a price they can afford or in some cases for free. The women purchase tickets for the meal, priced at tuppence for adults and a penny for children, at the door or, if they wish, they can buy a book of tickets in advance. Those without any means whatsoever are given a free ticket but, once inside the restaurant, none of the diners is aware of who has paid and who is eating for free. That way there is no stigma.'

'Now, what is stopping us doing the same here?' adds Gillian.

'Tarot cards and fortune telling may nourish the women spiritually,' says Sylvia, a hint of disdain in her voice. 'But they need long-term sustenance. And though it is very kind of you to throw in free bags of broken biscuits and stale rolls, I do rather blanch, and I expect much of the women do too, at such overt charity. It makes the women feel lesser, as though they are idle beggars on the street, not decent working women who have been treated abominably by this sorry excuse for a government in the pursuit of this wretched and frankly illegal war.'

She pauses, her pale face flushed pink from the exertion of her speech. Both Gillian and I stand regarding her, open-mouthed. In a matter of moments, the dour, do-gooding, brown lace-up shod Sylvia has metamorphosed into the Sylvia Pankhurst of the newspapers, the scourge of Downing Street, the woman who instils fear and loathing in the upper echelons of polite society and something close to hero worship amongst working-class women of the East End. Much as it pains me, I have to admit that seeing such a tour de force up close is quite something.

'Anyway,' says Sylvia, regaining her composure. 'What do you think, Kitty? Would you be happy to incorporate a much-needed social scheme like this into the bakery?'

Six months ago, my answer would have been a stern no and not just because it was Sylvia asking the question. From an early age, thanks to my father, I had been drilled in the ways of commerce and capitalism, the importance of profit and, if truth be told, the horrors of socialism.

But after what I have witnessed these last few months, the emaciated women with eyes dead from hunger and despair, the desperate choices they have had to make just to survive, I see the world and its mechanisms very differently.

'I would like to,' I say. 'But this is a bakery not a restaurant. I'm not sure we have the space or the facilities for such an undertaking.'

'We could convert the back room,' says Gillian, her green eyes animated.

'But that's my reading room,' I say, feeling rather cornered suddenly. 'I know you may disapprove of such things, Sylvia, but my Tarot card readings are a big part of the bakery's popularity. They're a lifeline for many of the women who shop here.'

'Can you not conduct your readings upstairs?' says Sylvia, turning to Gillian for approval. 'If I recall, there is a decent-sized sitting room up there and, I suppose, it offers your clients a little more privacy.'

'What a wonderful idea, Sylvia,' says Gillian, clasping her hands together. 'And really, Kitty, that back room is far too large for little old you and that tiny table. You're like a pea on a drum in there.'

They both look at me expectantly and it feels as though the decision has been made without my say-so.

'Well?' says Gillian, leaning towards me and taking my hand. 'What do you say?'

'I suppose my answer has to be yes,' I say grudgingly. 'After all, if we don't help these women, who will?'

'Oh, Kitty, thank you,' cries Gillian, throwing her arms around me. 'I knew I'd make a radical of you one day.'

'Splendid news,' says Sylvia, looking a little taken aback

183

at Gillian's blatant display of affection. 'I shall be in touch to talk over the logistics. Now I must run. I have a meeting at Millbank at seven.'

'Thank you, darling,' says Gillian, turning to Sylvia, her hand still clasping mine. 'Good luck with the meeting and I shall see you at Old Ford first thing.'

'You shall indeed,' says Sylvia briskly. 'Cheerio, the two of you.'

'Cheerio,' cries Gillian, as we stand on the step watching Sylvia depart. 'Sock it to the old duffers in Millbank, won't you?'

Sylvia raises her umbrella in the air to acknowledge the comment and Gillian shakes her head in awe. As she turns back to me, I try to read in her face whether her feelings for the sainted Sylvia go beyond mere admiration. After I had rejected her so coldly, who could blame her if she had sought solace in the arms of such a bold and brilliant woman as Sylvia?

'Thank you, Kitty,' she says, as we head back inside. 'Your joining the cause means everything to me.'

'I'm glad I could be of help,' I say, gazing out of the window. The sun is dipping in the sky, casting a reddish glow on the cobbled street. 'Those women and children would be lost without you and Sylvia and the work you've been doing. I'm just sorry I didn't see that sooner.'

Gillian looks at me, her eyes so warm and full of affection, and I am transported back to Hampstead Heath that summer day all those years ago. Hidden from prying eyes beneath the boughs of a weeping willow, the two of us lost in each other, our bodies entwined as closely as our hearts. Without thinking, I pull her towards me and for the first time in almost two years, I kiss her. Though, at my insistence, we have spent these last few months living platonically, there is nothing awkward about this embrace. In fact, it feels like the most natural thing to do. And as I sink into her familiar scent and the softness of her skin, the street, the bakery, Sylvia, the misery of war, the downtrodden women, all my worries and fears, begin to fall away

And yet, even as we kiss, a voice in my head tells me that nothing good will come of this. I cannot allow myself to risk being with Gillian in that way again. It is too dangerous. For now, 'friends' is all we can be. I pull away swiftly, then glimpse someone out of the corner of my eye. I turn and see an elderly man in frock coat and top hat looking over at the shop from across the street. His face, shadowed somewhat by the hat, is strangely familiar though I can't quite place it. I turn back to Gillian – her face is full of an old sorrow.

'I'd better get changed,' she says, composing herself. 'I have a meeting at the Federation this evening.'

As I watch her head upstairs, guilt gnaws inside me. I have rejected her again, but it is for our own good. There is no other way.

Just then the evening newspaper comes clattering through the door. I stoop to pick it up but as I do I see something that sends the room spinning around me.

ZEPPELIN RAID ON STREATHAM! screams the headline. MULTIPLE CIVILIANS, INCLUDING CHILDREN, FEARED DEAD. REPRISALS EXPECTED.

I read the third line again. Reprisals expected. Reprisals I had witnessed for myself just months earlier. As I stand clutching the newspaper, I can almost hear the men's voices screaming vengeance, hear the windows of a hundred German businesses smashing, the clatter of hooves on cobbles as the mob work out which 'dirty Kraut' to target next. Folding the paper and putting it on the counter, I place my hands on the wooden surface and try to steady my thoughts. You are safe here, I tell myself, you are an Englishwoman who bakes delicious cakes and buns and helps the poor people of the area. There is not a trace of German about the place. Katerina has gone. These people only know Kitty. There is nothing to worry about, nothing at all.

But as I extinguish the oil lamps and make my way upstairs, a sick feeling of dread lodges itself in my stomach. You are safe, Katerina, but for how long?

21

MIRIAM

Dänholm Prisoner-of-War Camp

October 1918

'So you do have a voice after all?' I say, astonished.

X smiles as he strokes my face. We are sitting by the fire, cradling mugs of warm broth. The fire blazes in the grate and I stretch out my stockinged feet to warm them in its glow.

'It's a nice voice,' I say, looking across at him. His eyes are fixed on me. 'A gentle one.'

He smiles and my mind tumbles back to the kiss we shared, the scent of him – musky with a hint of sugar – lingering on my lips. I do not know what was more shocking, hearing his voice or experiencing the intensity of his passion.

'It is an ordinary voice,' he replies, pausing to take a sip of broth. 'To suit an ordinary man.'

It is true that his voice is rather anodyne. Listening to him, I am reminded of the children of the army officers back in India, whose accents were not tied to any particular location, testament to a childhood spent travelling from country to country, nomads who never stayed long enough for any one dialect to stick.

'Ordinary is the last word I would use to describe you,' I say, feeling the heat from the fire burn into the soles of my feet. 'And as far as the men in this camp are concerned you are something of an enigma. Dangerous even. Take you and me, for example. We have just shared a kiss and yet I do not even know your name.'

'Names are irrelevant in war, don't you think?' he says, fixing me with that ice-blue stare. 'Everyone is a number out here, a statistic to place on the death tallies back home. Names humanize a person and you cannot be human while you're gouging out a man's insides with a bayonet.'

'That is true,' I say, blanching at the image. I reach across to my handbag and take out a box of cigarettes. 'But within these walls we can be human, don't you think? Though our countries are enemies we are not at war.'

I offer him a cigarette. He takes it, placing the empty mug on the floor beside him.

'All the same, I think it would be safest for both of us if we do not know each other's names,' he says, leaning towards me and cupping his hand around the cigarette as I light it. 'You are my Lady Lullaby, and I am, what is it that they call me again?'

'Prisoner X,' I say, waving the smoke from my face. 'The mystery man. The man without a voice. Though I cannot keep calling you that. It is too . . . too cold.'

He shakes his head and sighs.

'Call me Jo,' he says.

'Jo. Short for Josef?'

'No, but it was my nickname when I was a boy,' he says, his face growing sad. 'Many moons ago now.'

'Tell me, Jo,' I say, changing the subject as talk of his

boyhood has clearly touched a nerve. 'How is it that you can roam around the camp at night like this? As far as I know, it is forbidden for prisoners to come and go as they please. The hut doors are locked at night, no?'

'First, I suffer from sleeplessness,' he says, with a sigh. 'When you have been on duty for hours on end in the trenches, where falling asleep could cost you and your battalion your lives, you learn to adapt. Your body adjusts. Mine can't seem to return to how it was before. Lying in the hut, listening to my roommate, Boscombe, snoring, I find my mind assailed with dark thoughts. As for the doors, well, yes, you are right, they are locked each night. But I had noticed, when I first arrived here, that the small window above my bed had no bars on the outside. Though a normal grown man would never be able to fit through that window, I had lost so much weight in here, I gauged that I could slide myself out if I really tried. The first night I sneaked out I made it as far as the latrine block where I sat outside in the cool air and watched the stars. It was a new moon, a dark sky. I reasoned that if I followed the course of the moon then I could sneak out unseen, on the nights when the sky was black. Over time, I have noticed that new guards have been assigned to the watch-tower by my block. They are young and inexperienced with a love for poker games, which they begin at midnight each night. So engrossed are they, I can slip out unseen. I just have to remember to leave the window slightly ajar so I can get back in.'

'But if someone came to your hut, they would see you were not there?'

'Ah, I have thought of that already,' he says, with a

childish grin. 'Boscombe's bed is hard and uncomfortable, so I have bought his silence by letting him sleep in mine. The other one, I stuff with pillows. It is so dark in there, anyone coming in would see two occupied beds and would leave satisfied that we were both sound asleep, without bothering to light an oil lamp to take a closer look. What matters is that I am up and dressed and standing by my bed in time for roll call at six each morning. Which I always make sure I am. No one has noticed anything amiss so far.'

'It seems you have it all in hand,' I say, stubbing out my cigarette. 'And don't get me wrong, I am glad of your nocturnal visits.'

'I like your company,' he says. 'You remind me of . . .'

He pauses and gazes into the fire. The expression on his face is so melancholy I do not press him to finish what he was saying.

'Jo, may I ask you something?'

He looks up at me and nods.

'What had happened that night? The first night you came here? It was Reid who did that to you, wasn't it?'

He nods, then lifts his hand to take another drag of his cigarette, the cryptic words of his tattoo flashing momentarily before my eyes. *For Eternity.* I want to ask him what it means, what or who prompted him to etch them on his skin, but wary of bombarding him with questions or presenting myself as some jealous hysteric, I refrain.

'I didn't like what he did to you,' he says, fixing me with an intense stare. 'He needed to be taught that good men do not treat women like that.'

'I hope you haven't made an enemy of him on my

account,' I say, my thoughts returning to the repellent Scot. 'He is clearly not a man one would want to cross.'

'You were in danger,' says Jo, his expression hardening. 'When I saw him pinning you against the wall like that . . . what else could I do? This may be a prison camp, but have we lost all sense of ourselves that we would look the other way while a woman is violated, simply because her people are fighting ours?'

I think about the young men who broke into the kitchen, the hatred in their eyes when I walked into the sanatorium the other day and they accused me of being the snitch. How far did that hatred carry? I wonder. Would they have turned a blind eye if they had seen me being attacked? Would they have left me, the 'filthy Kraut', to my fate? The thought disturbs me, and I suddenly feel, sitting here, desperately vulnerable.

'Anyway, it seems the blow to his pride mattered more than the black eye I gave him,' says Jo, stubbing out the remains of his cigarette into the empty mug. 'Word in the camp is that he has placed a bounty on my head, commandeered the services of some half-starved thug to kill me – in exchange for a crate of beer he was gifted from the guards for informing on the men who raided the kitchens.'

'He betrayed his own men?' I cry, panic and anger gripping my bones. 'And now he wants to kill you? He is a monster! Well, there is nothing for it. You must go to the commandant, tell him what Reid is threatening. Tell him what he did to me, or almost did. He will be dealt with, punished.'

'You think the commandant will be bothered if one of his prisoners is killed?' he exclaims. 'Why, this would be sport for such a man. Punish Reid? Your commandant would be more likely to pit me and Reid against each other in a gladiatorial fight.'

'He is not *my* commandant,' I say, my voice trembling. 'I am simply here to assist Herr Garn in his project and tend to the sick. The politics of this war are not to be placed at my door.'

'I know, and I am sorry I said that,' he says, leaning towards me and taking my hand in his. 'I just want you to know that, despite what they may tell you, there are no rules in this place. It is dangerous and we must tread carefully at every turn. Look, if I told the commandant what Reid had done to you then I would have to explain why I was walking around the camp unaccompanied. God forbid, they might even accuse me of being Reid's accomplice in the attempted rape. Ever since I arrived here, they have viewed my silence as a threat. They think that I am a spy, that I am here with a grand plan. It's why they have pinned that clown Dieter to my side to shadow me, watch that I am not about to blow up the place.'

'They think you're a spy?' I say, the flesh on the back of my neck prickling. 'And are you? Is that what this is all about? Kissing me. Am I part of your plan?'

'Of course not,' he says, dropping my hand. 'I am not a spy. I swear to you on the life of my family.'

'Your family?' I say, glancing at the tattoo, the word *Eternity* temporarily obscured by the folds of his arms. 'You mean, your wife?'

With those words, I feel a knot of guilt in the pit of my stomach. I imagine a rosy-cheeked young Englishwoman, standing at the door of her pretty country cottage, a baby in her arms and small children running round her ankles. A woman full of hope, waiting for her love to return from war, and the love they both swore was for eternity. What are you doing, Miriam? I think to myself.

He turns to me, and his eyes are full of tears. It is then that it all makes sense: the sorrow at my mention of her, the tattoo, the silence. His wife is dead.

His pain is palpable – how awful to be widowed so young. No wonder he carries her photo with him always.

'By family,' he says, wiping away the tears with the heel of his hand and composing himself, 'I was referring to the people I grew up with. My kith and kin. Surely you have family too?'

I think of my father huddled at his desk in the Berlin town house that ceased to be a home with my mother's passing, and my aunt and uncle attending to their guests in the sprawling gardens of the Kerala plantation.

'I did once, yes,' I say sadly. 'Though now they are either dead or spread out across continents. I am, you could say, quite rootless.'

Leaning back in the chair, I find myself telling him about my mother's death, the intense silence that fell on our once vibrant home, and the weight of my father's grief, a leaden thing that filled every corner of the house. I tell him about my voyage to India, the seasickness, the terror of leaving my home and all that was familiar. And then I tell him the story of Kerala, the magical world of rare wildlife, spectacular forests and jungles, the colours of the sky and the lakes, the smoky scent of freshly picked tea, my first sighting of the leopard that prowled the plantation at night, his green eyes twinkling in the twilight.

'You reminded me of that leopard,' I say, looking across at him. 'Silent and beautiful, yet also dangerous, capable of . . .'

'Capable of what?'

'I don't know,' I say, my heart torn between longing and fear. 'What you said just now about the Germans thinking you're a spy. It has unsettled me. Planted a seed of mistrust that was not there before.'

'I was like you,' he says, his hand tracing the contours of the wooden chair arm. 'I moved around a lot as a child. Nowhere quite felt like home and if it did the feeling was temporary. Either the place or the people would not be what I had imagined, they would betray me in some way. I suppose, looking at it that way, I have never had a home. And the closest I have felt to belonging are these hours spent with you, sitting in that chair, listening to you sing.'

A tear drops from his eye onto his lap.

'Can I trust you?' he says, wiping his eye.

'Yes,' I whisper. 'Of course you can.'

'I ask you that because everyone in my life has betrayed me, one way or another. How could I ask such a thing of you if I couldn't afford you the same courtesy? My Lady Lullaby, I am not a spy, I swear to you.'

Outside, a dog begins to bark. The noise makes me flinch.

'But I am in danger,' he continues. 'Those yapping Dobermanns out there are valued more than the lives of us men. If Reid means to have me killed there is nothing I can do about it. Except . . .'

'Except?'

'Except spend each night here with you,' he says, his

voice softening. 'The man that Reid has hired works in the mines from dawn till sundown, so I am safe in the daylight hours. Come nightfall . . .'

He lets the sentence hang and looks sheepishly across at me.

'You are welcome to come here each evening,' I say. 'For as long as you need to.'

He kisses my hand and I press my forehead against his.

'So what is this project of yours all about, eh?' he whispers, lifting his head. 'All this Bible reciting. What is its purpose?'

'Well, for a start it is Herr Garn's project,' I say, closing my eyes as he entwines his fingers round mine. 'I am simply his assistant.'

'A very gifted one,' he says. 'I heard you that first day. You were in command.'

'I don't know about that,' I say, feeling my cheeks flush. 'I am still a student really. My university career was cut short due to the war and . . . well, Herr Garn's project has been a gift from heaven.'

'Manna,' he says, with a sigh. 'But what of all these voices? What is the point of recording them all? Some may suspect this Garn fellow of having sinister motives.'

'Oh, nothing could be further from the truth,' I say. 'Herr Garn is like me, a linguist. The purpose of it all is to analyse the various dialects of the men, to preserve them for posterity. You know, some of those accents, according to the professor, may not even exist one hundred years from now.'

'So, it is a matter of preservation,' he says. 'Like one would preserve an artefact for a museum?'

'That's right,' I say, excited to talk to someone other than Garn about my work. 'I have now managed to convince the professor to have the men tell their stories, instead of just reciting verse. It allows them to talk more freely, lets the accent come through better, more clearly.'

'So one could say, my dear,' he says with a smile, 'that you are a story collector. I knew someone like that once.'

That sorrowful look again as thoughts of his dead wife flash across both our minds, no doubt. I bat the image away, changing the subject.

'Jo, what happened to you in France? To make you lose your voice. I've heard talk of all sorts of terrible things. Shell shock, they are calling it. Trauma that can send a man mad . . . or mute.'

His body stiffens then, and he gently eases me off him.

'You're right,' he says, getting up from the chair. 'Both sides are facing unimaginable horrors out there, things that would freeze your blood. And, yes, some men are traumatized into silence. But others choose it. I fall into the latter category.'

'But why?' I say, watching as he pulls on his coat. 'Why would you choose to be silent?'

'Because when the world refuses to listen, what use is a voice?'

He puts on his boots and comes over to where I am sitting.

'I must go now,' he says gently. 'Before the sun rises and I'm spotted.'

He kisses my head and I follow him to the door, taking the blanket from the back of the chair and draping it over my shoulders.

'Goodbye, my love,' he says, opening the door and letting in a blast of freezing air. 'Go back into the warm now. Try to rest a while. It is still early.'

He turns and presses his lips softly to mine, and holding my face in his hands, stares at me so intently I feel he can see right through me. Then, without another word, he walks away into the half-light.

I watch as he disappears but as I turn to go back inside, my heart lurches. Someone is standing by the wall opposite. It is too dark to make out who it is, but the figure is short and portly, and I can smell the distinctive smell of pipe smoke.

Herr Garn. Surely it cannot be? But if it is, he must have seen us. Hurrying back inside, I bolt the door with trembling hands, knowing in the pit of my stomach that I am in serious trouble.

2 2

KITTY

Seven Dials

November 1916

Though the anti-German sentiment has still rumbled in the wake of the Zeppelin raids, the retaliation I have been dreading has failed to materialize.

In the end, it was not bombs but bitterness that threatened our survival, and as I sit here holed up in my room, my ears are alert to every sound on the darkened street outside my window, every clatter of footsteps, every raised voice. I hear Gillian bashing frantically at the typewriter in the living room next door, the room that has for the last few weeks played host to an eclectic stream of visitors hoping to hear their destiny from the cards of Miss Dexter, the woman they trust, the kindly baker with the pretty rouged cheeks and flowing silk skirts, the respectable proprietor of Kitty Kat's Bakery and cost-price restaurant, the philanthropist and seer who employs and feeds the needy while also nourishing their souls. What will those visitors be thinking now after what has just emerged? They will feel cheated and betrayed surely? They will feel they have been deceived, that the woman they thought was one of them has in fact been living a lie, hiding her true identity behind a smokescreen of sugar and smiles.

There is a pause in Gillian's typing and I hear her strike a match before resuming. The smell of cigarette smoke trickles under my door and I pull the heavy blanket up to my chin and turn to face the wall, placing my hands over my ears as cartwheels clatter along the cobbled street outside, my heart pulsating as the horse's hooves draw closer. How has it come to this, I think to myself, as the cart recedes, when yesterday began so well?

Let me try to explain.

We were three weeks into the cost-price restaurant scheme and business was booming. The back room was unrecognizable, decked with long trestle tables donated by Jean's widowed sister whose late husband had used them for his painting and decorating business, white starched tablecloths sewn and embroidered by the women employed in the Federation's clothing exchange, metal chairs salvaged from a derelict school in Soho, and glass milk bottles filled with wildflowers foraged by Connie from the lakeside in St James's Park. We had sourced unwanted cutlery and crockery from our loyal and generous customers, one of whom – a wealthy old lady of Russian descent who had fallen so much in love with our vanilla cream slices that she had a standing order of a dozen a week to be delivered to her Mayfair home – had donated the grand sum of £100 to help with getting the restaurant up and running. This allowed us to invest in new pots and pans for the kitchen as well as hiring new staff. By the time it opened its doors on 15 October, we had a whole new system and structure in place. Jean, with her experience of working at

Lyons Corner House, was appointed restaurant manager, a remarkable young cook, Rose Goodwin, who had worked at the Old Ford restaurant in its early days, came to us courtesy of Sylvia, while Connie combined evening waitressing with morning bakery shifts alongside assisting Gillian at the mother and baby clinic and milk station in Bow each afternoon.

Everything looked perfect that first day, but nothing could prepare us for the near stampede when we opened the doors. Almost one hundred people were fed and watered at the lunch and evening meal sessions that day, some through purchasing a tuppenny ticket, others eating free though, as Sylvia had stressed when she first suggested the idea, the diners would be unaware who had paid and who had not. There was to be no stigma in this restaurant, no whiff of charity. And that is exactly what came to pass. For three weeks the pervading mood in both the bakery and the restaurant was one of community, of friendly chat, of sated appetites and bonhomie. How gladdening it was to see mothers and their children sitting down to eat a healthy balanced meal without fear that it would leave them short for the rest of the month or that they'd have to resort to unspeakable practices in order to secure it; how heart-warming to see hungry children's eyes light up as steaming bowls of chicken soup, soft rolls fresh out of the oven, sweet and sticky jam roly-poly and rich egg custard were placed on the table in front of them. Sylvia was right, this initiative had been much needed in the district and it was one which, we hoped, would endure throughout the duration of this long and, if reports were to be believed, futile war.

And so it was with a renewed sense of purpose that I woke each day, lighting the ovens in the bakery kitchen which I now shared with the indomitable but charming Rose Goodwin, helping Connie lay the tables for the lunch session, blessing and preparing my cards at the small table by the window upstairs. As news of the catastrophic fatalities from the Battle of the Somme reached home, demand for my mediumship proved to be just as high as that for the cost-price meals in the restaurant. Life, it seemed, in this little corner of London, was sweet and good. Children were being fed, their mothers were finding friends and solace, Gillian and I were busy and focused and united in our common goal. What could possibly happen to disturb such peace?

My father used to have an expression he used in business: '*Never underestimate the sleeping dog – though he may look docile while he snores, he is always ready to bite.*' He had been talking about business associates feigning ignorance while negotiating deals, but I was reminded of the sentiment when I came downstairs yesterday morning.

Jean, Connie and Rose were huddled round the serving hatch, their backs to me as I entered the restaurant. 'Oh, my,' exclaimed Rose. 'Did you know about this, Jean?' 'I would say it is none of my business,' responded my restaurant manager. 'Shouldn't be anyone else's either. I don't think any less of her, no matter what it says here.' 'Well, I think it's beastly,' cried Connie, slamming her fist on the counter. 'The man who wrote this is an old Tory duffer. I've heard them talk about him at the Federation. He once wrote a piece demanding that all suffragettes be hanged for treason. That is what's behind this, he's trying to attack this place because of its socialist connections.'

'What's all this?' I said, still blissfully unaware of the horror that was about to unfold. 'I must say I've never heard you so animated, Connie. For a girl so young, you have acquired quite the political vocabulary. Gillian's zeal is clearly rubbing off on you.'

On hearing my voice, the girl turned round, her cheeks flushed. Her mother gestured to Rose, and I saw the cook swipe a newspaper from the counter and tuck it into her apron pocket.

'What was so interesting in there?' I said, pointing to the paper. 'It all seemed rather salacious.'

I could see that Rose, still new here, was reticent to share the information. She glanced at Jean, who shook her head gravely, then swiped the newspaper from Rose's pocket.

'I think you need to see this,' said Jean. 'I know I would want to if it was about me. Though I think it's best we leave you alone to read it.'

She handed me the newspaper, then ushered Rose and Connie out of the room. Taking a seat at the trestle table, the scent of shepherd's pie wafting from the kitchen behind me, I opened the newspaper and laid it flat in front of me.

FILTH! IS THIS WHAT OUR BRAVE SOLDIERS ARE FIGHTING FOR?

Underneath the headline were two photographs. The first was the one that had accompanied the interview I gave Maurice Newton for this newspaper last year, showing me outside the bakery with a silly grin on my face. The second looked as if it had been taken from a distance and focused on the bakery window. Though blurry, it showed the silhouettes of two women embracing. It was then I realized that it had been Newton I had glimpsed outside the window the night I kissed Gillian. He had seen us, taken a photograph, and, on the basis of that, decided to investigate further, writing an article in which he damned us, the bakery, and all who were part of it. From what he had written, it became clear that he had managed to slip into the cost-price restaurant unnoticed and made notes about what went on within its walls, resulting in an account that couldn't have been further from the truth. Newton gave pen portraits of the 'kind of person' frequenting this establishment. He described a child, likely Connie from the details given, 'strutting about' in a *Votes for Women* sash and doling out kisses to the female customers as they arrived. There were also detailed descriptions in which Newton recounted the horror of seeing a group of women pawing and fondling each other in a debased manner. I knew the moment he was referring to and it was all perfectly innocent. We had just completed the first lunch session, feeding almost fifty people, and the happy diners had erupted into a rousing 'hip hip hooray'. With joy in our hearts, we had fallen into an exhausted embrace. It was a group of friends sharing a happy moment, but Maurice Newton had found a way to twist all that was good into something lewd and unsavoury.

After lengthy paragraphs detailing how the bakery was nothing but a front for *a Socialist Sapphic brothel, where bored housewives can indulge in immoral behaviour with a group of deviants led by a lesbian fortune teller who had hoodwinked this newspaper and its loyal readers into promoting her 'bakery'*, he concluded with the following: *To think that our brave men are risking their lives in the bloody trenches of the Somme, fighting for their country and for the freedom of all of us, the proprietor and her ilk included, while their wives make a mockery of their efforts by allowing themselves to be brainwashed into perversity in this sordid, left-wing den of vice.*

My mind immediately emptied, my body entering the blankness of shock as it shut down all thought and feeling. I walked back into the bakery, the newspaper clutched in my hand, firmly telling Jean, Connie and Rose to go home. They protested, Connie telling me that it was all a lot of nonsense, but I couldn't respond. I simply locked the door behind them, hung the *Closed* sign on the door – as if we would ever get customers now anyway – and staggered upstairs.

Gillian had come home shortly afterwards. Connie had told her what had happened, and, like her protégée, she had tried to reassure me that it was all just a lot of hot air, the rantings of a right-wing journalist who obviously had a problem with the bakery being turned into a socialist enterprise and had concocted some ludicrous story with the aid of a few grainy photographs. 'We can't hide away, Kitty,' she had said, trying to coax me from the bed. 'There are hungry women and children waiting to be served lunch. We can't let them down.'

In the end, Gillian, with the help of Connie, Jean and Rose who had patiently waited outside after I had thrown them out, had cobbled together the rest of the day's meals. I knew that the story had spread, though. I could see, as I stood at the window looking out, that the numbers had diminished. *A Socialist Sapphic brothel.* Most of our customers are churchgoers and the references to their men being betrayed would have horrified them. Rather starvation than sapphism, that would have been the refrain.

Outside the door, I can hear voices. Gillian is not alone.

I get up from the bed and peer out. Sylvia is sitting at the typewriter, Gillian wedged on the seat beside her. They both look up as I walk into the room.

'Sylvia has written a letter to the *Standard*,' she says, getting to her feet. 'Addressing each ludicrous accusation in turn and demanding a printed apology and retraction.'

I am both touched and taken aback by how supportive Sylvia is being and I feel more than a little ashamed that I have been so rude to her in the past. Still, despite her kindness, I can see no way out of the mess Newton's article has plunged us into.

'I am grateful, Sylvia, for your efforts but it won't change anything,' I say, pouring myself a tumbler of brandy from the glass decanter. 'The article has already been read by the whole of London. You saw the trickle of customers today. We're ruined. And the worst thing is, I have no idea what I did to offend that man, Maurice Newton, or why he chose to write such a vitriolic and damning article.'

'Maurice Newton is a known Tory propagandist,' says Sylvia, pulling the finished letter from the typewriter and folding it into a neat rectangle. 'His father-in-law is a wealthy industrialist and Newton himself has business interests in various commercial endeavours, aside from his journalism. He is also vehemently opposed to women's suffrage. I crossed paths with him a few years ago when he attended a meeting at Whitehall where the infamous Cat and Mouse Act was being discussed.'

'Revolting business,' says Gillian, shaking her head.

'Pardon my ignorance,' I say, taking a sip of brandy. 'But what is the Cat and Mouse Act? It sounds like some sort of vaudeville turn.'

I smile but it is clear that Sylvia does not share my mirth.

'It was the government's weak-willed attempt to deal with the problem of hunger strikers,' says Sylvia, buttoning her coat. 'I was one of those strikers, as were my mother and sister, Emmeline and Christabel.'

She grimaces slightly at the mention of her family, and I recall Gillian saying that they were now estranged. I think of Otto, how close we were and how he had slipped from my life. I wonder if Sylvia misses her mother and sister as much as I miss Otto, but the formidable Pankhurst shows little sign of emotion as she explains the intricacies of the Cat and Mouse Act to me.

'In short, it allowed the hunger strikers to be released from prison to regain their strength,' she says, her eyes hardening at the memory of her own struggle. 'And they were then taken back to jail once they recovered. Newton, I recall, was all in favour of this and wrote article after article admonishing the "wicked" suffragettes and calling for them to be flogged in a public place, to teach "decent women" not to fall out of line. The man is a disgrace to his profession, Kitty, and, though you may think my letter futile, I assure you it will be dealt with. This was an attack on me, not you and Gillian. He doesn't give a fig about sapphic relationships, it is the socialist enterprise that has fired his blood. That was why he wrote that garbage, so that he could stop me and the work of the Federation at every turn.'

'But what about the legal ramifications?' I say, draining my brandy. 'Homosexuality is punishable by prison or death in this country. This article threatens more than just the business, it puts both Gillian and me in grave danger. I thought the anti-German threats were bad, not to mention what I had to endure in Germany because of my psychic gifts, but this is worse. It is one thing being German but this – this is illegal.'

'Only if you are a man,' says Sylvia drily. 'For women, as with most things in life, homosexuality is not illegal, it is not even recognized. In the eyes of the law, just as with votes for women, female homosexuality simply does not exist.'

I slump onto the armchair, my body limp with relief.

'You mean we are not going to be arrested?'

'Only for the crime of keeping this fine establishment closed when there are hungry people in need of food,' says Sylvia, raising her eyebrow and smiling. 'Now, leave me to deal with the Newton creature and I suggest you get an early night and be ready to open those doors first thing tomorrow. It is the only way to get through this.'

'Sylvia is right,' says Gillian, guiding our guest to the door. 'And as for that article, well, it'll be wrapping wet fish at Billingsgate by now. We're safe, Kitty, don't worry.'

I nod my head and smile but as I watch Sylvia depart, the letter clasped in her hands, I feel an unsettling sense of foreboding. Though Gillian reassures me that disaster has been averted, I fear it has only just begun.

23

EDIE

Stepney Green

Present Day

I am sitting in the back room of Tony George's repair shop when my phone buzzes. It is a WhatsApp from Alexander:

Heading from Canary Wharf now. Meet you at the Tube?

I type out a quick reply, then put my phone away and return my attention to Tony and the wax cylinder.

After scrutinizing both the cylinder and its handwritten label, Tony, a plump sixty-something Cypriot with a mop of white hair and a beaming smile, had led me through the shop, which was crammed with old gramophones, radios and speakers, and into a small, soundproofed studio where he presented me with a strange metal box on top of which was fixed what looked like a plastic kitchen-paper dispenser.

'This is the archéophone,' he had proclaimed proudly. 'Bet you've never seen one of these before.'

He was right. I had never seen anything like it, and I sat mesmerized as he slid the wax cylinder out of its cardboard tube and fitted it onto the plastic roll. As we waited for it to play, Tony warned me that due to the age of the cylinder and the fact that it had basically been left to rot behind a wall, we might not be able to hear much.

'In fact, it may be unsalvageable,' he said, his cheery face growing serious. 'That's the tragedy of old recordings like this.'

Yet now, as we sit here watching as the cylinder turns round the plastic roll in a frenzy of clicks and static, popping like the bubbles from a scuba diver's nozzle, the strange aquatic ripples give way to something else. A voice. Faint and muffled, as though speaking underwater.

'Oh, what have we here?' says Tony excitedly.

We both lean into the archéophone, but the voice is soon overcome by static. It is impossible to hear what the person is saying.

'As I thought,' says Tony, shaking his head. 'It's what happens when you're dealing with something as fragile as a wax cylinder recording. They must be properly conserved, or else damage sets in, yet most of them end up gathering dust in an attic or, in your case, behind a load of plasterboard.'

He casts me a disapproving look and I stop myself from assuring him that it wasn't me who put the cylinder in that hole.

'So it's unsalvageable then,' I say despondently. 'Is that what you're saying?'

'Not entirely,' he replies, pressing a button on the archéophone which brings the cylinder and the crackling noises to a halt. 'This was just the initial play. Most cylinders sound like this when you're playing them raw. My job now is to use this archéophone to extract the original audio from the cylinder and transfer it onto a digital file. And if I can do that without damaging it then we may – and I'm making no promises here – be able to hear what the person on the recording is saying.'

'That is wonderful news,' I say, feeling strangely invested in both Tony George's specialist work and the strange, ghostly voice that filled the air just now. 'How long will it take you to do?'

Tony clicks his tongue.

'Well, I've got a backlog of commissions to clear,' he says, shaking his head. 'Normally, I'd say two to three months minimum but as it's for Alexander I'm willing to push it up the list a few rungs. If you leave it with me, I'll aim to get it ready for this time next week. How does that sound?'

'It sounds perfect,' I say. 'And thank you so much for fast-tracking it. I really appreciate it.'

'Like I said, Alexander's an old friend and a solid bloke,' says Tony, as we walk back through the shop. 'I've lost count of the number of old recordings we've uncovered over the years. Good to know that people still want to hear them, eh? That they haven't given up on the past altogether.'

I smile and bid him farewell.

'And don't worry,' he says, opening the door for me. 'I'll take good care of it.'

Yet as I step out onto the street, I feel a sense of relief to have left the cylinder behind. My curiosity as to what is on that recording has dissipated since hearing that strange, disembodied voice and given way to a deep sense of unease. Until this afternoon, the wax cylinder had been a harmless, benign object, yet now, like the Tarot cards, the eerie engravings and the Devil-worshipping tenant who shares my late husband's name, it has been imbued with something rather more sinister. And yet, despite my revulsion, I realize that I am bound up with this mystery now. I want to solve it even while it is terrifying me. Why is that, when just a few days ago, I had been blissfully unaware of its existence? Maybe it is as Tony said, that people still do have a fascination with history and what has gone before, that there is a strange comfort to be found in unearthing hidden lives, hearing long-lost voices.

Or maybe it is because there is another mystery that I will never be able to solve, and the box is providing some much-needed distraction. The mystery of 12 October.

As I walk down the cobbled walkway that skirts Stepney Green, the events of that night return to me in muted shades. I had been in a deep sleep, partly due to the bottle of red wine David and I had shared at dinner and partly as I had spent the last few weeks putting in sixteen-hour days to get my latest commission – a series of paintings to commemorate the anniversary of the Cable Street riots – finished and delivered on time. David had cooked roast chicken and the smell of it greeted me as I stumbled from my office, bleary-eyed, into the warmth of the kitchen. We had both been working crazy hours. David had two books on the go as well as his teaching work and what with various conferences and speaking events we had barely seen each other in months. I remember him saying, as he carved the chicken, that we were due some time to ourselves. Maybe we should book a holiday, he had said, what about Cornwall? I know how much you love it. Walking across the green blanket of St Dunstan's churchyard, the place where David and I were married, Dora was christened and many a Sunday afternoon was spent collecting acorns from the foot of the mighty oak whose branches extended across the churchyard like a benevolent grandfather, I realize that, in the tumult that followed, I had completely forgotten David's suggestion we go to Cornwall.

Heading towards the ornate iron bench where I last sat the day of David's funeral, I find myself turning that conversation over in my head, trying to find some answers, some clarity. Though I know the fact that the tenant shared his name has to be just a coincidence, I cannot shake the feeling that David, particularly in his final months, had been keeping something from me. I think back to the night he left to go to Düsseldorf for the Writers in Education conference. We'd had a silly row. About what? I honestly, for the life of me, can't remember. David left without saying goodbye and I stood at the window watching him go and wondering why he was walking in the opposite direction to the Tube. I'd told myself perhaps he'd decided to take a cab to Heathrow instead of braving the hordes on the rush-hour train. The trip was financed by the university so taking a cab would be a sensible choice. I hadn't thought anything of it, or the fact that he seemed to have more luggage than usual and was dressed in casual clothes, until now.

Oh, stop this Edie, I tell myself, as I reach the bench and remember how empty I had felt the last time I sat here. Dora, Ronke and my parents had offered to stay with me, but I told them to go on to the wake, that I would catch up with them shortly. But as I sat there, watching them go, the words and images of the funeral flitting in and out of my mind – David's casket being brought in to 'You're the Best

Thing' by the Style Council, the song we had played at our wedding, the vicar talking about the wonderful father, husband and scholar, Ronke's eulogy, the words of Siegfried Sassoon – I had realized with devastating clarity that he had gone. My David, my husband, my love, the man and the life that we had lived had gone and were never coming back.

My chest tightens with sorrow and a dull sense of panic as I make my way out of the churchyard and scurry down the blue cobbles I used to skip along as a child. I need to be around people who know and love me, need to stop torturing myself with questions and try to find solid answers, I think to myself, as I take a left turn towards Stepney Green Tube.

Alexander is waiting for me at the entrance when I arrive. The sight of him standing there in his dark overcoat, a friendly face among a sea of strangers, reassures me and I feel my nerves start to settle. Though he is almost a decade younger than me, he has a steadiness about him that makes me feel safe. The only other person who has ever had that effect on me before was David. It is a surprising realization and, as Alexander greets me with a kiss to my cheek, I feel calm and guilty in equal measure.

'Fancy a spot of lunch?' he says, heading back into the station. 'Thought we could head West. There's a great Yemeni place just opened on Greek Street. They do the most amazing *fahsa*. You can tell me how it went with Tony while we stuff our faces.'

'Actually, Alexander,' I say, taking his arm and guiding him back onto the road that leads to Mile End, 'would you mind if we stick to the East End? There's a couple of people I'd like you to meet.'

24

EDIE

Mile End

Present Day

'He's talking cobblers! I was left that cottage by my grand-mother. Her name was Jane and I've got her will to prove it. I don't know, who is this old fool, anyway?'

My father's rheumy eyes flash with indignation as he sits in the cramped kitchen of my childhood home, a two-up, two-down terraced house just off the Mile End Road, sipping sweet tea from his favourite chipped mug. Poor dad had been rather shaken when I told him about the box I had found in the cottage. The strangeness of it and the mystery of its contents seemed to unsettle him somehow. My throwing in Ned's theory about Jane seems to have only served to agitate him even more.

'Oh, Frank, don't get so het up,' says my mother, coming into the room with an armful of patchy leather photo albums which she places with a thud on the table. 'At least not in front of our guest.'

She smiles at Alexander, who is making his way through a slice of my father's legendary apple cake.

'Oh, it's all right, Frank,' he says. 'I completely agree

with you. Ned's just an old eccentric who's clearly got his wires crossed. He claims to know everything there is to know about the village but he's getting on a bit now and his memory can't be that good. Though I have to say, he's a damned good workman.'

'Hmm,' mutters Dad, unconvinced, as he opens an album.

I sit opposite, sketchbook on my lap, tracing the contours of his familiar, lived-in face. It's been years since I've drawn my parents and I'm suddenly aware of how age has crept up on them both. If anything, this Tarot project is giving me an opportunity to reconnect with them the only way I know how, through my pencil and paper.

'It's in here somewhere, I'm sure of it,' says Dad, taking his thick-rimmed glasses from their case. 'The only photo I have of her. It was taken on my father's wedding day. A group shot, outside the church.'

'Grandad Wilf?' I say, putting my sketchbook down for a moment and taking a Garibaldi biscuit from the packet to dunk in my tea, a habit from childhood.

It feels safe here in the cocoon of my parents' house, to be back in the East End, though I could never face venturing towards my old home. The flat I shared with David, once a haven for me, will now for ever be associated with what happened that night. Walking through St Dunstan's, which sits just moments from the flat, was the nearest I was going to get to returning. Still, even in the safety of this kitchen in the house I grew up in, I feel uneasy, as though any minute now some unseen force will come crashing through the door. It is part of the reason why I decided to bring Alexander here. His presence is like having a piece of Cornwall and my new life with me, a place where there is no danger, no threat, a place untainted by the events of 12 October.

'Well, here's the thing, Edith, love,' says Dad, interrupting my thoughts. 'Wilf wasn't my real father. My actual old man was killed in the Second World War, when I was just a baby.'

'What?' I say, spluttering into my tea. 'And you're only just telling me now?'

'People didn't talk about things like that back then,' says my mother, frowning as I wipe the tea from the table with the back of my sleeve. 'We didn't think you needed to know. Wilf was a good father to your dad and grandfather to you.'

'I didn't know it myself until I was in my twenties,' says Dad, looking up from the photo album. 'My mother only told me about him when I was about to get married and I needed to find my birth certificate.'

'Yes, that's right,' says my mother, taking the album from my father's hands and turning to the front. 'It was ever such a shock. Especially as your dad looked so much like Wilf. But according to Hazel, she had been married before. To someone called Sam.'

'My real father,' adds Dad. Nodding at Alexander, he says, 'Do you want another slice of cake?'

'No, thank you, Frank,' says Alexander, patting his stomach. 'I've got a meeting later and if I have any more cake they'll have to roll me in there.'

He turns to me and laughs awkwardly. I feel rather bad for dragging him here. He had been set for a swanky lunch in Soho and he ends up in the chaos of my parents' kitchen.

'There it is, Edie,' says Mum, as my father stops at a page of black-and-white photos. 'The only picture we have of your great-gran and the only one of your real grandad. Jane left it to your dad in her will, alongside the cottage.'

She pushes the album into the middle of the table, and I lean forward to get a closer look at the faded image. It shows a bride and groom – a baby-faced young man with fair hair styled in a side parting and a pretty young woman with blonde curls and the same snub nose as me, who I immediately recognize as my grandmother, Hazel. There are two women either side of the couple. A tall, rather stern-faced woman with large pale eyes and grey hair piled in a loose bun on top of her head; and a shorter woman of a similar age wearing thick spectacles and a wide-brimmed hat.

'Gran looks the same as she always did,' I say, recalling the playful character who had been such an integral part of my childhood. An East Ender through and through, she had run a market stall selling bric-a-brac on Columbia Road right up until her eighties. 'Though they both look so young.'

'She was only eighteen, your gran,' says Dad, pulling the album towards him. 'And he was just nineteen. Broke her heart, it did. That's what she told me all those years later. In confidence, though. She didn't want to feel disloyal to Wilf in saying that she'd loved another man. See that woman there?'

He points to the tall woman with the grey bun.

'That there is your great-grandmother, Jane,' he says, jabbing his finger on the cellophane covering. 'Handsome, wasn't she?'

'She was. And who is this?' I say, turning my attention to the rather dowdy woman standing next to the bride. 'I feel like I know her, somehow.'

'No idea,' says my father. 'Always thought she must be a family friend.'

'Didn't you ask Gran who she was?' I say, staring at the woman and wondering why her pensive expression is so familiar.

'If I'm not mistaken,' says Dad, taking the photo from me, 'I think it might say so on the back.'

He turns the photo over and looks and narrows his eyes.

'Here, you read it,' he says, handing me it. 'My eyesight's shot.'

I take the photo and turn it over to where, in pretty calligraphy, someone has written the names of the people featured.

'"From left to right,"' I read aloud. '"Sixth of March 1939. St Dunstan's Church, Stepney Green. Mummy-Jane, Mr and Mrs Samuel Dexter, and Miss Miriam Ziegler."'

25

MIRIAM

Dänholm Prisoner-of-War Camp

October 1918

When I was a child living in Berlin, we found that our house had an infestation of mice. The vermin appeared to be clustering in the back of the kitchens that spanned the entire basement level of the building. Determined to solve the problem, our cook, Marta, took in a large tabby cat that she had found on the street. Now, as a little girl I was something of an animal lover and was the proud owner of two canaries, a curly-haired spaniel named Hugo, and Frederik, a large goldfish, who I had won at a funfair. And yet this cat, which was never given a name, instilled in me a sense of fear I have not felt with any animal before or since. It was his stillness that troubled me the most, the way he would sit in the back yard, half in shadow, watching the mice as they scurried among the food scraps. Watching, waiting. And I in turn, from my vantage point at the drawing-room window above, would watch the cat watching the mice. He would pounce eventually and polish off the mice within minutes, yet it was the moments when those creatures were oblivious, when his eyes were fixed upon them, that I found most terrifying. I could see what was about to happen and yet there was nothing I could do about it.

This memory has returned to me over the last few days as I find myself in the same position as those mice with Herr Garn taking on the role of the ever-watchful cat. It has been four days since I saw him outside my cabin as Jo was leaving and still he has not spoken a word of what he may have witnessed.

'I think you are worrying unnecessarily,' says Jo, as he sits by the fire and pulls on his boots. 'I didn't see anyone that night and if it had been Herr Garn then he would have said something by now.'

Though I know that we are taking great risks in spending the nights together like this, we have no choice. Reid's man is primed to target Jo when he least expects it, and the obvious place would be to ambush him in his bed. Once again, my mind returns to that strange cat, his body rigid and taut as he prepared to pounce.

'Now, try to rest before your shift,' he says, kissing me gently on my forehead. 'Otherwise you will have no energy for your work. You must think about your life beyond this camp, beyond this war. You will want to resume your studies, no?'

I nod my head, though the university and all its promise seem like a world away now.

'Then you must not let pointless worry get in the way of your work,' he says, getting up from the chair and putting on his greatcoat. 'You have much to accomplish, my love. And I know you will do it.'

Buoyed by his words, I throw myself into the day's

work, making sure the recording equipment is set up well in advance of the men's arrival, laying out Herr Garn's Bible, pencil and paper, and spending more time than usual writing up the observation notes when the session is over. Every so often I feel Herr Garn's eyes upon me but each time I meet his stare with a confident smile, a smile that says I am every inch his diligent assistant and not a traitor who seduced a British prisoner.

This improved mood carries me through the rest of the day, even causing Julia, whom I am assisting with a round of tuberculosis inoculations for the new intake of prisoners this afternoon, to ask me if I have had good news – to which I reply I have not, I am simply in the mood for smiling.

'Well, it suits you,' says Julia, as we stand side by side at the sink, sterilizing the last of the needles. 'And smiles are such a rarity in this place. Tell me, Miriam, do you have a sweetheart back home?'

The question temporarily stuns me.

'I'm sorry, I have overstepped the mark,' says Julia, taking a clean cloth and drying her hands. 'I forget that we are at war and most girls have men fighting out there. It must be a very worrying time for you.'

She looks at me with heartfelt concern and for a moment I see another side to the diligent young girl with whom I have spent this last couple of weeks tending to the broken bodies of enemy prisoners; there's a spark in her sharp blue eyes that reminds me of my late mother and, before I know it, I find myself opening up.

'In answer to your question, I do indeed have a beau,' I whisper, shaking the soap suds from my hands. 'Though he is not fighting in the war.'

'Ah,' says Julia, her eyes widening. 'He is . . . an objector?'

'Oh, no, no,' I say, taking the cloth from her so that I can dry my hands. 'He is no refusenik. He has played his part in the war most gallantly.'

'I do not understand, then,' she says. 'If he is not fighting and he is not a coward then where can he . . .? Oh, Miriam, are you telling me it is someone in the camp? A guard? I know those men can be flirtatious, but you must be careful. Some of them are simply brutes. I have seen their behaviour with my own eyes.'

'He is not a guard, no,' I say, my mouth running away with me.

'Not a guard,' she says, her voice quivering. 'Then all that is left is . . . the prisoners.'

'Nurse!'

At the sound of Frida's voice, I almost drop the measuring cup I am holding. Did she hear us?

Sheepishly, Julia and I turn from the sink. Frida stands in front of us, her face wrought with fury. She is holding a syringe in her hands.

'What is the problem, Matron?' I ask, swallowing the terror that is rising through my bones.

'I was addressing Nurse Mueller, not you,' snaps Frida, her eyes bulging with anger. Beside me I hear Julia gasp.

'What is this?' demands Frida, pointing the syringe at Julia.

'It . . . it is the typhoid inoculation, Matron,' stammers Julia, her body trembling.

'I asked you to prepare 0.5 millilitres, the standard dose,' cries Frida. 'This is 0.9.'

She throws the syringe at the basin. It misses and clatters to the floor.

'If I hadn't noticed at the last moment, I would have administered it to the patient and then my nursing career of thirty years' standing would have been over.'

'Matron, I . . . I can explain,' begins Julia, tears streaming down her face.

'I do not want to hear it, Mueller,' cries Frida. 'This is cause for instant dismissal.'

Beside me, Julia's knees buckle. I've gleaned from our easy chatter while we've worked side by side that she was a student nurse back in Germany and that she hopes to pursue a career in the profession when the war is over. I also know that she is a diligent and hard-working young woman. This is a terrible mistake but one I am convinced she will not repeat. I cannot let her life be ruined because of this.

'Matron, it wasn't Julia who prepared that syringe,' I say, my heart pulsating as I step forward. 'It was me.'

'You?' exclaims Frida, horrified. 'Nurse Ziegler, how on earth did this happen?'

'I was distracted by a query from one of the men,' I say, the reasoning coming to me as I go along. 'As I was filling the syringe. I turned from my work and . . . I must have overfilled it.'

Frida stares at me aghast. I look down at my feet, waiting for the words to come, for her to tell me that I am dismissed from my duties. But instead, I hear her sigh.

'I will put this down to a most unfortunate, and out-of-character, error,' she says, sternly. 'I cannot afford to lose a nurse of your calibre and experience. But if this happens again, Nurse Ziegler, you will be on the boat bound for Germany and the munitions factory so fast your feet won't touch the ground, do you understand?'

'Yes, Matron,' I say, relief coursing through my body. 'And please, be assured it will never happen again.'

Frida nods briskly, then turns to Julia.

'Another syringe, Nurse Mueller,' she snaps. 'With the correct measurement. Now.'

As Frida walks away, Julia turns to me, her eyes still red with tears.

'Thank you, Miriam,' she whispers, her voice cracking with fear and relief. 'I will never forget what you have done for me today. Never.'

Later, as I step outside, the cold October air seems to snap me to my senses. What were you thinking, Miriam? I chide myself as I pull my coat around me and make my way back to the hut. Talking so loosely about Jo with Julia when Frida was in earshot, then taking responsibility for the girl's error. If it hadn't been for Frida's leniency, I could be halfway to Germany and the dreaded munitions factory by now. Though, thankfully, Frida only thinks me guilty of complacency rather than having taken up with a prisoner. I shall have to be more careful in future, I tell myself as I cross the quadrant. There are eyes everywhere.

In the darkness, I can make out the shape of the watch-towers ahead of me, see the swirl of cold air as the guards blow on their hands to keep warm. I think about the evening ahead, the notes I have to finish for Herr Garn as well as my own private research that I have been collating these last few months. As Jo reminded me, I must be prepared for when this war is over, when I can leave this camp and resume my studies. I must keep my brain focused and engaged.

As I turn the corner at the block that houses the officer prisoners, I see a group of officials gathered on the grass, their faces illuminated in the glow of the searchlights from the tower behind them. Two of the men step aside and as they walk away, I see, in the centre of the gathering, the distinctive form of the commandant, his broad shoulders almost bursting out of his uniform, his thick moustache moving up and down as he talks intently to a man on his right. As I draw closer, the man comes into focus, and my insides turn to liquid.

It is Herr Garn talking to the commandant.

I turn on my heels, catching, as I do, Garn's voice and the words 'something I have suspected for some time'.

He is talking about me, about us. There is no doubt. My legs almost give way under me as I half-run, half-stagger back to my cabin. Once inside, I bolt the door and throw myself onto the bed where I lie frozen, not moving to undress or to prepare food. I stay like that for the rest of the night. I tell myself that when he arrives, I will not let him in. I will ignore him, for my own safety. And his. But when the knock comes, and I hear Jo whisper, 'It is just me. Let me in,' all my good intentions fall away.

But something is the matter. When I open the door, he almost falls inside. Beads of moisture are gathered on his forehead, his knuckles are grazed and bloody, his coat damp with sweat.

'You are hurt?' I say, as he takes me in his arms. 'I will clean you up . . . I . . .'

'No,' he says, breathlessly, leading me to the bed. 'I'll

deal with it later. For now, all I want is to forget about the world. All I want is you.'

Afterwards, I lie in his arms, feeling, just as he wished, that the world has fallen away, that we, and the love we have made, are the only things that exist. The sheets are twisted and damp with sweat, our clothes strewn on the floor. I close my eyes, feel the warmth of his hand as it caresses my face, my neck, the curve of my breasts, and wonder if this is just a strange and vivid dream. I had begun this day a virgin. Now, as the clock creeps towards midnight, I lie here an altered woman. Nothing will ever be the same again.

I wake what seems like moments later – though it must be morning as the light is pouring through the windows – to the sound of dogs barking and sirens blaring. I glance at the empty space beside me. 'Jo?' Sitting up, I see that his boots and coat are gone. The barking grows louder. In a panic, I jump from the bed and unbolt the door. Outside is a hive of activity. Guards and dogs are lined across the path all the way up to the block that houses Jo's hut. A white medical vehicle is parked on the grass by the entrance to the block. Up ahead, I see the familiar figure of Frida standing by the sanatorium. I call out to her, and she looks in my direction but doesn't seem to hear me. Instead, she turns on her heels and heads back inside.

Grabbing my coat from the back of the door, I run towards the line of guards, recognizing Dieter, though his usually animated face is now grave.

'What has happened?' I say, trying to catch my breath. 'Has there been an accident?'

Dieter shakes his head.

'I am not sure if you could call it an accident,' he says, a sick smile appearing on his face. 'But it seems the prisoners are turning on each other now.'

'What do you mean?'

He gestures across the quadrant to where two guards are emerging from the block. As they draw closer, I see, to my utter horror and despair, that they are carrying a body.

26

KITTY

Seven Dials

September 1918

Two years have passed since the Zeppelin raid and Maurice Newton's inflammatory article yet, despite Gillian's reassurances that nothing would come of his spiteful rant, things have gone from bad to worse at the bakery.

At first, we had thought, disaster had been averted. Thanks to Sylvia, the editor of the newspaper issued a full apology, explaining to us that Newton had been experiencing some 'personal problems' and had taken extended sickness leave. I thought of my vision – his wife and the younger man – and wondered if it had been that and not his hatred of socialism that had spurred him into writing the piece. Was he jealous of the warmth he witnessed between the women at the bakery? Had his cuckolded marriage made him angry and bitter? Had he developed a hatred for women in general because of this and saw a chance to destroy two of them in one fell swoop?

I have seen first-hand the consequences of his hatred. The dwindling customers, the random acts of vandalism including a smashed window and vile slurs daubed across the door. A handful of customers, mainly women, who we have helped over the years both financially – through the cost-price restaurant – and spiritually – through my readings – have stayed loyal though our takings are disastrously low. Some days we have no customers at all, and I have to send Connie home for lack of any work to be done. Worst of all, I have lost Jean, a woman I considered a friend as well as an employee. And for that I only have myself to blame.

Tonight, to coincide with the anniversary of the bakery and cost-price restaurant, we have decided to extend our opening hours later into the evening, to try to drum up business from the women employed in the newly opened garment workshops nearby. Connie has dropped leaflets in to them, inviting the workers to come and claim their discounted meal at the restaurant.

We have a long night ahead of us but, despite my worries over the dwindling business, as I stand at the shop window watching Jean's young daughter, Connie, and Aggie, the young widow who had come for a reading all those years ago, set up the trestle tables on the street outside, I cannot help but feel a deep sense of pride.

'How healthy they both look,' says Gillian, appearing beside me. 'It's touching to see.'

She rests her head on my shoulder. Her hair smells of violets. For a moment, I am back in 1912 and my first night attending a meeting of the Divine Order. What a time that was. Otto, still my loving big brother; Father alive and thriving in his busy bakery. And the only time we Germans fell out with our English friends was over the football scores. To think that back then, the only thing I had to worry about was making sure I addressed the high masters in the correct way. But, oh, how I remember every detail of that first night. The candlelit apartment that looked out onto Soho Square Gardens, the floor strewn with embroidered cushions, the High Master chanting hypnotically in the centre, while I hid timidly behind my brother, clutching my Tarot cards to my chest. Otto and I had taken an omnibus from Liverpool Street to the West End. It was a warm April evening, and we sat on the top deck, the wind rippling through my hair as the bus trundled down the cobbled streets. Beside me, Otto chatted about the people I would meet that night, the conversations that might be had.

It had been Otto's idea to bring me along. He had joined the Order six months earlier on the invitation of its High Master, the enigmatic Arthur Rubelle-Jones, who had placed an advertisement for an editor to help work on his 'book of universal truth' as he referred to it. Otto, newly graduated from University College London with a first in English Language and Literature, had answered the advertisement and secured the job. I had never seen my brother so happy. His pale face had taken on a rosy bloom, and he appeared to be intoxicated by life. Through Arthur he had been pulled further into the life of the Order, attending meetings and socials where there were lively discussions to be had on a range of subjects from art to philosophy, poetry to transcendental meditation. It was, Otto told me when he visited Father and me at the bakery afterwards, like having one's eyes opened, like being born again into a new world of debate, analysis and free thinking. 'But better still,' he had whispered, out of earshot of Father who was busy slicing a batch of poppyseed cakes, 'they are tolerant of people like you, people with your gift. You wouldn't believe it. There was a woman at the Order last night, a seer like you. She gave a reading, and nobody laughed at her or demanded she be locked up. They listened to her, respected her. You should come along, Kitty. See what you think.'

I accepted my brother's invitation and found, to my surprise, that he was right. For a time, the world of the Order opened its arms to me. My gift, as Otto predicted, was respected and embraced by the other members. I soon found myself being called to give readings not only at the Soho Square headquarters but at select gatherings across London. And, best of all, I got to do all of this with my darling brother. For the first time since we came to England, Otto and I felt we were truly a part of things, that we were fully accepted in our adopted city.

Not only that, but we found love in the form of Gillian and Nancy. Those early, heady days of first love were something Otto and I could share. I recognized that far-away look in his eyes whenever he mentioned Nancy because it mirrored my own. I had never been able to talk about my secret, the love that dare not speak its name, to anyone before. Goodness, if I had been threatened with the asylum for being a psychic, who knows what they would have done to me had my queerness come to light. But none of that mattered in the closed-off world of the Divine Order. Love was an energy, it was not defined by gender or social codes – that is what the higher masters believed and for the two years between 1912, when I was initiated into the Order, and 1914, when everything fell apart, I allowed myself to think the wider world agreed.

How wrong I was. And yet, though I despise those small-minded souls who wish to diminish this love, there is still a part of me that cowers in fear from them, that will do whatever it takes to avoid social exile. It is why, despite our stolen kiss, I still keep Gillian at arm's length, making sure the world, as well as she, knows that we are simply two platonic friends living under one roof. But, oh, how the sight of her, the scent of her, taunts me day and night, how the past moments I shared with her return to me again and again in my dreams. How I would love to take the clock and wind it back to 1912, to be safe within the walls of the Divine Order and Gillian's arms. A time of love and safety and inclusion, before the world lost its collective mind and sent its young men off to fight a futile and senseless war, that seems, like so much in life, impossible to win.

'This bloody war,' sighs Gillian, almost reading my mind. 'The damage it has inflicted will take generations to heal. Sylvia tells me that the returning soldiers are being abandoned just as much as their wives and children were. I hear Jean's husband didn't make it back.'

'Killed at the Battle of St Quentin,' I say, recalling the moment Jean read the telegram two weeks earlier, the horror in her eyes. I shudder at the memory, recalling how she had turned to me and cried, '*But you said he'd be safe. You said he'd come back to us,*' and walk across to the counter where I busy myself arranging the choux pastry display. 'You should know Jean has left.'

'Left?' exclaims Gillian. 'That's a shame. I suppose she'll need time to get over the shock of her husband's death but, as Sylvia says, work is a distraction. It might help her more to be here, to keep busy.'

'I'm afraid it's not the work she's walked out on. It's me.'

'What do you mean?'

I explain to Gillian about the first reading I gave to Jean, how I had wanted to bring some light to the emaciated, distressed woman sitting in front of me.

'It seems I gave her false hope.'

'Oh, Kitty,' says Gillian.

'I'm beginning to think all of this has been a mistake,' I say, gesturing to my skirts. 'The subterfuge, the clothes, the name. I can't help but think that if I had stayed as Katerina, faced up to that mob, stayed true to myself, then . . .'

'Then what?' says Gillian. 'Look at the lives you have saved through this bakery and the restaurant. Even the Tarot readings, despite what you think you should have said or done with Jean. If the mob hadn't raided Mile End that day, then all those women would still be where they were two years ago, starving, penniless and alone. Now they have meat on their bones, hope in their hearts and a sense of belonging, or purpose. It was Kitty, not Katerina, who gave them that, silly skirts and all.'

In that moment, I couldn't love Gillian more. Though of course I do not tell her this.

'Kitty!'

Connie's excited voice fills the air and I look up to see her standing in the doorway, her arms full of leftover sweet peas.

'Aggie said to tell you that the guests have arrived and they're bloody famished.'

'What a greeting,' laughs Gillian, taking a tray of pies from the top of the counter and heading for the door. 'Come on, Connie, put those flowers down and let's go and feed them.'

An hour later, the women are still at the tables. It is a perfect late summer evening, and the air is full of their chatter and laughter. While Connie and Aggie attend to them, Gillian and I return to the shop to serve the steady stream of customers who, hearing of the late-night opening, have come to take advantage of the cost-price bread. I haven't seen the bakery so busy in years.

'We did it,' whispers Gillian, putting her arm around me as we stand behind the counter later. 'I'm so proud of you, Kitty.'

Just then I hear a commotion coming from the back of the queue.

'Let me through, you pathetic old crone.'

I look up to see the shambolic figure of Alfred Jennings, a man I had hoped I'd seen the last of back in Mile End all those years ago, pushing his way to the front, his face burning with cheap booze and fury. Beside me, I hear Gillian gasp.

'There's something you bird-brained women need to know,' he slurs, wobbling on his feet as he approaches the counter.

He slams his fist down and a hush descends on the room.

'This . . . this person here,' he begins, his drunken voice reverberating round the room, 'this woman serving you here is not what you think she is.'

He turns and points a fat finger at my face. Behind him, some of the customers start to mutter. 'If this is about the newspaper article,' says Connie, pushing her way to the front of the queue, 'then we've heard it all before. It's old news and none of us gathered here give a flying fig about it.

Bird-brained? Ha! We have more brains in our little fingers than you have in your entire body, you old drunk.'

Though I am grateful to Connie for leaping to my defence, I know that it is futile because I know, in my bones, what Jennings is working himself up towards. I knew it from the moment I heard his voice. My body starts to tremble as he slams his fist down once more.

'Pipe down, stupid girl,' Jennings snarls at Connie. 'This woman has corrupted you enough. It is time these poor people knew the truth. Now, how many of you ladies have husbands and sons fighting for our country?'

There is a show of hands and I spot Jean standing at the back, her face etched with confusion.

'As I thought,' he continues, turning to me with a hateful smile. 'And what would your good husbands and sons think if they knew that you were spending their well-earned money in this establishment, that you were lining the pockets of the enemy?'

There is an audible gasp which Jennings savours before continuing.

'That's right, ladies,' he says, nodding his head. 'Unbeknownst to you, the proprietor of this establishment is not an innocent young Englishwoman named Kitty Dexter. She is a German who fled her family business in the East End, my manor, to come here and take you all for fools. Not only that but her brother is serving in the German army and killing your husbands and sons as we speak. May I introduce you to Miss Katerina Drechsler.'

'Get out! You vile and wicked man.'

Gillian's voice is the last thing I hear as I flee the shop and run up the stairs to the flat.

*

It is dark outside when I hear her footsteps on the stairs.

'Kitty,' she cries, bursting into the room where I have been sitting on the threadbare armchair in a catatonic state for the last two hours. 'I am so sorry. The wicked, wicked man.'

'Are we ruined?' I say, looking up at Gillian. Her eyes are raw and swollen with tears. 'Our customers are horrified, I presume.'

'Some were,' she says, coming to me and kneeling at my feet. 'But Aggie and Connie and most of the women from the garment factory were understanding. As Connie said, you are just Kitty the baker to them, the woman who has always offered them food and kindness.'

At those words, a tear escapes from my eye, though I feel numb inside.

'Why does he hate me so?' I say, as Gillian takes a handkerchief from her pocket and gently dabs my eye. 'What have I ever done to him?'

'Nothing, my darling,' says Gillian, her face crumbling. 'People like Jennings simply see the world in black and white. He's been indoctrinated, like most people through this war, to believe that the battles should be fought on the streets as well as at the Front, that neighbour should fight neighbour. It makes me sick. It is all so futile. Poor young men being slaughtered – British and German – their lives, their hopes, their dreams, snuffed out, and for what? No, my darling, you did not bring this upon yourself, you just got caught in the crossfire of something much bigger and darker.'

'That seems to be happening a lot lately,' I say.

She kisses me lightly on the forehead and I feel my body loosen. I am tired of resisting, tired of shutting her out. I want to escape this feeling of shame and horror, want to lose myself in the soft warmth of Gillian's body. Pulling her towards me, I kiss her lips, let my tongue explore the softness of her mouth. A thousand memories cascade through me as I inhale her familiar scent, a mix of orange blossom and sugar cane, and with every kiss, every touch, I feel her returning to me.

'Are you sure you want this?' she whispers in my ear. 'You said it was over, that we could only ever be friends.'

'I want it more than I have ever wanted anything in this life,' I say, taking her hand in mine and pressing it to my heart. 'But perhaps it is too late. Perhaps you no longer want me, I . . .'

'Shh,' she says, her eyes sparkling with passion as she presses a finger to my lips. 'I want you, my darling. More than you know.'

'Do you mean it?' I say, as tears cloud my vision. 'After everything I have done?'

She nods her head and then, as gentle as a feather, kisses my tears away.

'I do,' she whispers. 'Always.'

With that, she takes my hand, and leads me to her bed.

Later, as Gillian sleeps soundly in my arms, and the moon casts a silver glow about the room, my eyes are instinctively drawn to the window. I hear voices outside and the clatter of horses' hooves.

'Darling,' I whisper, my blood turning to ice. 'Wake up. I think there's . . .'

Before the words have left my mouth, there is an almighty crash as the window shatters, glass raining down on the bed.

'What's happening?' cries Gillian, leaping up and rushing to the window.

'Gillian, no! Come away from there!'

She turns to me. I am still half-asleep. A male voice I recognize as Jennings's shouts expletives from the street below. Then, time seems to slow down. I see an object come through the gap that was once the window and hit Gillian on the back of the head with a sick thud.

I rush towards her, my legs as heavy as lead.

'Gillian,' I cry, as I hold her in my arms. There is a single line of blood running from her head to her mouth. 'My darling, please wake up. Talk to me, I beg you.'

But all I hear is a suffocating silence as Gillian grows limp in my arms, and somewhere in the distance, the sound of horses' hooves slowly beating a retreat.

27

EDIE

Mile End

Present Day

'That's the name,' says Dad, clicking his fingers. 'Miriam Ziegler. I remember it now. Sounds German, doesn't it. Which is odd, considering my old man was just about to go and off and get killed by a load of them.'

'Yes, definitely German,' says Alexander.

'They married in St Dunstan's,' I say, tears pricking my eyes. 'Just like we did . . .'

I feel the warmth of my mother's hand on my arm, but I can't bring myself to look up at her face, see the sadness, the pity in her eyes. Perhaps it was a mistake coming back here today, particularly with Alexander, dredging up the past.

I look down again at the photo in my hand and at Miriam, the slight, birdlike woman standing awkwardly in her oversized hat and horn-rimmed spectacles, as though she doesn't quite belong.

'I wonder if she was a relative?' I say, handing the photo to my father and taking my jacket from the back of the chair.

'Or perhaps a family friend,' says Alexander, shaking his head at my mother who is offering more tea.

'Yes, Miss Ziegler was more than likely a friend,' says Dad, fixing the photo back into the album. 'There's no German on our side as far as I know. We're East End through and through.'

He smiles at me and slams the album shut with a thud.

'Though, speaking of Germans,' says Dad, easing himself up from the chair, 'you've just reminded me of something. Hang on two minutes while I get it.'

'I'll have to be going, Dad,' I say, taking my cup and placing it in the sink. 'My train leaves King's Cross in just under an hour. And Alexander's got a meeting with a client.'

But my father is already hobbling out of the kitchen. I hear his footsteps on the stairs and wonder what he's up to now.

'I really do have to go now, Edie,' says Alexander, getting up from the chair.

He bids farewell to my mother, thanking her for the tea and cake, then I walk him to the door where he calls a goodbye up the stairs to my father. Dad, being partially deaf, doesn't hear him.

'I've enjoyed this afternoon,' he says, as I open the door. 'Your parents are good people.'

'If a little full on,' I say, with a wry laugh. 'Listen, thanks for all your help with Tony. I really appreciate it.'

'Any time,' he says softly. 'Safe journey home, Edie. Hopefully, if this meeting doesn't drag on, I'll be back before you. Give me a shout if you need me.'

With that he kisses me gently on the cheek and a warmth I haven't felt in months envelops me.

Closing the door after him, I feel like something is returning to me, though I am not sure what.

'Shall I make you some sandwiches to take with you, love?' says my mother when I come back into the kitchen. 'Your dad baked a lovely wholemeal loaf fresh this morning. I could slice up some ham and tomatoes to go inside. I know how you used to love that when you were a tot. You'll need a bite to eat. It's such a long journey, Edie.'

'It's fine, Mum,' I say, the familiar oppressive weight of my mother's concern pressing down on me. 'I'll buy something on the train if I get hungry.'

I hear her mutter something about wasting money and processed muck as my dad appears at the door. He is holding a rather tattered hardback book.

'I always meant to give this to David as he was into all that war stuff,' says Dad, handing me the book. 'It was one of the only things I took from our trips to the cottage back in the day. Oh, where's the young chap gone? I thought he might like this too.'

'He had a meeting to attend, Frank,' says Mum, rolling her eyes at my father. 'He told you that before you went upstairs. Honestly, I wish you'd listen to people.'

Ignoring my parents' bickering, I look at the book. It has a red dust jacket and the words *The Life and Work of Wolfgang Schumi: Forgotten Poet of Expressionist Berlin* written in embossed gold lettering across the top.

'I wanted something to read on the journey home,' chuckles Dad. 'So I grabbed that from the shelf in the cottage. When I got on the train, I opened it and found the whole thing was in German. Anyway, it had a bookmark in it, or what I thought was a bookmark, a folded-up bit of paper. Looks like a letter of some sort but that's written in German too.'

'Dad, I don't understand what any of this has to do with me,' I say impatiently. 'David's . . . David's gone. And I don't know anything about German poetry.'

'It was the postmark of the letter,' he says, pointing a shaky, arthritic finger at the back of the book. 'November 1918. Thought it might be a soldier writing to his sweetheart. Just with what you were telling us about the box and the recording, well, it might be connected somehow.'

'Possibly,' I say, stuffing the book into my bag, one more heavy load to carry. 'Thanks, Dad. Now, I really had better be off.'

'I'll walk with you to the Tube,' he says, grabbing his blue fleece jacket from the hook by the door. 'Could do with some fresh air.'

After saying my goodbyes to Mum and assuring her that I'll call to let her know I've got home to the cottage safely and that I'm fifty-six years old not twelve, Dad and I set out along Mile End Road towards the station.

'You're looking well, Edie, despite it all,' he says, his voice rasping with the exertion of keeping up with my brisk walking. 'Your mother and I do worry, though, what with you living so far away. Are you sure it's the right thing, love? After all, times like this you should be around family and this place is your home, always has been, always will be.'

With that, a police car rushes past, its piercing siren causing my dad to cover his ears. We watch as the car pulls up outside the off-licence where two young men are engaged in a heated argument. As they're bundled into the police car, I'm reminded of the two shadowy figures standing in the living room, the way David paused at the door, then turned and mouthed to me, 'Call the police.' I remember my hands were shaking so violently I could barely press the numbers 999. I could hear raised voices, one of them addressing David by his full name, and then a thud. For as long as I live, I will never forget that sound.

'It's peaceful in Cornwall,' I say, turning to Dad as the police car pulls away. 'And that's what I need now. I can think clearly, and the great thing is that I'm painting again. I'll never get over him, Dad, and this place, well, it's just full of memories.'

My father nods, his eyes clouding.

'I understand,' he says, squeezing my arm. 'And I can't imagine how someone ever recovers from what you've been through. We just miss you, that's all.'

'And I miss you both too. You should come down to Cornwall soon. I'd love that.'

'We'll see, love,' he says unconvincingly. 'My arthritis is getting worse, though, and your mother's never been the same since she had that knee operation. We're falling apart, the pair of us.'

I smile, knowing full well that though they do have health issues, wild horses wouldn't drag my father away from the East End.

''Ere,' he says, as we pass a row of shops. 'All that talk of Sam earlier reminded me. This was his shop. He was a baker, you know? Must be where I get my bread-making skills from.'

He has stopped outside a boarded-up premises, wedged between a pawnshop and a fried chicken joint.

'Hang on, wasn't this an estate agent back in the eighties?'

I say, looking up at the tall Victorian windows. 'I seem to recall coming here with David when we were bought our first flat.'

'I think it was, yes,' says Dad. 'But they closed in 2008, probably went online like the rest of them. Anyway, a few years back, I was walking by here and saw that some builders were working on the front of it. They'd scraped off all the plastic signage and you could see the old shop sign underneath. Have a look, you can see it if you look closely.'

He points to a wooden sign above the boarded-up window. The lettering is very faint, but I can just about make out the word.

'Dexter?' I say, squinting my eyes.

'That's right,' says my father, grinning proudly. 'Dexter's bakery, Sam's place until he died in the war. Your grandma said that when they met he was running a bakery on the Mile End Road though I never knew the specific location until I walked past that day and saw them removing that plastic sign. Talk about serendipity. State of it now though, eh? Probably get knocked down or renovated into million-pound apartments. Shame. Though strange to think it was here, just round the corner from us, all this time and we never knew. It's like my old man was looking over us.'

'I think he must have been, Dad,' I say, as we walk on towards the Tube. 'Seems we really are East End through and through.'

At the station entrance, I hug Dad goodbye and watch as he shuffles back down Mile End Road, an ancient relic stepping over the detritus of a lost world. As I make my way towards the ticket gates, a sadness wells up deep inside me. I think of my mother's warm kitchen, the concern on her face: '*It's such a long journey, Edie.*' Isn't it just?

When I emerge at King's Cross station twenty minutes later, I find my train has been delayed by an hour, so I buy a coffee at Pret and settle myself into a corner table. My phone starts to ping with a dozen or so notifications, including, to my surprise, an email from Stephen Mountjoy, the curator from the British Library I messaged last week. Taking a sip of coffee, I open it and begin to read.

In it, he says that he is curious to learn more about my discovery and that the fact that the wax cylinder is labelled with the name of a German POW camp is of particular interest. He goes on to say that the Dänholm POW camp was one of the sites used in a project known as the Stimme Projekt, conducted by German linguistics professor Josef Garn, during the First World War. Most strikingly, he tells me that neither he nor his colleagues had been aware that any of the 1,600 recordings made by Garn were still at large as all had been accounted for. He ends by saying he would love to talk to me about it further and includes his phone number.

I glance at the station clock. I have plenty of time before my train arrives. Settling in my seat, I dial the number. Mountjoy answers after two rings. He sounds rather hurried but tells me he is so glad I have called.

'You see, after I emailed you I explored a little further,' he says excitedly. 'We have access to a database here at the library which details the personnel involved in each stage of the project,' he says. 'When I typed in the Dänholm sessions, Josef Garn is listed as project leader. According to the records, Garn was assisted by a young woman who was also believed to be working as a nurse in the camp. Unfortunately, her name has been erased from the records, seemingly by Garn himself, though the reason remains a mystery.'

'How odd,' I say, taking a sip of coffee. 'Why would he remove all trace of this woman if she had been such an integral part of the recording?'

'I have no idea,' says Mountjoy, sighing. 'As you say, it is most odd and, I might add, unprecedented. The project had been conducted, from its conception, in a precise academic way, every participant had been logged and photographed, the name of every poem recited, the dates and times, they are all meticulously documented. In this instance, I am inclined to believe, since the label was handwritten and the cylinder showed up in a cottage in Cornwall, that whatever is on your recording was never intended to be part of the official project. It's almost as if it was conducted in secret, a one-off that was never intended for release. Then I asked myself why? What could be on there?'

'I am just as much in the dark as you when it comes to that,' I reply, my heart sinking. 'But thank you anyway, Mr Mountjoy. For getting back to me and doing some digging. I really appreciate it.'

'Oh, sorry, Mrs Hart, I wasn't quite finished,' he says. 'I was intrigued by the fact that this woman had been erased from the records, but I found a reference, through a recording of a man named Boscombe, where he is heard addressing someone in the room as Miss Ziegler. I did a bit of digging and found a woman who fits the bill. A rather illustrious twentieth-century linguistics professor who did indeed spend time in the Dänholm Camp during the war.'

'Sorry,' I say, sitting up in my chair. 'Did you say Ziegler?'

'Yes,' says Mountjoy. 'Or to use her full name, Miss Miriam Ziegler.'

I spend most of the four-hour train journey turning the revelations of the day over and over in my head and when I arrive back at the cottage, watching the lights of the taxi disappear over the brow of the hill and fumbling with my keys, I find I am still no closer to making sense of them. As I walk up the path, I notice that Alexander's bedroom light is on. His meeting must have finished early if he is home so soon.

Once inside, I take off my shoes and pad towards the kitchen where I open the fridge and stand idly for a few moments eating the overnight oats, which were meant for tomorrow's breakfast, with a teaspoon. As I stand here, my thoughts turn to the photograph Dad showed me. What links Miriam Ziegler to Jane, my great-grandmother, and Sam, the father Dad never knew? Something brought them together, but what?

Closing the fridge, I go into the living room and take the box down from the sideboard. Lifting out the photo of the man and woman, I hold it up to the light. And it is then that I realize why Miriam Ziegler, the woman in the wedding photo Dad showed me earlier, looked so familiar. Though she is clearly much younger here, and a lot less dowdy, she has the same curled hair, the same slim figure and birdlike face, the same thoughtful expression. There is no doubt that the woman in this picture and Miriam Ziegler are one and the same. I notice something else too. The way she and the man are looking at one another. There is an intensity about it, a sense of longing. Were they having a relationship? How could that be so when, according to Stephen Mountjoy, Miriam was a German woman working on the voice project, and this man, from the clothes he is wearing, is quite clearly a British prisoner of war? So how did this German woman come to be at my grandfather's wedding? What link did she have to my family?

As usual, there are more questions than answers and my aching body is longing for bed. But as I head upstairs, there is a knock at the door.

My heart thuds in my chest. It is 2.a.m. Nobody knocks on the door at this hour unless . . . Calm yourself, Edie, I tell myself, as I tiptoe towards the door.

'Who is it?' I call out, my voice echoing off the walls.

Gripping my phone in my hand, I wait for a reply, my mouth dry with fear. Then I hear footsteps disappearing down the gravel path. I wait a couple of moments before opening the door a fraction. There is no sign of anybody. But as I go to close the door, something crackles on the other side. Opening it a little wider, I see a piece of paper tied with string around the door handle. With shaking hands, I untie it and then shut the door hurriedly, double-bolting it for good measure.

I take the piece of paper into the kitchen and sit down at the table to examine it. The paper is yellowed with age and covered with faded handwriting. The margins have been decorated with intricate drawings – a young man peering round a fence, a sword snapped in two, a hooded figure astride a horse – and their style is so distinctive, I instantly recognize them as Kitty's work. Holding the paper up to the light, I begin to read:

The Page of Swords likes to watch people. He thinks, by doing this, he can observe their motives, keep one step ahead. But the Page uses his sword to keep people at bay. He distrusts his fellow men and women, like the cruel King whose blood runs in his veins. Though the Queens of Cups and Pentacles offer him kindness, the Page shuts them out. He gives his time to those who need help of a practical nature, but he keeps his heart as sheathed as his sword. Fear will stalk his days until he sees the error of his ways. Only when he meets the Queen of Swords will he be forced to face the consequences of his actions but by then it will be too late, as Death will be knocking at his door.

My skin prickles as I put the paper down. Someone has been to the house just now and pinned this to my door. Someone who thinks I need to see it. But who? And why? I feel an old terror rippling through me as I turn off the kitchen light and make my way upstairs, Kitty's words spooling around my head: *Death will be knocking at his door.*

28

KITTY

Seven Dials

September 1918

'I thought I'd lost you,' I whisper. 'When I saw you lying there, not moving, not breathing, I . . . I was terrified.'

I wait for Gillian to respond but she just stares at me blankly from the bed where she is sitting propped up on plump pillows.

'Gillian, please talk to me,' I implore, taking her hand and pressing it to my lips. Her familiar scent of sugared violets has been replaced by the pungent, medicinal tang of camphor oil. 'I know you're in there somewhere. I can sense it.'

'Come now, dear,' says a voice behind me, a voice I have grown to depend on these last few weeks. 'You need a break. I've made a fresh pot of tea.'

I turn to see Sylvia standing in the bedroom doorway, her solid frame clad in black coat and scarf. Though I have spent years railing against this woman, this formidable phantom I had imagined to be a rival for Gillian's affections, I am now forced to admit that Gillian was right all along. Not only is Sylvia a good egg, she has also been a tower of strength to me. From organizing the best possible care for Gillian at the hospital to making sure the bakery was in safe hands as I spent day and night keeping vigil beside her bed.

'I don't know what has happened to her,' I say, getting up from my chair and following Sylvia into the living room where a pot of tea and a plate of Jean's ginger biscuits are set up on the table. 'It's as though she's here in body, but her spirit is elsewhere.'

'The doctor said it would take some time,' says Sylvia, sitting down on the armchair and pouring the tea. 'Injuries to the brain are complex, though we will have to wait and see if Gillian's silence is physical or psychological. One wonders whether the shock of the attack has affected her in a greater sense than the injury itself. Time will tell.'

'It is my fault,' I say. The events of that evening play out in front of me as they have done every day since. The hatred on Jennings's face, the smashing of glass, then the terrifying thud as the brick struck Gillian's head. 'None of this would have happened if it wasn't for me. I brought this upon her just as surely as if I had thrown that brick myself. I am cursed.'

'Come now, my dear, you are upset,' says Sylvia, handing me a cup of tea. 'And I for one set no store by curses. You and Gillian were the innocent victims of a drunken man and a baying mob. This is the price ordinary people are paying in this wretched war.'

'No, you don't understand,' I say, placing the cup on the table. 'I am not an ordinary person. I read the Tarot. I commune with the dead. I have had this . . . this ailment I will call it, for that is what it is – it was never a gift no matter how much my father tried to sugar-coat it. I have had this with me since I was six years old. It cost me my mother and my brother and now it has cost me the love of my life.'

'That is not true, Kitty.'

'Gillian?' I gasp as she walks into the room, her frail body trembling. 'Come and sit. I'll fetch your blankets.'

'No, I'm fine,' she says, taking a seat on the sofa next to me. 'I . . . I heard what you said just now. You've got it all wrong.'

'I think we need another cup,' says Sylvia, getting up from the armchair. 'And I'll warm the tea too.'

'Thank you, Sylvia,' I say, as she takes the pot into the kitchen.

Beside me, I can feel Gillian's shallow breathing.

'Darling, you really ought to be in bed,' I say, taking my shawl from the back of the sofa and spreading it over her lap. 'The doctor said you must rest.'

'I have to tell you something,' she says, turning to me, her left eye still bruised and swollen from where she fell. 'About Otto.'

'What about him?' I say, alarmed. 'Have you heard news from the Front? Is he . . .?'

'It's not that,' she says, placing her cold hand on mine. 'It's about what happened, that last time. The reading you gave. I didn't know that you were holding yourself responsible for what happened with Otto and Nancy.'

'Of course I hold myself responsible,' I say, Otto's face, twisted with anger, returning to me with vivid clarity. 'I told them they were not meant to be, that there was another love for Otto. Then Nancy broke off their engagement and he never forgave me. It is why he left to fight for Germany.

He told me I was dead to him, Gillian. What more proof do I need that it was all my fault?'

'Because it wasn't,' says Gillian, her voice barely a whisper. 'It was Nancy's father. He had already lined up a suitable man for her to marry, an Englishman with a sizeable income and good prospects. She told me this herself, shortly afterwards.'

'But Nancy loved Otto,' I say, unable to fully take in what Gillian is telling me. 'She would never let him go just because her father told her to.'

'I'm afraid that is precisely what she did,' says Gillian softly. 'When it came down to it, despite all her protestations at the Divine Order meetings, her so-called rebelliousness and independence, Nancy did as she was told. If Daddy decreed that she should drop the German and marry a solid Englishman, then that is what she would do. And she did. She broke it off for that reason alone. It had nothing to do with your reading. Like I said, Kitty, none of this is your fault. And as for saying you were responsible for my attack, well, you know that is absolute rot.'

'I was so scared,' I say, tears overwhelming me. 'I thought I'd lost you. And I knew that if you had died then I would be unable to go on. I know I'm not perfect. I'm reserved and aloof and I let my fear of being outed destroy our relationship but after today, I swear to you, I will never lose you again.'

As I hold her in my arms, my mind returns to New Year's Eve 1913. We had spent the day walking the length and breadth of Hampstead Heath, visited Kenwood House, then taken tea at a sweet little place in Highgate Village. Linking arms, we had returned to Rutland Place, Gillian's parents' grand house, in time to ring in the New Year. That day felt like a turning point for me. We were walking out in public arm in arm, not secreted in the confines of the Divine Order headquarters or darting through the shadowy labyrinthine streets of Soho. We were out in the open, a real couple at last, and no one who saw us had batted an eyelid. Letting my guard down in such a way, I had pulled Gillian to me as we stood in her parents' drawing room listening as Big Ben counted down the minutes to 1914, and I had kissed her deeply. I thought that was the beginning of us. But then her mother walked in, and I saw in her eyes that it had to be the end. I can hear myself now, the bitterness and sadness in my voice as I fled the room, telling Gillian that it was over.

'I was a coward.' I wiped the tears from my eyes. 'All I could see was my own ruin. I didn't consider you. I'm so sorry, my darling. Truly I am. And I love you. From the bottom of my heart. I love you.'

'I love you, too, Kitty,' says Gillian. 'We all do.'

She gestures to the kitchen door where Sylvia is standing.

'That's right,' she says. Then, glancing at the clock, she nods her head. 'Gillian, I think it's time.'

Gillian smiles, then turns to me.

'Sylvia and the girls have a surprise for you,' she says, easing herself from the sofa. 'Will you give me a hand to get down the stairs? I don't want to miss this.'

Taking one arm each, Sylvia and I gently guide Gillian down the stairs. When we reach the hallway, I am overcome with the delicious scent of warm baked bread.

'What is happening?' I say, as Sylvia strides on ahead before pausing at the bakery door. 'I thought we'd closed the bakery for good? As Jennings said, no one wants to do business with a German.'

'Are you sure about that?' says Sylvia, giving me a wink as she pushes the door open.

The sight that greets me as I step into the shop almost takes my breath away. The counter is decked with bell jars of biscuits and confectionery, the glass display cabinets groan with tartlets and fruit buns, jam sponges and Father's famous vanilla creams and, the most delightful sight of all, the shop is crammed with women and children clutching shopping bags. When I step behind the counter, a cheer goes up.

'Hooray for Kitty,' they cry. 'Hip hip . . .'

'Aggie and Connie have worked day and night cleaning up the mess from the looting and getting it all spick and span,' says Sylvia, coming to stand beside me. 'Connie's also been filling in for Gillian at the Federation. It seems I may have a budding suffragette on my hands.'

She gestures to Connie, who is merrily chatting to the customers while offering them free samples of cake.

'You taught her well, Kitty.'

I look up and, to my astonishment, see Jean standing in the doorway. She comes over to where I am standing behind the counter and clasps my hand in hers.

'Jean, I . . .' I say, tears coming unbidden to my eyes. 'I am so sorry for what happened, truly. I thought I was help-ing by giving you a glimmer of hope. It was wrong of me.'

'But you did give us hope, don't you see,' says Jean, ges-turing to Connie and the beaming women gathered in the room. 'My daughter was half-starved and fearful when I first came to see you. Look at her now.'

I smile as I recall Connie's timid face peeping out from

behind the curtain as I gave her mother a reading that first time, and the look of pride as she created her first sugar loaf just a few weeks later.

'I think Connie is going to surprise us all,' says Sylvia. 'She has a fine mind as well as fine baking skills.'

'Sounds like someone else I know,' says Gillian, squeezing in beside us and gently taking my hand. 'See, Kitty,' she whispers. 'I told you everything would turn out fine.'

She is right, but there is one last thing I must resolve. The following morning, while Gillian is sleeping, I sit at the small dining table and write a letter to my Uncle Klaus in Switzerland. Otto stayed with him when he fled in 1914 and, as far as I know, it was there that he made the decision to sign up to fight. Neither Father nor I had any idea which battalion Otto had joined or where he was stationed. He had kept us both in the dark for, as my father refused to condemn me for what I had done, my brother had deemed us both the enemy.

When I have finished the letter, I put on my coat and take it to the post office. The clerk looks at the address on the front of the envelope, then back at me. 'Switzerland is neutral,' I tell him, and, feeling emboldened by yesterday's events, this time I do not even attempt to disguise my German accent. He mutters something under his breath but processes the letter all the same.

As I step outside onto Shaftesbury Avenue, I feel an odd sense of release. There is nothing to hide any more, no need to run.

For the next few days, I fall back into a routine I thought had been lost for ever. While Jean serves in the shop, I once again take up residence upstairs to give my readings.

At my little table, I am privy to a myriad of stories, from the heart-warming – a recently passed grandfather coming through to tell his granddaughter that the toy rabbit she thought she'd lost in the Lyons Corner House is safe in the staff quarters – to the tragic – a young gunner killed in the first weeks of the war imploring his sweetheart to move on and find new love. It takes it out of me, emotionally and physically, so that by the time I return to the apartment in the evening where Gillian is being fed warm chicken broth by Connie, I feel utterly spent.

This evening, however, something feels different. I sense it as I ascend the staircase and place my hand on the door handle. Before I have even entered the room, I know what is coming. Death, as I have always said to my clients, is a palpable thing for me: I can smell it, taste it, touch it. I know when it is near. So tonight, as I walk into the flat and see the letter propped up on the table, the Swiss postmark stamped in red, I do not even have to open it – though in the end I will – to know what is written inside.

Hours later, when Gillian finds me sitting at the table, the letter open in my hands, she will take it and read what I already knew, what, if I am honest, I have known in my heart all along:

My dearest Katerina,

Thank you for your letter, which arrived today, and sincerest apologies that the news I am about to impart has come to you so late. When it happened I sent word, along with a parcel of your brother's possessions, to your family address in East London – though I see from your letter that you have had a change of residence.

Katerina, it is with great sadness that I must inform you of the death of your brother, Otto. I hope that you are not alone when you read these words and that you have someone to support you in your hour of grief. According to reports from his battalion leader, your brother was found in an abandoned barn in Northern France in September of this year. He had a gunshot wound to the head. As he had recently fled his battalion on the eve of battle, his officers concluded that he must, tragically, have taken his own life.

29

MIRIAM

Dänholm Prisoner-of-War Camp

October/November 1918

For as long as I live, I shall associate the Welsh accent with a sorrow and despair so deep I fear it will take my breath away.

Today we are recording the stories of a recently captured Welsh battalion. As each man steps up to the recording horn, waxing lyrical about his blissful childhood, the lamb cawl his mother cooked, the smell of the colliery furnace, the soul-lifting fervour of the male voice choir, the pride of the valleys, I search his face for answers. Because, for now, I do not care about their stories. I just care about Jo. Do they know that he has been killed? Were they there? And, more chillingly, could one of them be his murderer?

'Thank you, Mr Evans,' says Herr Garn, as a slight young man with a pronounced lisp steps down from the platform.

The professor's voice shows no trace of emotion, no sense that he is distracted by the news of a prisoner's death. I watch him closely as he sits at the small desk beside the recording platform, spectacles perched on the edge of his nose, silver pen scratching his observations of each man's diction, dialect and tone. Could he have alerted the killer to Jo's movements? Could he have seen him knock on my door and walk away?

At this thought, I relive the events of the previous evening as though they are being performed on a stage in front of me: Herr Garn, his face rendered silver in the glare of the searchlight, talking intently to the commandant, his words stabbing at my head as I run back to my room. Jo's stricken face at the door. His need for me. The warmth and urgency of our lovemaking.

'Next, please?'

As the young man, who introduces himself as Private Lownes, a farmer's son from Pembrokeshire, begins to tell his story, I hear Jo's voice whisper, '*Are you there?*'

Why, oh, why did I fall asleep after we made love? Why didn't I stay awake for him? I am as bad as the disciples who let Christ suffer alone in the Garden of Gethsemane. For though I suspect Herr Garn was the informant and any of these young men could be the killer, it was me who slept through his agony, me who made him feel he was alone. If I had stayed awake, I could have stopped him from leaving. Instead, he walked out to his death. 'My God,' I exclaim, 'I have killed him.'

'Fräulein Ziegler?'

Snapping out of my agitation, I look up to see Herr Garn and the remaining prisoners looking at me. Herr Garn has got to his feet, the young man on the platform smiles uneasily.

'Fräulein Ziegler,' says Herr Garn, taking me by the arm and leading me to the back of the room. 'What is the meaning of this?'

'I don't know what you are talking about, Herr Professor.'

'Your outburst just now, talking of killing somebody. What kind of impression are you giving to these men? That we Germans are insane, that we flash our eyes and bare our teeth and speak absurdities?'

'I . . . I am sorry,' I begin, as the realization that I have inadvertently spoken those words aloud dawns on me. 'I forgot myself momentarily.'

'Fräulein Ziegler,' says Herr Garn, his voice grave. 'May I remind you that we are here as representatives of the University of Berlin, an exemplary institution of research and learning, and that we must conduct ourselves in a way befitting such an institution at all times.'

'Yes, Herr Professor.'

'We are not here to get close to these men or their situation,' he says, his eyes blazing. 'Or to let emotions get the better of us. I have been informed of the prisoner's death as, I suspect, have you but we cannot allow such an incident to get in the way of this project. Do I make myself clear, Fräulein Ziegler?'

I nod my head, but my eyes are full of tears and Herr Garn, the room, the men, the wretched recording horn, are but an indistinct blur of colour and sound as I make my way back to the platform to resume my duties.

The last of the men is just finishing his story when the door opens, and the formidable figure of the commandant enters the room. I freeze as I watch him speak to Herr Garn, then cast his eyes around the room. The young man on the platform seems to sense my discomfort.

'Don't worry, love,' he says, flashing a grey-toothed smile at me. 'His bark's worse than his bite. We've already had a visit from him and his thugs this morning. They're trying to find out who killed Boscombe.'

'Boscombe?' I say, my body growing limp. 'The man who was killed last night was Harry Boscombe?'

'That's right,' says the young man. 'God rest his soul. He was a good lad too. Wouldn't hurt a fly. Which begs the question, why would anyone want to kill him?'

Relief courses through my body. The same question runs around my mind as I make my way back to my room later that evening. My darling Jo is alive. I will see him again. The dark thoughts that have invaded my mind all day – of him suffering in his final moments, of the fact that I never got to say goodbye, of the indescribable pain he must have felt as he slipped away – begin to lift. But then another troubling thought comes to me, as I recall the words of the young soldier in the studio earlier. Why would anyone want to kill Harry Boscombe? The question festers inside me as I fumble for my keys in the darkness, oblivious to the oil lamp glowing in the window. So preoccupied am I with thoughts of poor Boscombe's demise, for a few moments I do not notice that the door is unlocked. Until I hear movement from inside and, with a sickening dread, I stand frozen on the other side of the door, still holding the key in the lock.

'Who . . . who is there?' I call, my voice trembling both with fear and with the biting cold.

Tentatively, I push the door open. There is a man standing by the fireplace, his back to me. He turns as I enter, and I am relieved yet puzzled to see that it is Private Singh.

'My sincere apologies for letting myself into your rooms,' he says, coming towards me. 'I did not want to arouse suspicion from the guards by loitering outside. And when I found the door unlocked, I thought it safer if I wait inside for your return.'

I think back to this morning. I had been in such a state when I heard the sirens, I had fled the room without thinking to lock the door.

'What are you doing here?' I ask, keeping my hand on the door handle. 'What do you want?'

'I have come with a message,' he says, his dark eyes solemn. 'From your friend. I take it you've heard about Boscombe?'

'Yes,' I say, tears coming to me unbidden. 'It's . . . it is terrible. But when I first heard the news I thought it was . . . you see, we have been . . .'

I stop, emotion getting the better of me.

'I know, Fräulein Ziegler,' says Singh softly. 'And really, you do not need to explain yourselves to me. You are both consenting adults. What you do is your business not mine. He wanted me to give you this. He said it explains everything.'

He hands me a piece of paper, army-issue lined notepaper. It has been folded in two and on the front in beautiful cursive handwriting are the words '*Lady Lullaby*'.

'I will leave you to read it in private,' says Singh. 'And apologies again for my intrusion.'

'Thank you, Private Singh,' I say, clutching the letter in my hands. 'And take care out there, won't you?'

He smiles and nods his head, then, opening the door, scurries out into the freezing night.

As Singh's footsteps disappear round the back of the hut, I remove my hat, coat and scarf and sit on the bed.

Opening the letter I begin to read, and as I do I feel that Jo is lying beside me, speaking softly into my ear.

My Darling,

Please forgive me for writing and not coming to see you in person but when you read what I have to say you will understand that it is important I lie low for a while.

As you are probably aware by now, Harry Boscombe has been killed – and it is all my fault. It seems that Reid had grown impatient with the man he'd tasked with killing me and decided to take matters into his own hands and do the job himself. He broke into the hut by climbing through the window I had left ajar, and killed a sleeping man in my bed who he thought was me.

It was dark, my greatcoat was hanging on the bedpost. As far as Reid was concerned, it was me. He had a carving knife he'd stolen from the kitchen. Harry didn't stand a chance.

Darling, all of this is down to my cowardice. If I had faced up to Reid instead of running to you every night like a frightened child, leaving the window open for anyone to climb in, then poor Boscombe would still be alive.

So now I must do what I should have done in the first place and deal with Reid once and for all. There is no more running now, my love. I must do what is right.

Please do not try to contact me. I will come and find you once the deed is done.

Pray for me . . .

Jo

I read the letter over and over until its words are imprinted on my mind. Fear grips my bones as I contemplate its meaning. Jo is going to avenge Boscombe's death by taking on a violent killer. It cannot end well. I know that, deep in my core. But as sleep finally comes, I do as Jo asked of me, and pray for him. Keep him safe, I whisper as my eyes grow heavy and the letter drops to the floor, please God, keep him safe.

The following morning, I report for duty at the sanatorium where all the talk is of Boscombe and his grisly fate. There is a new nurse, Anna, come to replace Julia, who was sent to provide emergency cover in the high security wing, after three of the nurses there were struck down with dysentery. Anna, who looks barely sixteen, does not possess Julia's quiet efficiency and as I walk into the room she buzzes around me like a sugar-stuffed wasp.

'The doctor says he had twenty-seven stab wounds all over his body,' she whispers, as we stand by the dressing station cutting cloth into squares. 'The walls were dripping with his blood.'

'Enough of that, Nurse Matthias,' hisses Frida, appearing beside us. 'We have work to do. Now, collect the gauze and attend to Mr Preston who has scalded himself with boiling water this morning in the kitchens.'

She claps her hands and gestures to the examination table where a young prisoner is waiting.

As Anna retreats, Frida turns to me with a stone-cold expression.

'As for you, I hope there won't be a repeat of the mistake you made the other day. Now, wash your hands. I need your help stitching a head wound.'

'Yes, Matron,' I say, my heart palpitating. But as I stand at the sink and plunge my hands into the hot soapy water, a horrifying thought comes to me. Did Frida overhear what I had confessed to Julia? Has she passed this information on to anyone else? After Boscombe's death, I fear no one is to be trusted now. We are all in danger.

Weeks pass and still Jo does not come to me, though I spot Reid strutting round the exercise yard like the cock of the walk. My nights are long and lonely without him, and I spend much of them praying that he will see sense and stay out of Reid's way. I torture myself by imagining a life for both of us when the war is over. Perhaps a little apartment in Freiburg where the two of us can live while I finish my studies. I see a balcony overlooking a court-yard garden where we sit each evening, the evocative night scent of jasmine filling the air, while we sip wine and discuss the events of the day. But then, in darker moments, I chastise myself for harbouring such dreams. After all, Jo is a British soldier and I, as a German, am his enemy. What hope have we of building a life together when so much blood has been spilt in the name of our respective nations?

Yet such thoughts have sustained me these last few weeks, given me hope, however tenuous, that he may return to me. They are still there in my head this morning as I assist Frida at the surgical station, attending to a young man with a very low pain threshold, who screams out with every stitch Frida makes in the surface wound above his left ear. She is just finishing up when we hear shouts and screams coming from outside.

Anna, leaving her young patient with half a gauze stuck to his hand, rushes past me and opens the door.

'Nurse Matthias,' cries Frida, her face turning beetroot. 'Get back to your work this instant.'

But Anna is oblivious to the matron's strictures.

'They've got him,' she cries, rushing down the steps. 'The murderer has been caught.'

With that, both the injured prisoners leap from their respective tables and rush outside. Frida and I reluctantly follow but what I see makes my blood run cold.

Jo, covered in blood and with his hands cuffed in front of him, is being escorted across the grass by two burly guards.

'They're taking him to the solitary confinement cells,' cries the young nurse breathlessly. 'He'll be executed for this.'

'No,' I cry, rushing down the steps towards him and shouting to the guards in German. 'You have made a mistake. This is not the man who killed Boscombe.'

But as they draw closer, I see that Jo is not injured, that the blood on his uniform is fresh but not his own.

When he sees me, he calmly nods his head. It is a simple gesture, but I understand at once what it means. He has exacted his revenge on Reid.

It is done.

30

EDIE

Cornwall

Present Day

'Whatever can it mean?' says Alexander, frowning, as he reads the strange story a second time.

I had turned up on his doorstep with fresh croissants from the bakery, hoping he might be able to help shed light on the strange message but also because, after what happened last night, I really didn't want to be alone in my cottage.

'I have no idea,' I say, shading my eyes from the bright sunshine beaming in through the living-room window where Alexander and I sit huddled side by side on his sofa. 'But it's obviously Kitty's work. I recognize her style from the drawings in the margin, and the story has a lot of Tarot references throughout. Perhaps it was a reading.'

'A bit dark, though, if it was,' says Alexander, handing me back the piece of paper. 'I pity the poor sod who got that as a prediction. "You're a bit of a loser as well as a stalker. You'll amount to nothing and all you can look forward to is death knocking at your door." You can imagine their response. "Oh, thanks, cheers for that."'

'But why would someone pin that to my door?' I say, as Alexander pours us both a coffee from the cafetière. 'And who for that matter?'

'Well, that's what happens when you start digging ruddy great holes in old Cornish cottages,' says Alexander, chuckling as he hands me my drink. 'This place is gorgeous, don't get me wrong, but when you've been here a while you start to realize just how ancient it is, and secretive. You only have to spend a couple of minutes with Ned, or Sue in the bakery, to see how guarded the older folk are round here.'

'You're right. But I have to be honest – it's really starting to unsettle me now,' I say, cradling the warm mug in my hands. 'I came here to heal from my husband's death, to get some peace and quiet, and now it seems I've dredged up something that should have been left well alone. And my deadline for finishing those bloody Tarot cards is growing ever closer. I just want to scream.'

Alexander smiles at me awkwardly.

'I'm sorry,' I say, aware that I'm ranting. 'I don't mean to unload like this. It's just . . .'

'Edie, I understand,' he says. 'Most people come here to escape one thing or another. I know I did but that's a whole other story. You're lucky you have your painting as an outlet, and I don't mean that as patronizingly as it sounds. I used to draw a lot when I was younger and had set my heart on becoming an illustrator, but my parents told me I needed to do something useful and I, being a coward, listened to them.'

'I didn't realize,' I say.

'You look surprised,' says Alexander, his cheeks flushing.

'Not surprised,' I say. 'It's just that you never mentioned it before. I'd thought you were more . . .'

I pause, trying to find the words.

'More city wanker?' says Alexander, raising his eyebrow. 'Hedge fund hoorah?'

'Not in the slightest. I was going to say more academically minded. You've always got a book on the go. You remind me of David in that respect.'

I regret the words as soon as they come out. Beside me, Alexander shuffles uncomfortably in his seat.

'Listen,' I say, putting my cup down on the table. 'Why don't you come with me next time I go to the beach? Bring your sketchbook. Draw something too. I'd really appreciate the company. And besides, now you've met my crazy parents, I think we've cemented our friendship, wouldn't you say?'

He looks at me aghast, as though I've just suggested we go skinny dipping. I realize that, with my reference to David just now, he may think I am overstepping the mark or, worse, flirting with him.

'Of course, if you'd rather not, I completely understand.'

'No, it's not that,' he says, smiling gently. 'It's just . . . well, oh God, here goes. Edie, I feel things have changed recently. In a good way. Since Mile End, I can't stop thinking about you. And not simply as a friend.'

He edges closer. I feel his breath on my face. For a blissful moment, I allow myself to fall into this feeling, of being desired. His lips are warm and soft against mine as we kiss. It feels different to David, it is new and unfamiliar. But then I feel his tongue press against mine. This is moving too fast. What am I doing? How could I be so disloyal to David?

'Sorry,' I say, pulling away from him. 'I . . . I can't do this.'

'No, I'm sorry,' he says, his cheeks flushing again with embarrassment. 'Edie, I didn't mean to push it. God, I'm an idiot. Look, I'll make us another coffee. Let's forget this ever happened, eh?'

He gets up, grabbing the cafetière and almost dropping it in his haste to escape. I hear him filling the kettle in the kitchen and my heart sinks. Have we just ruined the beginnings of a good friendship? Getting up from the sofa, I go across to the window and stand looking out at Alexander's carefully tended garden. Jupiter has commandeered a sunny spot on the drystone wall where he lies basking in the sun. Don't let this spoil things, I tell myself, but as I turn from the window, I notice something on the seat below. An A4 notepad, folded open. Looking closer I see, written in Alexander's distinctive neat hand, the following:

Re: Planning App. Things to consider:
Funding.
Timing.
Approval.
Villagers?
Consent.
Kerb appeal?
Edie? Will she be happy with this? Get her on side.

Get her on side? Then, with a sinking feeling, I realize what this has all been about. The friendship, the helping me find Tony George, the little speech about how he can't stop thinking about me, the bloody kiss. He has just been buttering me up so he can get his hands on my cottage or extend into it or whatever that bloody application is all about. I am furious with myself as I march out of the house and head back to Moonstone. How can I have been so stupid?

When I reach my gate, I see a figure standing by the front door and my heart sinks. Not him. Not now. I'm really not in the mood.

'Hello, Ned,' I say wearily. 'What can I do for you?'

The old man turns and walks towards me down the gravel path.

'I've come to fix that slate,' he says, dispensing with any need for small talk. 'Like I said I would. I came over yesterday but you weren't in. Didn't like to start without your permission.'

'Yes, I was up in London on business,' I say impatiently. 'Again, it's rather late in the day, though, Ned. Might it be better if you come back in the morning?'

'Got another job on tomorrow,' he says, folding his arms. 'And I'm working the rest of the week in St Ives. I can do it now or come back next week, but there's rain forecast this weekend and I don't fancy your chances of avoiding a leak. Your choice.'

'All right,' I sigh. 'Go ahead. I'll bring you a cup of tea out.'

He nods his head and as I leave him to assemble the ladder, I actually feel rather reassured that he will be here for the next few hours, an extra pair of eyes to watch for any unwanted visitors. Now that I know Alexander cannot be trusted I will not be calling on him for help any time soon.

I head into the house and fill the kettle. I can hear Ned clambering onto the roof above me and I pray, for both our sakes, that he doesn't come crashing through the ceiling. As

I wait for the kettle to boil – and I don't know whether it is guilt at the kiss with Alexander just now – I find my mind returning to the night of 12 October and another detail I had blocked out. They had been wearing steel-capped boots. The sound of Ned's footsteps on the roof brought it back to me. Thud, thud, thud, as they made their escape, the noise mirroring the pounding of my heart.

Just then the phone rings in my hand and I get such a fright I almost send it clattering to the floor.

'Hello,' I say, my nerves settling when I see my father's name on the screen.

'Edie, is that you?' he says, speaking extra loud as he always does on the telephone.

'Who else would it be, Dad?'

'Ever the comedian,' he says, pausing to deliver a succession of hacking coughs. 'Sorry about that. Your mother's been burning scented candles and they're playing havoc with my lungs. Anyhow, listen, I've found something out about my grandmother. About Jane.'

'Really? What?'

'Well, I couldn't rest after hearing what that old fella was saying about us not being related to the owner of the house,' he says, his voice muffled by the sound of shuffling papers in the background.

I smile. Old fella? Ned is about the same age as Dad though my father, who sees himself as eternally twenty-five, would be horrified to admit this.

'Ah, here it is,' he says. 'Like I said, all that talk about us not having a legal claim to the cottage was bothering me, so I dug out the will again, and you'll never believe it.'

'What, Dad? What is it?'

'I can't believe I'd forgotten, but it was so long ago when I got the will, and I was just a young man excited to have been left a cottage. I didn't care what name was on there. Also, you know how my eyesight's always been bad.'

'Dad, what does it say?'

'Well, it looks as though my grandmother simply liked to be known as Jane,' he says, 'though it wasn't her legal name. People like to do that, you know. Your mother's father always went by his middle name, Raymond, though his first name was John.'

'Dad,' I say impatiently, as Ned hammers the roof above my head, 'will you cut to the chase.'

'Sorry, love,' he says, his voice booming over his deafness. 'Now, let me just put my glasses on to make sure I've got it right. But, yes, here we are, her real name, her legal name, according to this was Gillian. Ms Gillian Huffingham Barnes.'

KITTY

East London

September 1918

In the end, there was only one place to go if I wanted to feel closer to my brother but as I wander through the streets of the East End, dressed in my own clothes, my Katerina trousers, jacket and cap, past boarded-up shops and houses that once bristled with life, I feel like I am experiencing the end of days.

The Tower moment I had dreaded all my life had come when I least expected it, in a moment of rare gladness. I had thought the attack on Gillian was the worst that could happen, thought that, in its aftermath, I was blooded, ready to take on whatever the world wanted to throw at me. Seeing how Sylvia, Connie and Aggie had rallied round and cleaned up the bakery after Jennings's mob had looted it, how our loyal customers had come out to support us. That evening, as I stood in the bakery among friends, I had felt for just a few moments more welcome, more accepted than I have ever felt before in London. These women, whose lives I had been privy to through the cards and in their daily chatter as they bought their bread or sat down to their cost-price meals, had opened their arms to me, had seen the Katerina that existed long ago, before the balloon incident, before Mother's death; the innocent child who loved her parents and idolized her big brother, whose greatest wish was for them all to be happy and safe.

How is it, then, that of all of us – my quiet yet stoic mother, my robust, proud father, my strong-minded, brilliant brother – it is me, the misfit sister, the girl who heard voices in her head and never fitted in, who has survived?

The air grows stale and putrid as I make my way along Mile End Road, where despair and poverty appear to have created a miasma so thick it feels like wading through quicksand.

'Look at the state of it.'

Glancing up, I see two men standing outside the tavern on the corner of the street, cigarettes pressed between their lips, tankards of ale grasped in their hands. They look at me with contempt as I pass, one of them even spits on the ground. Growing up here, dressing as I do, loving as I do, I have become immune to such reactions, but today, for the first time, I feel their hatred like a dagger to my heart. For now, the world is different. It has been tilted on its axis, for that is what it feels like when someone you love has died. They take not only something of you with them but something of the world. The thick layer of protection I had acquired around me all these years, that kept me safe from the jeers of men like these two, had been put there by my brother. He was my winter coat in a snowstorm, my sunshade in the midday heat; without him I am as I was born, thin-skinned, vulnerable to every sling and arrow flung at me, from both the living and the dead.

Now that he has gone, I am exposed, defenceless, naked with grief as I stand on the threshold of what was once our home, now a hollow box, a dolls' house left to rot. Pushing open the door, now devoid of glass, I step over a pile of post, spotting the Swiss postmark on the small parcel sent by my uncle months ago. It is matted with green mould from lying so long in this damp, dark place.

The rest of the post is so water damaged it is beyond salvaging. Kicking it aside, like a mulch of sodden autumn leaves, I take the parcel over to what remains of the counter.

In the three years since I fled, the shop has sustained further damage. The floor is rotten and full of holes, there are mouse droppings across every available surface and damp patches ooze up the walls. The portrait of my parents that once hung above the counter and that was defaced that fateful evening has been looted, leaving a dark rectangular stain on the wall. Some enterprising intruders obviously saw the value in its mahogany frame and snaffled it, likely discarding the painting on some rubbish heap along the way.

My poor father, I think to myself, as I look around this scene of devastation. He put everything into this business, all his time and expertise and every penny of his money. Unlike the other shopkeepers round here, he had bought the premises rather than take a lease, thinking it would offer security and provide a legacy for his children in the years ahead.

The parcel sits like a festering wound in my hands. Though part of me is desperate to see what is inside, another part wishes to throw it away so I don't have to suffer the sorrow I know will come from seeing Otto's things. After all, there is only so much pain a person can take before they fall to pieces.

I look down at the parcel, my uncle's elegant cursive handwriting blurred with damp, and with a trembling hand rip away the sodden brown paper. But before I get it open, I hear something overhead. Footsteps. Someone is upstairs. Grabbing the parcel, I run out of the shop and do not stop until I reach the relative safety of the number 7 omnibus.

When I alight at Shaftesbury Avenue it is quite dark, the dulled street lights and blacked-out theatres adding to the velvet-deep gloom. As I walk, my thoughts turn to the parcel. I will open it as soon as I get home. Once again, the unquiet truth returns to me, like a hammer blow. My brother is dead, I tell myself as I turn the corner onto Seven Dials; he died fighting for a country he barely knew because he thought that there was no love left for him in this place.

It haunts me to think of the fear he must have felt in those final hours, the loneliness. For if there is one thing Otto couldn't bear it was to be alone.

A flash of light fills the night sky and I look up to see plumes of orange flames rising like strange birds from the rooftops of the row of buildings. At first, I do not make the connection. Only when I see the figures huddled outside the shop, hear the heart-piercing screams and almost choke on the thick black smoke curling towards me, does the horrifying reality of what is happening sink in.

Kitty Kat's is on fire.

32

MIRIAM

Dänholm Prisoner-of-War Camp

November 1918

'*In the midst of life, we are in death,*' so the Bible tells us. This week, those two polarities have been brought to my door with a sickening reality.

On the day Jo was sentenced to death for the murder of Douglas Reid, I, oblivious to his fate, had taken a fainting turn while administering an injection to a newly arrived young prisoner. Frida had sent me to the sickbay where a flustered doctor had examined me, telling me that I was likely just overworked or underfed, and then he had muttered the immortal words, 'Well, Miriam, after four years of drought, at least we can rule out one thing – you definitely can't be pregnant.'

Until that moment, the thought had not even entered my mind. But as I lay there on the bed, I began to calculate the dates in my head. I had my last bleed in mid-September. I first slept with Jo in October. There had been no period in the meantime, but I had been so preoccupied I had not noticed the absence.

'You're right,' I said, pushing the doctor's hands from

my abdomen before he made the discovery himself. 'There is no chance of that. As you say, it is probably just exhaustion. Thank you, Doctor. I won't waste any more of your time.'

And with that I had fled the sickbay, praying that the doctor didn't suspect anything. I must keep the pregnancy a secret for as long as possible, I tell myself, let out the seams of my clothes to disguise the bump if need be, for if it is revealed I will be ruined.

And yet there is a part of me that is joyful at the thought of being with child. Though there is no way of confirming the pregnancy, I know, deep in my bones, the truth of it. I can feel it in the heaviness of my breasts and the nausea that wakes me each morning, the sudden aversion to strong smells and my revulsion to the taste of coffee. There is a life growing inside me, a life that I must nurture and care for, and yet the man who created this life with me will soon have his own taken from him.

The news that Jo had been sentenced to death came just hours after his arrest. As always in this godforsaken place, news swept through the camp rapidly, reaching the studio via a group of young prisoners, their hair freshly shorn, who whispered amongst themselves the story of the psychotic mute soldier who had embarked on a murderous spree, killing one of his own, and who will now face the firing squad.

My fainting fit had followed shortly after and as I lay in my bed that night, waves of nausea and terror bouncing back and forth throughout my body, all I could think of was that my child would grow up without a father, and I would have to live my life without the man I had given myself to, the man I had fallen in love with. And then, a horrifying thought came to me. Jo would die without knowledge of his unborn child. He would die, as he had always told me he feared most of all, alone. I had to find some way of telling him.

My answer came in the form of Julia, the young nurse I had trained and who had now been seconded to the high security wing. Julia trusted me, both as her mentor and as the person who took the blame for her error with the typhoid dosage, and when I told her that I needed her to get a note to Prisoner X, the name he goes by to all but me, she agreed to do it without question, promising to deliver it that afternoon and to be ready to receive a reply from the prisoner once he had read it.

Yet, now, two days later, there has been no response though Julia assures me that the note was delivered, and that Jo is still very much alive, his execution date not yet set. I try to get on with my duties as normal, walking from the sanatorium to the studio and back to my hut in a daze, stunned with grief but unable to share it with anyone. By its very nature, a secret love must become a secret sorrow when the end comes.

Despite my sadness, I am glad for the routine of work, the reassuring numbness of performing familiar tasks, for while I am occupied the dark thoughts are safely held at bay.

And yet I know, somewhere deep inside me, that I cannot rely on that routine, that eventually, as all things do, it will come crashing down around me. This morning, when I walk into the studio and see Herr Garn packing up the recording equipment, I know that moment has come.

'Ah, Fräulein Ziegler,' he says, looking up from his packing. 'I have been looking for you. Your matron said you had been ill. I hope you are feeling better.'

'I am fine, Herr Professor,' I say, taking short breaths to ward off the nausea rising up my gullet. 'It was just a head cold, that is all. What is happening here? Are we moving to new quarters?'

'Completely new quarters,' he says brightly. 'It is why I was trying to find you. The project has now concluded. Word has been sent from Berlin that there is no more funding.'

'Oh, Herr Professor, that is terrible news.'

'It is . . . disappointing,' he says, his moustache twitching. 'But understandable considering the circumstances. To have been able to get this far is a great feat when almost every piece of research was stalled as soon as the war broke out.'

'What will you do?' I say, looking at the recording horn which now sits redundant on the table.

'I shall return to Berlin, of course,' he says, stapling a pile of papers and placing them into a box. 'I have enough data to begin writing up my thesis. More than I thought I would have, to be honest. It is an exciting prospect. For both of us.'

'Both of us?'

'That is what I wanted to talk to you about, Fräulein Ziegler,' he says, taking off his glasses and fixing me with his sharp grey eyes. 'I have been greatly impressed by your diligence and your insight over the course of this project, particularly your insistence that we have the men tell their stories, which has proved invaluable. I see in you the makings of a fine academic. I understand you were in the middle of a philosophy degree at Freiburg, but I believe your strengths lie in the field of linguistics. If you would like to accompany me back to Berlin, I would be delighted to offer you the role of research assistant.'

The opportunity is incredible, a dream come true. It is everything I hoped and wished for as a student back in Freiburg. But now, the thought of leaving the camp while Jo is still here is unimaginable. And then there is the pregnancy. Even if I took the post at the university, once my bump began to show, I would have to resign immediately under a cloud of shame.

'Herr Professor,' I say, my voice trembling. 'That is the most gracious offer, but I am afraid I cannot accept it. I must stay here, you see. There are . . . circumstances that bind me here now.'

'Circumstances? Or people?' says Herr Garn, with a sigh.

'You . . . you know, don't you?' I whisper. 'I knew you did. You told the commandant, didn't you?'

'My dear girl, calm yourself,' says Herr Garn, leaving his box of papers and coming to sit next to me. 'If you are referring to your . . . acquaintance with Prisoner X then, yes, I do know. You are right, I did see him leaving your hut one evening. But telling the commandant? I am afraid I have no idea where that came from.'

'I . . . I overheard you talking to him a few weeks ago,' I say, dabbing my eyes with the back of my sleeve. 'On the quadrant. You were saying you had suspected it for some time. I assumed you were talking about me.'

'Ah,' says Garn, with a sigh. 'I remember now. We were

discussing the progress of the war. Both the commandant and I fear that Germany is facing certain defeat – a fear, I may add, that is becoming more real as each day passes. When it comes to you and your prisoner friend, well, as far I am concerned, your private life is your business.'

'Oh, Herr Professor,' I say, the tears I have been trying to supress for so many days finally coming forth. 'Thank you. Thank you for understanding.'

'Now, Fräulein Ziegler, I did not say I understood, I said that it was none of my business. There is a difference. What I do feel is a deep sense of concern for you. There is no happy ending to be had here, you know that, don't you?'

I nod my head, feeling my heart sink in my chest as if laden with lead.

'And even if he wasn't facing the firing squad in a matter of days there would still be no future for you,' he says sternly. 'Fräulein Ziegler, whether you like it or not, Prisoner X and his comrades are British. They are the enemy; they have killed our countrymen in battle and are no less a danger to us just because they recited some lines of poetry and recounted their childhood memories in the course of our experiment.'

'Herr Professor, it is not like that,' I cry. 'Jo . . . Prisoner X is different. He hates the war and sees no sense in killing innocent people. He loves me and I love him.'

'Fräulein Ziegler,' he says, raising his voice. 'You have lost control of your senses. As I said to you once, you have everything it takes to become a fine academic, but the first rule of academia is to remain objective. You have let your heart overrule your head. You have forgotten that we are at war.'

'I'm sorry,' I cry, putting my head in my hands. 'I didn't mean for this to happen. I was focused on my work as I have always been and then he turned up and . . . I can't explain it, Herr Professor.'

'Hush now, child,' he says, his voice softening. 'Some things cannot be explained. What do they say? Love makes fools of us all. Or, in my case, it provided the inspiration for all of this.'

He gestures to his notes, the recording equipment, the Bible still open at the Parable of the Prodigal Son.

'When I was a student, I won a year's scholarship to Oxford University,' he says, his eyes glistening. 'It was a dream come true for a young man like me, born to a labourer and a domestic servant, neither of whom could read or write. I had thought gaining entry to my provincial university in Bavaria was grand enough but Oxford, well, it was another world.'

He smiles and his face alters. The middle-aged grey academic is suddenly twenty-one again, full of life and hope.

'The problem with Oxford, as I soon discovered,' he continues, 'was that though they would let you into their lecture halls, the inner sanctum, the social hierarchy, remained firmly closed to people like me. To the men who ran the societies, I would always be the son of a Bavarian labourer and no quantity of first-class grades would change that. So I looked elsewhere for my social nourishment and that is when I met Sally.'

'Sally was your sweetheart?'

He nods his head and smiles wistfully.

'She worked behind the bar in the Fox and Grapes in Thame, a small town outside of Oxford,' he says.

'Her father was the landlord and she and her mother cooked the meals and served the ale. She was a shy girl with a mop of straw-coloured hair that would fall across her eyes as she spoke. But it was her voice that sealed it for me. When I first heard it, I was mesmerized. It had a lilt to it I have never encountered before or since, a cadence that, upon hearing it, made you feel like you had fallen under a spell.'

His voice falters then and he clears his throat.

'We spent a blissful summer together and then, come autumn, I had to return to Germany,' he says, taking a handkerchief from his pocket and dabbing his eye. 'But we parted on good terms, and we wrote to each other almost every day, pledging that when the time was right, she would visit me and . . . well, I had planned to propose to her though I never told her this in my letters. I wanted it to be a surprise.'

He takes a deep breath, then continues.

'One morning, I came down to the post room in my university halls,' he says. 'And I saw an envelope with an Oxfordshire postmark though the handwriting on the front was not Sally's. I opened it and what I read tore my world apart. It was Sally's mother, writing to inform me that her daughter, my love, had died of influenza.'

'Oh, Herr Professor,' I say, placing my hand on his sleeve. 'I am so sorry. You must have been devastated.'

'I was,' he says, wiping his eyes. 'But instead of brooding on it, I threw myself into my work for I now had a mission. As I said to you, what drew me to Sally, what had caused me to fall in love with her so deeply, was her beautiful voice, that melodious accent I had never heard before. So I vowed to find it again, dedicating my life to collecting voices, like butterflies in a net, in the hope that I would one day hear hers again. Though in all my years of searching, I have never found an accent or a voice to match hers, not even close. I suppose that is the mystery and heartache of love.'

'I suppose it is,' I say.

'Before I forget,' he says, taking the square cardboard box we use to store the records of the participants, 'I have something for you.'

I watch as he flicks through the various documents before pulling out a photograph.

'I took this by accident,' he says, handing it to me. 'I was testing the light and inadvertently managed to capture the two of you. Of course, you should have the photograph. It is of no use to me or the project as Prisoner X was not a participant.'

I look down and see a rather blurred image of me, sitting at my desk, looking up into Jo's face. The moment we first met. My eyes fill with tears as I notice the fear in his face, the sorrow he was hiding.

'Thank you, Herr Professor,' I say, slipping the photograph safely into my pocket. 'This means so much to me.'

'You're very welcome,' says Herr Garn, collecting himself. 'Now, Fräulein Ziegler, I have a meeting with the commandant to discuss my transport arrangements to the mainland. Can I leave you to pack away the rest of the equipment?'

'Of course, Herr Professor,' I say, resuming my professional head. 'Leave it to me.'

It is getting late when I finally finish stacking Herr

Garn's books into the packing boxes. My arms ache and I feel rather faint as I slump into the rigid wooden chair by the recording platform. Leaning forward to offset the light-headedness, I hear something, a noise coming from the corridor.

'Is that you, Herr Professor?' I say, going to the door where I press my ear to the glass and listen.

'It is me,' says a voice that makes my whole body constrict. 'I have to see you. Let me in.'

I open the door and fall into his arms.

'Jo,' I cry, as he guides me back into the room, closing the door behind us. 'What are you doing here? How did you get out?'

'Your friend Julia,' he says, casting his eyes across the packed boxes. 'I bribed her. Said I would translate a letter she had received from her British sweetheart in exchange for a few hours with you.'

'Julia has a sweetheart?' I exclaim. 'She told me she had never—'

'It is none of my business,' he says. 'And under the circumstances, it hardly matters.'

'Jo, why did you do it?' I say, wishing that I could freeze this moment, make time stand still. 'Why did you kill Reid? I know Boscombe's death affected you, but to sacrifice your life like this. I do not understand.'

'I tried to reason with Reid,' he sighs, his voice hitching as he speaks, 'to call a truce and stop this crazed vendetta of his. But he crossed a line, said that he would come and find you and . . .'

'And what?'

'And finish what he had set out to do the day I rescued

you,' says Jo, his eyes flashing with rage. 'He meant . . .
he meant to violate you. At that, I saw red and lurched
for him. He took out a knife he had swiped from the
kitchens. I wrestled it from him and . . . Look, I want you
to know that I am not some cold-hearted killer. You must
believe me.'

'I do,' I say, a shiver rippling through me at the thought
of Reid coming for me.

'Good. Now, there is something I want you to do for
me. We must be quick. I do not have long.'

I look at him in bewilderment. He has not mentioned
the baby. Did he even receive the letter? Does he care that
I am pregnant?

'What is it?' I ask, watching as he roots around amongst
the boxes. 'What do you want?'

'I want you to record me,' he says, looking up at me, his
eyes wild.

'Record you? But why?'

'Please,' he says, coming to me and taking my hands. 'I
don't have much time. Will you do it?'

'I don't know if I can,' I say. 'Everything has been packed
away except the recording horn.'

'What about these?' he says, holding up a box of wax
cylinders.

'Those are spent cylinders,' I say, going over to him.
'Spoiled recordings that will not be used.'

'Can you record over them?' he says, taking one and
handing it to me. 'Is that possible?'

'I suppose so,' I say, taking the cylinder. 'Though I don't
know why you feel the need to do this. I didn't know the
Parable of the Prodigal Son meant so much to you.'

I let out a hollow laugh, but it is clear he is in no mood for joking. And to tell the truth, neither am I.

'Please, Miriam,' he says. 'Set it up for me.'

I nod my head and make my way over to the recording horn, realizing, as I switch it on, that he has just used my name for the first time. It should be a poignant moment, but it feels like an elegy.

I hear him pacing behind me as I set the cylinder into the coil, muttering under his breath.

'It is ready,' I say, turning to him. He stops, his face red, beads of sweat gathered on his forehead.

He nods, then steps up to the platform, his face inches from the recording horn.

'On a count of three,' I say, my heart pulsating. 'One, two, three . . . go.'

He clears his throat and then begins.

And I do not know what is more astonishing, the message that follows or the fact that he imparts it in an accent that is as German as my own.

33

EDIE

Cornwall

Present Day

It is almost midday by the time I get to the beach, and I chide myself for sleeping late as I have missed the best of the morning light. It had been almost eleven by the time Ned finished fixing the slate and after he had left, I had spent the night tossing and turning, plagued by disturbing dreams of hooded men armed with swords.

My body aches with tiredness as I slip off my flip-flops and sink my bare feet into the warm, golden sand, but aware that I have two drawings to complete today, I shrug off my exhaustion and focus on the task at hand. As I settle into my usual spot, however, I turn to see a familiar figure heading across the beach towards me.

Alexander.

'Fancy some company?' he says, smiling as he places a large jute bag and deckchair on the sand beside me. 'I brought some sandwiches with me. Egg and cress and cheese and tomato seems to be all they have in the bakery. Do say if you'd rather be alone, though. I'd completely understand.'

'It's a public beach,' I say frostily. 'I can't dictate who does or doesn't come here.'

'Edie, I wanted to apologize,' he says, lowering himself gingerly onto the deckchair. 'About yesterday. The kiss. I feel I crossed a line and . . . well, I hate to think that I've upset you.'

'It didn't upset me,' I say, keeping my eyes fixed on the horizon.

'Oh, that's a relief,' he says. 'It really is. I would hate you to think I was taking advantage. I value our friendship and I know how difficult it must be for you to move away from London and start a new life here, particularly after . . .'

'After David?' I say, staring into the sea as sharp golden sunlight glints on the waves. How far away that life seems now, how out of reach. And yet how beautiful it was, how happy we were, until that night. 'To be honest, there was no other way. The London I knew with David has ceased to exist for me.'

'I can relate to that,' says Alexander. 'When Carole – my ex-wife, that is – left, I spent six months sitting on the sofa in some sort of vegetative state. I only left the flat to go to work and even then, I made sure I was out of there at six on the dot so I could avoid having to socialize. In the end, it was an old friend who brought me to my senses. Graham came over one Sunday afternoon, told me that it was ridiculous to be sitting wallowing in an empty penthouse flat when, in his words, "There's a world of happiness out there, waiting to be found." It was through him that I found this place. He'd just come back from a holiday here and spoke so warmly of Cornwall and the beautiful beaches I decided to come and find out for myself. It was then I finally came to my senses about Carole and how trapped I felt with my whole situation.'

'You felt trapped?' I say, intrigued despite myself.

'It's like I was telling you about the drawing,' he says. 'All my life I've felt that I should do as I'm told, follow convention, not take the road less travelled. I did it with my studies and I did it with Carole, sadly. We met at university. She was intelligent, beautiful and, though there wasn't much of a spark, she got on with my parents and that's what sealed it for me. It sounds so lame, doesn't it? I married a woman who I didn't love because my dad approved of her. But I'd been brought up to believe that passionate love, following your dreams and all that, only happened in the movies.'

'So what changed?'

'She had an affair,' he says, with a sigh. 'Though I don't blame her. It seems she was just as unhappy as me. And who was I to deny her the great love she was seeking? I was actually grateful to her for doing it, for saying enough is enough. If she hadn't then we'd probably still be together, flittering miserably around our sterile penthouse flat thinking about the lives we could have had.'

'So you set your sights on Cornwall,' I say, turning to him. 'You must have big plans for the cottage?'

'Plans?' he says, his eyes fixed on the distant sea. 'My only plan was to find some solace. Though everyone said I was making a big mistake. With the exception of Graham, my old uni mate, all my friends said I was having a mid-life crisis and my parents predicted I would be back in West London with my tail between my legs within six months. And yet all I've felt since coming here is a great sense of freedom and relief. I feel like I'm eighteen years old again but this time I'm in charge of my choices.'

'If David's death has taught me anything,' I say, still unable to shake the feeling that he is not telling me the whole story, 'it's that life is precious. You can't waste it living a lie.'

'That man has inspired me, and I never even met him,' says Alexander. 'His wife is doing a pretty good job of inspiring me too.'

He smiles and his cheeks flush.

'Again, I am so sorry for what happened yesterday,' he says, turning in his seat to face me. 'That kiss, I—'

'Oh, for goodness' sake, Alexander,' I cry, hating this feeling of being duped. 'I've told you it wasn't the kiss that shocked me. I know you're hiding something from me. I saw my name on the—'

A piercing noise cuts through my words. I look down and see my mobile flashing at my feet with a number I do not recognize. With Alexander's eyes upon me, I grab the phone and press Answer.

'Hello,' I snap.

'Mrs Hart, is that you?' It's a woman speaking – she sounds agitated and out of breath.

'Yes,' I say. 'Who is this? Is everything all right?'

'Oh, Mrs Hart, it's Sue from the bakery. Listen, I'm at your cottage. You have to come quickly. Something's happened.'

34

KITTY

Seven Dials

September 1918

'I am not welcome here any more. That is quite clear.'

Standing in the burnt-out shell that was once Kitty Kat's, amid the blackened walls, the smashed glass and the acrid scent of petrol fumes and smoking cinders, I know that my time is up.

'It could have been much worse,' says Sylvia, lending Gillian her arm as she comes up the step from the street. 'Thank goodness Connie and the girls were at my talk yesterday evening. If not, I dread to think what would have happened.'

'Oh, Kitty,' cries Gillian when she sees the extent of the damage. 'How could they do this to us? How could they be so cruel?'

'They haven't done it to "us", Gillian,' I say, trying to repress the anger in my voice. 'They have done it to me. You, Sylvia, Aggie and Connie are not the targets here. It is the crazy German woman they wanted to kill. Like I said, I am not welcome here. There is nothing else for it but to leave London.'

'Leave London?' says Gillian, sobbing. 'But where will we go?'

'I don't include you in that statement, Gillian,' I say. 'I'm the one who should leave. I can't keep putting you in danger like this. You will be safe here without me.'

'What are you talking about?' cries Gillian, loosening herself from Sylvia and hobbling to my side. 'You can't abandon me. Not after everything we've been through.'

'I'm not abandoning you,' I say, pulling her towards me. 'I'm setting you free. You could have died on two occasions because of me. Next time, we won't be so lucky.'

'Well, wherever you're going I'm coming with you,' she says, wiping her eyes with the back of her sleeve. 'I can't lose you again. I won't.'

'Gillian, you have your work with the Federation here,' I say, glancing over at Sylvia who appears to be lost in thought. 'I know how much that means to you. I can't drag you away from that. You would never forgive me.'

'I think what you both need is a little holiday,' says Sylvia, her calm voice a balm amid the mayhem of the last twenty-four hours. 'A chance to take stock, and for Gillian to recuperate properly. And I think I may have the solution.'

'My friend owns a cottage in Cornwall that has lain empty since the beginning of the war,' she tells us over a pot of tea in the dining room of the Roseberry Hotel in Covent Garden to where Gillian and I have temporarily decamped. 'It's a sweet little place on the outskirts of the village of Holton. Very close to the coast too, so Gillian could take advantage of the bracing sea air. I know Vivienne has been looking for tenants but they're thin on the ground. I could write to her this afternoon and tell her you're interested. What do you think?'

'Cornwall?' says Gillian, spitting out the word as though it is a piece of gristle. 'But that's so far away. Whatever would we do there?'

'Nothing much is the answer,' says Sylvia, stirring her tea. 'And that is the whole point. You would be going there to rest and to get well. Then once things have settled here you can come back.'

'But what about the Federation?' says Gillian. 'And the families I've been helping? I can't just abandon them.'

'No, you can't,' says Sylvia briskly. 'And you won't. You will be taking a period of convalescence, during which time Connie can fill in for you. She's been doing a sterling job since your accident.'

Gillian's cheeks flush. I can see it rattles her to think that the fifteen-year-old shop girl she took pity on is rising through the ranks of the Federation and winning the admiration of Sylvia.

'You've taught her well,' adds Sylvia, sensing Gillian's unease. 'And you can continue to mentor her when you return. Now, Kitty, what do you say? How does Holton sound to you?'

Holton. I roll the name around my tongue. It feels warm and enveloping, crisp and new. It feels like space to breathe and room to grow, away from the prying eyes of London and the ever-present threat of the mob. It feels like waking up to birdsong and susurrating waves, sleeping soundly, and finding peace.

'It sounds,' I say, turning to Sylvia, my mind full of sunlight and sea foam, 'just right.'

'Wonderful,' says Sylvia, clasping her hands together. 'I shall write to Vivienne this afternoon. Now, drink up you two, you have packing to do.'

'This must be what purgatory feels like,' says Gillian two weeks later, sitting on the window seat and looking out at the grey Cornish drizzle. 'The only good thing is that you've started dressing like you again. No more frightful frilly blouses. But as for this place, I can't believe Sylvia thought it would be restorative. Healing? Good Lord, I'm more likely to die of boredom.'

'Come now, Gillian, it's not that bad,' I say, looking up from the large leather trunk we brought with us from London to Holton. 'Granted, it's horrid weather today but surely you can occupy yourself while I finish the last of the unpacking. Haven't you a book to read? Or what about the *Dreadnought*? Sylvia sent the latest copy in the post though it looks like it's taken half the week to get here. Apparently, Connie's written something for this issue. An opinion piece on extending the vote to working women.'

'I should be there with her,' says Gillian, sliding off the window seat. 'Not simply reading about it.'

'All in good time, darling,' I say patiently, although my irritation at Gillian's general demeanour is growing daily. 'You are still recovering. Connie is doing a sterling job covering for you in the meantime.'

'I told you, I'm feeling much better,' cries Gillian, grabbing her raincoat and galoshes from the porch. 'And I need to get back to work. I am not an invalid, Kitty. It really isn't helping me to be stuck out here in the middle of nowhere.'

'Oh, I haven't told you about my discovery,' I say, trying

in vain to lift her spirits. 'There's a deep hollow in the wall over there. I noticed it when I was setting up my reading table. I'm curious as to what its function is. Perhaps it's some sort of hidey-hole.'

'Or a catacomb,' says Gillian, shuddering. 'God, I need some air.'

She pulls the door open, letting in a flurry of wind and sodden leaves.

'Where are you going?' I say, watching as she wrestles with the buttons on her raincoat. 'It's blowing a gale out there. You'll catch your death.'

'Kitty, please. I'm not a child,' she says, slamming the door behind her.

I make to go after her but then stop myself. Let her blow off some steam. Who knows, the bracing weather might just do her some good.

While the wind whistles down the chimney breast, I take the trunk over to the fireside and settle myself onto the thick woven rug. A warm sensation fills my body as I absorb the sounds of the cottage, the whistling wind, the creaking joists, the caw of the seagulls as they chatter on the roof. Gillian may not feel rejuvenated by Cornwall, but I certainly do. The peace here is like nothing I have ever experienced before. I can hear my thoughts as well as the voices that were always clamouring to be heard amid the noise of London and the loved ones of the numerous people I read for.

My cards sit on the reading table I have set up by the wall next to the fireplace. I cast a glance at them, my fingers tingling. Do I have time for a reading? Just a quick one while Gillian is out. But then I turn to the trunk and its overflowing contents, my father's voice in my head: '*Attend to the task in hand, Katerina. There will be time for leisure when the day's work is done.*'

He is right, of course, and I feel a deep sense of satisfaction as I remove and fold various items of clothing from the trunk, stacking them into neat piles beside me. When the clothes are clear, I reach my hand into the box and pull out something heavy and damp.

It is the parcel sent from Otto's battalion, the parcel I had intended to open the night of the fire. A deep sense of dread washes over me as I look at the sodden brown paper, the faded handwriting. Am I ready to see what is inside? Should I wait until Gillian returns and we can open it together?

'*Enough procrastination, Katerina,*' implores my father, his voice hovering over me. '*Open the damn thing.*'

I do as he says and tear off the paper, my heart thudding in time with the rain pounding on the windowpane.

Inside there is a pocket notebook, a cap and a locket. I steel myself, preparing for the gut punch when I see Otto's handwriting and Nancy's picture which, despite what happened, will undoubtably be in the locket.

But when I open the book I see, to my astonishment, another man's handwriting, page after page of it. Looking closer, I see that the writing is in English and littered with misspellings. It is a dry and dull account of a British battalion's food supply in the trenches which, after the seventh page of listing cabbages, tea and canned meat, the writer – thankfully – gives up on. It must be a mistake, I say, grabbing the locket and digging my fingernails into the thin clasp, that is not Otto's pocketbook. The locket snaps open, and the image inside confirms my suspicions: a heavyset, dark-haired woman stares sternly out from the photograph. She looks to be in her late thirties, and is quite clearly not the blonde, birdlike Nancy.

Turning to the damp remains of the parcel, I see a piece of lined notepaper stuck inside. The handwriting is faded but I see the insignia of Otto's German battalion clearly stamped at the top. *Found alongside the body*, it reads. *Returned to you with regret and condolences.*

The overworked clerical officer who posted this obviously did not have time to scrutinize either the contents of the pocketbook or the label in the cap which, on close inspection, is printed with the words *Property of the British Army.*

It is disappointing but I am strangely gladdened by this silly administrative error, relieved that I did not have to endure the heartache of seeing Otto's effects. But then another thought creeps into my head, so fantastical I can barely let it in.

If the contents of this package do not belong to Otto, then what other errors have been made? Could it be that the dead man they found that day wasn't my brother after all but the dull British private with the stern-faced sweetheart and a pocketbook full of lists? Could this mean that . . . I almost do not want to let the thought enter my head for fear that such a hope will be dashed, but I allow it in all the same. If the man they found in that barn was the same man whose possessions I hold in my hand right now it means only one thing.

My brother may still be alive.

35

EDIE

Cornwall

Present Day

'The body's still warm,' says Sue, her face riven with fear and disgust. 'All that blood too. Just horrible.'

We are standing in my living room watching as Ned Kendal retrieves the limp and bloodied body of a gull from the floor. The poor bird had crashed through the window, sending shards of glass flying and leaving a trail of blood on the ledge outside.

'Hmmm, looks like it's still breathing,' says the old man, pragmatic as ever. 'Those of a nervous disposition, you might want to avert your eyes.'

As he squeezes a gnarled hand around the neck of the bird, my legs begin to tremble, and my head feels as light as air.

'Come on,' says Alexander, sensing my discomfort. He takes my arm and guides me out of the room. 'There's no point making ourselves ill watching such a spectacle. Let's leave him to it and go to my place. I'll make us all a cup of tea. Sue, will you join us?'

'Well, I should get back to the shop, but I think a restorative cuppa might be a good idea first.'

As we accompany Alexander to his cottage, I am in a daze, rigid with shock from the sight of that bird.

'Ooh, hello, puss,' says Sue, crouching to stroke Jupiter, who greets us at the door. 'I bet you'd have made light work of that bird, eh?'

The cat, sociable as ever, wriggles away from her and flees up the wooden stairs.

'Take a seat in the front room, both of you,' says Alexander, his face pale and drawn. 'I'll go and put the kettle on.'

'I couldn't believe my eyes when I saw it,' says Sue, flopping onto the sofa with a sigh. 'That horrible bloodstain on your lovely windows. I thought it was some kind of painting at first. Ned told me you were an artist and I thought you might have – oh, I don't know – painted some decorative scene on your windows.'

'Dead seagull?' I say, trying to dismiss the image that has already burnt itself into my brain. 'I'm not sure that's the look I was going for when I decided to renovate a coastal cottage.'

'Well, quite,' says the old woman, shaking her head. 'But you never know with these modern fads, do you? There was a family moved into the village a few years back and they painted their house dark grey. It looked like something out of a horror film though my daughter tells me it's all the rage in London.'

'What's all the rage?' says Alexander, entering with a tray of mugs.

'Painting your house grey,' says Sue, taking a mug of tea. 'Have you ever heard of such a thing?'

'I'm afraid I haven't,' says Alexander, sitting down on the

leather pouffe by the fireplace. 'Though it doesn't sound quite as startling as bird kamikaze.'

'Is that what you think it was?' I say, cradling my own hot mug of tea in my hands.

'Not quite as dramatic,' he says, with a wry smile. 'But it seems as though that kind of thing can happen. According to Ned, the poor bird got blinded by the sunlight and went crashing into the window.'

'All that blood for just one little bird,' says Sue, shaking her head. 'It was a shocking sight, I can tell you. Luckily, Ned was in when I phoned him, and he removed the worst of the blood from the window by the time you got here. It was Ned that gave me your number. He said you'd been having all sorts of problems with the cottage, which doesn't surprise me, knowing what we know about the place.'

'What do you mean?' I say.

'Well, you've heard about the previous tenant, I expect,' she says, lowering her voice as though he is actually hiding behind the sofa. 'And his – what do they call it – dubious practices?'

'The devil worshipper,' says Alexander gleefully. 'Load of nonsense all that, though, isn't it?'

'We may think so,' says Sue, pursing her lips, 'good Christian folk as we are, but you can't know what dark forces that sort of thing could unleash.'

'You think the cottage is possessed?' says Alexander, leaning forward in his seat like an excited child listening to a bedtime story.

'Well, I didn't say that, but what I will say is that there was talk about Moonstone Cottage even before Mr Reynolds moved in.'

'Mr Reynolds?' I say.

'The previous tenant of Moonstone Cottage,' says Sue, smiling as Jupiter slinks into the room and jumps onto Alexander's lap. 'We all thought he was a respectable young man. A teacher, he was, at a sixth form college up at St Ives. Chemistry, I think that's what he taught. One of the sciences anyway. You'd think, wouldn't you, a man of such logical mind would not be dabbling in . . . in such dark matters as he did. But then, as Ned said, there's something rather satanic about science, isn't there, when you break it down? The lack of God. And he did tell me one day in the bakery when he came in to buy some buns and I asked if he was coming to the carol service that – what were his words again? – that was it, he said he "didn't believe in fairy tales". Can you imagine it? The baby Jesus a fairy tale? "Well," I said to him, "you can think what you like but—"'

'Mr Reynolds?' I say, stopping Sue in her tracks. 'The previous tenant was called Mr Reynolds?'

'Yes,' says Sue, taken aback at my interruption. 'Kevin Reynolds. I remember that because I have a nephew called Kevin. Lovely young man. Has a big house on Dartmoor and—'

'But I thought his name was David,' I say, placing my mug down on the table. 'David Hart.'

Alexander looks up from stroking Jupiter and gives me a quizzical stare.

'No, dear,' says Sue, shaking her head. 'There's never been anybody of that name living in the village, and I get to know everyone.'

She laughs and the sound of it puts my nerves on edge.

305

Just then there is a knock at the door. Alexander shoos Jupiter from his lap and goes to answer it.

'Probably Ned saying he's finished,' says Sue. 'He'll be off down to the beach now to dispose of the bird. And I really must be getting back to the shop. I've got a new woman working for me and though she's great with the customers she's ever so lax with the oven timings.'

I try to focus on what Sue is saying but all I can think about is the name of the previous tenant. Ned had been adamant that it was David Hart. I am suddenly gripped with an awful feeling. Did Ned actually say that, or did I imagine it? Is this another aspect of the grief fog I am wading through each day?

'Oh, by the way,' says Sue, leaning towards me, 'has Alexander told you the big news yet?'

'What news?'

'Edie?'

I turn to see my father standing in the doorway, his face ashen.

'Dad?' I say, rushing towards him. He is wearing his smart coat – the black wool peacoat he wore for David's funeral – and his best liver-coloured brogues. 'What are you doing here? Is it Mum? Is she all right?'

'Your mum's fine, darling,' he says, taking off his cap and putting it in his pocket. 'She's waiting in the car outside. I was going to call you, but I thought it best you hear this in person.'

'Hear what?' I say, while behind me Sue clears her throat. 'What is it, Dad? What's happened?'

'It's the scum that broke in that night,' he says, his voice raw with anger. 'The ones that . . .'

He pauses, gathering himself.

'Dad, please, you're scaring me now.'

'They've been released, love,' he says, taking my trembling hands in his, just as he did when I was a child and I woke from a nightmare. 'From prison. About a month ago, according to the papers.'

'Released?' I say, the room and everything in it spinning around me. 'But how is that possible? How are they out already?'

'I don't know, love,' says Dad, his eyes filling with tears at my distress. 'Good behaviour. Isn't that what they say? Anyway, we wanted to come down and check you were all right, that you were safe.'

He looks at me then and in his eyes I see what he is trying to tell me. The two men that my witness statement helped put behind bars are free. As my father guides me out of the cottage towards his car, I hear Sue whisper something about 'a dead gull – I'm sure that's a bad omen', and I realize to my horror that while I was preoccupied with that silly box and talk of devilish tenants, the real danger had been hiding in the shadows, just as it did that night. Watching me. Waiting.

36

MIRIAM

Dänholm Prisoner-of-War Camp

November 1918

Jo falls silent. The recording was only a couple of minutes long but, in that time, he managed to convey enough feeling, emotion and love to last a lifetime.

'My darling . . . I . . . that was beautiful,' I say, my eyes welling with tears. 'And I captured every word of it.'

'I'm sorry, Miriam. Truly, I am.'

'Sorry for what?'

'For everything. For killing Douglas Reid, for leaving you alone like this.'

'What's done is done. There is nothing I . . .'

The recording stops. There is no more space left on the cylinder. Thank heaven, there was just enough to capture his voice. I walk over to the platform where he is still standing, his body rigid.

'My love,' I say, holding out my hand. 'Sit with me a moment. While we still have time.'

He takes my hand and presses his mouth to it, the damp of his tears mingling with the kiss. I want to pause this moment as I have paused so many of the recordings these last few months when a hesitant young prisoner stumbled over his words, or a book clattered to the floor. I want to hold Jo's warm, solid body against mine and never let go. As we sink to the floor, pulling at each other's clothes, a blur of limbs and bare skin, I pray to be frozen in time, a fossil imprinted onto this man's body for ever, our love surviving catastrophe, the downfall of civilizations, even death itself.

'Speak often of me,' he says afterwards, as we lie together, his hand gently stroking the curve of my belly. 'To the baby. Make sure he or she knows who I was, not what I did.'

He looks up at me, his face glistening with sweat, his pale eyes full of sorrow.

'How can I?' I say. 'When I do not know that myself. You have kept so much secret, Jo. Including the fact that you are German. If you want your child to know you then you must tell me, once and for all, who you are.'

'You are right,' he says, gently extricating himself from me and grabbing his clothes that are scattered about us. 'I must tell you. Though I do not know where to begin.'

'How about the start?' I say, taking my dress from the crumpled heap of clothes and slipping it over my head. 'Where were you born?'

'Before I tell you, I want you to place that cylinder somewhere safe.' He gestures to the phonograph.

'Is this safe enough?' I say, lifting the cylinder out and placing it in my medical bag. 'If anyone asks, I shall tell them it is a new-fangled suppository.'

He smiles but his eyes are filled with sadness.

'In answer to your question, I was born in Bernau, just north of Berlin,' he says, composing himself as he buttons his shirt.

'How did a boy from Bernau end up fighting in the British army?'

'It is a long story but, I suppose, one as old as time,' he says, with a sigh.

He sits up, then takes a brown envelope out of his coat pocket.

'Here,' he says, handing it to me. 'This will tell you everything you need to know. There is another letter in there too that I would like you to pass on for me.'

'Pass on to who?'

'There is no time to get into that now,' he says. 'It is all in there.' He pauses then, his eyes darting to the door. 'Did you hear that?'

'No,' I say, getting to my feet. 'What is it?'

'Voices,' he says, the colour draining from his face. 'They may have come looking for me. I must go. Will you promise me you will deliver the other letter?'

'I will,' I say, taking his hand and kissing it. 'But I ask for something in return.'

'What is that?'

'That you tell me your name.'

He smiles and shrugs his shoulders.

'That is not much to ask,' he says, stroking my face. 'And it is a rather boring name anyway, not worthy of such mystery. It is—'

With that, the door is pushed open, and half a dozen guards armed with rifles storm into the room. Two of them seize Jo, while another pair, one with a spiderweb tattooed on his cheek, the other grinning menacingly, grab me from behind and haul me into the air.

'What are you doing?' I cry, in German, clutching my

medical bag to my chest. 'Put me down. I am . . . I am not well.'

Seeing that I am being manhandled, Jo lashes out at the men holding him, elbowing one in the face and kneeing the other in the groin.

'Let go of her,' he cries, storming towards my captors with fists raised. 'Do you hear me? Let go of her. She is pregnant.'

With that, the men that had been guarding the door run at Jo. One of them takes his rifle and smashes the butt into Jo's head. He slumps to the floor and then, bearing down over him, one guard takes his arms, the other his legs.

'My darling,' I cry, as they drag him out of the room. 'I won't forget you. I promise.'

'You'll shut your mouth, whore,' hisses the tattooed man holding me. 'Like you should have shut your legs.'

He slaps me across the face, the blow making my eyes water. Then, with his grinning comrade, they carry me out of the building and into the dark and frozen night.

37

EDIE

Cornwall

Present Day

'It's probably nothing,' says my mother, laying out a large tartan blanket on the beach. 'But your dad thought it best we come and check on you, make sure you're all right.'

I watch as she and Ronke, who has driven my parents down here, empty the large blue plastic icebox which my mother has filled to the brim with sandwiches, fairy cakes, biscuits, cheeses, cooked meats and hard-boiled eggs. We have left Ned back at the cottage fixing the broken window. After hearing the news, I couldn't face sitting cooped up inside amid the old man's hammering and my own troubled thoughts, so was relieved when Mum suggested we take her ample picnic and set it up at Lytton Cove.

'I smuggled this in,' whispers Ronke, conspiratorially, taking a miniature bottle of gin out of her handbag and pouring it into my plastic beaker of orange juice, while my parents bicker over the correct way to slice the apple sponge. 'Thought you could do with it. Look, Edie, I know your folks are worried, but I don't think those lads are going to come anywhere near you. There are all sorts of conditions attached to their release, including restrictions on travel. I doubt they'll be able to go as far as Canning Town, let alone Cornwall. And besides, no one outside family and close friends knows that you're here.'

'I hope you're right,' I say, taking a long glug of my gin and orange, its burning warmth helping to soften my nerves. 'It's just – well, I haven't told anybody this, but there's been some strange occurrences lately, at the cottage. I'd put it down to the weather and a previous tenant who was into devil worship, but now I think it could be them. They might have found me.'

'Hang on,' says Ronke, her eyes widening. 'Did you say devil worship? Oh my days, Edie. You see, this is why I could never live somewhere like this. Too many *Wicker Man* vibes for my liking.'

'Hey, I thought you were here to reassure me,' I say, shading my eyes from the sun as my mother appears above us brandishing a packed plate of food. 'Though seriously, nothing, not even devil worship, terrifies me as much as those two men. I have replayed that night over and over in my head for the last year and just when I thought I was turning a corner, when I was finding some semblance of peace, they come back.'

'I've sent your father into the village to buy a knife,' says my mother, settling herself on the blanket between Ronke and me.

'A knife,' laughs Ronke. 'Look, I know things are tense, Mrs L, but I don't think octogenarian violence is going to help.'

'For the apple sponge,' says Mum, rolling her eyes. 'In the rush to leave we forgot to pack the cake slice.'

'Oh, Mum, we could have brought a knife from the cottage,' I say, my head tightening with tension as it often does when my parents start fussing. 'You didn't have to send him off into the village. It's uphill all the way.'

'The walk will do him good,' says Mum, unscrewing the ancient tea flask they've had since I was a child. 'He's been ever so agitated, all the way here.'

'He kept telling me to go faster,' says Ronke, stretching her legs out in front of her. 'I was terrified I was going to be done for speeding.'

'He worries about me, I know he does,' I say, remembering Dad's face when he came to the hospital where I was keeping a vigil by David's bed, the stricken expression, the way he held me while I sobbed like a baby. 'After that night, I guess he felt like I did, that nothing and nowhere was safe any more.'

'I hope prison has made them think on what happened,' says Mum, cradling her plastic cup of tea in her hands. 'Made them reflect. I mean, they may not have killed poor David, but they certainly contributed to . . . to what happened.'

A shadow passes across the sun then, plunging the beach into a dull grey light. The temperature drops as we sit here in silence, the grieving widow, sister and mother-in-law, thinking about that night and its consequences. Draining my drink, I see the events of 12 October unfold on the grey horizon ahead of me as though I am watching them on some open-air cinema screen. I see me and David curled up together in bed, my arm wrapped loosely around his waist, his hand placed on mine. The street light that stands directly outside our window casts a greenish glow across

314

the room, illuminating the bulky antique French wardrobe, the chest of drawers, the bedside tables – mine stacked with magazines, tubes of hand cream, a half-drunk mug of peppermint tea, a sketchbook, my phone and charger; David's side bare but for his reading glasses and a copy of *Parade's End*, the book he has always meant to read but never got round to it – the hook on the back of the door where David's bottle-green silk dressing gown hangs on top of my dove-grey hooded fleece one, the painting, over the bed, of St Dunstan's Church that I sketched for David as an anniversary gift. It is a scene of serenity, of perfect domestic solitude. But then the scene shifts. Downstairs, two young men, high on drugs and desperate for their next fix, have smashed the kitchen window and are rooting around the living room in search of cash, credit cards or sellable items. One of them is rifling through the pile of post on the coffee table. He picks up an envelope and reads the name on the front of it. He is saying the name aloud when the owner of it comes into the room holding a battered old baseball bat in his hands. 'David Hart?' says the young man with a sneer. Behind him, his accomplice is busy pulling out the plugs on the TV and laptops before stuffing them into a massive black bin sack. I am standing at the door, hidden in the shadows, waiting for the police to arrive, my hands still gripping the phone from which I made the emergency call. But I can see, even from this restricted view, that while one of the young men just wants to grab some valuables and get out of here, the other is looking for sport. 'Is that for me?' he says, gesturing to the baseball bat David is gripping in his hands. 'Come on then? Let's have it, Dr David Hart?' But David doesn't move. 'I said, let's have it?' Something is wrong. David is rooted to the spot. Then sirens, faint at first but growing louder. A car pulls up outside, a door slams. The young man with the black sack makes a run for the kitchen, escaping the way he came in, while the other one, in a sick display of bravado, lurches towards David, kneeing him in the stomach before joining his mate. I rush to my husband's side. He is clutching his chest, telling me he can't breathe. It's OK, I tell him, it was just a kick. He's only winded you, that's all. Thankfully, they didn't have a knife or a gun, I tell the police officers when I let them in a few moments later. Thankfully, it was no more than the TV and laptops. Thankfully, thankfully, thankfully. I repeat it as a mantra all the way to the hospital. I whisper it to myself as I wait with my father outside the cubicle in A & E where a team of medics tries to resuscitate my dying husband. I say it as a way of blocking out the truth of the situation, that it wasn't just a kick to the stomach, that the shock of the break-in and violence brought about a heart attack that would end David's life at 11.59 p.m. on 12 October 2022.

'Edie.'

I blink into the dank afternoon light. Ronke is nudging me.

'Your phone's ringing.'

She hands it to me but as I click the green button my mind and soul are still in that East London hospital, dazed and numb.

'Hello,' I say, watching as my father strides across the beach towards us.

'Mrs Hart? It's Tony from Vintage Digital.'

It takes me a couple of moments to twig. Then I

remember. The cylinder. The box. It all feels like a lifetime ago now.

'I'm calling about the wax cylinder,' he says, his voice muffled by the wind. 'I have news. It took quite a bit of work, but I've managed to extract the recording for you.'

'Oh,' I say, placing my finger to my lips as my dad starts proclaiming loudly about the quality of the cakes in the bakery. 'That's great.'

'I just wanted to let you know that I've sent it to your Cornwall address via courier,' he says. 'It should be with you this afternoon, all being well. And I must say, Mrs Hart, that sometimes, in my line of work, I come across stuff that makes the hairs stand up on the back of my neck but this recording – well, I'll let you hear it for yourself. Cheerio now.'

He clicks off and I sit with the phone clasped in my hands, wondering how I had ever summoned up the energy to pursue the contents of that box. It all seems so trivial now, so pointless.

'I couldn't believe it.'

I look up to see my father, face flushed, standing over my mother, who is slicing the apple sponge with a borrowed knife.

'What couldn't you believe, Dad?' I say, turning down my mother's offer of a slice of cake.

'Here, I'll show you.'

He gestures me over to him, complaining that if he tries to sit on the sand, he will never be able to get up.

'My knees haven't been right since 1987,' he says, while Ronke giggles into her gin and orange. 'Anyway, look at this.'

317

He hands me an A4 clear plastic wallet. Inside is an old newspaper cutting from the *Lytton Herald*, dated June 1932. I carefully remove the cutting and see a photo of two women, one fair-haired and tiny, the other tall and dark, their arms draped around each other, standing outside the bakery.

'Guess who that is?' says Dad.

I look closer. I recognize the blonde woman as Kitty, older here than in the photo that hangs above the counter in the bakery, her hair now loosely bobbed, her clothes subdued and rather drab. The other woman is familiar though the photograph has faded with age and her face is difficult to make out. She is much taller than Kitty and towers above her despite wearing flat lace-up shoes. Her long hair falls loose around her shoulders, and she is wearing a dropped-waist dress that ties in a bow at her neck. The most remarkable thing about the photo, though, is the body language between the two women, the easy intimacy. If this had been taken in 1930s London and not a small village in Cornwall, I would have sworn that the two were lovers.

'The blonde one is Kitty,' I say, handing the newspaper back to Dad. 'As for the other one, I have no idea.'

'Fancy not recognizing your great-grandmother,' he says, with a chuckle. 'That's Jane – or Gillian as she was known in London.'

'My goodness,' I say, taking the paper back for another look. 'Where did you get this?'

'The nice woman who runs the bakery gave it to me,' he says, his eyes twinkling in the sunlight. 'She said that she was chatting to you about Kitty the other day and it had prompted her to dig out her mother's photographs. She found this among them.'

'So Kitty and Jane knew each other,' I say, scrutinizing the photo. 'They were friends.'

'Looks like they were more than friends to me,' says Ronke, appearing beside me.

'Well, I don't know about that,' says Frank, clearing his throat. 'But if you read the article attached to the photo, there's an interview with the pair of them. Kitty talks about how she lived in Mile End and ran the family bakery there until her father died just before the First World War.'

'Mile End,' I say, turning the paper over to read the article. 'What a coincidence.'

'Isn't it?' says my father, sipping his tea. 'It also says that Gillian was a suffragette who worked for Sylvia Pankhurst and she and Kitty ran a charity bakery in the West End for a few years until a fire destroyed the business and they moved down here. I never knew till now that your great-grandmother had had any connection to the bakery trade. Still, I suppose it makes sense if her friend was a baker.'

'Her friend?' says Ronke incredulously. 'Yeah, right.'

'Well, whatever they were, this is another piece of family history that I intend to hold on to,' says Dad, taking the paper and putting it back into the plastic envelope. 'And by the look of that black cloud, I'd say it's time we headed back to the cottage.'

Ned is just finishing the window when we arrive, sodden with rain. While my parents and Ronke head inside in search of hot tea and warm blankets, I stay behind to thank Ned for his swift work.

'Not a problem,' he says, putting up the hood of his

waxy raincoat so that his face is partially obscured. 'It's as good as new now. Not a trace of blood. And there was such a lot of it.'

'You must let me know how much I owe you,' I say, trying not to think of the dead bird lying on the floor. 'I can drop it over to you later.'

'Let's call it two hundred,' he says, with a nod. 'And let's hope that's the last of these . . . mishaps. I can't say I've seen anything this bad since David Hart's time.'

The mention of my dead husband's name in this context unsettles me and I find myself feeling rather angry. I am about to confront him with the fact that the former tenant's name was Kevin Reynolds and not David Hart when Alexander appears beside me.

'Edie, have you got a minute?'

He is holding a parcel in his hands.

'I'll leave you to your friend,' says Ned. 'I'll pop back later for the money.'

As Ned stalks off, I turn to Alexander.

'What is it?' I say, irritated both at Ned and at this man who's claimed to be my friend but who I can't help feeling is hiding something from me. 'I don't have much time. My parents and sister-in-law are visiting.'

'I just want to give you this,' he says, handing me the parcel. 'It came earlier while Ned was fixing the window. I hope you don't mind but I signed for it. Thought it might be important and I know from bitter experience that if they take the parcel back in these parts it can be weeks until the redelivery.'

'Thank you,' I say, taking it. 'But can I ask, in future, that you leave my post alone?'

I turn and head back to the cottage.

Inside, Mum, Dad and Ronke are huddled round the kitchen table sipping hot chocolate and eating the remains of the picnic. Dad looks up as I enter.

'Aren't you inviting him in?' he says, gesturing to the garden where Alexander is making his way forlornly down the path. 'Thought you two would have a lot to talk about what with his big purchase and everything. Thought it would be right up your street.'

'What big purchase?' I say, placing the package on the table.

'The bakery?' says Dad, swiping a crisp from my mother's plate. 'When I was in there earlier, Sue told me she was retiring and selling up. Apparently, Alexander's made her an offer she can't refuse.'

'Alexander is buying the bakery?' I exclaim. 'Whatever for? I know he likes eating cakes but baking them?'

'Oh, he's not keeping it as a bakery,' says Dad. 'He's going to turn it into an art gallery.'

38

MIRIAM

Dänholm Prisoner-of-War Camp

November 1918

Daylight slowly seeps through the metal bars of the cell where I have sat amongst straw and rat droppings and goodness knows what else for the last four hours. They deposited me here, in the solitary confinement wing on the edge of the camp by the harbour walls, without ceremony, kindly pointing out the execution yard as we passed. 'See that wall,' the tattooed guard sneered. 'All white and clean. For now. Come the morning it will be spattered with your man's blood. British murdering scum. How could you sink so low as to lie with the enemy? You are no German. You are a traitor. And the commandant has no mercy for traitors.'

Morning. That is what he said. When morning comes, they will lead Jo out into the yard, blindfold him, and then, with his back to the wall, they will line up and open fire. The man I held in my arms just a few hours ago, the man whose child I now carry, and whose legacy I have been tasked with upholding. And then, with a sickening feeling, I realize that I do not have the letters. I dropped them when the guards grabbed me. Jo's story, and the message to our child, hidden away in the wax cylinder I secreted inside my medical bag, will remain untold. He seemed to me, when I first met him, little more than a ghost, and, despite everything we have shared, he remains, still, nothing more than an enigma.

All I know of him is the pet name his mother gave him. Jo. The man who found his voice.

A stronger glare of sunlight beams into the cell, illuminating the dank walls. The light is almost an affront and I want to yell at it, and all it represents, tell it to leave well alone. I feel like Donne in the poem I had to memorize for an English grammar class at university, raging at the 'unruly sun' for chiding him and his sweetheart from their bed. But this sun is different, this sun brings more than just another day, it brings death.

I mutter the words of the poem under my breath as heavy footsteps pound the yard outside the window.

'Busy old fool, unruly sun.'

Voices now. A command bellowed in German; the sound of rifles being cocked.

I put my hands to my ears, the words of a long-dead poet running round my mind in a sickening loop.

'Busy old fool, unruly sun.'

Voices, muffled by my hands, then a crack and six staccato shots.

'Busy old fool . . .'

Six more.

A pause.

The sound of footsteps walking away.

Silence. Then the sensation of a heart breaking into a thousand pieces.

Hours pass. The winter light fades and gives way to a darkness so opaque it feels as though I am a part of it. A human shadow bleeding into the black void, the smell of straw and vermin excrement seeping into my skin, my hair, my clothes.

When the cell door opens, letting in a dull grey light, I lift my head, expecting to see the face of the man who has been standing guard all through the night, the tattooed brute who struck me and called me a whore and a traitor. But the figure I see as I blink into the light is short and plump and, as it steps towards me in a cloud of pipe smoke, I let out an anguished cry.

'Herr Professor. Is that you?'

'Hush, child,' he says, putting his finger to my lips. 'We must move fast. Here, put this on and pull up the hood.'

He hands me a coat that is several sizes too big. I slip it on, pick up my bag, and follow Herr Garn out into the deserted corridor.

'The guard,' I say, noticing the empty chair outside the door. 'Where is he?'

'Don't worry about him,' he whispers, taking my arm and leading me down the corridor. 'He has been dealt with. Now, I am going to slip some papers into your pocket and when we get to the gates you will present the guard with them. Do you understand?'

'Papers? What kind of papers?'

'Identification papers,' he says, pulling me into a doorway as another guard approaches. Huddling in the shadows, I feel Herr Garn's breath on my face, his heart perhaps racing in his chest like mine. Finally, when the guard's footsteps recede, we creep out and continue on our way.

'They belong to a British woman named Winifred Foster,' he whispers as we skirt the edge of the prison block. 'She has been in the camp as part of a Red Cross delegation sent to inspect and report on conditions.'

'A British Red Cross worker?' I say, lowering my head as the bright searchlights of a watchtower illuminate the path ahead. 'How do you come to have her papers?'

'Miriam, my time here in this camp has allowed me access to . . . how can I put it, certain favours,' he says, gripping my arm tighter as the exit gates come into view. 'I don't want to give away the details but let's just say I had a little help from someone who owed me something. That's all you need to know.'

'What about the guards?' I say, my heart twisting inside my chest at the thought of this subterfuge. 'They are sure to see through this.'

'That is a risk we have to take,' whispers Garn, as we draw closer to the gates. 'But at this point, I can see no other way, my dear.'

It all sounds so messy, I think to myself, as I grip my bag tightly. Surely I will be caught?

'I also found these,' whispers Garn, shoving two narrow envelopes into my hands. 'You must have dropped them on the floor in the studio.'

I look down at the envelopes, see Jo's elegant handwriting, and I am filled with a new-found vigour. He wanted me to pass one of these letters on to someone, said it was of vital importance. I cannot let him down now. I can do this. I can be brave. For Jo.

'Now,' continues Garn, his voice low and steady. 'All you need to remember is that your name is Winifred Foster, you are a British Red Cross inspector, and you are headed to the port where you are being taken to another camp. I will go on ahead. We are not to be seen together. Now wait here and when you see me leave the gates, wait for at least fifteen minutes, then proceed to the checkpoint. Do you understand?'

I nod my head.

'Good. Now keep calm, remember what I've told you and I will see you on the other side.'

I watch as he walks toward the gates. When he gets closer, I hear the guard dog bark furiously, then a figure appears, shining a torch. I jump back against the wall, my heart racing. After a couple of moments, I peep out and see Herr Garn with his hands raised in the air. At first, I fear he has been arrested but then I see the guard patting him down and realize that he is being searched. Once that is over, he hands his papers to the guard who, with a cursory glance and nod of the head, opens the gates and lets him pass.

The fifteen minutes that follow feel like hours. I count each second, tears filling my eyes as I put my hand to my stomach and think of Jo's words, his final message to the child he will never know.

'I won't let you down, my darling,' I whisper, unclipping my bag and placing the letters inside along with the cylinder. 'I will make sure your voice is heard.'

Then, on a count of ten I make my way across the grass to the checkpoint. As I walk, I think back to Herr Garn's words when he first heard my English accent: 'My dear girl, I haven't heard such perfect RP since Oxford.' Bolstered by the memory, I rehearse the lines under my breath: 'My name is Winifred Foster and I am a British Red Cross inspector. My name is Winifred Foster and I am a British Red Cross inspector. My name is . . .'

The dog is at my heels and the light of the torch temporarily blinds me.

'Name!'

The voice is unsettlingly familiar.

Peering out from under my hood, I come face to face with the checkpoint guard and am struck with such terror I almost collapse.

It is Dieter. My heart sinks at the sight of the guard who, despite his flirtatiousness, is a stickler for the rules. But he is always on the south watchtower by the sanatorium. What in God's name is he doing here?

'Name,' he repeats, his voice hoarse.

I have no choice. I must take the risk and suffer the consequences.

'My name is Winifred Foster,' I say, handing him the papers without meeting his eye, and pulling my hood tighter. 'I am a British Red Cross inspector heading to the port.'

He snatches the papers, takes a look and then, to my horror, yanks my hood away. There is no going back now. I am finished.

He regards me for a moment before taking a step back as if to summon assistance.

'Please,' I say, my insides turning to liquid. 'I can explain, I—'

He comes towards me and presses his finger to my lips.

'Shh,' he says sternly. Then something, a memory of the way I always accepted his compliments good-naturedly or just a new-found sense of decency, causes him to back away. Returning the papers to me, he gestures to the exit.

'Go through, Winifred Foster,' he hisses. 'Quickly now.'

I freeze, fearful that this may be a trap.

'You heard me, woman,' he yells, raising his rifle. 'Go.'

'But I—'

'You have not heard,' he says, lowering the weapon. 'The war is over. As of eleven o'clock this morning. They have won, Nurse. And we are doomed.'

39

EDIE

Cornwall

Present Day

'I didn't want to tell you until the sale had gone through,' says Alexander, when I go to find him at his cottage. 'But now that Sue has blabbed, I guess the news is out.'

'An art gallery,' I say. 'In Holton. You're going to try to give St Ives a run for its money?'

'Nothing as ambitious as that,' he says. 'Listen, Edie, I have been trying to escape London for a long time. My job, the flat, everywhere I turn there are reminders, not just of my failed marriage, but of the dreams I didn't pursue. I told you how my folks discouraged me from studying art when I was a teenager and, well, it seems my life since then has been all about making other people happy. The gallery is my chance to make myself happy and, hopefully, lots of artists and patrons too. You included, if you're not still mad at me.'

'Oh, Alexander, I saw a piece of paper with my name on it when I came to feed the cat and I thought . . . well, it sounds so foolish now . . . I came to the conclusion that you were planning some mega extension that was going to encroach on Moonstone Cottage. I thought you were trying to win me over or scare me away. I feel ever so silly now.'

'Don't,' he says, coming towards me and stroking my arm. His touch feels warm and comforting. 'It was me who was silly. I should have just been honest with you. About everything.'

He looks at me, his dark eyes loaded with everything we haven't yet expressed.

'Come on,' I say, breaking the moment. 'Come and listen to this recording. Hopefully we can solve two mysteries today.'

After introducing himself to Ronke, Alexander joins her and my parents at the table while I open the parcel. Inside it are a slim silver memory stick and a folded piece of paper. It is a brief note from Tony, telling me that he managed to salvage most of what was on the wax cylinder and that the memory stick should be compatible with my laptop. *Any problems*, he concludes, *give me a shout.*

'What's that you've got there, Edie?' says Mum, looking up from slicing a large wedge of apple cake for a delighted Alexander.

'It's the recording,' I say, coming to join them at the table. 'The chap Alexander recommended in East London has managed to digitalize it.'

I place the memory stick down in front of me. All the intrigue and enthusiasm I had felt when I left the cylinder with Tony has dissipated now. In the light of what has happened, I have no urge to listen to some old recording, no desire to dredge up even more of the past.

'That thing doesn't look big enough to store a flea, let alone a whole recording,' says Dad, shaking his head as he sips his tea. 'Amazing, the technology these days.'

'Shall we give it a listen?' says Alexander, looking across at me, his face bright and eager. 'Solve the mystery of the box?'

'Oh, I don't know,' I sigh. 'I'm starting to think that I unleashed some sort of dark energy when I ripped open that wall. Maybe I should just get rid of the lot of it. Take it down to the sea and let the tide carry it away.'

'Oh, come on, Edie, it would be a shame not to find out,' says Ronke, taking the plates over to the sink. 'After going to all that trouble of having it digitalized.'

'All right, all right,' I say, throwing my hands in the air. 'I'll go and get my laptop. Hopefully, whatever is on there will put this nonsense to rest once and for all.'

When I come back downstairs with my laptop, the table has been cleared and a fresh pot of tea brewed. Alexander leans back in his chair and pats his stomach.

'Well, Mr Lowe,' he says, smiling at my father, who is pouring the tea. 'I have to say that your apple sponge is still the best I have ever tasted, and I do regard myself as something of a baked-goods connoisseur.'

'Ah, so that's what you do for gainful employment,' laughs Ronke. 'I did wonder. Single man living with his cat in a remote coastal village. What else is there to do but eat cake?'

'Right,' I say, placing the laptop in the middle of the table. 'Enough stalling. Let's hear what's on this bloody thing.'

'All this build-up,' whispers Mum, as I insert the memory stick. 'It'd better be worth it.'

Beside me Alexander drums his fingers nervously on the table, while the others lean forward.

'Ready?' I say.

'As we'll ever be,' Dad sighs.

'OK, here goes,' I say. I click Play and my hands tremble. Calm down, Edie, I tell myself, as I sit down and wait for it to begin. It's just an old recording, nothing to be scared about.

There is a hissing sound, then a long pause, and as we sit there tentatively I recall how Tony said he'd been unable to remove a lot of the background noise and hope that after all this effort we can actually hear what is being said. Finally, a man's voice starts up, the room falls silent and the hairs on the back of my hand prickle.

'The Parable of the Prodigal Son,' says the man, in a distinct West Country accent.

He goes on to recite a couple more lines, then stumbles over a word and starts to cough.

'Take your time, Mr Hughes.' Another man's voice. German. 'Fräulein Ziegler, can we start again, please.'

'Ziegler,' I say, looking across at my dad, who is staring at the laptop as though it is a flying saucer come to land on the table. 'That must be Miriam he's talking to.'

There is a fizzing noise then, followed by a long pause.

'This is the strangest thing I've ever heard,' says Alexander. 'Why are they reciting passages from the Bible? Do you think it's some sort of torture method? I know it would be for me.'

'Well, if it is, I have never heard of such a thing,' says my father, shaking his head.

'Death by Bible,' laughs Ronke. 'David and I used to

feel the same when we went to Sunday school as kids. Utter torture.'

'Is that it?' says my mother, taking a sip of tea. 'I thought that Tony chap said there was something amazing on it. If that's his idea of amazing then—'

She stops as a man's voice strikes up. A different man this time, more assured and quite clearly German.

'*As it looks increasingly likely, from the mutterings in this camp, that Germany is about to lose this war, I have decided to deliver my message in English. Who knows, by the time you hear this, the German language may have been outlawed altogether. Still, whatever happens, your wise and multilingual mama will ensure you speak with many tongues.*

'*This is, and ever will be, a prayer for my unborn child.*

'*By the time you hear these words I will be gone. To you, I will be but a name carved in stone, faded and without form, a relic you stumble across in the vaults of some country church, gathering dust, largely forgotten.*

'*You will never feel the warmth of my hand in yours nor the solidity of my arms as I rock you to sleep. You will never sit beside me at idle dinners, laughing until tears spring from our eyes at some silly shared joke.*

'*You will never see me greet your mother with a kiss and listen as we tell you, for the hundredth time, the story of how we met. You will never scribble my name on birthday cards or tell your friends just what it is I do for a living. You will never gaze upon my face and see yourself reflected in it, see the aquiline nose, the curl of your mouth, the freckles on your forehead, passed on to you from me.*

'*You will never know me but be reassured that I will be there in the quiet moments when, retreating from a raucous party, you seek solace in some peaceful study and, taking down a book, your hand is guided to a poem that speaks directly to your soul.*

'*I will be there in the hopeless moments where you sink to your knees in despair, wondering if there is any point in going on, and you look up and see a vixen lying on the roadside feeding a litter of cubs and realize that there is always hope, even in the darkest times.*'

There is a pause of about thirty seconds, then a female voice comes in.

'*My darling . . . I . . . that was beautiful. And I captured every word of it.*'

'*I'm sorry, Miriam. Truly, I am.*'

'*Sorry for what?*'

'*For everything. For killing Douglas Reid, for leaving you alone like this.*'

'*What's done is done. There is nothing I . . .*'

With that, the recording ends. We sit in silence, like Victorian ghouls gathered at a seance, all of us lost in the world of 1918, a man speaking his last words to his unborn child, to his lover. A man confessing to a murder.

'What do you make of it?' I say, looking up at the others. My father sits open-mouthed. My mother has tears in her eyes. Ronke, for once, is lost for words.

'I wish my dad had left me something like that,' says Mum, dabbing her eyes. 'He died when I was a girl, as you know. All I have of him is a bunch of old photos. If I could have heard his voice . . .'

'Same with my grandmother,' says Ronke, handing her a tissue. 'She died before David and I were born. Though my mum always said Gran lived on through the recipes she passed down. I still get emotional when I cook her jollof rice and I never knew the woman.'

'He had a kind voice,' I say, my thoughts returning to

the doomed father on the recording. 'Thoughtful and eloquent.'

'He sounded like a poet,' says Alexander. 'If he'd lived he could have become the German Siegfried Sassoon. Though he *was* German, wasn't he, going way back? Oh, I don't know, I wish I knew more about that period.'

I smile, thinking of David. He would know. Then, remembering the boxes crammed with his books in the spare room, I tell Alexander to go and have a look. There are plenty of Sassoon volumes up there. His eyes light up when I say he is welcome to borrow a few. 'It's good to think someone is still reading them,' I say.

As he walks out of the room, he gently pats my arm and I feel a strange sensation through my body, a sense of peace I haven't felt in a long time.

'It's just so sad,' says Mum, dabbing her eyes with a ball of tissue. 'They loved each other, and he was about to go to his death. He would never get to meet his baby. Oh, Edie, are you OK?'

I realize then that I have tears streaming down my face.

'It's just when he said, "To you, I will be but a name carved in stone",' I say, taking a tissue from the box on the sideboard. 'That's what I feared would happen after David . . . that everything that was him would disappear – his laugh, his smell, his presence – and all we'd have would be his name printed on those books.'

'You will never guess what I've just found?'

Wiping my eyes, I turn to see Alexander standing at the door. He is holding a book and a faded piece of paper.

'Hey, that's the one I gave you, Edie,' says Dad, as

Alexander comes to join us at the table. 'The one I found here.'

'It's extraordinary,' says Alexander, placing the book and the piece of paper on the table.

'*The Life and Work of Wolfgang Schumi: Forgotten Poet of Expressionist Berlin*,' says Ronke, craning her neck to read the title. 'Sounds scintillating.'

'It's not the book,' says Alexander, taking his reading glasses out of the top pocket of his shirt. 'It's this letter. It explains everything. Edie, you're not going to believe it.'

'I told you there was a letter,' says Dad excitedly. 'But it was written in German, so I had no idea what it said.'

'This is where my A-level German comes in handy,' says Alexander, placing his glasses on and unfolding the paper. 'Hopefully, it hasn't let me down, though after reading it, everything makes sense.'

'Well, go on, lad,' says my father impatiently. 'Don't keep us all in suspense. What does it say?'

With a smile, Alexander clears his throat and begins to read.

40

KITTY

Cornwall

July 1919

'The war is over, Kitty. It has been for months.'

Gillian stands by the window, arms folded defiantly across her chest.

'And yet we are still here in this . . . this pitiless place in the middle of nowhere,' she cries. 'I don't understand it, Kitty. Anyone would think you didn't want to return to London.'

I let her get it out, her frustration, her anger, while I sit at my desk, putting the finishing touches to the new deck of Tarot cards I am working on. The old set contained too much past energy, too many dark memories. Whenever I picked them up, I saw the faces of those poor widows I met at the bakery, starved and haunted, desperate to hear news of their men; or else I saw Otto, the wind knocked out of him as I imparted the news that he and Nancy were not to be. I saw myself running through the streets of Mile End while the mob ripped the bakery apart. Those cards have been privy to every horror, every sadness, every scar, and, as tools of divination, they have absorbed it all.

I knew, when we arrived in Cornwall, that I would need a fresh start, and that it would begin with my cards.

'Kitty? Are you even listening?'

I look up from my pencil drawing of the Queen of Wands, a formidable figure with Sylvia's placards and Gillian's face, and my heart sinks.

'Yes, darling, I am listening,' I say, laying my pencil down. 'You want us to return to London.'

'Why do you say that as though it is an outrageous request?' she exclaims, sitting down with a thud on the window seat. 'This trip to Cornwall was only ever meant to be temporary, a bit of respite while I regained my health. We weren't supposed to stay here for good. And, anyway, Sylvia's friend is bound to want the cottage back soon now the men are returned from the war. She'll need the rental income.'

'Sylvia's friend has said we can stay as long as we like,' I say, gazing past Gillian's head to the garden where, in a burst of colour, the roses have begun to bloom. 'And as for rent, well, I have worked out an agreeable sum with her. We had quite a bit put away from the bakery takings and I'm sure I will be able to pick up a couple of shifts at Mrs Banks's tea room in the village. I hear the old lady plans to retire soon. If that happens then Holton will be in need of a new baker and I—'

'Stop right there, Kitty,' says Gillian, puffing out her cheeks in indignation. 'Are you seriously telling me you want to stay here for the foreseeable future? In this tumbledown cottage in the middle of nowhere? Away from London? Away from everything!'

I think back over the last few years, the sense of

hopelessness and fear that pervaded every waking moment: from Otto leaving to my father dying, the attack on the bakery, then Gillian's accident and the fire. And all the while, London loomed there in the background, a witness but also an accomplice to it all, never letting up the relentless pressure, even in the darkest moments. I could try telling Gillian that I feel a sense of peace here in Cornwall that I haven't felt since early childhood, since before that blasted balloon, but I don't think she would understand, not really. For Gillian loved the London version of me, the fearless extrovert who charmed the members of the Divine Order and strode through the East End in hobnail boots and herringbone suit like some avenging angel. I realize, as I sit watching her twitching and fretting by the window, that she has never known the other side of me, the one who craves peace, the one who has come alive since moving to Cornwall. And that, perhaps, now that she has seen this other side, she may find she doesn't like it. But fearful of causing another argument, I do not raise this with Gillian. Instead, I take up my pencil and draw the face of the Queen of Wands – bold, defiant, fearless and ambitious, she is Gillian through and through.

'Kitty? I asked you a question,' says the real Gillian, from her spot by the window. 'Do you plan to stay here in Cornwall and not come back to London?'

Looking up at this woman who I have loved for so long, I feel a knot of sadness as I see the years unfold ahead of us. We will go our separate ways again. I know that. I have always known.

'I think I do, Gillian,' I say, my voice almost a whisper. 'Yes.'

With that, she jumps up from the seat, her eyes blazing.

'I can't believe it,' she cries. 'This is madness. Are you sure you didn't get a blow to the head as well as me?'

'Gillian, stop.'

'No, I won't stop,' she says, revealing a petulant side I have never seen before. 'I rescued you from the rubble of your father's bakery. I was there for you through thick and thin and this is how you thank me.'

I am about to respond when there is a knock at the door.

'Wonderful,' I say, taking up my pencil and resisting the urge to scribble out Gillian's face from my Queen. 'All your shouting has probably roused the neighbours. Well done.'

She scowls at me, then stomps off to answer the door.

I breathe a sigh of relief and return to my drawing, hoping that whoever is at the door is here to take Gillian back to London. It is a terrible thought, but her constant griping is draining my energy and I find I can only concentrate when she is not around.

'Er, Kitty, there is someone here to see you.'

I turn to see Gillian standing in the doorway. Next to her is a woman of around my age. She is wearing a rather shabby felt hat and a thin, black coat that has seen better days. Most surprisingly of all she is, quite clearly, heavily pregnant.

'Hello,' I say tentatively, getting up from my chair. 'What can I do for you? Please, do take a seat. You look exhausted.'

'I'll make some tea,' says Gillian, giving me a puzzled shrug as the woman sits down on the chair by the window.

'My name is Miriam Ziegler,' she says, removing her hat. 'And I have spent the last eight months trying to find you.'

'That sounds ominous,' I say, wondering if she is a

bereaved widow looking for comfort. 'But if it's Tarot you've come for, I'm afraid I only read for myself nowadays. The readings at the bakery took it out of me, somewhat.'

I smile but the woman does not return it.

'Tarot? No. I have no interest in any of that,' she says, frowning as she puts her hand to the small of her back.

It is then I catch her accent. I am about to ask whereabouts in Germany she is from when she says something that almost knocks me off my chair.

'I am here with a message for you,' she says, opening her handbag which has been wedged under her sizeable belly. 'From your brother.'

She takes a brown envelope out of the bag and hands it to me. When I read the words *For Kitty*, written in my brother's beautiful handwriting, I let out a cry of anguish, just as Gillian returns with the tea.

'Kitty,' she says, placing the tea tray on the side. 'What is it?'

In a daze, I hand her the envelope. She looks down at it, then at Miriam and her bump, and at that moment the penny drops for both of us. Miriam, sensing this, begins to speak.

When she has finished, the room falls silent and then, almost unbidden, I hear myself say, 'I am cursed, Miriam. It is as simple as that. I am cursed and I destroy everyone around me.'

Minutes turn to hours, evening comes, the tea grows cold, and despite Gillian's protestations that I should eat something, and our visitor's frequent trips to the outside privy as, she so kindly informed us, the baby is now pressing on her bladder, I find I cannot move from my seat.

The letter lies unopened on my desk, its grubby envelope obscuring the face of the Queen of Wands.

'Kitty,' says Gillian, coming to sit at my feet, and placing my hands in hers. 'Talk to me. I can't bear to see you like this. And I know you didn't mean what you said earlier about being cursed. That was just the shock talking. Miriam is resting in the spare room. I have told her she can stay as long as she likes. She looked wretched, poor thing, and was complaining of having twinges. I made her some soup, and she seemed a little more comfortable. She's sleeping now, thankfully. My darling, it is just you and me in this room now. Whatever you are feeling, you can tell me.'

The truth is I do not know what I am feeling. In a strange way, it seems that all the grief I felt for Otto was used up when I received the letter from my uncle. There had been brief hope when I opened that parcel and found it belonged to another man, but deep down, in the place where intuition lives, I had known: my brother, my childhood playmate and protector, the man I loved more than any other, including my father, was dead.

'She seems very pleasant,' says Gillian, stroking my hand. 'Intelligent too, from what she was telling us about her work. You can see why Otto was drawn to her.'

It is then that it falls into place, the final piece of the puzzle.

'She was the one,' I say, looking up into Gillian's soft green eyes. 'The one I foretold that night. She is the one he was destined to be with, not Nancy.'

'Yes, even if it was for such a short time,' says Gillian. 'It is so very sad.'

'But there was something else,' I say, the shock of the news triggering a cascade of recollections from the past. 'I remember it now. It came to me when I left the party that night, a message as clear as the sound of the seagulls outside that window. But Otto had already fled so I never got the chance to tell him. I never really understood it at the time, which is likely why I forgot about it, but seeing Miriam standing there, suddenly it made sense.'

'What was it?'

'I heard the word "orphan" over and over again,' I say, shivering, though the room is warm. 'And then "a child that will never know its father or its mother".'

'Oh, Kitty,' says Gillian, the colour drained from her cheeks. 'Whatever you do, don't tell Miriam that. Not in her condition.'

We go to bed and while Gillian falls into a deep sleep, I lie awake trying not to think of my brother's final moments, the fear he must have felt as they blindfolded him and prepared to fire. His countrymen. Fellow Germans. The very men he had been fighting alongside. I turn to face the window, try to block out the dark thoughts that are crawling through my head by listening to the faint murmuring of the sea. I breathe with the waves – in and out, in and out – and am just on the point of sleep when I am woken by a high-pitched scream.

My reflexes tricking me that I am back in London, and someone is attacking Gillian, I leap from the bed and grab the iron bar I now keep by me at all times, but as I come to, I see that Gillian is sleeping peacefully. Another scream pierces the air and I remember. Miriam. The large bump. The prophecy.

'Wake up,' I say, shaking Gillian out of her slumber. 'We need to fetch Dr Green.'

I leave Gillian staggering about the room, trying to locate Green's number, but when I reach the spare bedroom, with a heavy heart I realize we will very soon be beyond the need for doctors.

41

EDIE

Cornwall

Present Day

Dänholm Prisoner-of-War Camp
9th November 1918

My dear sister Katerina,

I am writing this on what will be my last night on earth. Tomorrow, I shall fly free with the spirits and, perhaps, in that form I will speak with you once more. For now, I have two requests to make of you.

The first is that you forgive me for leaving as I did. Youthful hubris and an inflated sense of importance caused me to act like a petulant child and abandon you and Father when you needed me most. I will never forgive myself for not being there when he passed away or for leaving you to cope with the grief and turmoil alone. All my life, I felt I never measured up to you. I envied your free-spiritedness, your resolute determination to be yourself and to defy convention. I envied your great gift, your ability to see right into the soul of a person, and I envied the love our parents bestowed on you, a love that came easily to them as it never did for me. But most of all I envied the love you shared with Gillian, the love you told me of though it was your deepest secret, and I wished that one day I would find the same for myself. I thought I had in Nancy – a love to be proud of, a love for the ages, one that would inspire me to write poetry and conquer the world. Yet I knew deep inside me that I was fooling myself. Your prophecy only confirmed that, though I was too proud to admit it. As always, sweet Katerina, you knew me better than I knew myself.

My second request is a direct consequence of that realization for, in the direst of circumstances, I found the love you foretold for me. You may ask, upon seeing the place name at the top of this letter, how I came to be incarcerated in a German prisoner-of-war camp where British soldiers are detained. The answer is rather shameful, I am afraid, but I feel I must be honest with you. All I ask, dear sister, is that you will not let my revelation taint your memory of me or what I will go on to ask of you. For it is not just me who will be dependent on your kindness and forgiveness but two people you will discover shortly.

My involvement in this savage and futile war did not come with medals for valour or great acts of bravery. The truth is I was terrified, out of my depth. I had been a literature student, a dreamer, devoid of practicality – even the simple mechanics of the ovens at Father's bakery were beyond my limits. When I was given a rifle, my hands trembled so much the officers thought I had the tremors or was suffering from some medical condition undisclosed on my papers. I had no idea how to look after a weapon, how to think strategically, how to second-guess the enemy. I was hopeless. Yet over time I learned how to use the gun and to defend, if not the Fatherland, then at least myself. My transportation to Dänholm stemmed from an act of self-defence gone horribly wrong.

It was after the Third Battle of Picardy, a bloody and drawn-out conflict that went on for several weeks. During a particularly frenzied few hours of fighting, I was blasted with a cloud of mustard gas that rendered me temporarily blind. I staggered across the battlefield, *trying to locate the German trench. But with my vision seriously impaired by the gas, I drifted out into open countryside where, exhausted and with eyes streaming, I ended up collapsing in a heap inside an old cattle shed. I woke to find a man bearing down on me. A British soldier, holding a rifle to my head. I cannot recall much about the moments that followed, only that my survival instinct overcame any sense of fear. I remember grabbing the rifle and trying to wrest it from the man's hands. The next thing I knew there was a gunshot, and I felt a damp sensation creeping up my chest. I had been shot, I reasoned, and now I was going to die in a cattle shed, far from home and all I loved. But when I regained my senses, I saw that the blood on my chest was not mine but was coming from the soldier who lay dead at my feet. After that, everything happened in a sickening blur. Panicking, I stripped the man of his uniform and dressed him in my filthy, blood-spattered German one, which had my identification papers in the pocket. Then I left him, hoping that he would be found, that he would be given a proper burial. As Otto Drechsler.*

My decision to take his uniform, I realize now, came from a desperate fear not to return to the trenches. Those moments of temporary blindness as I staggered across No Man's Land were the most terrifying of my life. I could not repeat it. I was not brave enough. I remembered from a conversation I'd had with my commanding officer that morning that the British soldiers captured the previous day were due to be taken by train to various camps across Germany later that day. So with my head down, I walked across the fields to the town of Amiens where I joined the prisoners just as they were boarding a train to Stralsund. I made sure not to have my German identity revealed by posing as a mute. Shell shock is so rife amongst the men, I was not treated with any kind of suspicion but accepted as an enigma known simply as 'Prisoner X'.

Oh, Katerina, the conditions in this camp are brutal and I am afraid I have become hardened to the point where I have killed again, and this time, though it was justified, I have been reprimanded. Now I sit here in this solitary cell awaiting my execution. Please do not weep for me, dear sister, for I am resigned to my fate.

And so to my final request. As I told you, the brutality of this war and this camp has almost broken me, in fact this moment would have come a lot sooner had it not been for the presence and love of a woman named Miriam Ziegler. I fear she may be in some peril now for her involvement with me and this chills my blood as she has just informed me that she is carrying our child. Katerina, I am going to get this letter to Miriam and have her deliver it to you when the war is over. When that happens, I ask that you look after her and our child as Father and Mother looked after us. Treat her with the love and kindness she deserves but that I cannot give her.

I trust you, Katerina. I always have done.

For ever your loving brother,
Otto

'Otto was the man on the recording,' says Alexander, folding the letter and placing it back into the book. 'The reference to Miriam Ziegler and the fact that he wouldn't live to see his baby born. It has to be.'

'It's so sad,' sighs Ronke.

'Heartbreaking,' adds Mum. 'Imagine writing that, knowing you're going to be shot, that you'll never see your loved ones again.'

'Hmm,' says Dad, frowning. 'Aren't we're forgetting the bit where he said he killed someone? What was the name again? Douglas Reid?'

'That's right,' says a voice behind us.

I almost jump out of my skin with fright until I see who it is.

'Goodness,' I say, getting up from the table. 'How did you get in here?'

'Door was open,' he says, his eyes fixed on my father.

'I'm afraid I'll have to go to the cashpoint for your money,' I say, aware that the atmosphere in the room has altered. 'I can drop it in to you later today.'

'I haven't come for money. I've come to do something I should have done years ago.'

It is then that I notice the crowbar in his hands, the anger dripping from his every pore.

'Ned?' I say tentatively. 'What . . . what is this?'

'That man you're talking about,' he says, turning to me, his face taut with fury. 'The one who was murdered in that camp. Well, he wasn't some random soldier, some poor unfortunate sap. Douglas Reid was my grandfather and that man, your relative, Drechsler, killed him in cold blood.'

42

KITTY

Cornwall

July 1919

'We're going to have to deliver it ourselves,' I say, as Gillian appears behind me.

I am standing by the narrow bed in the spare room, in which Miriam Ziegler, who only a few hours earlier was a perfect stranger, lies with her skirts about her waist, her face sickly yellow and contorted in pain. The screams that summoned me to her side have now subsided, her energy spent.

'What are you talking about, Kitty?' cries Gillian, horrified. 'We can't do that.'

'We have no choice,' I say, placing my hand on Miriam's forehead. 'I can see the baby's head, and she is burning up.'

'I've telephoned Dr Green,' says Gillian, sounding agitated. 'Shouldn't we wait for him to come?'

'Dr Green lives two villages away,' I snap, trying to gather my thoughts. 'This baby won't wait that long.'

'Please,' gasps Miriam, gripping my arm. 'It doesn't matter about me. Just don't let . . . don't let the baby die. I beg you.'

Her eyes rest on the faint inking on my forearm, one that I share with my late brother. We had the idea after Arthur Rubelle-Jones had brought in a tattoo artist to the Divine Order one evening. Though it was frowned upon for a woman to be marked in this way, Rubelle-Jones had approved of the idea that, as loyal believers, Otto and I should have a matching stamp, that the infinity symbol and the words *For Eternity* would be burnt into our skin until we drew our last breath.

'No one is going to die,' I say, trying not to think about the orphan I had seen in my vision. 'Now, Gillian, go and get some boiling water and some fresh blankets. A tot of brandy wouldn't go amiss, either.'

'Are you sure you should be drinking, Kitty?' says Gillian, voice trembling. 'Won't you need a clear head?'

'For Miriam, not for me,' I say, exasperated.

'I . . . I . . . don't need brandy,' says Miriam, between contractions. 'I'm a nurse . . . I know what to do . . . let me . . . let me talk you through it.'

She grips my hand and stares at me imploringly. She is scared, that is clear to see, but there is something about her, a steeliness, that reminds me of my brother. I can see now why he loved her so much and I cannot let her down.

'I am listening, Miriam,' I say, as Gillian staggers back into the room with an overflowing bucket of water. 'Tell me what I need to do.'

Between laboured gasps and screams of pain, she guides us through the birthing process.

At one point, I feel the air grow heavy as it does when a spirit is near. Fear grips me as Miriam's body grows limp.

'Come on, Miriam,' cries Gillian, sensing my concern. 'One more push and this baby is here.'

I look up at Miriam, she is pointing towards the door behind me.

'Jo,' she says, her face softening. 'You came?'

I can smell my brother's cologne on the air as Miriam grips my hand and prepares for one final push.

'We can do this,' cries Gillian, from the base of the bed. 'One last push, Miriam. That's all it's going to take.'

'We'll do it together,' I say, as the heaviness of the air intensifies. 'You're not alone, Miriam. We can do this.'

And so we breathe with her, we share her pain, her exhaustion – and her elation as the baby is delivered safely, a feline cry heralding his entry.

'Scissors, Gillian,' Miriam gasps, as I lift the child, a purple mound of hot flesh and mucus, and place him on his mother's stomach. 'You'll find them in my medical bag . . . along with . . . the surgical clamps. They'll need to be sterilized. Boiling water will do.'

Gillian leaps to attention and heads in search of the instruments, while I wrap a blanket around the child.

'I can see my father in him,' says Miriam, tears mingling with the sweat on her exhausted face. 'He has his frown.'

She looks up at me and smiles and I ache for her, for Otto, and the moment he has missed.

'He was here,' she says, gesturing to the doorway. 'I have never believed in such things before, but I saw him, standing there, just as the baby was born.'

'I know,' I whisper, taking a cold flannel and mopping her brow. 'He is always here.'

'He told me to call him Jo,' she says, her voice reed thin. 'Said . . . said it was a pet name.'

I smile sadly.

'Ah, yes,' I say, tumbling back through the years. 'From Joachim, his middle name. Mother always preferred that to Otto, which had been my father's choice, and throughout our childhood she insisted on calling him Jo.'

As Miriam lies back on the pillow, her body limp with exhaustion, I wonder to myself if Otto, in asking her to call him Jo, had been returning in his mind to those happy days in Germany, before the balloon hit the ground, before Mother died, before it all fell apart.

'Here we are,' cries Gillian, rushing into the room. 'I've had a large brandy,' she whispers to me, with a wink, as she hands me the scissors and Miriam the clamps. 'For the shock.'

I smile. She is still my Gillian. My love. 'Right,' I say, watching as Miriam carefully secures the cord. 'Who is going to do the honours?'

'Not me, thank you,' says Gillian, backing away. 'I've seen enough blood for one day.'

'Miriam?'

'I would like you to do it, Kitty,' she says, placing the baby on the bed in front of her, the stubby umbilical cord still connecting the two of them. 'For luck.'

'It would be my honour,' I say. Then, with one clean cut, my brother's baby, my nephew, is released fully into the world.

43

EDIE

Cornwall

Present Day

'Douglas Reid,' says Ned Kendal, pulling out a chair and sitting down, placing the crowbar at his feet, 'was a fine Highland soldier, a brave man who died at the hands of a German.'

His nostrils flare as he speaks. I try to catch my father's eye, try to communicate to him, through silent gestures, that perhaps we should call the police, but he is transfixed by Ned. They all are. Except Alexander, who glances at me and nods reassuringly. After all, this is an elderly man, not two young thugs. And yet, in this moment, Ned Kendal terrifies me more than they did that night. Something about the way he is sitting, so calm and poised, the crowbar within arm's reach.

'At least, that is the story I have told myself all these years,' he says, his face softening suddenly. 'I'm afraid I owe you an apology, Mrs Hart.'

He turns and looks at me, his eyes clouded with age and sadness.

'Me?' I say, rather flustered. 'Whatever for?'

'All the problems you've been having,' he says, looking down at the floor. 'The flooding, the dead bird, the note. It was me who did those things.'

'Now, hang on one minute,' cries my father, leaping up from the table, his face pink with rage.

'Dad,' I say, aware of his high blood pressure. 'Let me deal with this.'

'Why would you do such a thing, Ned?' says Alexander, horrified. 'I gave Edie your number in good faith. You've always been an exemplary worker. I don't understand.'

'I think I do,' I say, an odd sense of relief washing over me. 'As Douglas Reid's grandson, this cottage, because of the people connected to it, is a constant reminder of his murder. I get that.'

And it's true, I do get it. Hadn't I felt the same about my beloved flat in Brick Lane after it had been violated by those young men? Hadn't I seen David's lifeless body lying on the living-room carpet every time I came downstairs? But I had left the flat and come here, removed myself from the source of the hurt. Why hadn't Ned done the same?

'There is no excuse for my behaviour, Mrs Hart,' Ned says, as I pull out a chair and sit down next to him. 'None at all. But, you see, ever since I was a lad I've had this anger inside me, a burning rage I could never subdue. I didn't know where it came from. My parents were salt of the earth, gentle folk, I had a wonderful upbringing. We didn't have much, but I wanted for nothing.'

Across the table, my father opens his mouth to speak but my mother places her hand on his and shakes her head.

'There was nothing in my life that would explain the

anger,' says Ned, looking at each of us in turn, his rheumy eyes pleading. 'But it persisted. I got expelled from school for fighting, joined the army but got kicked out after six weeks, couldn't hold down a job. My folks despaired of me. I ended up living with my grandmother and she told me something that explained everything.'

'She told you about your grandfather?' I say.

He nods his head and then, taking a deep breath, he tells us his story.

'Gran came here in 1919,' he says, his voice quivering with emotion. 'A widow with a toddler to look after. My mother. Her husband had been killed in a prisoner-of-war camp, leaving her penniless. The letter informing her of his death mentioned the name of his killer. Otto Drechsler. There was some story behind it, how he had masqueraded as a Brit in a German prisoner-of-war camp, but when he was arrested for my grandfather's murder it all came out. He confessed to who he was, then ended up facing a firing squad. The letter was meant to reassure my grandmother that this man had been punished accordingly, that justice had been served, but to Gran it was a spur. She took the name and did some digging. Found a Katerina Drechsler, a woman who'd run a bakery in Mile End. Gran went down there but the place had been abandoned. As she was leaving, a young girl stopped her, asked if she could help. When Gran mentioned Katerina Drechsler, the girl said she used to work for her at the bakery and that her old boss now went by the name of Kitty Dexter. Talk was she'd upped sticks after the war and moved to Holton. Armed with this information, Gran decided to pay "Kitty" a visit, dole out some justice of her own. You have to remember that my grandparents were from the tenements of Glasgow. They were tough people.'

'What happened?' asks Alexander, next to me. 'When your grandmother came here?'

'What happened is that she ended up being charmed by Kitty,' says Ned ruefully. 'Like everybody did who met her. My mother, who was just a toddler, got sick with scarlet fever. They were staying in lodgings in the village. Kitty heard and rushed to help, nursed her back to life, she did. After that, how could my grandmother have anything in her heart but gratitude for this woman? After all, she told herself, it wasn't Kitty who killed Douglas, it was her brother, and he was dead. God had dealt his justice, that was what she believed after that, and he had sent Kitty to save my mother when she was ill. You can't go against the Lord, that's what Gran told me.'

'So, if everything was resolved with your grandmother and Kitty, why did you keep the grudge going?' asks Ronke, perplexed. 'What would it matter to you or your grandad if someone like Edie comes to live in this cottage all these years later?'

'I suppose it's a matter of pride,' he says, with a sigh. 'When I found out about my grandfather, and this was a few years after Kitty had died, I started thinking about the way she had treated me. Though everyone in the village loved her, she seemed to see something in me when I was a kid that . . . well, that sickened her. Now, I was no angel, I dabbled in petty theft, but it was innocent stuff – pilfering a few bits from the bakery and the shop, apple scrumping from people's gardens, that sort of thing. But this one time, Gran and I were invited to tea with Kitty here at

Moonstone Cottage and she asked me if I would like her to do a reading. Now, I knew nothing about the occult back then and thought she was going to tell me a story, so when she pulled out a deck of Tarot cards, I didn't know what was going on. Ironically, she did end up telling me a story though not the one I was hoping for.'

He pauses, clearly overcome with emotion.

'She wrote it all down,' he says, his voice trembling. 'My life. My future. In the form of a story. And when she handed it to me, I felt like someone had socked me right in the stomach. She painted such a bleak picture, though she disguised it in all that Tarot nonsense. Imagine being a nine-year-old boy and being told you'll lead a sad and lonely life and all you can look forward to is—'

'Death knocking at your door?' I say. Across the table, my father looks at me as though I have lost my mind. 'So, you're the Page of Swords? And you've admitted you pinned that disturbing story to my door.'

'Yes,' says Ned meekly. 'And I'm not proud of my actions. I didn't mean to hurt you or that poor tenant, the teacher chap. I feel ashamed for saying the things I did about him. But you see, it was nothing personal to you or him or anyone else who lived here over the years. It was just that I wanted to punish Kitty for what she'd said to me, for what her brother had done to my grandfather. Seeing people happy in this cottage made me sick. Why should they be happy, when my life had been so empty? But I can see you're a good person, Mrs Hart. Kitty predicted that much, at least. The Queen of Swords will make you see the error of your ways, she said. And it's true. Once I got to know you, I knew I couldn't continue this behaviour.'

'But accusing people of devil worship, Ned,' says Alexander. 'That's pretty strong stuff, not to mention over-stepping quite a lot of boundaries of the legal variety.'

Ned bows his head in shame. He looks old and beaten, and for a split second I feel sorry for him, but then I remember.

'You told me the previous tenant's name was David Hart,' I say, my voice catching in my throat. 'When that wasn't true. Did you . . . did you know that that was my late husband's name? Were you deliberately trying to scare me off by smearing him?'

'I told you, Mrs Hart,' he says, his eyes widening with fear and remorse, 'I am not proud of my actions. I looked you up when Alexander here gave me your details and I read about what had happened to your husband. I wasn't thinking straight . . . I just . . .'

'I think it's time you left, Mr Kendal, don't you?'

My father has risen from the table, standing erect, suddenly appearing twice his height.

'I'll go,' says Ned, shrinking into his seat. 'And I promise you I will never bother you again. But please, first, there is something I think you should know, something that, after speaking to Mrs Hart and hearing about this box and its contents, just clicked into place.'

'What is it?' I say, feeling repulsed by this man and what he has put me through. 'Go on, tell us.'

'Oh, Edie, love,' cries Dad, throwing his hands in the air. 'Don't give the old crook any more of our time. It'll be more nonsense or bile that he's spouting. Now, come on, Alexander, help me escort this man to the door.'

Alexander goes to get up, but Ned lifts his hand.

359

'Please,' he says, turning to my father. 'Just a couple of minutes. You see, Mr Lowe, this concerns you and your family. Your real family.'

My father slumps down in his seat.

'What's he talking about, Frank?' implores my mother.

'Mr Kendal, either tell us what you are getting at, or we will call the police,' says Alexander firmly. 'You have three minutes.'

'All right then,' says Ned, his hands visibly trembling. 'Kitty told my grandmother that the boy she had raised, Sam, was actually her nephew. His real parents were that murdering brother of Kitty's and some German woman.'

'Miriam Ziegler?' I say.

'That was the name, yes,' says Ned. 'Kitty said she arrived one afternoon in a state of – how can I put it – I think we used to refer to it as the family way.'

'Yes,' I say, recalling the letter Otto had written to Kitty.

'Almost ready to drop,' says Ned. 'Gillian and Kitty delivered the baby and cared for Miriam. According to my grandmother, the boy idolized them. It's from him that Gillian took on a new name. Apparently, little Sam couldn't pronounce Gillian properly so called her Jane instead. It was quite a—'

'Did you say Sam?' asks my dad, placing his hands on the table to steady himself. 'The boy's name was Sam?'

'That's right,' says Ned, smiling sadly. 'Sam Dexter.'

'My real father,' says Dad, his shoulders sinking.

'Hang on, I'm confused,' says Alexander, frowning. 'You're saying that the man on that recording and the woman on the photo are your grandparents, Frank?'

'That's right,' says Dad, tearful now. 'I never knew my

real father, Sam. He died in the Second World War, and I was brought up by Wilf Lowe, the man I called Dad. My mother had lost touch with Kitty and Gillian when she remarried so my real father's family remained a mystery.'

'Until now,' whispers Ronke.

I sit dumbfounded, trying to take it all in. These people – Kitty, Otto, Miriam – are related by blood. They are part of me and my story. They too had grown up in the East End and, in Kitty's case, found solace here in Cornwall. All these years there was a missing piece of our family's puzzle, a puzzle we were unaware existed until I found that box. And this strange little cottage that my father, and most of its tenants, had thought was cursed, had solved it for us. It had brought us all, both the living and the dead, back home.

44

KITTY

Cornwall

July 1919

'I'm worried about her,' says Gillian, coming into the kitchen with a tray of uneaten food. 'Something's not right.'

It is a week since the baby, named Samuel after Miriam's father, the man he so resembles, was born and in that time the cottage has been a hive of cleaning and cooking and waking several times through the night to the mewling sound of baby Sam. It is everything I thought I would despise – housework, domesticity, the mess and clutter of babies – but I have found, to my astonishment, that I rather like it. I feel as I did when Father was alive: busy, engaged. Dealing with practical matters rather than the jumbled contents of my head is liberating. I had forgotten that. The whole tumult is made all the easier by the fact that baby Sam is such a cherub, a darling, placid child with the softest skin and the most inquisitive eyes. Gillian has chided me on more than one occasion this past week for dissolving into a marshmallow whenever I see him. 'Honestly, Kitty, anyone would think the little chap was yours.'

Well, he may not be mine, but he is Otto's and that is the next best thing.

Yet in the midst of all this baby hysteria, one person has faded into the shadows. When Miriam spent the first two days sleeping, waking intermittently to rather begrudgingly feed Sam, I had put it down to exhaustion from the birth, but by the third day when she still refused to engage with the child, both Gillian and I had begun to worry. I had braved the heat to walk to the chemist's shop where I bought a strange crescent-shaped contraption that the chemist assured me was a baby's bottle, as well as a hearty supply of powdered milk. When I returned, I found baby Sam screaming with hunger while poor Gillian paced round the room with him in her arms, in a desperate attempt to soothe.

Meanwhile, Miriam stayed in bed, facing the wall, her hands clasped over her ears.

'We have to do something to help her,' says Gillian, taking a piece of my home-made fruit cake from the tray and munching it greedily while I sit on the chair nursing Sam, who has taken nicely to his new bottle. 'For one thing, she can't just stay in our spare bedroom for ever, and for another, well, I saw this kind of thing with some of the new mothers I dealt with at the Federation. In the days and weeks after the birth, they became diffident, listless, unable to love their babies as they should.'

'What happened to them?' I say, tilting Sam into an upright position where he lets out a glorious burp.

'Well, that's just it,' says Gillian, sitting down next to me with the rest of the cake. 'A lot of them just got on with it, though you could see they were a shadow of their former selves, while others found it impossible and ended up completely rejecting their babies.'

'That doesn't sound encouraging,' I say, pinching a piece of cake from the plate. 'We must try to get her to have another go at breastfeeding him. Perhaps I was too rash in putting him on the bottle.'

'Don't be silly. It was either that or let him starve,' says Gillian, stroking Sam's soft head. 'You did what you thought was best under very difficult circumstances. No, my biggest fear is that she is slipping into some sort of depression. Sylvia used to tell me about a woman she had been helping who, after giving birth, was in such a state she ended up in a lunatic asylum.'

'Good grief,' I say, looking down at baby Sam, who is gurgling, oblivious, on my lap. 'Surely it won't come to that with Miriam. She's simply . . . in shock. Remember, she lost her sweetheart just a few months ago. I heard her calling for him in her sleep the other night. I fear Sam has brought it all back, all those painful memories.'

'I must say, you seem more at peace with everything,' says Gillian, brushing cake crumbs from her skirt as she gets up from the table. 'With Otto, I mean. You seem less . . . haunted by it all now.'

'I read his letter,' I say, inhaling the powdery scent of Sam's skin as he nuzzles into my arms. 'And it explained everything. You were right, Gillian. Though Nancy wasn't completely honest when she ended the relationship. She didn't tell Otto that her father had ordered her to do it but used my reading as an excuse. Otto fell for it, initially, which is why he stormed off to Germany in a rage, but in the letter he tells me that meeting Miriam made him realize

I had been right, that there was a great love out there waiting for him, and it wasn't Nancy.'

'You're my great love,' says Gillian, kissing the top of my head as she makes her way to the sink. 'And I'm sorry I've been such a grump these last few months. I just, well, I'm not cut out for remote coastal living, I'm a London girl through and through. I need grime and belching chimneys and omnibuses and crowds.'

'Yet I've discovered I need none of those things, only this,' I say, looking down at the sleeping baby in my arms. 'And you.'

'And you will always have me,' she says, her eyes filling with tears. 'We've survived bricks and burning buildings – we can survive this. I'll get my London fix through the week and come back at weekends, and you can have your peaceful Cornwall. We'll find a way to make it work. I promise you. Who knows, I might even tempt you to come swimming with me.'

She laughs and I am about to retort with a salty quip when the front door slams.

'Who can that be?' I say, startled.

'Likely the wind has blown it open,' says Gillian, going to investigate. 'We really ought to get that door frame looked at.'

I sit for a moment, rocking Sam, who was woken by the noise, back to sleep. Suddenly Gillian reappears, looking troubled. She is holding something in her hand.

'I think you'd better read this,' she says, handing me the paper which, I now see, is a piece of cardboard, ripped from the box of baby formula.

Placing Sam in his crib, I take the note over to the light of the window so I can see it clearly. It is brief, just a few lines, and written in an almost illegible, manic handwriting, but what I read makes my heart both sink and soar, if such a thing is possible, and I feel guilty at once for reacting in such a way.

Kitty and Gillian, forgive me. I cannot be the mother this child deserves for I have nothing in the world to give him. Hopefully, one day I will, but until then I ask you to love and care for him as your own.

Yours,
Miriam
PS You are not cursed, dear Kitty. You never were.

'She also left these,' says Gillian, coming to join me at the window. 'On the bedside table.'

She hands me a photograph and a peculiar tube-like object with the words *STIMME PROJEKT* written on the side. A relic from Miriam's voice project, perhaps? Placing it on the window seat, I turn my attention to the photograph. What I see makes my heart hurt. There is my beloved brother, bone thin, battered and bruised, his lovely hair shorn to the scalp.

'I don't want to see these again,' I say to Gillian. 'For as long as I live.'

Then, taking the carved box Otto had given me when I was initiated into the Divine Order, I place the tube, the photograph and my old Tarot deck, wrapped in purple silk, inside and lock the latch firmly.

'I shall call a tradesman tomorrow and get him to seal it up,' I say, placing the box into the hidey-hole.

'And then?' says Gillian.

'And then,' I say, as Sam snores peacefully in his cot, 'we concentrate on living and let the dead rest in peace.'

Epilogue

EDIE

Cornwall

Eighteen Months Later

The air is ripe with energy as I stand, champagne glass in hand, looking at the view, the late-afternoon light turning the winter sea silver. It is the perfect vantage point, this enchanting roof terrace, to behold the breath-taking beauty of Lytton Cove and remind myself how far I have come, how much I have healed.

The terrace, with its whitewashed brick walls, terracotta pots filled with herbs and, in summertime, glorious seasonal blooms, started life as a series of architectural drawings presented to me, and the rest of the village, at a meeting held by Alexander in the municipal hall, a few weeks after Ned's revelations.

Thankfully, in the wake of his behaviour, Ned has taken his caravan and moved away from the village. No one knows where he is, just that he disappeared in the night leaving no trace. I should feel relieved that this man who caused me so much fear and anxiety is gone, but there is a part of me that feels sorry for him. Like me, Ned and his family lost a loved one, and though we found out later from Stephen Mountjoy's research that Douglas Reid was far from the upstanding, brave soldier Ned had made him out to be, he was still his grandfather, still blood.

'A gallery,' Alexander had exclaimed, standing on the makeshift stage, with a PowerPoint presentation displayed on a screen behind him. 'The first of its kind in Lytton Cove.'

I felt so proud as he pitched the idea to the villagers, complete with plans, drawings and projected forecasts, extolling the possibilities of an arts festival and fringe events, with major names and budding artists being given equal wall space. The man whose parents told him to get a proper job, that art was just a hobby, was now bringing his passion to the people of Holton and he was doing it in the most unlikely of spaces.

'The truth is I'm tired, Edie,' Sue had confided to me when Alexander had shared his news. 'I've run this bakery for almost sixty years. It's time to let go, give someone else a chance. Alexander is the perfect person to take it on.'

There was one stipulation, however, that Sue required Alexander to agree to before she confirmed the sale. There would have to be a bakery of some kind, be it a café or takeaway, on the premises, and it would have to bear the name of the woman who started it all, over a hundred years earlier. 'I'll go even better,' Alexander had enthused. 'Not only will we incorporate the bakery, but we shall also commemorate its founder in the gallery too. After all, she was just as renowned for her drawings as her cakes.'

And so, Kitty Kat's Gallery was born. A place where artists can come and create, a place where, like its namesake all those years ago, one can nourish the body as well as the soul.

While the gallery was being renovated I completed the seventy-eight Tarot cards, hitting the deadline just in time. And as I placed my signature on the very last card, the World, the symbol of completion, the card heralding the end of the Fool's journey and the start of another, I felt Kitty's presence in the room with me. Since discovering I was related to the enigmatic woman who had lived in the cottage before me, the mystic who had communicated messages between this world and the next, I have found a sense of peace I have never felt before. The feeling that everything that has happened in my life, from the triumphs to the heartbreak, has been for my greater good. And though some of those things, David's death in particular, left me feeling broken, I also know that the thirty years I had with him were a gift so many others are denied. My great-grandfather only had a few weeks with Miriam and never got to know and love his child, never got to build a life with them or create precious memories.

My own memories of the life I shared with David, as well as the portraits I made of my family and friends, were so strong and vivid they ended up setting the theme for the entire deck of cards. I hadn't planned for that to happen and felt rather self-indulgent when I presented them to Rebecca Young at her London office. What if she hated them and told me I had to start all over again? But to my surprise, Rebecca's response couldn't have been more positive. The images had answered the brief perfectly: telling the universal story of love and life through the stories of ordinary people.

It had been wonderful to see the portraits transformed

into Tarot cards when the deck, titled YOUR STORY, was released. Opening my complimentary pack, I had smiled at the familiar faces laid out in front of me: David and Dora playing in the sea at Lytton Cove, a perfect encapsulation of the happy family energy of the Ten of Cups; Mum and Dad, my King and Queen of Pentacles, sitting at their kitchen table drinking tea and eating home-made cake, stable and secure in their beloved East End; Ronke dressed in her favourite sparkling red dress, raising a glass of champagne at her birthday party at the Groucho Club, my glamorous and strong sister-in-law and friend, every inch the Queen of Wands; Sue sitting, pink-faced and cheery, in the old bakery surrounded by images of the past, a tray of delicious cakes displayed in the cabinet behind her, the abundant Empress in her domain; troubled Ned, who I had been tempted to draw as the Devil, but who I ended up giving the happy ending he had craved, depicting him driving out of Holton in his caravan, the Fool, ready to embark on a whole new story; and then Alexander, my King of Cups, cutting the ribbon to open the new gallery, pouring his heart into something he believes in at last. And though I am not a major player in the deck, if you look closely you will see that I have drawn myself into each of the cards – sometimes standing in the background, sometimes just my hand or the back of my head – because though it took me a long time to realize it, I am part of these people's stories, the invisible thread that brings them all together.

I would be a liar if I said that spending so much time immersed in the Tarot as well as discovering my connection to Kitty, a woman who had dedicated her life to it, had not left its mark on me. Not least in the sense that I now firmly believe there are signs and synchronicities around us everywhere, little messages being conveyed to us from both the living and the dead. One of those came in the shape of my darling Dora, who surprised me last Christmas with a gift that took my breath away: an award from a German arts foundation for International Portrait Artist of the Year. What Dora told me next not only put to rest any doubts that had lingered in the wake of Ned's lies but also reinforced the idea that the thread that ties me to my darling husband will never be undone. According to Dora, David had entered me for the prize after hearing about it from a colleague and had taken the painting I'd made of him on his trip to Düsseldorf, where the foundation is based, hence his bulky luggage and surreptitious behaviour that day. 'He'd wanted it to be a surprise,' said Dora, when she handed me the letter with the details of the award. 'So he gave both his and my contact details to the organizers. The email announcing that you'd won arrived last week. Just in time for Christmas.' And with that a mystery was solved and a whole new world opened up, for accompanying the award was an invitation to give a series of workshops to art students across Germany. Germany, the land of my great-grandparents, was about to become part of my story too.

'There you are. I was wondering where you'd got to.'

I look up and see Alexander striding across the terrace, black peacoat buttoned up to his chin, hair as unruly as ever.

'You must be freezing,' he says, taking my empty glass and placing it on the ledge, then slipping my hands into his pockets. 'Are you ready for the announcement?'

'I think so,' I say, smiling as he kisses me gently on my cold nose. 'Though I'm rather nervous. It's a big one.'

'I'll be right next to you,' he says, pulling me towards him. 'Every step. Now, shall we?'

The gallery is packed with people. Some I recognize – Dora and her friends, Mum and Dad, Ronke and her new boyfriend, Sue, Tony George – others I can see from their hopeful expressions and youthful energy are here for my announcement. As I make my way to the makeshift stage, I catch a glimpse of myself in the mirrored wall. My blonde hair is now fully grey though, and with the help of an excellent hairdresser in St Ives, it has been teased into a glossy silver pixie cut which Alexander thinks brings out the blue of my eyes. As my appetite for life returned, I found I could eat better, sleep better. My gaunt face has filled out and a certain bloom has returned. Some might say I am myself again but that would not be quite true. The Edie who existed before David's death has gone for ever. The one standing here now is older, wiser, toughened, and yet a little softer round the edges. My dad even pointed out a resemblance to the older Kitty, the one pictured with Gillian outside the bakery, and I took this as the greatest compliment.

As I step up to the lectern, I see Stephen Mountjoy and his wife standing at the back of the room. He catches my eye and raises his champagne glass at me with a smile. When we discovered the family link to Otto and the Voice Project, Stephen had offered to create an exhibition space at the British Library where visitors could listen to Otto's recording as they viewed the photographs and writings made by Professor Garn in the Dänholm prisoner-of-war camp. 'We already had those in storage here,' Stephen told me when I went to visit the space. 'Otto's recording was the missing piece, the story that brought the whole thing to life. It really was worth every penny.'

He was referring to the generous sum the library had paid me for this rare recording. A payment that I had felt troubled by. It didn't feel right that I was profiting from my ancestor's pain, but as I made my way through the exhibition, seeing in grainy black-and-white images the realities Otto had to endure, the barbed-wire fencing, the watchtowers guarded by ferocious dogs and merciless soldiers, and listening to his heartbreaking message to his unborn child, a seed was planted in my head, an idea that would take me all the way to this packed room in our little corner of Cornwall.

'Good evening, everyone,' I say, my trembling voice magnified by the microphone in front of me. 'And thank you for coming here. The bursary that will be awarded tonight, in the name of my late husband, Dr David Hart, will allow one literature student to spend a year working on a project of their choosing free from financial hardship. My husband was passionate about the arts and believed that they should be open to everybody. Yet, as we know, there are many who view the arts as frivolous, indulgent, not a real job.'

At this Alexander, who had encouraged me to add that, raises his glass at me and beams.

'Yet, as David often used to remind me, if there is no art, there is no soul. That is why I, and all of you gathered here tonight, continue to create, because it feeds something deep within us. But we have to feed our bodies too, and our bloody electric meters.'

There is a chorus of cheers from the young students gathered by the stage.

'This bursary was made possible by a discovery I made: a recording of a young soldier incarcerated in a prisoner-of-war camp. His story, and his voice, hidden for over a century, has inspired and informed thousands of people. And I know that it would have given him great pleasure to see that he played some part in helping others find their voice. So now, without further ado, this year's David Hart Bursary goes to . . .'

Later, when the last of the guests have left, Alexander and I sit on the roof terrace, huddled under blankets, sharing a bottle of champagne he pilfered from the drinks table.

'That went well, I thought,' he says, his breath visible on the freezing air. 'A very worthy winner too.'

'I agree,' I say, resting my head on his shoulder. 'Their work reminded me of David's early stuff, the same mixture of anger and grace. I can't wait to see what they produce.'

'Speaking of great works of literature,' says Alexander, sitting up and taking a small paperback from his inside pocket, 'look what I have. Gillian's memoirs. Stephen Mountjoy located it in the Bishopsgate Institute and brought it along tonight. Apparently, there are only three in circulation. It was published as part of Sylvia Pankhurst's commemorations after her death.'

'How wonderful,' I say, filling up my glass and taking it to the ledge, the lights of the cove flickering below. 'Have you read any of it? What does it say?'

'I had a flick through while you were chatting to the students,' he says. 'It's quite short but it fills in a lot of gaps.'

'Really? How so?'

'Well, she writes that, over time, Kitty returned to the East End less and less. Though Sam, your grandfather, had discovered it for himself and had resurrected the family bakery in Mile End. It seems there were too many painful memories there for Kitty and, when Sam got married, Gillian attended in her place with Miriam Ziegler.'

'So it was all there,' I say, shaking my head. 'All this time. Hidden away in a dusty book in East London.'

'Yep,' says Alexander, shining his phone torch over the page. 'According to Gillian, Miriam felt that baby Sam would be better off staying with his aunts in Cornwall. She saw him sporadically throughout his life but more as a friend than a mother. Kitty and Gillian had taken on that role, but Sam understood, and he loved Miriam. She went on to become a prominent German linguist at Berkeley University in the US. I looked her up and she has a faculty named after her there. After Sam's wedding, Gillian never saw her again but heard, years later, that she had died in 1950, the same year as Kitty.'

'Does it say what Kitty died of?'

'She doesn't specify but it seems she had a weak heart,' says Alexander, closing the book and coming to join me.

'She had a big heart,' I say, the tears I have spent the evening trying to contain finally coming forth. 'Like David.'

'There's something else,' says Alexander gently, handing me the book. 'At the end, Gillian included a note written by Kitty. Have a read.'

He hands me the book and, with the light of his phone

illuminating the page, I read the words of the woman whose ghostly footsteps I have followed in, the woman who brought so much healing to the people she encountered, including myself. And as I read, I feel a breeze ripple through my hair, faint but clear enough to sound like a voice.

Kitty's voice.

Another World War has begun, she whispers into the night. *And though I would like to think this one will be short and swift and will not incur much bloodshed, my spirit guides, one of whom is now my beloved Otto, tell me otherwise. So, I ask you, dear brother, to keep my precious Sam, who has signed up, safe, and if that is not meant to be then hold him in your arms until the day comes when we will all be reunited.*

Until then I will continue to use my cards to light the way.

My wish, on this Libra new moon of 12th October 1939, is that people will find my Tarot in the years to come, people from all walks of life, from all over the world, and they will use my images, my stories, to create stories of their own, stories to comfort and to inspire, to teach and to advise. Countless people will be guided to shape the stories of their lives from this simple deck of cards. What are they, after all, these seventy-eight little cards, but a never-ending journey, a story without end?

Acknowledgements

I would like to thank the following people for their encouragement and support as I wrote and researched *The Story Collector*.

My editor, Vikki Moynes, for providing a wealth of editorial magic, and for believing in this story, and its author, right from the start. It has been such a joy to work with you.

My agent, Liv Maidment, and all the team at the Madeleine Milburn Literary, TV & Film Agency – the best support team an author could wish for!

Ellie Hudson, Rosie Safaty, Lydia Fried, and the incredible team at Viking Penguin. It takes a village . . .

Thanks also to Mary Chamberlain for the meticulous copy-editing.

The idea for *The Story Collector* came to me several years ago after watching the BBC Four documentary *How the Edwardians Spoke*, which included extracts from a very unusual linguistic project that took place during the First World War. The study, conducted by German linguist Wilhelm Doegen, and his collaborator, the philologist Alois Brandl, as part of the German Phonographic Commission between 1915 and 1918, took place in various prisoner-of-war camps across Germany where Doegen and Brandl recorded thousands of speech samples from the inmates. The aim of the project was to investigate how 'ordinary people' spoke, and, in doing so, managed to capture certain Edwardian dialects that have now become obsolete. Listening to these recordings, and the disembodied voices of the imprisoned men, many of whom were reciting verses from the Bible, sent shivers through me, and the seeds of a story began to gestate in my mind, a story that would take several years to come to fruition. Though the characters of Herr Garn, Miriam Ziegler and the prisoners in my novel are fictional, the 'voice project' they are working on has its roots in this remarkable piece of linguistic study. A selection of the Berliner Lautarchiv British & Commonwealth Recordings was acquired by the British Library in 2008 and consists of over eight hundred digital copies of shellac discs. For those interested in finding out more about the real 'voice project' there is a wealth of information on the British Library website – www.bl.uk – and in the work of Jonnie Robinson, Curator of Spoken English at the British Library. His Twitter page can be found here: @VoicesofEnglish.

I also owe a debt of gratitude to Julian Walker whose excellent seminar, 'Language and the First World War', which I attended at the Bishopsgate Institute, proved invaluable as I set about developing the characters and dialects of Boscombe, Reid, Singh and Prisoner X.

Thanks also to the Bishopsgate Institute Library for providing much-needed inspiration, quietude and resources during the research phase of the novel.

The voices of the past come to us in many forms, and I loved exploring the world of divination in *The Story Collector*, through the character of Kitty. I first discovered Tarot at the age of thirteen and it has been an integral part of my life ever since. Over the years, my fascination with the symbolism and imagery of Tarot has led me to the work of Pamela Colman Smith, the enigmatic, and largely overlooked, artist behind the iconic Rider-Waite-Smith Tarot deck. Pamela's story, her links with W. B. Yeats and the Hermetic Order of the Golden Dawn, provided a lot of inspiration for my character of Kitty and the fictional Divine Order of Universal Truth. Many thanks also to the spiritual guides and mentors – the inspirational Michele Knight-Waite, in particular – who helped shape and further my understanding of this subject.

It was an honour to be able to include one of my real-life heroes, Sylvia Pankhurst, in this novel and, though her appearance in *The Story Collector* is fictional, it has given me an opportunity to shine a light on the extraordinary work she did in improving the lives of working-class women during this period.

I have always been captivated by the glorious coastline around St Ives in Cornwall and, though the village of Holton is also fictional, it has been a true delight to capture the beauty and magic of this unique part of the world through the characters of Edie and her family.

Love and thanks to my family and friends for their unending support. It really does mean the world to me.

And to my son, Luke, who was revising for his GCSEs as I wrote this book. Thank you for inspiring and delighting me on a daily basis. Here's to the next exciting chapter!

While I was writing this novel, my beloved parents, Luke and Mavis Casey, passed away within nine months of each other. My dad, an award-winning newspaper and television journalist, spent his life writing stories, a gift and passion he shared with me from an early age. 'Words have value,' he once said, and his will stay with me forever. My mother was a free spirit who didn't follow the rules but made her own instead. She was a Pisces dreamer with a wonderful imagination, who believed wholeheartedly in fairytales and angels, astrology and signs from the universe. In their own different ways, they inspired me to tell stories of my own. This novel, and the sentiment behind it, is dedicated, with all my love, to them.

For those interested in discovering more about the subjects explored in *The Story Collector*, I found the following books, pamphlets and blogs invaluable as I wrote and researched the novel:

Forgotten Voices of the Great War: Told by those who were there by Max Arthur

Pamela Colman Smith: Tarot artist, the Pious Pixie by Dawn G. Robinson

The Home Front: A mirror to life in England during the First World War by E. Sylvia Pankhurst

British Prisoners of War in First World War Germany by Oliver Wilkinson

Secrets of the Waite-Smith Tarot: The true story of the World's Most Popular Tarot by Marcus Katz and Tali Goodwin

Trench Talk: Words of the First World War by Peter Doyle and Julian Walker

Out and About London: Your soul the shrine whereat I kneel and pray. Lady, the world grows old. Let us be young by Thomas Burke

The Enemy in Our Midst: Germans in Britain During the First World War by Panikos Panayi

'While the Kettle Boils': Internment in the prisoner of war camp at Danholm-Stralsund – www.thedanishscheme.co.uk

Anti-German Riots in London – www.nationalarchives. gov.uk

UNRAVEL THIS SPELLBINDING TALE OF
FAMILY DRAMA, LOVE AND BETRAYAL

THE SECRETS OF
ROCHESTER PLACE

A LOST CHILD.
A LONG-KEPT SECRET.
THE HOUSE THAT HOLDS THE KEY

Spring 1937: Teresa is evacuated to London in the wake of
the Guernica bombing. She thinks she's found safety in the soothing
arms of Mary Davidson and the lofty halls of Rochester Place,
but trouble pursues her wherever she goes.

Autumn 2020: Corinne, an emergency dispatcher, receives a call
from a distressed woman named Mary. But when the ambulance
arrives at the address, Mary is nowhere to be found. Intrigued,
Corinne investigates and, in doing so, disturbs secrets that have
long-dwelt in Rochester Place's crumbling walls. Secrets that,
once revealed, will change her life for ever . . .

Who is Mary Davidson? And what happened at Rochester Place
all those years ago?

*This intricately layered mystery tells the spellbinding story of
two people, separated by time, yet mysteriously connected through
an enchanting Georgian house and the secrets within its walls.*

Read on for a sneak peak . . .

I

Corinne
PRESENT DAY

'The ambulance has arrived at the house, Anthony. The paramedics will be with you any moment now.'

I breathe a deep sigh of relief as the red dot that has been flashing across the screen for the past five minutes finally settles on the address.

'Oh, thank God. Thank God,' says the man on the other end of the line, his voice trembling. 'And thanks, Corinne. For everything. I couldn't have done this without you.'

I have spent ten minutes talking this young man through CPR for his mother, who had collapsed with a suspected heart attack. He was so panic-stricken at first, I didn't think he would be able to perform the procedure. There was also the added stress of a child screaming in the background. Yet, thankfully, using all my skills as an emergency call handler, I managed to calmly coax this man into focusing on his mother until he could detect a pulse.

'You're welcome, Anthony. All part of the service.'

I hear the voices of the paramedics in the background

before Anthony clicks off and my shoulders loosen. The ambulance got there in time. Anthony's mother is in good hands now.

As I wait for the next call, I lean back in my seat and look around at my colleagues, who are dotted about the room. There is something about the dispatch centre – the broad, windowless room, the weighted silence broken in sporadic bursts by the voices of the operators – that makes me feel calm. No matter what might be going on in my life, when I get to my pod and put my headphones on, see the familiar red lines streaking across the map of London on the computer monitor in front of me, I enter what we refer to as 'the zone'. For the duration of the twelve-hour shift, we cannot see the outside world. We have no idea whether it is night or day, warm or cold, stormy or still out there. Our thoughts and focus are directed solely on the disembodied voices on the other end of the line.

I see Ed, leaning forward in his seat, talking urgently into his headset. Ed has only been here a few months, but he was thrown in at the deep end with a major traffic accident on his first night. That's the thing about this job: nothing can prepare you for what's going to come in. It's how you deal with it that proves whether you are going to cut it long-term. Ed, though visibly terrified, kept his nerve and handled the emergency with a calm efficiency that impressed even the old-timers like me.

I've been here ten years – my first job after university – and during that time have been privy to the worst that life can throw at a person. I have heard people gasping for breath, listened as anguished relatives tried to resuscitate their loved ones, heard screams so blood-curdling they penetrated my bones. Yet I manage to keep all those horrors contained in my pod. I never take them home.

That is because, if I let my emotions take over, I will sink. Ever since I was a child, I have been able to tap into the feelings of those around me. At school the air would buzz with the other children's thoughts, their happiness, their pain, their insecurities. It was so intense I would sometimes put my hands over my ears to try to block it all out. As I grew up, I learned how to deal with those feelings, how to keep calm and centre myself so I wouldn't become overwhelmed. Over time, this centring has become a kind of shield I place between myself and others, to the point where most people think that I am aloof or impassive. Little do they know that, if I allowed my true nature to come through, then I would be so overcome with the emotions of the people on the other end of the line I wouldn't be able to do my job. Better to have people think me cold than have that happen.

After a hysterical sous chef in Clapham suffering third-degree burns and a motorbike accident on Streatham Hill, my headset falls momentarily silent, and I feel my stomach rumble. Time for my break. I gesture to Ed then take myself off to the staffroom.

Sitting on the soft green beanbag chair, my usual spot, tucked away in the far corner of the room, I peel open my plastic takeaway box and greedily devour mouthfuls of cold – yet delicious – dosa, the hit of potato, pancake, mustard seeds and spice sending me into a temporary food coma. While I eat, I take my phone and go through my inbox, skim-reading, and make a mental note of the HR email outlining the details of an upcoming staff training day in Kent. Then I click on an online petition calling for the preservation of an ancient yew tree located in an East London churchyard, sent by my Uncle Robin at midnight. I smile as I read his accompanying message: *It would be much appreciated if you could add your name to stop the heartless bastards destroying yet another piece of London's history. Oh, and a gentle reminder that my new series starts this Thursday at 9 pm . . .*

All signed, I hastily reply. *Working night shifts this week but will watch the first episode on catch-up. Can't wait to see it xx.*

Closing my emails, I pause for a moment to scrape every last crumb from the box, the hungry feeling suddenly replaced with a shiver of adrenalin. Time to get back to it. I go to wash out the box and am just trying to locate a clean tea towel when my phone starts vibrating. My chest tightens. Calls at this time of night are never a good sign. I yank the phone out of my pocket and see the words *Unknown Number* flash onto the screen.

'Hello,' I say, placing the box on the draining board to air-dry.

There is a hissing sound on the other end of the line, like the static on an old recording. The person must be in an area with poor signal.

'Hello. Who is this?'

I can hear a woman speaking. Her voice sounds muffled, as though she is in a windowless room, or trapped underground.

'Please, you have to help me,' she cries. 'You have to find my little girl. She's trapped.'

I abruptly switch back into work mode. With the phone pressed tightly to my ear I rush back to my pod.

'It's the big old Georgian house,' she says, her words tumbling out so fast I can barely keep up. 'Rochester Place it's called, you can't miss it. It's hidden away, behind Larkin Road, down the little pathway. It has a bright red door and a magnolia tree in the garden. Telephone number: BAL 672. Please hurry. I think the house might have been hit. There's so much smoke. You have to help her. Do you promise me you will? She's just a little girl. Eleven years old. Just make sure she's okay, will you do that? My name is Mary. Did you get that? Mary.'

'Mary, can you tell me where you are?' I say, wondering if this person is someone I know, a neighbour perhaps. They are all aware that I am a first responder. 'Hello? Are you there?'

With a sick feeling I realize that the line has gone dead. And as it was an unknown number, I can't retrieve the call.

'Everything okay?' says Ed, peering over the top of my screen from his pod. 'What was that?'

'Someone called my mobile,' I say, looking down at the notes I've scribbled. *Child trapped. House has been hit. Smoke. Rochester Place. Georgian house off Larkin Road. Red door. Magnolia tree. BAL 672.* 'A woman. She said there's a child trapped in a house. I'm going to have to call it in.'

'Strange that they called your mobile and not 999,' says Ed, frowning. 'Could it be someone you know?'

'I don't think so,' I say, as I type *Larkin Road* into the system, prompting the computer to automatically dispatch the fire service. 'It came up as an unknown number and I didn't recognize the voice. She had an Irish accent, sounded quite elderly.'

Almost immediately a red dot appears on the map, hovering over the familiar broad stretch of Larkin Road. Zooming in, I see what looks to be a square patch halfway down the road, jutting off to the left. Larkin Road is just minutes from where I live, yet I had no idea it had a side street leading off it.

'Did you say the child was trapped?' says Ed, adjusting his headset. 'If so, you might want to alert the fire service first. It could be an explosion.'

'Already done it,' I say, watching as the dot on the map stops moving.

With a potential gas leak or explosion, the fire service must attend first in order to deem the area safe. I also have an ambulance on standby, waiting for the all-clear. I sit, my eyes fixed on the screen. This part can take a while, and every second feels like a lifetime. But, after just a few minutes, a male voice comes through my headset.

'Hello, it's Ian Turner, fire and rescue. We're at the address and there's nothing here. No house at all – just a back alley. We've done a door-to-door of the houses on Larkin Road that back onto the side street and there's no one here needing assistance. Are you sure you got the right address?'

I look down at my notes.

'The caller said it was a large Georgian house called Rochester Place, just off Larkin Road,' I say, aware of Ed's eyes on me and hoping I didn't mishear the woman. 'She said it had a red door and a magnolia tree in the garden.'

'Well, if there was a house like that here we'd notice it,' he says with a sigh. 'There's just a load of bins and what looks like some sort of compost heap.'

'Are you sure?' I say. 'The caller was very clear and—'

'I am sure, yes,' he says, cutting in with more than a hint of irritation in his voice. 'Now, we're leaving the scene.'

He clicks off, and I lean back in my chair, my heart racing.

'Hoax call,' says Ed, shrugging his shoulders. 'It happens to the best of us.'

I nod my head. He's right, of course. I have dealt with hundreds of hoax calls in my time. This was just the latest. I adjust my headset and try to refocus, try to block out what has just happened, but as I sit, waiting for the next call to come in, all I can hear is Mary's voice: *Please . . . You have to help her . . . She's just a little girl.*